The

Parth Path

Oliver Eade

Best wishes
Oliver

Once made equal to man,
woman becomes his superior

Socrates
(circa 470-399 BC)

For Yvonne...

Wonderful wife, much-loved mother and
adored grandmother

Acknowledgements:

I wish to thank David Jones and Iona McGregor for helpful advice with the manuscript, and Wendy Leighton-Porter and others at Silver Quill Publishing for keeping an enthusiastic group of writers, of which I feel privileged to be a member, afloat after the demise of Mauve Square. I thank my family, and particularly my dearest wife, Yvonne, for keeping *me* afloat, and last, although by no means least, I am grateful to that little South Vietnamese lizard with a hard-to-pronounce name that gave me the inspiration. If she can do it, why not 'womankind'? A question with which I struggled for two years whilst writing this novel.

Chapter 1

They call me a Single X-Why. I don't know anything about chromosomes, but I do know this much: the 'y' of the 'Why', as written, has a curve. Like the curling arteries that keep our bodies alive, curves are essential...

Curves from a troubled past that we pray might one day lead us to a future paradise, the curved course of the sun as it follows time from East to West, and the barely-perceptible curve of the horizon lost in the curves of those hills ahead. There are also the curved bumps and dips that cause me to jolt with each stumbling footfall. But all these things are of vanishing importance compared with the curves of the woman ahead, a woman fleeing from unspeakable horror. I attempted, but failed, to force her to complete her personal curve and turn back, for to flee from me and pretend she'd been kidnapped is her only sensible course of action. And now? *If she had but listened*, I'm thinking whilst the curve of our story to date pumps power into my muscles, forcing them to take us in a widely-curving arc.

The bouncing hills get no closer. Only more distinct as the pinking sky to the East sharpens their black shoulders. Beyond these, it will surely be easier. A woman called Texta told us that the land slopes down towards the coast where we're sure to find shelter in a hidden cove until the boat shows up, and where I'll be able to ponder my crime.

I killed a man. No shame in that. Barely a crime, nowadays. No real punishment for it. Only admonishment and maybe a flogging. But killing that dog? Far too serious for a bullet through the brain, the Commandant's humane method of disposal, although, if Rea is lucky, this could be her fate. As for mine: to be butchered like a pig whilst still alive, I was warned. Muscles, now propelling each of my four frantic

1

limbs, would be stripped from bones, belly by belly, and fed *au poivre* to the Commandant (I'm told she likes pepper) and her chosen few. This, I was assured, I shall be able to watch from a jar whilst they continue to perfuse my brain. *My* bones, picked clean and washed, will be ground down to provide minerals for *their* bones, and my body fat—what there is of it for I'm as lean as a stick insect—processed for generator and helicopter fuel.

But the dog had to go.

I learned about the curve of the horizon and the earth being spherical from illegal books, although this is the first time, since they took me as a child, that I've seen it without a twenty-foot-high barrier of barbed wire in the way. I barely remember that open space of the Reservation, the wooden huts, Moira and those other ratties.

Ratties?

I'll explain later. Too concerned at present with the shape of the curve I should create to confuse the Commandant's dogs.

That stream ahead? Why not? We could backtrack downstream towards Man Camp 7, then take off in the direction of that clump of trees decorating the brow of the centremost hill ahead in yet another, wider, curve.

Curved horizon? Really?

Hardly seems so, but I've no time to stop and gawp in the dim light of dawn. Like me, those hills are on the move, bobbing up, down and every which way. I see only hazed contours impossibly far away, but these are my only hope.

'My only hope'? Shouldn't I say, '*our* only hope'? Maybe it's guilt that encourages me to singularise this futile attempt to escape.

Anger at what they might do to her if caught pushes the blood round faster, hammering frenzy into those pistons called legs, whilst never-ending obstacles clutter my consciousness: jutting stones, pits and holes left by rabbits, knotted heather and unexpected gullies that bring much-needed water to Man Camp 7 by feeding the meandering burn which might just save us from capture. My muscles do the work and I force my brain to remain connected with my feet. Periodically, I halt to fill my lungs with the heady air of freedom and to briefly dwell on the curves that started it all: delightful curves that change so alluringly with the girl's nimble steps.

* * *

I knew Rea was different the first time I spotted her. My purpose at Man Camp 7, together with that of the other fifty or more men, has always been a mystery. I'm known as a Wrathie rattie —a reminder of the camp's previous cumbersome title: M.O.D. Cape Wrath Training Centre. 'Rattie' is short for 'reservation nattie', nattie referring to all males and those women who enter this world through natural (sexual) reproduction. The reason for new-liner girls like Rea is obvious: playthings for the Commandant, plus wealth. At least, that's how it seemed, but if I'd had a mere inkling of what was really going on in a place that was once a stronghold of male dominance—an army base—over a land now run by the superior sex, I would have thought twice about fixing my gaze on the curves of the new girl in the canteen.

How snugly she fitted into the drab, grey uniform dress, with her black belt pulled just that much more tightly around her waist than those of the other girls, revealing hips so beautifully curved for what we rattie men talk about when out of range of both biological and electronic ears: sex. Even the jagged course of my life up to that point had failed to suppress a primordial male desire that lies dormant within every full-blooded man.

Thinking back, I'm certain it's the belt that made a difference. Added an extra few centimetres of curve to the girl. Hooked by that vision, and between mouthfuls of mash, my eyes travelled up and down those curves till they came to rest just below the twin curves of her dark eyebrows and met with hers. The curve of her smile warmed my soul. A moment of bliss which, from that moment on, began to metamorphose into torment.

I went for seconds. Another helping allowed only for the privileged amongst us ratties. Perhaps I should have questioned why Hellcat never vented her insatiable fury on *my* back with her whip, or why no one cautioned me about asking for more. Just considered myself lucky, I guess.

"Not seen you here before," I whispered after the girl dolloped another mound of mash and oats onto my plate. She glanced sideways at Hellcat before responding:

"New," she whispered shyly, but her eyes said so much more.

Hellcat, a woman in her late fifties, and built like one of the rusting army trucks left behind by the men who once controlled the camp, wears a red belt around her grey uniform dress. She broadens out from shoulders down to belly. No shapely curves. The belt, a sign of authority, makes no impression on her fortress abdomen. Some reckon it stays there only because of the thick handle of the whip wedged between belt and uniform.

Boy, how Hellcat loves to wield that whip. A curve-less smile is the first warning given to some hapless victim. Next, a pink, pudding hand fondles the whip handle. No need for words since Hellcat's reptilian eyes say it all. As hard as cork-board pins, they fix her prey as if he's an insect to be displayed for public amusement. Oh, and that's another thing: those experiments with insects and lizards. But I'll get around to

4

these later. Meanwhile, the man in her sights remains motionless as the fat hand flicks the whip free from that belt. She only stops when the screams threaten to burst her eardrums.

Rea's fearful sideways glance, when I first saw her, informed me that the woman's anger can also be directed against the girls who work in the canteen, many of whom are exquisitely pretty new-liners. Some surely bear fading scars of her fury under their dresses. As far as the red wardens are concerned, canteen girls, and other lower forms of the superior sex in Man Camp 7, are not so very different from men. But new-liners do have privileges for which a price must be paid: the nocturnal company of the Commandant.

When I winked at the girl, her smile gave me hope. Hellcat was engrossed in intimidating a group of new boys, barely men, the poor young things.

"I only arrived yesterday," she added softly. I adored the timid mischief in her expression and her voice almost melted my insides, the words rising and falling in gentle curves of sound.

"Oh," I answered, unable to take my eyes off her small hand as it spooned an extra-large helping of mash onto my plate. That's all I could say: "Oh!" The longing began with seeing that hand, so alive. The mash, by contrast, suddenly looked dead and unappealing. Back at the table, I forced mouthfuls of the stuff into my stomach, all the time eyeing Rea. She reminded me of the Reservation.

I often dream of my life as a boy on the Reservation. Men, women, boys and girls were all equal in that place. I had a little friend there. A girl called Moira. We ratties had such funny names. Mine was Peter. When chores were finished, Moira and I would play by the loch connected to the sea. Chores were shared between us whenever possible. In the evening, we would run as I am running now, but for joy, not fear. Run to the water's edge. And, her being a girl, I would wade in, waist deep, to show off. I can still hear that shrill, young female voice calling out:

"Peter, not so far! Daddy said not to."

I did it because she cared, and I liked to know that she cared, but I lost caring about anything after they destroyed the Reservation together with my mother and sister and my friendship with dear little Moira.

I lost my name, too.

My mother told me that Peter had been a saint, a special sort of a person whom others should respect. Her name was Mary. Apparently, Mary had been an extra-special saint. That other Peter had something to do with a place called 'heaven' and, after I lost my family and Moira, the word heaven, in my mind, got blended with the word 'Reservation':

Heresaver-venation!

Moira wasn't particularly pretty. On the looks front, rattie females cannot possibly compete with the genetic perfection of new-liners like Rea, but she was full of fun and happiness. In cold, windy weather, when even I saw sense not to swim in the sea, I would run from our hut to seek her out. We played all manner of games, our favourite being 'family'. I was 'father', she 'mother', and at some appropriate time during our play she would stuff a cushion under her dress and proudly announce that she was 'pregnant'.

We knew the word spelt danger, for mothers and/or babies in the Reservation often died during childbirth, but it was a word of great mystery. For new-liners like Rea, natural birth has been replaced by test-tubes. The most perfect, the most beautiful of the young female ratties are taken to special places called 'laboratories' where women in white coats work with insects, lizards, scientific paraphernalia and nurtured chemicals to produce genetically-identical lines of cloned girls. 'New-liners' for the commandants and their favoured underlings. What they do with the rattie girls whose stem cells initiate the new-lines, I sometimes wonder. Who mothered the genetic origin of that perfection called Rea? Before we met, I used to think (almost exclusively) about what we men ache to do with such feminine beauty but can't. I did not consider where that beauty came from. And our Commandant? What does she do with (or to) such beauty? Rea never revealed details to me. Only blushed and looked away.

Whatever happens behind closed doors, new-liner 'clonies', identical in every respect, appear in orderly batches, then disappear, not to be seen again. Probably traded with other man camps as 'currency', although a few of the most jaw-dropping, like Rea (and she is the best of the best), are preserved, possibly as investment. Hence the privileges for my girl, if such a term can be applied to extra nights in the Commandant's bed.

Other man camps? How many and where?

I have no idea, but such thoughts jerk my fear upwards by several notches as I run to catch up with Rea. And the knowledge that there are Rea clonies elsewhere both excites and disturbs me. If I lose her, as happened with Moira, could there be another Rea in another place? Whatever, nothing can compete with the memory of what we shared that first night behind the store shed. Even with a Rea lookalike, I doubt it would have been the same. It's not only her liquid eyes, lingering lips and sweet nose—the things that can be copied by cloning—it's her soul. I love Rea. And this means I could not bear to see her hurt. It also means she owns me, my life and everything I have.

Certain?

Can I be certain about anything in this world of women? Is Rea the real Rea? What about that original version after her cells were scientifically crafted into twenty lookalike clonies? Was she kept deep-frozen? Or discarded? And how old would she now be? Maybe, to look at, not that much older than my version, for Rea tells me they did 'things' to her ever since she was little. Chemical things to do with producing and perpetuating perfection and altering biological processes. Perhaps, being so perfect, they plan to use the woman, preserved, for other new-lines. Rea never knew her mother and her 'father', she was told, was a syringe.

But Moira?

There will only ever be one Moira. How I howled when I saw them drag her away from the Reservation. Louder even than after Mother got silenced by a bullet to the head, though perhaps that was simply too unreal—a bad dream from which I was sure to awaken, screaming, to be comforted once more by a mother's loving embrace.

The bad dream got worse. I never discovered what happened to my little friend, my only friend, after I and many other young males in the Reservation were bundled into a covered truck and driven for hours with neither food nor water till we'd reached the first man camp—then the second, third, fourth and so on. In ones, twos and threes, terrified rattie boys were tipped from the truck which then drove on, finally reaching Man Camp 7 in the dark. When off-loaded onto the tarmac, I was the only boy left. A red warden twice my size immediately grabbed me.

And Moira? No way pretty enough to be considered for a new-line, but she was my one, true friend. I adored her. Whatever happened to little Moira?

***

That's how my nightmare began.

8

Life for males in Man Camp 7 is as fragile as a glass bauble in a cement mixer. Being the only one from our highland reservation, I had no friends. All part of the Parth Path plan, of course, but the penny never dropped whenever boys I grew to like disappeared. Whether they had been chosen to help mass produce girls via molecules in syringes, become playthings for red wardens, or whether they were re-located to other man camps, or simply recycled (meat, minerals and man-fuel), there was no way of finding out, and it upset me. Now I wonder whether this is precisely what the Commandant wanted: to keep me in the dark… to test me.

As for rattie reservations, I now know that they are only temporary, something over which even commandants have no control. They belong to the Controller who has as much power over our Commandant as the latter has over the red wardens.

I was too young to understand why my mother was shot and Moira, screaming, got dragged away, but now it's obvious. Ratties, the only pure source of genetically-strong new-liners, are a danger to the system. This danger is reduced by periodic 'cleansing' of reservations: effectively, destruction of everything. We men are as human as women. We're not all stupid. Grouped together in reservations, with women who think of us as equals, sooner or later rebellion is inevitable. I believe those in power, under the leadership of the Controller, will do anything to prevent a return to the old ways when men with armies were in control and almost destroyed the world. But they went too far by separating me from Moira. A seed of dissent was sown on a bed of anger.

The impossibly-beautiful new-liner was there every time I visited the canteen. Lured by her curves, I went up for seconds each day and always got a special smile from Rea—a smile that on the seventh day emboldened me to incubate a plan. Each subsequent smile added substance to my plan whilst her

9

hip-hugging dress, tightly gathered about her slim waist, gave me the courage I needed.

One day, as Hellcat slow-stepped towards an errant new boy from a far-flung reservation, I went up, as usual, for another helping. Momentarily out of the red-belted bully's line of vision, I raised my right hand, palm foremost, at Rea. She frowned, enough for me to know that she understood. No shake of the head or any other gesture of refusal, so, with a grin almost wide enough to accommodate the plate I held, I returned to my seat, ignoring the shrieks of pain extracted from the whipped newcomer.

***

Yes, I killed a dog.

Dogs are scarcer than guns. Will they risk losing another in pursuit of a running stick of man-flesh? I must assume they will—my reason for creating a generous curve. Better chance of confusing a dog if I and my curvy companion-in-crime splash through gullies and change the course of another curve by wading downstream for a few hundred metres back towards the hell from which we're trying to escape. But because of this, it's taking forever to reach the brow of a hill that seemed so close after cutting a woman-sized hole through the perimeter wire fence. Will they have yet discovered the lifeless eyes of the man in the tower, now staring at oblivion, whilst their precious guard dog experiences eternal canine sleep in an expanding pool of blood?

We had no dogs on the reservation. Far too valuable a resource to waste on ratties, so, in Man Camp 7, I've always been frightened by their barks and teeth, for that's all the Commandant's dogs seem to be: barks, teeth and unbridled aggression. Thank the Great Controller, Rea's plan—sausages—worked.

Once a week, on a Sunday, we rattie men are fed sausages. Not sure what they put in them. Recycled males, perhaps? Yesterday was Sunday. Hellcat was playing a cat-and-mouse game with another new boy whilst the new-liner with the face of an angel slipped two sausages into the top of her dress where they lodged unnoticed between the tempting hillocks of her young breasts. She winked and those sweetly-kissable lips curved a knowing smile for me alone. A woman called Texta, who occasionally appeared in the canteen, and who had access to the Commandant's chambers (her unofficial title: 'the boss's bed-maid'), got hold of sleeping pills retrieved from the dead town.

All these years after the Revolution, a couple of women still drive an old army truck once a week to the dead town, a ghost of a city where two hundred thousand once lived before the Great Man War. They return with it filled to near bursting with things that might please, or be of use to, the Commandant. Amongst these are 'medicines' that make her feel better, highly prized even decades after their expiry dates. Perhaps her slumber needs to be chemically induced after the excitement of sharing a bed with a beautiful new-liner.

Rea has not only beauty but brains. I didn't willingly go along with the second stage of her plan. When she climbed the watch tower ladder, smiled at the male guard and unbuttoned her dress to expose her breasts, I felt cheated, but anger gave me an excuse to kill him.

What she did isn't unusual in Man Camp 7. Women are encouraged to tease and excite men, then denounce them to a red warden to be dealt with accordingly. It comes under the banner of 'resource re-allocation': more male-meat, minerals and man-fuel, I guess. But my beloved Rea? It isn't in her nature to do such a cruel thing. Nevertheless, it worked. The sausages fell to floor, but the guard had no interest in these.

11

The dog growled contentment as he chewed on the sedative-laden meat whilst the guard stared in wonderment at the uncovered beauty before him. Meanwhile, I shinned my way up one of the posts supporting the tower.

"You can touch them," urged Rea. "Honest, I won't tell."

Didn't get that opportunity, of course, but later, when we stopped to catch breath, she faltered on describing his expression and I thought she was going to be sick. Nevertheless, her siren-like action had given me superhuman strength and agility. The thought of anyone touching Rea was bad enough, but for someone of my sex to touch her there, unbearable. Raw fury drove the knife into his back up to its hilt, my free hand cupping his mouth. No scream emerged when I slit his throat. It was all so easy, so quick and so quiet. The sedated dog suffered a similar fate before the girl—her breasts still bared—and I slid down the pole and set to work cutting that hole in the fence. Texta had provided the cutters. Once out of the compound, we ran—and ran and ran.

Why should Rea risk everything for a rattie oaf like me? I know I'm vastly inferior, coming from natural childbirth caused by a man called 'Father' penetrating a woman called 'Mother', and yet when Rea and I are alone something quite extraordinary happens.

I'll never forget the first time. Thinking about it powers my legs as we struggle together up the slowly-brightening slope of grass and heather. How I dared to brazenly hold up my hand to Rea as she stood on the other side of that large tin of mash and oats, I have no idea. On my palm were the words: 'behind store shed after bell'.

The night bell sounds when it officially becomes dark. For an hour or so, the red wardens are engaged in seeking out pretty bed companions for the Commandant and her senior officers amongst new-liners and other young women, far too busy to notice goings on in the compound courtyard, so it's a period when we men can exercise our legs and, in pairs only, talk. No way could they have imagined that one of those pairs might include a girl.

The store shed is out of bounds. I was taking a ridiculous risk, but the excitement of seeing Rea—the whole of Rea, and alone—erased all traces of fear. My chief concern was that she might be chosen for the Commandant that night. A resourceful girl, she chewed on a raw onion before Hellcat and her colleagues-in-fear came seeking a sex-toy for the Commandant. She stank like the waste-bin used for pig food, so was left in peace. But when we came together behind the store shed it would have taken more than a raw onion to prise me away from her. I cannot think of a word to describe the happiness I felt when we first became 'one' on that narrow strip of grass and gravel blanketed by the shadow of the grim, brick shed. One writhing shape, one self-exploring, double-headed living creature. I found out what the thing that dangled between my legs was really meant for, and how the difference between 'us' and 'them'—men and women—made supreme sense. Afterwards, Rea wept in my arms. For joy, she told me. She hated being bedded by the Commandant. Said it smelt and felt awful. And from those tears something unstoppable blossomed and grew inside me. A boldness that caused me to replace common sense and caution with a desire to know everything about Rea. Every curve, crease and cleft, every sweet expression, every secret thought.

The sex thing in the Commandant's bed?

Rea shrugged when I asked again, but she remained silent too long for my comfort.

"Erogenous zones," she finally answered. "They teach us. From when we're little. The red wardens. But—" She looked at me and I saw something in her eyes as if I had touched a no-go area walling off unwanted memories. "It's nothing. Truly. Not after—" Then she pressed herself against my chest and sobbed whilst I held her close. We never spoke of it again, but I did learn what little she knew of the 'experiments'.

Before working in the canteen, Rea was a cleaner until the Commandant said she was too precious for such manual work which was beginning to spoil the girl's delicate hands. Cleaners must clean the laboratory.

"Chosen men are kept in cages," she informed me. "They do things to them with needles and knives and after that you never see those men again. I found out about these things cleaning the lab building. And the insects and those horrid little lizards."

Chosen men? Insects and lizards? Like Rea, I was puzzled...

The all-female lizard, Leiolepis ngovantrii, once eaten in the Mekong Delta, Southeast Vietnam, was known locally as Nhông cát trinh sản – the 'sand lizard that reproduces by parthenogenesis'. As with the aphid, only females are produced. Inspired by a long-dead sheep called 'Dolly', a brilliant lesbian scientist, working in a makeshift laboratory in the remote Scottish Highlands, had worked out the genetics involved plus the cocktail of chemicals needed to try it out in women. Female human stem cells were encouraged to divide and turn into clones of embryos without the intervention of sex-defining spermatozoa. Human parthenogenesis was possible and the 'Parth Path' became the rallying cry of the Feminine Revolution in the wake of an all-out world war— part-nuclear, thanks to the U.S. President—that almost obliterated mankind. Men would become virtually obsolete in the breeding game, only required for one of the chemicals in that 'cocktail'. Humanity had been saved. In Scotland.

But lesbians were vastly outnumbered by 'hets', as women who preferred sex with men were called.

***

Rea slows then stops, gasping for air. I catch up then look back at the flickering lights on an old horizon: the horizon of my past. Rea is my future. Beyond, will the past of my dreams—my mother, little Moira and the sea—become the horizon of a new future? We must reach the coast to re-discover that past. Surely those confusing curves we've traced up the hill that sweeps down towards Man Camp 7 will befuddle the dogs of which there's still no sign. Perhaps the Commandant is too busy exploring the curves of some unwilling new-liner to be bothered about a dead dog.

Or perhaps...?

No, I cannot allow myself to fear the worst. Surely a dead dog plus a missing new-liner could never justify such a course of action:

The helicopter!

Many fat men (overfed specifically) would have to be killed off to produce enough man-fuel to power the helicopter for the thirty or so minutes required to sweep the hills in search of an escaped rattie and his stolen new-liner. How could the Commandant justify this to the Controller? It was a risk I had taken, but the fear remained. No way could Rea and I hide from the helicopter on the open moorland surrounding Man Camp 7.

She's still crying.

"Do you want to turn back?" I whisper. She shakes her head.

Whisper? Why, when there are at least three miles between us and any human ears?

Fear, I guess. Makes you whisper all the time. Perhaps it's because no one ever sees the Controller, and because of this we believe that she's everywhere.

I read once about an ancient belief in gods in a book that smelt of a long-gone age. It was passed around us men until some poor bugger got caught with it open at 'Genesis' and was flogged senseless. Before the Great Man War, exactly how long I don't know, people believed in beings called gods that were thought to exist but could never be seen. They would put their hands together and talk to the god(s) in the sincere belief that everything they did or said could be heard or seen by such beings. Perhaps this strange notion continued in rattie genes as an inbuilt fear that the Controller can hear and see everything that anyone in her realm is doing or saying. So, we whisper a lot.

Rea shakes her head.

"Why the tears?" I ask.

"I'm happy. That's all. This seems so... so right. To be with you. Without Hellcat. And the threat of... of it!"

"It?" I laugh, knowing she means the Commandant.

She, too, laughs through her tears:

"It! Yeah, 'it' just about describes her!"

Being men, guards are also natties and therefore held in disdain. Nattie men in the 'wilds', areas outside the man camps and the reservations, are usually killed and recycled if caught, but muscular ones are kept and trained as guards. Likewise, after a reservation is 'cleared', the larger, brutishly-stupid rattie men are taken to special camps and turned into guards.

I prefer to think about the kind ratties of my childhood, like my mother and father and little Moira and her family, but we weren't all like that. For the Great Man War to have occurred means that natties can be every bit as brutal as the red wardens. I feel no more guilt about slitting the throat of that guard than the Commandant will feel sadness over the loss of him. Indeed, for her another dead man means extra fuel and fertilizer over and above her monthly Man Camp 7 allowance, unless the helicopter is deployed.

Or is this wishful thinking?

Still no dogs, but I can't take the risk of following a straight course over those hills to the coast. Taking Rea by the hand, I retrace my steps to the stream we forded. Rea giggles nervously as we splash back towards Man Camp 7 for a few hundred yards before clambering up the bank and heading off in a direction indicated by Texta on her hand-drawn map. And I'm reminded of running up a similar heather-laden slope of my childhood with another girl, Moira. I would always let her be ahead of me if only to hear her giggle when I caught up with the child.

Oh Moira, are you still alive somewhere?

***

Moira bit the podgy arm that was strangling her.

"Why, you little bitch!" screamed its owner. "I'll have you whipped, you bet I will."

Vision, cut off by that python-like arm through lack blood to her brain, slowly returned to the girl.

"She's only trying to breathe," said another voice, calm and assured. "You were killing her."

Moira backed away from the fat woman into a corner of the truck. The other woman was a silhouetted shadow, though the girl recognised the voice: that of the red warden who was once about to shoot her but didn't.

"No more than she deserves, the little whore!" scorned the fat one.

"She's one reason we came here," emphasised the red warden who had ordered Peter to club Moira to death instead

17

of her shooting the girl. As back then, she held a gun. "The boy is the other," she added. A third figure climbed into the back of the truck. A living skeleton.

"But it's just a clearance!" remarked the skeleton.

"Is it?"

The van lurched forward, stopped abruptly, then shot backwards. Moira was flung to the floor and banged her head. The fat woman's cackles almost drowned the screams and groans of injured and dying villagers until overridden by the revs of the truck's engine as the vehicle accelerated onto the bumpy road that led to the shore. Although confined under the canvas cover of the truck, the girl knew that's where they were heading from the smell of the air breezing through the open window up front. She thought of Peter, terrified of what they might do to him.

After the vehicle slammed to a halt, the fat woman gave vent to her mirth when Moira again ended up on the floor. Her chubby hand grabbed a fistful of Moira's dress. The girl was pleased to see red, bruised tooth impressions in the blubber of her arm. To Moira's delight, she had drawn blood. The arm yanked her backwards out of the truck and threw her to the gravel. Its hand pulled out the whip of authority, but the thin woman caught hold of the tail of the lash before it could be used on Moira.

"Leave her be, Bukla!"

The fat woman spat on Moira, then waddled off like a beached walrus.

"See there," said the older red guard with the gun as she helped Moira to her feet. She pointed to a boat bobbing alongside the quay. "That'll be the start of your new life."

"What about Peter?" the girl asked. "What's happening to him."

"Peter? Surely you know? He's special and will be well cared for."

"I don't believe you! He's only special because he's my friend. I want to see him. We're going to come together when I've started."

"Not possible. And he's on his way to Man Camp 7 this very minute."

"Why did you kill Mother Mary? And Peter's sister?"

"Did we? Must've been their fault if it happened. Look, get yourself onto that—"

Moira turned and started to run back towards the village, but the thin warden quickly caught up with her and grabbed her arm. She was surprisingly strong for someone with jointed bone-sticks for limbs.

"Come quietly or my friend really will use her whip."

Moira, being Moira, didn't. Reluctant and struggling, with her wrists now bound, the girl from the Reservation got frog-marched to the quay where Bukla took obvious pleasure in using her lash. Later, as Moira sat in the pitching stern nursing her wounds, she vowed she would never forget the faces of the three women who took her away from the only life she knew and from her only true friend. Particularly that of the fat one who had whipped her.

Chapter 2

"Tell me more about Texta," I ask Rea as my mind flips back to when we first made love. "But only if you want to," I add.

Texta is the woman who secured the sausages and got hold of the knife I'm still holding. She, too, hates the Commandant, Rea once said, and is old enough to remember the time before the Revolution. Rea's frown informs me of a closeness between her and the older woman. I wish to know everything about Rea, plus whether a physical relationship between the two women has been an integral part of the girl's life at Man Camp 7. I fear the worst but need to have it spelt out.

"What else do you have to know?" she asks, frowning.

Have to know?

Rea's eyes warn me to keep away from the subject. We men know little about what goes on between women. All we can do is to guess and keep our disgust to ourselves. But Rea has already told me about bed-sharing with the Commandant in the dark, which she hates, about erogenous zones, which bore her, and about stuff called poetry: something to do with words with which women can excite each other when erogenous zones fail to work their 'magic'. But words, it seems, are not the Commandant's thing. Only silent fumbling is. In the dark. Rea has never seen her face.

Magic?

Our love-making is magical beyond my wildest dreams. For Rea too, I have no doubt whatsoever. Nothing fake about the pleasure it so obviously gives her. So, what about Texta? Does she offer Rea similar pleasure? If so, why help the two of us? I take some comfort in the fact that she's as ugly as the backside of a cow.

"A mother," Rea finally replies, her frown gone. "She's like a mother. You had one once, right?"

One glance from those eyes disperses my fear. My mother, still struggling with two brutish women, before being shot in the head, rises up from a cranny in my brain. I see the panic in her eyes mixed with something I was too young to understand at the time, but which I now know only too well as Rea and I continue at a more relaxed pace towards the brow of the hill:

Love…

"Yes, I had a mother who loved me," I admit as we talk and walk. "After Moira, she was the most precious person in my little world. She did anything and everything for me. Even tried to stop them from taking me away, so they shot her. But Texta? How come you think of her as a mother when she has nothing to do with you? I mean, you didn't even come out of her belly. I know that much about mothers." Rea looks offended. I apologise. "Sorry. I'm only a man. And stupid because of this. It's just that…"

We come to a halt. Rea gently places two small fingers against my mouth to silence me. She grins.

"She told me," she says.

"Told you what?"

"What it would be like. With you."

"Oh—thanks!" I look the other way.

"No, you don't understand. She was married. Once. That is, she had a man to herself. Not a shared one. Before the Revolution. And the war."

"Halleluiah!"

"That too. They married young in something called a church. Where people talked to God. They both put rings on their fingers. To remind them."

"Of what?"

"Each other."

I hardly need a ring on my finger to remind me of Rea, but I am so relieved that Rea's and Texta's relationship is no more than that of mother and daughter. It must show in my face for Rea pats my cheek and smiles.

"So—what happened? To her man?" I ask.

"Wouldn't tell me. Probably recycled. Or became a slave."

A slave?

The illicit books informed me that there were no slaves to speak of before the Great Man War. People, both men and women, worked in the fields growing food and in buildings called factories making all sorts of things, and they were given something called money with which they could acquire their own food and toys for their children. So, what went wrong, I often asked myself during endless hours of doing nothing in Man Camp 7? Why the war? Rea must have shared my thoughts. After another lovemaking session between the fence and the storeroom, she posed the same question:

"Why do men fight?"

It's true. We fight all the time. I punched a guy in the face for explicitly describing to his grinning mate what he'd do with Rea behind the store shed given half a chance, unaware I was listening and had already done it.

"Because of you," I replied, feeling guilty since the man had ended up in the sick room.

"Me?"

"Women. Can't stop ourselves when—I dunno really. When we think it'll all get taken away. Like when I was a kid. Losing little Moira."

"You're always going on about Moira. What was so special about her?"

I stared at Rea for few moments before it dawned: jealousy. It had never occurred to me that women could feel the same things as men. Similar, perhaps, to the darkness that engulfed me when that guy used words to play with Rea's body—a darkness conjured by the fear that she might prefer his words to my groping hands.

"A friend. She cared. That's all," I answered.

And it was. Now I'd hardly give Moira a second glance, plain little thing that she was, but at that age a girl's looks seemed of secondary importance. Our souls had merged in our make-believe play and that meant so much more than the tits and bums I later only ogled, like most rattie men, before Rea appeared.

"D'you think *I* don't care, then?"

"Rea, what on earth put that into your sweet head?" I held her face fast between both hands and kissed her lips—once, twice… three times.

"Look what I'm risking for you!" she continued.

I dabbed, with my sleeve, at the tears that welled in her eyes.

"I know. And not for nothing, I promise. We will get away from here."

"How? Where?" Questions for which Rea later came up with answers.

Texta knows more about Rea and me than I do about the two women. As I continue up the hill, with the only person I've truly loved in *every* possible way, towards a pile of rocks on the crest that only Texta knows about because she created it, I'm beginning to wonder if there's anything that woman is not aware of.

"She's arranged for a boat to pick us up," Rea said one evening, smelling, this time, of rotting cabbage with which the older woman had smeared her to avoid the Commandant's

23

bed. Later, I almost had to hold the girl down for fear she might attract attention to herself by bouncing up above the store shed roof during an orgasm of ecstasy. "All we have to do is get to the coast. Over the hills. She's made a map— look!"

Lifting her dress, Rea extracted a folded sheet of paper tucked into the elastic waist of those panties I so love to remove. She indicated, with a trembling finger, Man Camp 7, the stream along which we've just back-tracked, the hills, Texta's stone pile and the old road that will lead us to the coast.

"Can't stick to the road, of course, but Texta says we can cut though those woods there, then sort of zig-zag to that place she's marked. By the sea." Rea tapped at a red cross on the sheet.

"Paper? Pen? Where did she get these things?"

"Just don't ask."

"Why is she doing this for you?"

Rea again placed two fingers over my lips. She likes to do this.

"Enough questions. She is, and that's all that matters. The boat will take us out to sea. To an island. *The* Island. Too far away for the helicopter, Texta says. She has connections there."

"An island could be worse."

Rea punched me playfully in the chest.

"You can be so miserable at times! How worse?"

"No escape." I too know things. Things from my past.

Rea took both my arms and wrapped them about her waist.

"Why should I want to escape if I'm with you all the time? Do you think—?" she began before looking over her shoulder as if to check the empty space wasn't listening. "A baby? You and me?"

I don't even know whether new-liners, after being interfered with in those laboratories, can reproduce naturally, but the thought of this pulsed excitement into that ever-changing member that had already entered Rea many times. A baby? Our very own child in a place free from red wardens, whips, brutish guards, and, for Rea, the Commandant's bed?

"Texta says things are happening on the Island. Things we couldn't even begin to understand."

Why did I ever doubt Texta? Because she's ugly? Or because she's a woman? But the penalty for her if discovered helping a rattie bum like me would be indescribably awful. What bravery!

When we arrive at the crest of the hill, and briefly rest up against Texta's pile of rocks, panting, I see shock in Rea's face. Her hearing is better than mine.

"What? You hear a dog?"

I scan the bracken and heather-clad slope below, tinged purple now that the sun has slipped above the horizon. Nothing!

"No—not a dog. Oh, curse the Parth Path—look! There!"

I hear it now. Like a frenzied wasp. The helicopter! But I see nothing.

"Where is it?"

"The other side of Man Camp 7. Beyond those buildings. Can't you see it?"

She's right. Flying low, tilted forwards, it sweeps the fields where slaves are already out digging potatoes at the break of dawn. I grab her hand and we're off again, down the slope, away from the helicopter wasp, the dead guard and his dog. I misjudged the Commandant's determination—or was the price she'd get for Rea greater than a helicopter tankful?

More rabbit holes, rocks and hidden roots. Rea stumbles, twisting her ankle. I support her as we part-run, part-scramble down the hill towards the woods in the valley. She's crying. I tell her to shut up. Extra noise cannot help our chances of escape. The engine whir being muffled by the hill gives no reassurance. I expect the helicopter, its wasp sound magnified a hundredfold, to suddenly swoop up and over the hill and bear down on us like a pterodactyl stripped of wings. Rea slows down. She's giving in to despair. The pain from her ankle must be driving her insane. Anger at seeing her suffer suffuses me with superhuman strength. I stop, momentarily. Rea goes limp, her eyes vacant. I stoop, heave her, a shapely living sack of human love and warmth, up over my thin shoulder and start to run again. No—sprint. Almost fly.

The blurred line of trees ahead bounces and jerks alive. Just as the drone of the helicopter engine breaks cover behind me, I spot a gully that'll take us to the trees. I scramble down, with Rea, into its trough, leaving us exposed for no more than a split second. Enough time for the female pilot to have seen us? Hopefully not.

In the wood, I stop, gasping for breath before gently lowering my precious burden to the ground. I tear a strip from Rea's dress to serve as a bandage to support her twisted ankle, then break off a branch, pluck it free of twigs and fashion a bob over one end, using another strip of her dress, to serve as a crutch. Meanwhile my stolen treasure, sitting with her back up against the trunk of a tree, and pleasingly showing more of her legs, stares oddly at me. I laugh.

"What? I can see more of those beautiful legs now!" I gloat. Then I worry. So, will other men when (if?) we meet them on the boat.

"You never told me you were that strong," she grins. "How did you do that?"

26

I shrug my shoulders.

"You," I reply. "No other reason. But I can't carry you all the way to the coast. Try walking with this."

I hand Rea the home-made crutch and help her to her feet. I drink in the admiration in her eyes when she looks up after taking a few successful steps along a path cutting through the wood in the direction of the coast. We set off again and I marvel at the girl's speed with the crutch.

"You must've been practising!" I joke.

"No!" she responds. "It's you! Don't want to lose you so I have to keep up." I laugh again. Rea too.

The noise of the helicopter diminishes until the only sounds are those of the crackle of twigs underfoot and the scuffing of fallen leaves from Rea's swinging leg. Now, as we cut through the woods heading for the coast, I must put my faith in Texta.

It takes half a day. Trees provide cover for most of the way. A deserted village leaves us dangerously exposed for a mile or so, then a tarmac road pocked with holes and tufted with grass and weeds makes us even more vulnerable. The road is marked on Texta's map and we must follow it to reach that cove on the coast.

Exhaustion, thirst and hunger tease at first but by late afternoon they sap our strength. Worse, they dig into my spirit and find doubts there. Ever since I hatched the plan with Rea, I've known this whole thing about escaping and living again as a rattie is ridiculous to the point of insanity. Glancing at Rea beside me, using her crutch with such determination, helps to dim the doubts, but only briefly. I begin to wonder whether we shouldn't turn around and give ourselves up—if only to get food and water. Then I spot a pitiful figure. Rea sees her, too. We halt and stare at the woman standing at the roadside a few hundred yards ahead.

She's old and bent and would offer no more resistance to the thrust of my knife than did the drugged dog. Plus, she's alone. I leave Rea leaning on her crutch as I go up to her. Her eyes are safe, so I beckon to Rea to join us.

"Her!" the old woman says. "The new-liner. What happened?"

How does she know? I look from Rea to the old woman and back. Rea shrugs her shoulders and I rest my hand on the handle of the knife slotted into my belt.

"What?" I ask.

"Rea. What's wrong with her?"

"You know her name?"

"Texta," she says as if that name explains everything. "I've been waiting so long I seriously thought the helicopter had caught you both. Or the dogs. But I see now what slowed you up."

"You know Texta?"

"Everyone does. So, what happened? Dog bite?"

"Twisted my ankle," Rea chips in before I can reply. "Solem is amazing. So strong. He carried me—"

"Yes, my dear," the old woman mutters. "I'll hear about it later. Just follow me."

Which we do after Rea sneaks me another shrug. We follow the lady for a mile or so before taking a small path that leads to a ruined stone farmhouse. On the other side of a wooden door hanging by one hinge, the old woman pours us glasses of water from a jug, then cuts two hunks of bread from a loaf on a table.

"Sit down," she says, pointing to chairs around the table. She joins us, pushing the bread and water in our direction. "So, they worked then. The poisoned sausages."

Rea glances at me as if it's my job to find out who or what the old lady is.

"Don't!" I warn as Rea reaches for the bread. Could she suffer the same fate as that dog? "Wait—" I turn to the woman. "How come you know Texta?"

The woman chuckles before replying.

"How does anyone here on the outside *not* know Texta?"

"But—this makes no sense. Is this whole thing a... a set-up?"

"A what?"

"Texta, you, the guard and the dog... is it all a trap?" I feel Rea's hand tighten on my fidgety arm. Perhaps she believes that controlling its movement will ease my mind—or maybe she's restraining me from myself. After all, she knows what happens when I see red. "Well? Is it?" I repeat.

The old woman, smiling, shakes her head.

"No traps. We don't belong to the Man Camp 7 Commandant. Which is why we still exist."

"You—exist? Look, I only want Rea to have a chance. To live as I used to in the Reservation before they destroyed it."

I glance at Rea and she shakes her head ever so slightly. Enough for me, but not the old woman, to notice.

"Explain!" I demand, ignoring Rea's tentative warning. "Texta, yourself, the Island—everything!"

"I can't do that. All I can do is ask that you trust me—and let me feed you, give you water and send you on your way. You must reach the coast by sundown. I really don't know whether... no, wait, I've an idea. But eat up first."

Rea grabs my arm.

"What?" Frowning, I pull free from Rea and stand up. The woman, too, gets up then heads for the door.

"If anyone knocks, if you hear anything, hide underneath that bed." The old woman points to a blanket-covered bed up against the wall behind Rea and me. "You might have to use your knife again."

29

She knows about the killing as well?

She's gone a good while. Neither Rea nor I dare utter a word but, as so often happens during periods of silence between us, our eyes share a myriad of thoughts, unspoken fears and a thousand yearnings. The old woman finally returns, but not alone. A man of similar age stands back from the doorway, close enough for me to take in his tattered trousers, his boots with gaping toe caps and a torn grey jumper with potato-sized holes in the front. I recognise the delivery fellow who occasionally smuggles illegal books into the man camp... therefore a friend.

"Don't ask again," she warns. "Watchem will take you there. He has a horse and cart. He's supposed to travel tonight to pick up the day's catch from the fishing boat to deliver to Man Camp 7 in the morning. He can go there early and sleep in the cart." Growls from Watchem inform me that he's not entirely happy with this arrangement. "Of course you will, you silly old bugger!" snaps the old woman. "Need anything else first? A pee, Rea? Even new-liners need to pee, I imagine."

If that's supposed to be funny, I don't find it so. As far as I'm concerned, Rea is the only person in the world—*my* little world—who matters. Rather than being some sort of a freak, she's totally human. Special, I grant you, but human. And perfect. What if there *are* other genetically-identical Reas in man camps across the country? *My* Rea is different. She's unique. I wait whilst Rea pees behind the cottage, still uneasy about the old woman's seemingly-limitless knowledge concerning our plan. Perhaps, I hope, the morose old man will open up.

This doesn't happen. Rea and I are bundled into the back of the cart and covered with a greasy tarpaulin that stinks of dead fish, whilst the man called Watchem climbs up front behind the horse and whips the animal

30

into a brisk trot. It's bloody uncomfortable but I feel heartened that, whoever Texta really is, we at last appear to be getting somewhere far away from Man Camp 7. After another hour or so—I have no measure of time with me—I smell something that triggers flashbacks of childhood: the sea. Mingled with the scents of seaweed and rock-pools, the reek of dead fish takes on a new meaning. I see images of me running free again with little Moira along a beach that goes on forever in a land that can never be destroyed...

A land that exists only in my head.

***

The movement of the boat, the nausea, plus fatigue from the lashing, caused Moira to drift off. With bound wrists, being unable to nurse the blood-flecked welts criss-crossing her back, sleep was her only escape from pain.

It was the rain that awoke her. It began in a dream where she and Peter were playing by the sea. Peter splashed water over her and she giggled and splashed back until dizzying waves returned the sleeping girl to the cruelty of reality. The wind drove the rain into every crease and hollow of her young body and she started to shiver. Through wet, narrowed eyes she watched Bukla, the skeleton colleague, and the woman with the gun, with a hatred such as she had never before experienced.

They must have killed her parents. Why else would those screams have been so abruptly aborted? A 'new life', that red warden said. Hers, not theirs, she decided in that boat. Her brain took command and controlled the nausea. It refused to allow her to vomit for the amusement of Bukla-the-Pig. She had a good brain. Peter often told her that. She would use it to overcome the Skeleton, the Pig and the gun woman.

And so, the bound girl, huddled in the stern, recorded in mental detail everything about the boat and its occupants. By the time land was sighted, and she knew this from the conversation, she had a good idea of who did what and how the craft was being steered.

She, Moira from the Cape Wrath Highland Reservation, would steer herself into this new life.

Chapter 3

Rea and I bump heads when the cart stops with a jolt.

"Ow!" she cries out before the tarpaulin is lifted. She's rubbing herself and scowling.

"Sorry!" I apologise and help her down.

"Not your fault! His! What's he staring at me like that for?"

Rea's anger surprises me. I glance at Watchem who stands holding the horse's bridle, his gaze fixed on Rea like a magnet stuck to a shapely metal statue. Her shortened dress reveals more of her legs than I'd wish him to see. But he's old. It must be decades since he last saw legs like that, let alone did anything about it. I approach him.

"I've just killed a man," I say. "If you think you can—"

"She told me everything!" He reaches into the cart and takes out a red and yellow polythene bag. It has writing on it. Never seen one of those before, a bag with writing. "And she said to give you this. Food. They might not have any, and if they do they're not likely to share it. Unless—" He looks again at Rea as he hands me the bag.

"I told you—take your bloody eyes off her."

He grabs my arm.

"A world of advice, son! The girl—her legs... cover them up. You've no idea, have you?"

"About what?"

"What it's like outside that little paradise called Man Camp 7."

"Paradise? Man, what the fuck have they been telling you?" I remove his hand from my arm and pull out my

33

knife. "I mean it, if you can't show Rea the respect she deserves I'll—" I wave the knife in a pointless gesture before Watchem erupts into laughter.

"No, you won't," he says. "It's not just about respect. Some of us know how important this girl is. More than you do, I'll wager."

"And what's that supposed to mean?"

"That you're special too, but only because of who Rea's going to become. Look, I'm trying to help. Like she told us to."

"Texta?"

"Of course!"

"What is it about that bloody woman?"

"She's only pretending to be one of them. I can't even begin to explain—perhaps because... Look, I need to warn you about the boat men. What the Commandant and the red wardens do in Man Camp 7 is... well, it's nothing compared with what those sea-faring apes might get up to. With a woman."

"Man Camp 7? Have you ever been there?"

Watchem glances awkwardly at his feet. He shifts his gaze towards the sea, then Rea.

"Not inside the buildings. But I've heard things. About gentle floggings."

Maybe it's thinking about those red wardens that does it, but whenever my anger shifts upwards a notch or two, I see red. Watchem's face turns red around the edges. I step towards him, grab him by the collars and lift him up so that his chin disappears down into his shirt.

"You know nothing about Man Camp 7! And you know nothing about me! And if you look at Rea like that again you'll know nothing about anything! Hear me?"

Rea pulls at my arm:

"Leave him alone, Solem. Please. He means no harm. He's only trying to do his best."

Pricked by shame, I let go of the old man.

"I'm sorry," I say. "I know. I should thank you for risking your own life. Thanks."

Watchem seems unconcerned as he readjusts his collar.

"Texta says I have a duty to warn you, and you have a duty to protect the girl. That's all. The boat will be here shortly after sundown. Too risky for them to land in the daylight. There's a watchtower beyond the next cove, see."

"You used to work there, right? Your name?"

"Know pretty much every pebble on the shore in these parts. Yes, I used to work for them. One way of staying alive with my woman. Then Texta found other uses for me. Told them I was too old to climb the steps to the tower. Nonsense of course, but—let's just say I have a different job now. See those rocks?"

He points to a cluster of rocks sticking out of the water beyond the cove. They remind me of Hellcat's teeth.

"Tide's going out. After night fall you'll see a large block of concrete from the old times emerge out of the water."

"Old times?"

"When we men were something in this world. We're not all like the boat men, you know. Anyway, that's where the boat comes in. They'll be looking out for you. But her? They won't be expecting anyone quite so—" For the first time, Watchem appears embarrassed and I suddenly feel sorry for him.

"So... what?" I ask, knowing exactly what he's trying to say.

"Beautiful. It'll bring out the worst in them. That knife there. Hide it carefully."

"What's in it for them? Why should they want to take us to the Island?"

"Don't ask. Better you know nothing. Follow that path down to the shore. There's a small cove. The helicopter won't see you even if they come out this far—which they won't."

Holding the bag in one hand, the other supporting Rea down the uneven, sloping path, I leave the old man standing and staring until he's out of sight.

A new sound peels off another layer that separates me from my past with Moira: the scrambles of thousands of wet pebbles drawn back by receding waves after breaking shore. I can almost hear my one-time friend's squeals of excitement as Rea and I clamber down towards the surf-glistened rocks. What, I ask myself, would I do if Moira were to appear out of the water and come running towards me? What would I do about Rea?

***

"Can Peter play now?"

I heard Moira at the door talking to my Mother. I grinned to myself for it was more of a begging than a question. What the child meant was "please ask Peter's father to let him come out and play." I'd told her only a short while earlier that I had to help my father fix some broken furniture and we'd barely got started on the table with a wonky leg. Moments later, I was looking pleadingly up at my father.

"Go on!" he chuckled. "Don't need a strong man for this job. Your sister can hold the leg whilst I fix it."

I liked it when he called me a 'strong man'. It meant I could protect little Moira from the mean sea spirits that we imagined to be lurking in the caves along the shore.

"You sure, Father?"

He smiled and nodded. I jumped up and ran to the door. Moira was holding her driftwood bat in one hand, and, in the other, a ball made from screwed up paper, soaked in sea water and dried in the sun. We called the game 'cricky'. I loved it—and I loved to let Moira win. A born winner, this always made her fizz with delight.

We ran together to the flat land beyond the fields where the men grew crops as people used to before the Great Man War. My father had lent us three sticks to drive into the soil to form a 'wicky', the aim of the game being for one of us to throw the ball at the other who had to hit it so hard that he or she could run in wide circles around the wicky before the 'bowler' went to retrieve the ball and 'stump' the player who wielded the bat. I would often pretend I couldn't find the ball to allow Moira extra 'runs' before throwing wide, giving her a better chance of winning. This was countered by a desire to show her how good I was at hitting the ball with such power that it 'almost touched the moon'. I wanted her to be proud of me plus win, so my runs would slow to a walking pace as she ran away from me then speed up for her return sprint.

How we loved to play cricky!

But that day was different. I remember it so clearly. Moira, laughing, had run on ahead when I stopped to pick wild flowers for her hair. When I say that she wasn't particularly pretty, I am of course comparing her to the genetic flawlessness of new-liners. To a boy of my age who had only ever seen rattie females, she was exceedingly attractive, and I loved to make flower crowns to place on her wavy, blonde hair. I couldn't resist a patch of yellow and pale blue flowers as she skipped on ahead. When I saw her stop, with her back to me, the bat

37

dangling, at the top of the path that led to our cricky pitch, I knew something was afoot.

"Moira!" I called out. She didn't even turn her head. I dropped the flowers and ran.

I'd never seen a gun before. Heard about them, of course. From Father. As teacher of me and my little sister, he would explain to us about the awful things of the past after lessons; about the Great Man War, how badly women were treated before the Revolution and about guns. No one fought in the Reservation, and the only weapons of my childhood were the spears and arrows used to hunt deer, birds and other game beyond our boundaries, plus knives to prepare the flesh for Mother.

Guns, however, fascinated Father.

"I could catch deer on my own if I had one of those," he once told me.

I knew they were banned from the Reservation, but mistakenly thought that was because our new Chief considered them to be evil; a reminder of the Great Man War. There was a rumour going around us boys that she possessed one, although Father told me this was nonsense. When I asked what a gun looked like, he drew one for me. So, on seeing the woman point a gun at Moira I knew what it was. My friend had no idea what it could do. It was fear of the unknown that had frozen her.

"Peter?" the woman asked.

I nodded. "And this is—" I began.

"A mother called Mary?" the woman interrupted.

I nodded again.

She wasn't one of us. Her clothes were different. She wore a grey dress with a red belt into which was slotted a whip. Perhaps it was this that terrified Moira rather than the gun, the barrel of which was still aimed at the girl.

38

The face of the ageing woman was as hard as the rocks left behind on the beach when the tide went out.

"Take the bat from the girl," she ordered.

I looked at Moira. I had an unpleasant hunch about what she was going to ask me to do. Moira offered me the bat and I reluctantly took it.

"Now hit her with it!" she said. "On the head! And hard!"

Moira cowered and protectively held up both hands when I raised the bat. Her eyes were tightly closed as if to say, 'get it over quickly, Peter, so I'll not know a thing.'

That's when I first realised how much I loved the girl. To hurt her feelings was, for me, awful; to harm her little body, impossible.

"Either you do it with that club or I shoot her with my gun."

Club? What's a club? I thought to myself. *This is a bat.*

My response was automatic. With the bat held aloft, I ran at the woman with the intention of doing to her what she'd asked me to do to Moira. A loud bang pulled me up short just yards from the sturdy, grey-haired figure. I turned. Thank the Great Controller, Moira was still standing, her panicked eyes wide in disbelief. The bullet must have missed her head by inches... deliberately.

"You pass," the woman said. "Or did you know we'll need her too, one day?"

"I don't know what—" I began.

"You don't have to know anything. Leave that to us. But know this. She's getting older and your silly little games can't go on forever."

"She's thirteen. Like me!"

"Not that girl! Oh, get back to your game. Only play properly. Allowing her to win is tantamount to cheating."

Moira frowned when I glanced at her. The woman held the gun up against her shoulder then pushed me aside as she swept past.

"Definitely pass!" she called out without looking back. "The girl too!"

Dumbfounded and confused, I watched as she disappeared over the embankment. For what seemed an age, but can't have been more than a few moments, Moira and I simply stood like dummies until I could hold back no longer. I ran to her and hugged her. She cried like never before. Happy, bubbly little Moira cried and cried as I remained with my arms wrapped around her, like a fool not knowing what to say. Not to her, to my parents or to myself. So, I said nothing. Moira and I never talked of it again, but we had played our very last game of cricky.

We kissed instead.

After that day, when I so nearly killed my friend, I began to grow up. Moira loved me all the more for what I did, or didn't do, never knowing I almost smashed in her skull for I preferred the idea of her dying from a blow with my bat-come-club than from that woman's bullet. I didn't truly know what a bullet might do to her. I imagined it might have magically caused her body to disappear, though my father obviously knew better than me if he wished for a gun to hunt deer. It was anger that caused me to confront the woman. Pure, blind, unashamed anger on seeing Moira screw up her eyes. Moira's eyes were the best part of her and that woman causing them to momentarily disappear made me see red. *Will the rest of Moira disappear too if that woman shoots her?* I wondered. So, the whole of the woman, not just her belt, turned red.

That wasn't the only time I saw red because of Moira. It happened with Luke too. Another saint, I was told, but one with the eyes of a devil. When those eyes took to seeking out Moira—he was a year older than us, and bigger than me—I questioned her about him.

"I hate him!" she said to my great relief. "Always staring at me during community meetings." Her lips comforted me with a kiss.

"I know," I said when we parted. "And I was worried that—"

"Shut up!" she exclaimed. "I don't want to ever hear his name mentioned again."

At least I knew where I stood as far as Luke, Moira and I were concerned, and this gave me the confidence I needed when, as we wandered one evening in summer, arm-in-arm, towards the hills, I became aware that we were being followed. I didn't look round. I assumed that the pimpled bully, the obvious stalker, would give up in the forest. As we sat with our backs to a tree, with spears of sunlight shafting through the silent pines, dappling the path with flickering gold, I started to relate to Moira some of the stories of old that my father had told me. Tales of what went in the cities that once teemed with people, of shops, of televisions that talked and showed moving pictures and of thousands upon thousands of cars and airplanes. Things we neither experienced nor imagined possible on the Reservation. Moira's bright eyes hung on every word until we were interrupted by a crackle.

I looked up. Something blue disappeared behind a tree trunk. Luke, I knew, had a blue top. I broke off a small branch from the tree under which we sat and

41

fashioned a club—my new word—before investigating in slow motion. Moira sat with one hand cupped over her mouth, watching. As I approached the tree concealing the boy, Luke darted out from the other side of it, dressed as I expected him to be, in a blue top and jeans. He sprinted towards Moira. A knife gleamed in his hand. He was too fast for me. He grabbed Moira by the arm, pulled her up and swung her around, securing her slender neck in the crux of his elbow whilst holding the knife point at her throat. Once again, fear in my friend's eyes made me see red. I walked on towards them.

"Go away!" barked Luke. "I want her. Why can't I have her?"

Perhaps I knew he'd not harm her. Not if he really 'wanted' Moira. I kept moving forwards. The older boy let go of my friend, who shot behind the tree, then backed away, now holding the knife pointed at me. I didn't stop coming and I had no answer to his question. With the club, I struck the knife from his hand then, whilst he nursed his injured arm, prodded him in the belly with it, forcing him to bend forwards, like a collapsing penknife, with his back against the tree. I raised the club high with the intention of doing to Luke what that woman told me to do to Moira. I couldn't think of anything to say. There was just me, the club and Luke's frightened face plus what he'd threatened to do to Moira.

Moira saved me from becoming a child killer. Emerging from behind the tree, she began to shake her head, slowly but deliberately. I lowered the club.

We'd known each other for as long as I could remember. It might have seemed as if I was the 'controller', but Moira had truly been the one in control because of who she was. I would let her win at cricky because she wanted to. It made her happy, as did the flower crowns. I told her stories because she loved them. So, when she shook her head, the red that covered Luke faded. He became a pathetic, pale pink creature, barely worth a punch on the chest let alone what I was intending to do to him. Moira took the club from me then led me by the hand out of the wood and down to the beach, leaving Luke to quake alone.

"My saviour!" she announced, before running off to look for shells amongst the pebbles and rocks. I found some for her. She had a large collection at the back of her family hut. Mostly ones I'd discovered during shell-seeking forays in the early mornings when there was only us, the gulls and the sea.

The wood had been special. Following our first kiss, before the incident with Luke, kissing was something we could do more and more of in the wood without fear of being seen. Afterwards, Moira refused to go there, so kisses were reduced to snatched, secret moments. But that didn't worry me too much. Moira said her mother told her she'd be 'starting' soon because of those breasts which so fascinated me. In the reservation, we all knew what starting meant for a girl. The games we'd played as children might soon happen for real. Our lives being short, as soon as a girl 'started' she had the chance of being bedded. This was the only way we ratties could continue our little heaven. And the girls always chose. I was over the moon to have been called her 'saviour'. Luke, poor wretch, never stood a chance. He must have been desperate, but the penalty for a male forcing himself upon a female was far worse than a blow to the head with a cricky bat. It involved doing unpleasant things to the offending organ.

***

43

The beach became our only place of privacy for stolen kisses, but how private is the beach ahead for Rea and me? Although hidden from the tower, there seems to be precious little shelter. Rea, limping, approaches the shore, then, as Moira used to do, starts to turn over wet stones, periodically picking up clumps of dripping seaweed. A fine, misty rain cools both face and spirit as I recall those days on another beach, in another time, spent with wee Moira.

"Come back!" I call out. "You heard what Watchem said. We must stay hidden in the cove back here."

Rea hobbles back to me. She becomes Moira the child in the days when we played fathers and mothers with a pillow under her dress.

"But I've never seen so much water before. It's—it's like—"

"Heaven?" I suggest as she walks up to me.

"What?"

"Heaven. A great and mysterious reservation without red wardens and commandants. Somewhere. Just this (I indicate the beach and sea)—and us—and babies."

"Babies?"

I take hold of Rea's hand, pull her up close and repeat the word.

"Babies. Little people. From you. And me. Together. Being together. New lives."

"I didn't know."

"What?"

"Until I was six. We clonies stayed together in the compound before then. Came as such a shock when we got merged."

"You mean when you joined other children? Children who looked different?"

44

"I was terrified. I knew grown-ups were all different, but I just thought all child girls were the same. Don't know why, but I just reckoned we'd someday grow up then turn different. I had no idea children could also look different."

"Or be boys?"

"They taught us about boys. And about what men did before the Great Man War. And the 'Glory of the Parth Path'. And how special we are!"

"Correct there. But that other thing?"

"The Parth Path?"

"Yes, the Parth Path. You know, getting given that little pink book when I first arrived at Man Camp 7 from the Reservation made me feel quite sick."

Rea looks taken aback. She pulls her hand free from mine.

"What do you mean? How could the Glory of the Parth Path make anyone feel sick? It says in the book how you men were killing the planet as well as each other. Didn't the women save you men as well?"

"To live on as slaves?"

Rea laughs.

"You—a slave?"

"Not me. And there is something big, I know. Plus, I feel in a way I'm a part of it. But those poor buggers out there in the fields working till they drop—or getting flogged to death! As for the red wardens! I'd sooner kiss a dog than—"

Rea chuckles again.

"No one's asking you to do either. Only me." She holds me in an embrace whilst planting a love field of warm kisses all over my face. "Telling you, not asking. Now it's your turn to kiss me!"

I oblige—on the lips and for so long that she has to break free to catch her breath.

"Yes," she says, patting my cheek. "Just like that!"

"No boys? No men at all?" I ask for the thousandth time. "When you were old enough, like?"

Old enough?

Moira, once, quite confidently, said she was 'old enough' because of what she felt for me, but her mother had firmly told her, 'No!' Not until she'd started. The 'starting' was a mystery to us boys. Something to do with blood coming out and babies and being fathers, but more than that we hadn't a clue. Moira, also, was ignorant of the sort of physical union that has already happened between Rea and me. What she felt for me, and I felt for her, was primal love. It needed no physicality. I feel this too with Rea, but with her I desperately need the other. An age thing, I suppose. What I don't know is what I'd do if Moira should emerge like a ghost from those waves and come running towards me as she used to. Which girl would I love? Both? Can such a feeling ever be unpicked?

"I wish you'd not keep asking me that. Why do you?" Rea asks.

Why indeed? She sounds cross. Fear of losing her as well, perhaps? Her being bedded by the Commandant no longer registers as a threat. Only an annoyance. But the thought of that male guard in the tower back in the man camp touching the twinned softness where I so happily rest my head after we make love—it drove me to kill with the ease of stamping on a wasp.

"Stay by my side in the boat. All the time. You heard what Watchem said. There are things men do that—"

"My saviour," interrupts Rea, putting her arm around me. "You're my saviour so why should I worry?"

"You—you just said—" I stutter. "Saviour? Where did you—?" All these years later, wee Moira's word still lies sacred amongst my memories. I felt stronger for saving Moira without clobbering Luke. But it seems wrong that Rea should come out with the same word for no obvious reason. "I'll do my best," I add tersely. "To protect you."

Separating Rea from Moira requires knowledge about her past. The ten-year gap between the two females of my life curiously merges them into one, yet I cannot conceive of Rea as little Moira or my childhood friend turning into the woman my hands explore whenever I have the opportunity. For now, the child I'd wish to know must join the adult I can never know.

But is it really like that?

"No boys at all when you were little?" I repeat. "In the fields—did they—?"

"No fields. There was a yard. With grass at one end. We were allowed out once a day. All twenty of us clonies."

"Twenty Reas? Heaven!" I pretend to joke.

"Shut up! I was me and they were—well, we all had different names. And—"

"Only one Rea, then! But if you were identical, didn't you share thoughts? If you played games—like cricky... did you never play cricky?"

"No games. Nothing that might damage us."

"Damage? Playing cricky?" I recall the last time Moira and I went to play the game and I nearly clubbed her to death to save her from being shot. But what I want to extract from Rea is how cloned girls relate to their genetically-budded sisters. I used to imagine that clonies have no need for speech to communicate with each other. Looking alike, they should think alike. Games would be pointless. But having lain with Rea, I know this to be

47

nonsense. So, what went on between those young new-liner girls?

Rea stares at the sea foam as it spreads over the pebbles whilst I stare at Rea and at a solitary tear that emerges from the corner of one eye. I follow its stop-go trail down her cheek. There's so much she's not told me—so much more I must know.

"We were very different," she says at last. She turns to face me. "Why do you keep asking the same questions all the time? Is there something wrong with me? Because I'm a clonie, perhaps?"

I kiss then stroke her tear-trailed cheek.

"I can't bear the thought of anyone else having you. That's all. So, if the other nineteen of you—"

"How many times do I have to tell you? We're different! I'm the only Rea. If you can't see that you can't love me!"

I hold her close.

"I do, I do. But there's a lot you have to learn about us men, too."

Rea breaks free then fixes her gaze on the pebbles at her feet. "The first boy I saw was at the man camp we first got sent to. We were all together there. He was in the canteen alone. We got herded in by the red warden. She was the first red warden I'd met, too. We clonies all stared at him. Twenty of us. Lined up. Then we started to giggle. He smiled. Until the red warden took out her whip. I can still see him. With his hands over his head as she struck him again and again across the back. I was the only one who cried. Some of the others laughed. I'd thought they were my friends, but after that—"

"That's enough," I say, comforting her. "I know now. About the soul."

"The what?"

48

"From a book that I read. Made long before the Great Man War. Got smuggled into Man Camp 7. Maybe by Watchem. Who knows? Anyway, it was full of stories and talked about the soul and so many other things. It was called The Holy Bible. Had lots of strange words in it, but—"

"Bible? That's odd. I'm sure I've heard that word before. At our school, perhaps. What's it mean?"

"No idea. Except that there has to be another way apart from the Parth Path. Like clonies, men and women are different but equal."

"Equal?"

I spy mischief in her eyes as she pokes me in the side.

"Ouch! What did you do that for?"

She laughs.

"Testing you. Yes, when that red warden whipped us girls we squealed just like that poor boy. Equal but different. How long do we have to wait?"

"You heard what Watchem said. Till the sun's gone down." I squat on a rock and beckon for her to join me. "Rest your head here. On my lap. Need to be alert on the boat. Both of us. Sleep now if you can. Then I'll take a rest. We're equal, see?"

Rea stretches out on the pebbles of the sheltered cove and rests her head on my lap. She closes her eyes as I run my fingers through her long, jet-black hair. And I think of little Moira and her blonde curls.

***

The rain had stopped, and the wind had dropped, by the time the boat approached the shore. Like a huge, curled, concrete finger luring the small craft towards it, a jetty stuck out into the bay. Moira was yanked to her feet by the Pig and pushed forwards to the side of the boat as it nudged up against the jetty finger. A rope was

49

thrown to secure the craft, then a landing plank with cross-struts positioned before the Skeleton and the gun woman disembarked. A group of red wardens stood on the quayside, so there was no hope of Moira putting into action her plan—to kick the Pig and her companions and make a run for it. By the time the others had left the boat, there were a dozen women on shore. Two men, one up front and the other at the tiller, remained aboard. Moira tried to trap their eyes with hers, as she'd done so often with Peter. Perhaps, like him, they found her pretty and would wish to help her. No such luck. Both looked away. Born into a reservation where, nominally, men were equal to women, she was, as yet, unaware of the powerlessness of the opposite sex in the real world.

"Is this the Island?" Moira asked.

"Shut up!"

A plump arm, decorated with a bite mark, pushed her towards the plank then grabbed and half-lifted her off the boat. If it hadn't held her so tightly she'd have jumped into the water—her second plan—but this proved impossible. That podgy hand secured her for a reason of which Moira was unaware: its owner would have been shot had Moira escaped.

And so, with her arms still bound, the girl was shoved into the back of a grey truck, followed by the Pig and the Skeleton. The engine powered up, and soon Moira was being bumped along a potholed track to start a new life journey that no one on board could have anticipated.

Chapter 4

It happened three sunsets after that incident with Luke. Shame had shoved me into a state of gloom from which Moira struggled to extract my sickened soul.

"Not your fault!" my little friend insisted. "He shouldn't have done that. You were my saviour for a second time. So, stop being miserable."

"It's not just that I really wanted to kill the bugger when he turned red in my mind. I'm afraid of losing our friendship. With someone other than Luke, you might have felt differently."

"No way! Look, it's beginning to rain. Come back to my place."

Moira's mother had once been our chief. She was a wonderful woman, like her daughter, and it was a mystery to me why she stopped being chief. Moira shrugged shoulders when I asked her.

"Dunno. She said it was the Controller's decision."

"Who's the Controller?" I asked. I knew nothing about what happened in the world beyond the Reservation, let alone the meaning of 'The Controller'. It seemed to me, a mere ignorant boy, that our chief controlled everything in our niche of heaven. I still have little understanding of the Parth Path, and, back then, wee Moira hadn't even heard of it. When I asked her mother, named, after another 'saint', Agnes, she said the Controller stood proud at one end of the 'Parth Path' overseeing everything that happened on earth following the Great Man War. She, Agnes, was apparently unimportant.

"What the Controller says, happens," Mother Agnes informed me.

My own mother was known as 'Mother Mary'.

"Which mother will become chief next?" I asked Agnes.

"Too many questions! Moira, show Peter the new doll your father made. Perfect for mothers and fathers."

"Mother, I'm too old for all that stuff now. Soon it'll be for real!"

Agnes gave my friend a funny look.

"Too young to start, too old to learn? Make up your mind."

"No, I mean... oh, come on Peter. I'll show her to you anyway. Mother will never give me any peace if I don't!"

I felt cross with the woman for upsetting Moira, but when able to examine the doll myself, and lifting up her dress, I saw things I now know about; things to do with making babies. The doll was a preparation and Agnes knew I was soon to be chosen by Moira. Now, looking back, it all seems so unreal and pointless.

The new chief was an old woman who lived by herself at the very edge of the Reservation, close to the fields. We children were scared of her, for her face would sometimes appear, like a spectre, at her window whenever we passed by. I wondered how she knew. I told Moira I thought she must be reading our minds to anticipate us, and that if we wanted to speak whilst passing her hut it should be in a whisper. It meant nothing to me then, but during the council meetings, when Reservation ratties could voice concerns or give vent to their anger, the old woman would wear a red belt, now so familiar to me, and hang around in the background, silent but watchful.

Whilst we played with Moira's new doll, I could hear the girl's parents' anxious voices discussing the new chief.

"How much does she know?" her father asked.

"Everything," replied Agnes.

"We must leave. For the mountains. They'll never find us there. Then head for the coast—and the Island. Should've done this years ago."

"But I thought we'd be safe when I was chief. Thought she'd put in a good word for me if, and when, she took over again. And that everything would be all right."

"Didn't your teachers tell you anything? About the real Parth Path? No reservation is safe from the Controller."

"Moira won't come without Peter."

Moira must have been listening too, for she glanced at me in such a strange way. Almost a smile, as if to imply she had no need to worry for I was her 'saviour'.

I took to going out after dark and watching the new chief's house. On seeing Luke emerge the night before it happened, I realise in retrospect that I should have warned Mother Agnes. But I still felt ashamed of my earlier angry outburst and I suppose I feared she might overrule Moira's choice after her 'starting'. I hardly slept that night, worried I might wake up to find Moira and her family gone. I wanted to talk to my mother about what I'd overheard but she had enough worries of her own what with my little sister Caitlin going down with fever and spots and our father complaining there wasn't enough food in the stores to see the Reservation through the winter. Later that morning, after lessons, Moira and I went down to the beach. Never, before, had I seen the loch so calm. Nothing disturbed its glassy surface. I

53

searched for a piece of driftwood then threw it as far as I could.

"Let's pretend it's a boat," I said to Moira. "Throw stones just behind it and drive it to that rock sticking up there. That could be the Island. If it reaches shore, we'll all be safe."

I started to throw the largest pebbles I could find that would reach the 'boat' of our future. And I imagined I was throwing them at Luke to stop him from saying anything bad about me to the chief. So engrossed was I, that I failed to notice the real boat when it appeared from beyond the headland. Moira saw it first.

"Peter—a real boat. There! Look! A big one."

I grabbed her by the hand and pulled her back from the shoreline.

"Quick! Warn your parents. I'll tell Mother Mary and my sister. Father's out in the fields."

"Why would they send a big boat to the Reservation?"

"No time to ask questions, Moira. Run!"

She streaked off. Back in our hut, I found my mother cradling Caitlin in her arms. My sister had been vomiting and had gone very pale. Her glazed eyes didn't seem to focus properly. I could tell Mother had been crying.

"Something's happening," I tried to warn her. "A big boat coming into shore. Full of red wardens."

Mother seemed unable to pick up on what I was saying, for Caitlin was so desperately ill. We had no medicines left in the Reservation. The pitiful few we used to have had been 'redistributed' to the man camps by decree from the Controller. A warning of what was to come that had been lost on me but not on Mother Agnes.

"That boat, Mother. Full of women with guns. They'll be here any moment. Moira and her parents are heading for the mountains. There's talk of an island—"

"Island?" Mother looked blankly through her tears. "*The* Island?"

"I don't know. Her father thinks we'll all be safe there. Hurry!"

She looked down at the skinny, limp body of my sister.

"I'll carry her!" I suggested.

I felt strong after being told twice that I was wee Moira's saviour. But when I tried to lift Caitlin up off Mother's knee she was even heavier than the potato sacks I would sometimes carry from the fields for Father. The girl made a weak attempt to support herself but immediately crumpled to the floor.

I had an idea.

"That screen panelling Moira and I were going to help Father put up! We'll lay her on that."

I ran to get this. As if half-asleep, Mother helped me lift Caitlin onto the panelling made from inter-twined twigs and remnants of cloth. Father was incredibly inventive and could always turn the most mundane of materials into something useful. Although light, bearing Caitlin it seemed to weigh a ton. We somehow managed to raise the makeshift stretcher off the ground, and struggled on towards the other huts. Everyone was now outside. Moira must have rushed around the compound to warn folk. At first, I panicked, for my friend's hut was empty and I couldn't see her amongst the crowd. Then I spotted them beyond the last hut, the chief's, and heading out towards the fields.

"Wait!" I cried out. Either Moira didn't hear, or they were in too much of a hurry. I looked pleadingly at

55

Mother, but she was lost to me. Caitlin was dying and only half in our world. I wanted to lower my sister and run to Moira; at the very least find out where they were heading to. Instead, I opened my mouth wide and shouted—no, screamed: "Moira!"

She turned, thank the Great Controller. Luke appeared at the same time. He ran past me, stopped, then turned to wave and grin before running on. To grab my friend and take her from me? No. He halted at the chief's house. The only brick house in the Reservation. I watched him knock on the door then disappear inside.

"Mother," I began, "we're gonna need help with Caitlin. Stay here. I'll—"

Too late! I had never before heard a gunshot. Two loud bangs cut short my sentence. I swivelled, expecting to see smoke and disintegrating buildings. All I saw were two fellow ratties stretched out on the gravel path, motionless. Beyond, a line of red-belted women in grey uniforms walked abreast towards me, their guns raised. At the same time, there were shouts coming from the other end of the Reservation in the direction of the fields—the direction Mother Agnes had taken with Moira and her father, carrying their few worldly possessions.

An old army truck drew up; similar to the one they now use to go to the city once a week from Man Camp 7, only filled not with provisions, but with armed, red-belted wardens. It must have driven straight across the fields destroying our fathers' crops in its path. Women scrambled out, ordering frenzied ratties to stand still. Some didn't and were shot. More screams ricocheted from both ends of the Reservation whilst I remained fixed to the ground in the middle of our village together with my dying sister and Mother. Until that moment, 'clearance' had been a word without meaning for me. In an instant it became the most feared word in my meagre vocabulary.

Luke emerged from the chief's house and talked to one of the guards, a colossus of a woman. She spoke with a group of her red-belted bullies who ran off along a path that zig-zagged up the hill towards the mountains; the path that Mother Agnes and her family had taken.

Saviour? No, instrument of failure!

Over and over I cursed myself for having lost it with Luke. What part he played in the clearance remains unclear. But just then, it seemed to me, he would get what he wanted: my friend. I wasn't prepared for what happened next.

The colossus pushed through the crowd, slapping aside those in the way as if she couldn't even be bothered to waste bullets on them. She stopped yards from where I stood.

"There he is," she called out, pointing at me. "Peter!"

I turned around hoping to see someone else called 'Peter', but there was only me in line with her stubby finger. Two guards marched up and seized my arms. I kicked and attempted to bite one. Not a good idea. She swiped me forcefully across the face, blurring my vision and twirling me to the ground and tipping Caitlin onto the gravel. My mother stepped forwards to stand between me and the guard.

"Leave him alone. We've done no harm. My daughter's—"

Her last words. The guard pulled out her gun and shot Mother in the head.

The horror of this was too absurd for me to take in. Mother was dead. She fell sideways, her sightless eyes now staring at nothing. Caitlin coughed and tried to get up onto her knees. She too was silenced with a single shot. I looked on as if the curled-up bodies of my mother and sister, with ribbons of blood trailing from their heads, had nothing to do with me. A curious feeling of complete detachment took over. All I could think about was little Moira. All I wanted was for her to escape from Luke.

They hadn't gone far. Moments after Mother and Caitlin were killed, Mother Agnes, followed by Moira and her father, appeared from over the embankment bordering the fields, half-pushed, half-dragged by three wardens, their hands bound. Moira fell as she stumbled down the slope towards the chief's hut. Luke emerged and shouted something at her, but I couldn't make out his words above the commotion. Moira's hair was a tangled mess of blonde curls and there were scratches on her face. Knowing my friend, she would have put up a struggle before allowing her wrists to be secured.

Perhaps it was because Mother's death had been so clinically quick that it affected me less than seeing Moira being dragged screaming towards the path that led to the shore and the boat, and where a truck was waiting; or perhaps death was too alien a concept for a boy of my age. Apart from Luke, life in the Reservation had been peaceful. People died of natural causes. In fact, I had never, before, seen anyone dead. The community gatherings after burials out in the fields were jolly, social occasions. I suppose the horror of the Clearance seemed too far removed from normality to allow my brain to accept that I would never again see Mother or Caitlin.

But Moira?

I fought with the fat devil woman restraining me, lashing out and trying to elbow her away whilst shrieking Moira's name and shouting obscenities at the invaders.

Luke began to laugh. I shouted "bastard!" and swore that I'd kill him the next time.

There wasn't to be a next time. Only more shootings whilst I and several other boys were bundled into another truck. Cries of panic had been replaced by groans from the wounded and sobs from the bereaved, many of whom were also slaughtered. I assumed Moira was being taken by truck to the boat, but had no assurance she, too, wouldn't be shot. My single hope was that I recognised the older woman taking her away—the one who had ordered me to club her to death. If she'd wanted my friend dead, she would have surely shot her the last time they met.

Sitting here with Rea on a beach not dissimilar to that of my childhood, where I and my little bosom friend would sometimes play from dawn to dusk, it all seems so vivid I can hardly believe ten years have passed since I and a handful of rattie boys were driven south in that truck. Not until I first saw Rea did I stop thinking about Moira.

***

"Take her to the school, though it's more than the little bitch deserves!" barked the Skeleton. Like her grip, her voice was surprisingly strong for someone whose skin seemed to be stretched over nothing but bones. The woman with the gun had gone on ahead.

Bukla-the-Pig took obvious delight in pulling the stubborn girl off the jetty and along a wide path that led away from the quay to a flight of steps. Here they were met by more red wardens who escorted Moira and her tormentor across a boulder-strewn terrain to yet another truck.

She'd heard the word 'school' from Peter's father. It was a place where children from before the Great Man

War, both boys and girls, were sent to learn about the world. Would this be the same? Would there be boys there? Would she be re-united with Peter? Or might it be that hateful Luke?

But one question burned brighter in her brain than all others: Was this the Island?

Chapter 5: Boat

With my back pressed up against the cliff, I soon learn that our overhang affords little shelter against the driving rain which begins to chill my love as she lies with her eyes closed. She shivers. I wish I had something with which to cover her legs.

Soaked through, I now sit astride a gap of ten years, half of me still a boy, starting a life without Moira as I got bumped along a potholed road that ended in Man Camp 7, the other half, a man returning to heaven, but with Rea, not Moira. Between us and this heaven is the boat, now darkened in my mind by Watchem's words.

Rea, awake, sits up. She's hungry. Like after we make love. We decide to eat and drink what little the old man gave us, then sit in sodden silence, waiting. Rea grows tired of staring at the mist-veiled sea and curls up beside me, resting her head once more on my lap. I trace the contours of her nose and lips with a finger and she smiles. She takes my hand and kisses it several times. I wish we were back behind the store shed in Man Camp 7. Well... perhaps not there, but somewhere... making love. Heaven? Could the Island of which Texta speaks be like the Reservation only without the threat of another clearance? Will I take the place of Father and Rea that of Mother? Will we produce little natties in a paradise where males are equal to the superior sex?

I must have fallen asleep. Rea's no longer beside me. Standing silhouetted against a sea without a horizon, for the mist is dense, she seems to be staring into oblivion when a sound springs me awake, and to my feet. Although the rain has stopped, she doesn't seem to hear me when I call out to her. With Moira still refusing to leave my mind, another boat from another time forces action into legs prickled with pins and needles. I half-run, half-stumble across the large pebbles towards Rea. Before I can grab her arm to pull her back, she turns. Her sweet mouth is stretched into a wide grin.

"What's a boat look like, Peter. Can I call you that? Please? Now that things are going to be different?"

For a few seconds, I don't know what to say. I look beyond Rea, my eyes attempting to penetrate the murk out of which the muffled chug-chug-chug of an engine motors into my ears.

"Back to the cliff, Rea! We don't know who they are. Not yet. Could be the Controller's red wardens for all I know."

"But I've never seen a boat before."

"Come away from water's edge. Quick!"

I pull her, like that bitch of a warden pulled Moira all those years ago, although Rea laughs rather than kicks and screams. By the time we reach the overhang, where I succumbed to sleep, the boat has appeared out of the mist, slowing in a chortle of churned up water before stopping. I see bobbing figures on its deck. Broad, heavy figures of men. One carries a gun. Rea's gone quiet. An anchor is flung over the side of the craft, its splash the only sound apart the patient putt-putt of the engine. A man climbs overboard and wades, in thigh-length boots, to the shore. He sees us but remains silent as he walks over the pebbles. I have one arm around Rea, the other hand on the handle of my knife.

"Solem?" he queries.

I nod, tightening my grip on the knife.

"Were you followed?"

I shake my head. He peers up the steep path we'd taken after being dropped off by Watchem, then glances back at the boat.

"My men seem to want one thing only," he said looking at Rea. "They never said she was so... well... never let on about her being such a perfect new-liner. I'm right, ay?"

I nod. It must be obvious to anyone. No rattie girl could be as perfect as Rea.

"The guy with the gun is to be trusted. The others are scum but they're all I can get. He and I are the only ones who can take that old tub across the water so don't count on us being your eyes, if you get my meaning."

"Why are you doing this?" I ask.

"Because of you two. And her. Texta. So, come with me if you wish, or stay here and get picked up by the Controller's coastguards. Your choice."

We have no choice. I help Rea to her feet, hand her the crutch and we follow the man. He turns, maybe to check that we're still with him, but more likely to absorb the beauty of the girl beside me.

"Just call me Captain. Like the others do. The one with a gun is Drackem. See him there by the gangplank? You don't need names for the scum. Just keep 'em away from her. If you can. And whatever you do, don't fall asleep."

He splashes through the still water. I scoop up Rea, still limping, and wade in up to my knees after him. Pairs of cold eyes dotting a row of ugly, bearded faces fix on us. I'm thinking Rea's crutch might serve as an extra weapon. By waving his gun at them, Drackem forces the other men to back away from the bow whilst the Captain helps us on board.

"A bullet through the brain for any of you scum who tries to fuck the girl," the Captain informs the crew. "Remember, these two are paying for your food for the next month... at least!"

Paying? So, the boat and her crew have been hired for this insane purpose? By someone? Whom? Texta?

"It's so small," whispers Rea. "I thought the boat would be really big. As big as a man camp building."

Drackem overhears.

"A ship? No. We're lucky to get enough fuel to power this little bucket of shit. But what he said about us paying for their food—did Texta say anything to you about payment?"

"The Island. A boat. That's all."

"In the back, you two," orders the Captain.

Holding the crutch aloft, I help Rea to the stern. The collective noses of the crew swivel to point at us as if they belong to a pack of dogs eager to familiarize themselves with our scent. Rea's, at least. There's a bench at the back and I lower Rea onto this then, like a guard dog myself, take up position beside her.

"Get on with your jobs, scum! Pull the anchor. Gotta get there by dawn. Before the bloody Parth Path boats track us down."

The putt-putting engine kicks into a chug. We move backwards, away from the shore, then forwards in a curve until the land is swallowed by the mist and there's only us, the boat and these men.

Rea snuggles up close to me as, reluctantly, and one by one, the crew disperses to get on with whatever is needed to steer a boat from the mainland to the Island. All, that is, except Drackem. He crouches beside me.

"It's not that lot you need to watch," he says quietly. "It's the Captain."

64

"What?"

"He only says those things to put you off the scent. Beware. What he says is only partly true. Sure, they'll be paid, in supplies, to get you to the Island. But that doesn't mean things will go how you'd like 'em to. Watch him!"

"But—what about you? You're the one with the gun."

The man holds a finger to his lips. He whispers:

"I'm one of Texta's. How much has she told you?"

"Bugger all! Just said to Rea here to follow her instructions if we want to escape from that hell-hole."

Drackem grins.

"Man Camp 7 a hell-hole? You should see the other man camps!"

"How can they be worse?"

"Hundreds up and down the country. Higher the number, the worse they get. They want to rebuild the cities, see. By using man-slaves from the camps. But you two have other uses. Which is where Texta comes in."

"She had a man once. Married," chips in Rea.

"I know, sweetheart," replies Drackem. "And that's where *you* fit in. Look, I'll do my best to get you both there safely. In fact, my life depends on it. And watch out for the Captain. But what about that leg of yours? Needing a crutch, I see?"

Sweetheart? Not a word I've heard before.

"Twisted it. Peter—I mean Solem—he's so strong. Carried me part of the way."

"Good for him. I'll get one of the lads to ease it for you. Has healing skills that he learned on his reservation."

"I don't think I should—" I begin looking at the man with suspicion.

"Thank you," interrupts Rea. "Anything but this pain, Peter!"

Drackem disappears below deck. Rea strokes my brow as if to erase my scowl.

"Please understand. It really hurts," she says. "You heard him. It's the Captain we have to watch."

Drackem soon returns with a man not much smaller than the bull I remember from my Reservation days. He crouches at our feet and Rea stretches out her leg, anxiously eyeing the brute. Very carefully, he eases off her shoe and removes her sock. Rea winces and I free the knife from my belt, keeping it hidden behind my back. Gently, he passes a spade-sized hand over and around her ankle before bringing it to rest on the instep.

"Here?" he asks, his voice as gentle as the caress of that enormous hand.

Rea nods.

"How did you know that's the spot?" she asks.

"He just does," answers Drackem. But he seems more interested in Rea's leg than what the giant is doing to it.

The giant, for that's truly what the man is, reaches into his pocket and takes out a jar from which he extracts a cherry blob of purple ointment. This, he works into the skin of Rea's injured ankle. Rea frowns, but when I ask if it hurts she shakes her head. The giant carefully flexes her foot clockwise then counter-clockwise, alternately, several times, causing her toes to trace circles in the air. He stops and looks at Rea. Even his eyes are kind.

"How does that feel?" he asks.

"I... I can't feel a thing. I mean it doesn't hurt any more. Not one bit."

"Stand," he says.

Rea stands up. Me too. I keep the knife concealed.

66

"Walk," he says.

Rea walks up and down, no longer hobbling.

"A miracle!" she exclaims. "Peter—I'm better!"

The healing giant returns the jar to his pocket, gets up and leaves us without another word.

"Now do you believe me? And you can put that knife away," suggests Drackem.

Feeling thoroughly foolish, I return the knife to my belt.

"What do you think the Captain will try to do?"

Drackem looks at Rea and I get his drift.

"But it's both of you that *they* want," he says to me. "Both of them."

"Them?"

"Texta and the other one."

"Other one."

"You'll not believe me if I tell you."

"Other what? Who?"

"The Controller."

I laugh. I've never heard anything so ridiculous. What on earth could the Controller herself want with a skinny escaped male rattie? I shrug my shoulders.

"Well, I'm game for anything so long as none of your lot touches Rea."

He chuckles.

"One already has! But I agree, Rolem the giant wouldn't hurt a fly, let alone a highly-prized new-liner."

"Highly-prized?"

My voice must reflect my concern, for he grins and pats my arm with his free hand. His gun is still held firmly in the other.

"Don't you know anything? Look, it's a long journey, but stay awake. I can't be with you all the time. I'm the navigator too. Helping the Captain. And only use your knife if you have to."

Drackem heads for the bow where he disappears into the cabin to join the Captain. Meanwhile I'm left not knowing whom to trust or what the bigger picture might be. All I do know is that I love Rea, that I want a life with her and that to escape from Man Camp 7 is the only way to achieve this.

We huddle together in the stern. Rea soon drifts off to sleep but I know to stay awake. Uneasy thoughts lap at my consciousness like the waves in the swell that curve from the bow of the boat in which we've put all our trust. They break against the slumber that yearns to take over; they bear me back to Man Camp 7 as a boy of thirteen who had seen his mother and sister killed, had lost the only friend he'd ever known, and had witnessed the destruction of a place he once called home.

***

Home?

The truck that prised me from my home followed an old road hugging the coast, so pock-marked with holes and gaps and sprouting plants that my backside soon became bruised from incessant bumping up and down. There must have been at least twenty of us squashed into the open back, though to tell the truth, my mind wasn't up to counting. It wasn't up to anything other than staying alive. I almost wished they had shot me instead, for without Moira I saw no point in living. It started to drizzle. A fine sea-salt drizzle. Soon we were soaked and sat like sponges tipped from a bucket of water.

Although I knew some of the faces in the truck, plus names that gave meaning to those faces, there were several not from our Reservation. I realised then that our little community wasn't the only one to be broken apart by the Parth Path. Overseeing us was a gaunt woman with a whip and a gun, so no one dared to speak during the interminable journey. Although we were sodden through to our bones, and shivering, the eyes of our guard were colder than anything the weather could come up with. They were like the ice that formed in those winter puddles that Moira and I loved to break with our heels, using frozen slivers in mock-dagger fights till they melted; they resembled the eyes of the dead fish we found floating in the sea, and the snowballs we once threw at a bunch of boys who chased us with taunting words:

Two little love birds sat by a tree
One tried to crap whilst the other had a pee...

I now realise how jealous they were, for there were not enough girls to please all of us boys for their 'startings'. This was mostly due to the disappearances. Several of the prettiest girls who were coming of age simply disappeared. Whether stolen by the Parth Path for laboratory use, for distribution to other reservations or intended for man camp commandants' bed chambers, I never found out, but it put pressure on our community and my friendship with Moira. So, little wonder that, when my eyes met with those of rivals from our reservation, with many, no doubt, as bitter as Luke, theirs were as unwelcoming as the wardens'.

My first plan for escape was hatched in that truck. Having survived, I had to return for wee Moira. I considered scrambling over the wet, miserable bodies of other ratties, jumping from the back of the truck and running, yes running, all the way to the Reservation, then heading straight for the shore, diving into the water and swimming after the boat that I assumed had taken Moira away from me. However, I already knew what guns could do. Each time the truck pulled into a man camp to disgorge a few boys, my eyes sought a hiding place where I might lie low before following the road back to the Reservation, but my brain knew that escape was only a dream. The cold finally did for my brain. It had become a useless thing. By the time we arrived at Man Camp 7, even my senses barely functioned. Only with focused concentration could I feel, smell and hear things.

After tumbling out of the truck, I was grabbed. Moments later I felt the sharp sting of the warden's lash across my back. My scream was little more than a disembodied noise that leapt from my throat without any conscious effort. The reason for the lash? Who knows? The smell of my sweat offensive to the red warden, perhaps? More likely, the anger lingering in my eyes annoyed the woman. After that, I was dragged off to a cleansing hut that stank of disinfectant.

I thought my nightmare might end there, either with a bullet to my head or a pleasant surprise. Was Moira in an adjoining building? Would she come running out to tell me about the wonderful things she'd seen and played with in a new home that I had fantasised about in the truck to ease the pain? Perhaps she didn't leave the Reservation by boat. Maybe she'd travelled in that other covered truck I saw in the yard.

But from that moment on there was no home, no Moira, no family... and no laughter. Not for ten years until I met Rea in the canteen. But I shouldn't complain. I was never flogged again. And I was given privileges denied to other ratties, which made me feel good—or, at least, 'special'—but I had no friends.

Did I just say 'no friends'? Correct to a point, but if you're 'special' you have no true enemies either. Not in the Luke sense. From day one, I was set apart to eat by myself until I told a pre-Hellcat-era red warden with ears that listened that I felt lonely. The other rattie boys used to talk and joke in the canteen, the hub of our existence, and to be separated off as 'special' sometimes seemed like punishment. The woman responded to my misery and subsequently others were allowed to join me... individually.

Should this have made me think why? Of course it should have, but when one loses everything that matters, as I had done, logic vanishes. I enjoyed talking to those other ratties at my canteen table in the evenings. I pretended to laugh at their jokes and, soon, we grew beyond that age when, in the reservations (Man Camp 7 has reservation ratties from all over the country), we would have either been selected by a girl who had 'started' or be envying other boys who had been granted such fortune.

Naturally, we talked about females. A lot. Although we were vastly inferior to 'Double Xs', as girls and women are called, this didn't stop us from discussing the delights of feminine attributes such as breasts, bottoms and legs. I suppose that's when my passion for curves started burst into flower like a dormant winter bud opening in a sexual spring, and why, on first seeing Rea, I asked for a second helping.

Double Xs always served in the canteen. Single X-Whys is how the red wardens teasingly refer to the inferior sex, the 'why' a question to which the answer was drummed into our skulls during lengthy and painful (for those who got whipped) Parth Path lessons. Males contaminated the planet, suppressed the superior sex and, during the Great Man War, destroyed not only almost everything humankind had achieved during its first two hundred thousand years, but also most living Single X-Whys of a species renamed *Femina sapiens*. Not required, like the others, to sit exams, I could afford to switch off during those yawn-inducing hours in the school room and dream about Moira turning into one of those busty girls who served us mash and mince, plus think about what I would do to Luke if she had been forced to choose him wherever it was they had taken her to. From the way he ogled her, and after seeing him emerge triumphantly from the chief's house, I could only assume the worst.

It's not entirely true that no friendships were formed by me in Man Camp 7. Some Single X-Whys I found easier to converse with than others. A few even talked freely about experiences in their reservations, about the girls there and how happy they had been in family units. We had a common past if not future, but somehow the red wardens saw to it that opportunities for developing close friendships never arose. We would be separated and the other rattie, sooner or later, moved to another hut or, as sometimes happened, disappeared altogether.

And the illicit books? I would wallow in the excitement of reading these before passing them on to those whom I trusted, hiding them in various secret places that only a few of us knew about, but never once did I, nor any of the others, question their source of origin. They were my true education and, in times of desperation, in the heart-break that I might never be re-united with Moira, my salvation.

Texta, who arrived at the man camp when I was fifteen, has always been a puzzle to me. Perhaps her direct access to the Commandant, whom neither I nor any other Single X-Why rattie has ever seen, adds mystery to the woman. The best thing I've heard about her is Rea's remark that she's like a 'mother' to the girl. I've often spoken to Rea about my own mother, about coming out of her as a baby, which makes me a 'nattie', and about that very special bond between us and between her and Caitlin. I saw the love in her eyes when Caitlin was dying of the fever, and the hurt in them when she knew she was about to lose me as well. We were both a part of her, and she of us. But Rea a part of Texta?

I often wonder whether Texta once had nattie children of her own. After all, she was 'married'. She had a man, as Rea has me. But where is he now? How did I lose him? Is Rea a man-substitute for her? This makes me uneasy, for a substitute could also be a possession. I must ask the girl. The first thing I'll do when Rea awakens will be to ask her whether Texta has a son or a daughter or both. Like Mother Mary.

Things seemed easier after Texta's arrival. For me, anyhow. Fewer obligatory lessons. I was allowed time alone in the yard. Time to wander and wonder. The red wardens avoided me altogether until Hellcat made her first appearance. I came closer to feeling happy. Happy like when I last played with Moira.

And *because* of Moira. You see, my friend remained in my head, almost as real as when she lived in a hut not two hundred yards from ours, and in my head, we played, talked and even kissed, for, having sprouted breasts, she had transformed, in my head, into a young woman. I must confess that there she was prettier than the reservation child, resembling those new-liners that passed through Man Camp 7, with my brain making allowances for changes effected by the passage of time.

Even I had changed beyond recognition. What, I would often ask myself, would Moira make of my beard?

I never gave up planning an escape. In addition to an image of a changed Moira, my brain housed a map of every niche and corner of Man Camp 7. This included spider-eye detail of all buildings, spaces, distances and materials. I had travelled the curves of the perimeter wire fence a thousand times over and knew the thickness of the wire and the precise diameters of those hexagonal empty spaces it patterned. Each tower had been imprinted upon my brain. My mind had climbed those metal ladders to kill the guards perched on their platforms so often that their bodies, as my brain saw them, had turned into flesh-dolls covered with knife slits of vivid blood red. Red has always been my personal colour of anger.

And yet...

And yet until I made love to Rea, none of this could happen. See how far I've come after getting a second helping of mash from the most perfect female to ever walk the face of Planet Earth!

One of twenty Rea lookalikes?

No, I can't let that spoil my triumph. Besides, she told me that, although they appear identical, new-liner clonies are as different from each other as are any other two people. But would *I* be able to tell them apart having entered Rea's body and shared with her soul the rapture of such a union? Of course I would, I keep telling myself. Rea is Rea. Others might look like her, but, with them not *being* Rea, I should be able to tell. Shouldn't I? Then Moira reappears in my head. A bigger, better more beautiful Moira. And Moira tells me that Rea is no more than a substitute for her, as Texta is a mother substitute for Rea.

74

My brain rebels. It clings to a future with Rea. The real-life mother and father game we started behind the store shed in Man Camp 7 will have new meaning on the Island. We'll have a hut to ourselves, grow potatoes and vegetables as Father once did, and those other nineteen Rea-lookalikes will become as irrelevant as the Controller herself.

What did Drackem mean by 'the Controller is the other one'? And to get to the Island and realise my dream, whom should I believe? Plus, whom can I trust—the Captain or Drackem?

***

Luke smiled as he watched the red wardens silence forever bothersome, injured, groaning fellow ratties. One day, he, too, would own a gun, he promised himself. He returned to the Chief's house.

"When can I have her?" he asked.

"Impatient boy! All in good time."

"But you said—"

"I said she'll be yours but didn't say when. Meanwhile you could do with a few slaves to help clean up this place. Anyone left alive you can call your slave. To help you prepare for the new arrivals."

"New arrivals?"

"Surely you knew?"

"What?"

"Starting over again. Natties from the City. Whilst we're rebuilding there."

"Another reservation?"

"Same reservation. New occupants. Now, go out there and put the survivors to work. They've spared the strongest men. Have them pile the bodies up, dowse these with fuel and burn them. Be sparing with the fuel, though. The ashes can be spread over the potato fields.

75

The big boat'll be here in two or three days. With new Wrathie Ratties. You and your slaves get to stay on."

"What about Moira? Will they bring her back for me?"

"Too many questions. Get to work."

Chapter 6

Rea screams. My eyes flick open. Holy Controller, I'd drifted off! She's not beside me.

In the darkness ahead, two figures struggle together. The larger one holds something.

A gun? Drackem and—

I jump to my feet and pull out my knife. Drackem points the gun at me.

"She smiled," he shouts. "I know what that means. You've had your time with her. After the scum have been paid off with provisions, there'll be little left for me. The Captain will pocket the rest. So, you'll not deny me a little pleasure, will you? She wants it. I can tell. And this time from me!"

"Peter, stop him. I can't—" She tries to bite at the hand gripping the front of her dress.

"Shut up you little clonie bitch. We're going to my cabin and no one's gonna stop us. Want me to kill him now or hand him over to the Controller? Come to think of it—AAARGH!"

Rea jabs her elbow into Drackem's ribs and breaks free. She runs to me. Drackem raises his gun. She protects me with her body. Behind the man something appears on the steps that lead below deck. Something very large.

Keep the bastard talking...

"You have to humour women, Drackem. Not upset them. You're going about this the wrong way," I suggest.

Even in the shadow of night, I detect confusion distorting the features of the man about to kill me. I can only guess he's never actually 'had' a woman.

"Humour? You mean tickle? Give her back here, Solem. Bit of slap and tickle will do the job, ay? Oh, and watching you die. That should make her laugh. Do they laugh like us, these new-liners? Never fucked one before. This'll be a glorious first."

Keep talking, you bastard. Just let it all come out. All your pent-up frustration. Never fucked anything, have you?

"Don't have to listen to the big bosses, do I? Either of them. Never get to see those women, anyway. Not even Texta. What's she like? Beautiful like this one or an old hag? Look, Solem, I've nothing against you. I only want a little—"

Aware of the huge figure looming right behind Drackem, I keep my gaze firmly fixed on the man's sad, tear-filled eyes. I feel strangely sorry for him. Two arms stretch out like the trunks of the trees Moira and I used to climb in the forest that skirted the mountains. Moments later they snap inwards, squeezing the breath out my would-be killer in a curious gurgled grunt. The gun drops to the deck and I run forwards to grab it. The gentle Rolem holds Drackem firm. Even a coil of nautical rope could not be as secure. Drackem, struggling for breath, kicks and wriggles, like a little worm, against the giant's python grip.

"Overboard, Master?" he asks.

Master? Me? A new word. I'd heard many a red warden demand to be addressed as 'mistress' from some cowering new boy, but 'master'? Never!

Rea holds onto my arm. Feeling her hand tremble, I know there is no other option. I nod. Drackem, his feet raised free from the ground, treading air, is taken with such ease to the side of the boat that it almost looks funny. Moira and I used to play with dolls and puppets. I believe I told you this. I try to suppress a giggle as Drackem-the-dancing-puppet is lifted up over the side. He screams, those monstrous arms release their grip and he's gone.

The gentle giant approaches me. I look for reassurance in his face that he won't do the same to me. It's there, in the kindest of eyes I've seen on anyone apart from Moira, Mother and Rea.

"I'll go back below deck, Master, if that's all right."

I release a laugh and pat him playfully on a shoulder reminiscent of the mountain rocks I once tried to persuade young Moira to climb with me. Rea is still shaking, so, after he's gone, clutching the gun (I know to pull back on that little curved catch called a 'trigger'). I hold her close and together we walk around to the small cabin at the front of the boat. The Captain stands alone, both hands on the tiller.

"I heard the screams," he says calmly. "Her and—?" He throws a quick glance. "Oh—you've got the gun from him, I see."

"Will you please tell me what the heck's going on?" I demand, pointing the accursed thing at him. "You accused that lot out there. Called them scum. Drackem accused you. Then he attacked Rea. And what's all that business between Texta and the Controller?"

"Between?" replies the captain. "They're together, that's for sure. So, you dispensed with our gunslinger single-handed using only a knife? No wonder they're after your genes."

"*My* genes?" I say nothing about Rolem's intervention.

"You want to know what it's all about? One word. Genes. The magic of our future. All our futures."

"But you said Drackem was to be trusted."

79

"He was. By *her*. Which is why I chose to use him. To test *you*." The Captain's grin threatens to split his face in two. It seems, now, that there are two captains, neither of whom I know. "As for Rea, she could have chosen him instead. But no, we got it right."

"You and who else?"

The Captain laughs.

"Yes, who else, ay? Who else is there? Look, I know you've got the gun now, as she said you would, and you really can trust Rolem—"

"Rolem?"

"The gentle giant. But he can't be in all places all the time. The others are truly scum. Stay in here with me. There's a bunk back there. Sleep. With Rea. Need to be awake when we get to the Island. Oh, and thanks for sorting out Drackem for me."

With a flick of his hand, he indicates a mattress-covered shelf on the wall behind me. I glance at Rea. She nods. Soon we're cuddled up together on the bunk, the gun in my hand, forefinger on the trigger. The Captain peers over his shoulder and winks. I know what he means, but I can't do it. Not here. I respect Rea too much. I'm angered that he should even expect me to make love to her in his presence. Bloody voyeur! Damn the man. Can I trust anyone?

Can I trust Texta? How come the maid of the Commandant's bed chamber, the woman who oversees the canteen girls and is distinctly inferior to the lowest of the red wardens, how come she's talked about as if on a par with the Controller herself? I realise I'll get nothing more from the Captain, but for some inexplicable reason I do trust him. Rea soon drifts off, one arm around my waist.

I fight to stay awake, but the next thing I know, it's become brighter. Rea is awake and looking at me, the gun now in her hand and therefore useless. I'm freezing, but her gaze is like a breath that warms my soul. I want only to fall into those loving eyes to escape from this hell. Her hand reaches out to stroke my cheek. I cup mine over hers and hold it, so alive, against my cheek. Then I take the gun from her.

"Dreaming?" she asks.

"As always," I answer.

"About?"

Can I say? About Moira? Why won't my past leave me alone? If ever Moira and Rea were to be placed side by side, there would be no questioning my choice. Poor wee Moira would not stand a chance. And yet memories of my childhood friend refuse to go away.

"About—" I roll over and study the solid, square back of the Captain. He barely moves as he steers the boat. "About what must never be. The past. It's gone. Hellcat, the Commandant, her slaves, her—"

"Her bed?" offers Rea. "And her smell?"

"Was it that bad?"

"It was like... you remember the blood on our hands from that guard in the tower? How it smelled?"

Yes, I can still smell the blood. And I can still hear Mother's screams and the bang of the bullet before exploding into her skull. I nod.

"Pretty bad, ay? And to think I once doubted you. With her. Texta. But never again. I promise."

"You can even smell it on Texta."

"What?"

"That awful smell. Of the Commandant. Do I—?" I take hold of her hand again, raise it up to my nose and draw in a deep breath, then laugh. "What?" she asks.

81

"Flowers," I reply. "You. Only flowers."

"Flowers? You silly man! Look, will you—?" Hesitant about finishing her question, Rea strokes my cheek with the back of her hand. For some reason, this makes me wish to make love to her there and then, Captain or no Captain. "Will you let me into your dreams one day?"

I frown.

"You might not enjoy them."

Her turn to frown:

"That girl called Moira! I wish I could put my hand into you, get hold of her and pull her out. Then... then throw her into the sea like the giant did with Drackem."

I laugh, then kiss her.

"So you shall. Throw Moira into the sea. With the Commandant and Hellcat and maybe even Texta."

Rea draws away from me.

"Why Texta?"

"The past, Rea. On the Island, the past will truly become the past."

I look to the Captain for a response. A shuffle of feet, a twist of the neck or a slight flick of a wrist? Nothing! It's obvious he's listening to everything we say, and that he's little more than a pair of ears for his boss—the Controller, Texta or some other unknown female with power—but I want him and that person to know it's over for them. Rea and I will start our new lives together, untarnished, and no one will separate us.

I ease myself up from the bunk, gun in hand, and reach out for Rea. She pulls herself upright and we leave the cabin for the deck outside. Three men are in the bow, uncoiling a rope. Rolem the giant stands between us and them. We're safe. I look at the dawning horizon. The mist has cleared. Resting on a wide curve that separates grey sea from grey sky is a row of dark mountains. The Island.

The island where I can lose the past and bury Moira for good, or, as Rea put it, from where her rival might be thrown—and lost forever—into the brine of forgotten memories.

***

The vehicle stopped. The rear door opened, smothering Moira in an explosion of light. With her hands still bound behind her back, all she could do was to turn her face away and screw up her eyes. The Skeleton leapt from the truck, followed by that pungent, globular roll of fat, Bukla-the-Pig. The Pig pulled Moira out of the truck by her feet, causing her to fall to the gravel whilst her skirt hem to rose up to her waist. The Pig, enjoying a pleasing display of female legs, and more, laughed.

Moira had only survived the painful truck journey by contemplating revenge on these three women. The worsening pain was balanced by increasingly cruel methods of getting her own back... these, for the present, remaining confined within her skull.

After struggling to her feet, Moira focused on the building: a huge, pink structure unlike anything in the Reservation. She looked at the third red warden to emerge from the front of the truck and saw, in the woman's face, a reflection of her own awe. Is this what the Parth Path is really about? *she wondered.*

"Yes," the woman said, stepping forward and grabbing the girl's arm. "It's where you're going, child! School! And it's a lot more than you deserve."

Inside the building, Moira forgot her whip welts, her bound wrists and her captors. She forgot Peter as well, momentarily. Not in her wildest, weirdest dreams could she have imagined such a place: long, window-lined corridors, doors sealing off unspoken mysteries

83

and a hall so huge it could have held the entire Reservation village with space to spare. At the far end of this was a raised platform or stage. Rows of chairs faced the stage like the lines of shells that she and Peter used to create together on the beach.

So, this is what a school should be, *she thought.* If only I could share it with Peter!

"*Is this all just for me?*" Moira asked as they passed by the back of the hall.

Bukla laughed.

"*Oh my, you do think a lot of yourself, don't you!*"

Halfway along the corridor, they halted at a door displaying a white plaque on which was written, in red, 'Parth Path School Directress'. The door was opened by Bukla. Moira got pushed into a room that smelt of leather and dust. Behind a high desk sat a white-haired woman wearing a long red cloak.

"*Took your time, didn't you?*"

"*But Directress, she caused so much—*"

"*Leave us! And free her wrists, for Controller's sake! What on earth came over you? Do you know who this child is?*"

"*But Directress, she was trying to—*"

"*I do not have time to listen to your excuses. Untie her hands and leave us! At once!*"

Freed from her bonds, Moira stood staring at the old lady whilst she rubbed, first the red rings created by the tight cord that had encircled her wrists then the smarting welts criss-crossing her back. Bukla left the room.

"*What's wrong with your back, girl?*" *The Directress got up from her chair and Moira noticed how curiously like a human question mark her old bent body was. She hobbled across the room to confront Moira. Although*

Moira was quite short, the top of the woman's head was no higher than the girl's eyes. "Anything wrong with your back, I asked? I can't do with imperfection."

Moira hesitated. She was about to say she'd been whipped by Bukla-the-Pig. Her mouth was open, and the words were forming, but they got no further. A survival instinct, somewhere in her brain, warned her to keep her mouth shut. So, she shut it and shook her head.

"Good," the old lady said. "Then keep your hands to your sides when I speak to you. I need to have them within my sights all the time. I know what hands can do. And so, too, will you, soon, if you're a good student. I hope to see you earn a red belt one day."

"Is this the Island?" Moira asked.

"I've no idea what you're talking about, child."

The girl decided not to mention the Island again. Maybe these people knew nothing about it. Maybe, if she were to use her brain, she'd find her own way there, and locate Peter. One day.

"Why am I here?" she asked.

"Why indeed? Well, I hope to find that out. The Controller never told me. The other girls are on the mountainside marking out a trail, but they'll soon be back. Meanwhile, I'll have Texta show you to your room."

"Who's Texta?"

"That's one question too many. Wait here."

The Directress shuffled to the door and left the room. Again, Moira entertained the idea of taking off, along the corridor and out of the building, but her back was too sore to endure another lashing. She remained rooted to the tiled floor till the old lady returned with *another woman; a woman of indeterminate age, dressed in grey. A woman with an unreadable face.*

Chapter 7

Drackem, not the sea voyage, nor the 'scum', had been my problem. Now, with the pathetic, female-deprived man overboard, plus Rolem's vast physical presence and a gun in my hand, there's been no further bother.

Rea is treated with the respect she deserves and something magical happens as the curved cut-out of the Island, balanced on the horizon, grows in both size and clarity. I feel genuine happiness. Something I last felt on the Reservation. There's been excitement, lust and sexual fulfilment behind the store shed, but always framed with fear. Now the fear, like Drackem, has gone. The Island seems like a magnet, drawing the boat towards her, whilst filling my future with mountains of pure, solid happiness. I believe Rea feels this too. I daren't ask her, for I know from my past how easily happiness can turn into illusion—like the day they killed Mother and Caitlin and took Moira away. All I want is to be with the only girl I've loved in a way that has true meaning, and wallow in the happiness of it. I nestle my face against Rea's wind-blown black hair, breathing in lungfuls of this happiness laced with smell of the sea and the fragrance of the girl.

But can I ever be truly happy without little Moira? I still ask myself.

Not until she's dead. One thousand percent dead. Whatever happened back then, in the Reservation, here she must die, over and over, to allow Rea to rise up, above the other girl's spirit, and live free like the rattie woman Moira should have become. Rea has already 'chosen' me many times. With Moira it was perhaps but a fanciful illusion.

Leave Moira on the boat if you can't kill her off, I suggest to myself. *Hmm! If only!*

Ahead is a concrete jetty. Two men stand there. Not a woman in sight, apart from Rea. The boat slows and begins to bob, curving slightly before chugging sideways, like a large floating crab, towards the waiting figures. One of the Captain's 'scum' throws a rope ashore. A man somewhat older than me (why does this give me a sense of relief?) picks it up and winds it around a stout metal bollard proudly protruding from the concrete quay like a disembodied phallus. The boat jerks and shudders on bumping into the concrete. A gate swings back, then a landing plank is slid through the gap to connect us with *terra firma*.

"I've done my bit," says the Captain. "Go now. Make history or become history. It's up to you, Solem."

"Peter," corrects Rea. I agree, for Peter is who I really am.

Will Peter be able to leave Moira behind on the boat as easily as he can abandon Solem?

"One at a time," insists the Captain as I help Rea up onto the plank.

Oh no! He's not gonna try that one on me!

I push in front of her, hand the gun to the Captain then immediately swivel round and lift the girl over my shoulder. I must be getting used to this!

"One pair of feet," I call back to the Captain.

He laughs.

"Yes, I've already seen why they chose you. Hurry now. It's getting brighter. We'll be more visible. The Controller's boats have an unpleasant habit of appearing out of nowhere."

I turn to look at him. *Maybe he's not with the Controller after all?*

"And what about you, now?" I'm curious about this mysterious ocean traveller who perhaps belongs only to himself and to the sea, and who surrounds himself with 'scum'.

"I have things to do, places to visit. But believe me, never before has a mission had such a purpose as this one. Suddenly, it all seems worthwhile."

Whether the Captain knows nothing more or too much I cannot tell. I continue down the gangplank, carrying in my arms the only reason for my continued existence. Rea giggles as I take her off the boat onto the shore where, with the care and respect that she deserves, I lower the girl to her feet. Thanks to Rolem the giant, we can leave the homemade crutch behind. I turn to wave, but the Captain has already left the boat side. The plank is pulled up and the boat, freed from the quayside, edges backwards before swinging her bow away from the shore.

As she does this, something extraordinary happens. I stand stupefied, mouth open, when a huge form bursts forth from the cabin and leaps into the water, causing a miniature tsunami to lick along jetty. Rolem's head breaks the surface before the massive man swims strongly towards us. After a flurry of activity on board, a row of bearded men leans over the ship's side. Voices call out. Something gets flung into the water but Rolem ignores it. His great paddle arms claw the surf until he reaches the quay where a series of rungs embedded in the concrete allows him to easily scale the ten-foot-high jetty wall. More shouts, more frantic movement on the boat. The Captain appears. He yells something, the men disperse, and he returns to the cabin. The boat moves away, gathering speed.

My mouth remains open. Rea squeezes my hand then smiles up at me. I grin back as the giant approaches, more than happy to have him with us.

"I thought to myself, 'suppose she gets hurt again'," he says. "Or there's another Drackem on the Island. I know this place only too well!"

I turn to face our welcoming party of two: the older man and the other one, not so old but ugly enough to pose only minimal threat as a rival for Rea's attentions. I'm starting to learn how different this world outside Man Camp 7 is going to be. In that realm of women, a girl like Rea, who hates being bedded by the Commandant, is mine for the asking. In this shady world of men, my supremacy over her has already been challenged. If it wasn't for Rolem, my story might have a very different ending. Now, every fit, younger man, except for the giant, must be treated with suspicion.

"Solem?" enquires the older man, clearly the other's superior.

"Yes. And this is—"

"Rea?"

How come everyone bloody knows?

I scowl.

"Uh-huh! And that's Rolem." The man and the giant exchange brief nods as if already acquainted. "Look, let's get this right. We've been sent by Texta. You know the woman, right?"

"My wife," he answers.

Wife? I've heard the word. Before the Great Man War, most men paired up with a woman, and the word 'wife' was used. My father once told me.

"Oh!" I offer. What else can I say as unformed questions still scramble around inside my head? Why am

I here? What have Texta and the Controller to do with any of this? Will we be left to live in peace?

'Live' is the only word that makes sense following what happened after I lost Moira. To be paired with Rea = Life. No more scuffling behind the store-shed. No more blocking out the whip-cut screams or imagining what the Commandant does with my beloved's breasts in her bed. Lucky for that invisible woman, I've never seen her, for even the word 'Commandant' turns whatever I'm looking at red. To send her to the watery depths to join Drackem in eternal slumber would be hard to resist should we ever meet. I know my temper as well as Moira once understood it.

Moira—dear little Moira—please leave me now. Much as I still love you I do not
want you here. Not in my new life.

"Texta promised us a new life here," I say to the man who claims that Texta is his wife. "At least, my understanding was—*is*..."

"She's not Texta to me," the man buts in. "Anna. From when we lived together in a reservation many years ago."

I glance at Rea. She shrugs her shoulders.

"I never knew," she says.

"We—Rea and me, only know her as Texta. So, you, too, got separated?"

"You'll both be tired," he replies, avoiding my question. "Long journey. Uncomfortable, I bet," I know now not to ask too many questions. "The Captain's not famous for his hospitality."

"He's okay. But he might've warned me. About that bastard with a gun."

"No. That's the whole point. It's why you're here. But we'll talk later. Better get you to your hut first. Rolem will be your neighbour. So, you'll have no need to worry."

"And *you* are?" I hate the nameless. But they make me see black, not red, for there's a darkness about those who refuse to give up their names.

"Tommy."

"Funny name. Like the ones in the Reservation I came from. Let me get one thing straight, Tommy. Who's really in control here on the Island? Reservations are only—" Words dance in my brain dressed as unanswered questions. What are reservations for? Have they any purpose beyond the amusement of the Controller's bullies? And is the Island going to be more of the same? "—Only temporary. I see that now. But not then."

"She can't touch you here," he replies without convincing me.

But why was the Captain so scared? I can tell that there's something Tommy isn't saying. He man frowns, then shrugs his shoulders:

"The Captain has his moments," Tommy adds as if reading my thoughts. "Most of us do. But you're right. There's a new life here waiting for you two. Just follow me."

He sets off along the jetty towards a wide path that disappears into a dark green splash of pine woods fringing the mountain. He turns around.

"Sorry. Too much talking. I should've introduced my friend. He's called Matt. Need to know anything, ask Matt." Matt acknowledges his presence with a tight-lipped grimace.

Tommy's hair is as white as a summer cloud. Matt's is grey like an approaching winter storm. His thin, wiry frame is clothed in the tattiest garments I've seen on anyone other than Watchem: grey, like his hair and expression, and dappled with darker stains and gaping holes with torn edges. Although Rea could never desire anyone dressed or looking like Matt, he, on the other hand, might lust after her. He follows behind us and I'm relieved to see the faithful giant ambling along in his wake.

The village beyond the woods hugs the hillside in a sweeping curve. The lower slopes of the hill are decorated with a complex patchwork of geometric fields, some brown, some corn-coloured, others green or vivid yellow. On this side of the village is a small lake fed by a stream that snakes down from the mountains before draining into a gully that courses through the woods like an artery before entering the lake. Men stand statue-still around the lake's rim. Yes, men with their fishing rods curved over the motionless water resembling a row of alien stick-creature phalluses.

Why should I fear other men so much? Apart from Drackem, none have ever threatened me or taken away what's mine. So, is the Parth Path correct after all? Is there an innate destructiveness in the 'y' chromosome that justifies even the cruellest of the Path's practices?

Rolem sees me stop to stare at the village.

"Are you thinking this is how it must've been before the Great Man War, Master?"

Master again?

I look into his eyes for something to dislike; a giveaway that will tell me he's teasing and not to be trusted, but I see only warmth and a wish to please.

"If only I could believe that," I reply. "No, I can only go back as far as my childhood."

Tommy and Matt, some way ahead, are safely out of ear-shot. They stop to find out why they're now alone.

"You can't believe this is for real, ay, Solem?" Tommy shouts back at me. "Hurry now. I'll show you. There's so much more."

The three of us catch up and we enter the village together. Immediately, people appear from nowhere. A crowd gathers around us, touching, feeling and grinning. Small children skip in circles around Rea.

"Why is this woman so pretty, Mummy?" a girl asks. "Can you make me look like that?"

"She's special," comes the answer. "*Very* special."

Of course! My reason for doubting any male within shouting distance of us. Rea is 'special'. I guess children here have never, before, seen the perfection of a new-liner.

"Angela, take Solem and Rea to their hut. Give them food. Get your children to show Solem their fields once they've rested."

A sad-looking woman of indeterminate age, with a small boy and an older girl in tow, steps forward and leads us through the village to a hut that would dwarf the canteen of Man Camp 7. At an acceptable distance on either side of this are two smaller huts. One of these somehow manages to absorb Rolem, despite his size. Angela's children run to the third. The girl looks back at us in silence, as if to inform me that this is their property and I'll only be welcome if I first ask permission from her. Using a key, Angela opens the door of the larger hut. She places the key in my hand. Rea and I enter together whilst Angela stands back.

Instead of one big open space, like the canteen and the dormitories of Man Camp 7, the hut is divided into rooms. Rea barely conceals her excitement as she goes from one to another, turning taps on and off, opening

94

empty cupboards, switching on the oven and peering in wonder at the reddening coils inside.

Electricity! We had been told, at Man Camp 7, that this, an invention of the First Controller, was only available in man camps and those places from where new-liners emerge. Laboratories. Should this revelation of deceit worry me? I flick on a wall switch. A light shines down from the ceiling, as in Man Camp 7. But I don't share Rea's delight. Something, I sense, is wrong. It's all been too easy.

We enter the bed chamber. At first Rea holds back. There's fear in her eyes.

"The Commandant?" I ask.

She nods.

I encircle her delicious curves in my arms, kiss the nape of her neck and reassure her that this particular bed is hers and mine only and that I'll kill anyone or anything, Commandant included, who tries to use it to extract pleasure from her body. I leave her staring at the bed, confronting her fear, and go to speak with Angela who remains standing patiently in the doorway.

A woman who is neither attractive nor ugly, neither tall nor short and with hair a colour I find impossible to describe, her expression is like a door that leads nowhere. Her children, a boy of around ten and a girl, three or four years older, could not be more different. Their faces tell a million stories. Their wide eyes reflect fleeting fears, moments of joy, wonder, anger and bemusement like ever-changing living kaleidoscopes. The children, I decide, must tell me what I need to know, not Angela or that dour creature Matt.

"Thank you," I say to their mother. "And what are the children's names?"

She looks oddly at me.

"Your two children. Don't they have names?"

"Oh—Daniel and Sara. Daniel's the boy and—"

"Sara's the girl. Yes. Tell them not to be frightened of me. Tell them that—" I look back through the door at Rea whose gaze is still fixed on the bed. I reckon I'll have my work cut out to persuade her to use it. "Tell them that there'll be more children here soon. Little ones. Babies."

What I say causes no reaction from the woman but her children, still standing in the doorway of the house next door, must have overheard for they suddenly run to us, grinning insanely. Sara claps her hands together. Her eyes beg me for information for she seems lost for words.

"Sara wants to know when," explains Daniel, the one with a voice.

I wish I knew, but it's why I'm here. Plus, to be with Rea. What I don't know is whether cloned new-liners can reverse the laboratory process and achieve natural reproduction, the norm for our species before this got tinkered with by Parth Path scientists. Where is the wisdom in the Latin name applied to our species? *Femina sapiens* is as misleading a classification of our kind as was *Homo sapiens* before the Great Man War.

I have no answers for Sara. Only hopes. But I have an idea that just might relieve Rea of her fear of beds.

"Do you children like bouncing?" I cheerfully ask, looking at the bed.

At last, a reaction from their dummy of a mother. She appears shocked, which pleases me. But it's ecstasy, not shock, that lights up her children's faces.

"Bouncing?" questions Daniel. "Like a ball?"

Rea once told me something about the Commandant's bed that has always intrigued me. Apparently, it's springy. Not hard, like the man camp bunks. The groping of the older woman, as she used to writhe and jerk about on top of Rea, pleasuring only herself, apparently caused the bed to bounce. Rea once told me:

"Must be something inside that makes it go up and down," she said. "Or it's the rattie."

"Rattie? Like me?" I suggested, tongue half in cheek. "Or a soft springy rat inside the mattress. Jumping up and down!"

"Neither!" my girl replied shaking her head. "Her! She's the worst kind of rat. Evil! And bouncing away on top of me. Yuk!"

I'd never truly considered how awful it must have been for Rea to face a long night of torment in the Commandant's bed. And not to see the face of the silent woman controlling those groping hands, for there was no light. The Commandant must never be seen by anyone other than Texta, apparently. But perhaps these two bright children might be able to undo some of the damage done to Rea.

I smile at Daniel and Sara.

"You two may bounce like balls on our bed. Get Rea to join you. Teach her to be happy. Go on!"

They look briefly at their mother for permission, but her expression reveals neither approval nor disapproval. Daniel shrugs his shoulders.

"Come on, Sara! It's what I've always wanted to do on Mummy's bed."

They skip past me into the bedroom. Soon the hut echoes with the delighted shrieks of two children and a woman so beautiful that to look at her for the first time is a divine revelation. All three bounce on our bed as if in competition to see who can break it first.

But the bed is strong. And they soon tire and collapse into a giggling heap.

"Can you tell us a story?" asks Daniel of Rea.

Panic straightens Rea's grin. I realise she has no stories to tell. Only the one we're now living, and who knows how it will end? I see my chance. I suggest to Angela, who at least now looks miserable, an improvement on 'nothing', that she should return to her hut. She has to know that the children will be safe with the two who have been 'chosen' as would appear to be common knowledge here on the Island.

There were no children in Man Camp 7. The last time I saw a child was in the Reservation. Being a child myself back then, it was the adults who seemed odd. Children were normal. Back in this world of natties, watching Daniel and Sara at play, despite a time-slip of ten years, feels more 'normal' for me than sailing in a boat full of bearded men, or talking, in whispers, to other ratties in Man Camp 7.

"Children, *I* have a story. A true one. About a sheep, a baby duck and a little girl," I offer.

Two young faces fix on me with an eagerness I'd not seen since my own childhood. I sit on the edge of the bed on which Daniel and Sara lie snug on either side of Rea, and I watch three pairs of eyes hang on every word as I tell them about the yellow duckling Moira found abandoned in the fields one evening:

We were eight at the time. Moira loved animals and, sensing this, they always loved her. We went around all the huts asking if anyone had lost a duckling, but the wee creature appeared to be ownerless. It was a particularly cold spring, snow continued to cover the top halves of the mountains well after sowing and planting had begun in the fields, and we thought it a miracle that the duckling hadn't died out there on her own. Moira wanted to keep the lively little yellow ball of

*fluff in her bed that night, but Mother Agnes said, 'No!'
It was known in the Reservation that animals,
particularly birds, carry diseases and, although we had
some medicines, no risks could be taken. The duckling,
who got named 'Quack', was forced to sleep in a box of
straw outside the family hut. I remember trying,
unsuccessfully, to comfort my friend. I thought the girl's
tears would never stop. I even worried that she might
dry out and die. I had to find a solution. And I did.*

*There were some baby lambs in a pen at the far end
of the village, and I knew the sheep got shorn to make
warm clothes for us in the winter. I ran back to my
friend's hut and excitedly explained my idea to her
mother: a baby lamb would become a surrogate mother
duck. Not only did it work, but I became the talk of the
Reservation.*

Unwittingly I had, perhaps, sown the seeds of both
my selection and of our Reservation's destruction,
though this is pure speculation.

"And so, the little girl carried the duckling in her wee
hands and placed her on a cosy, fleecy, living bed. The
next morning, she and I met up at the break of dawn
beside the sheep pen. The lamb and the duckling had not
only become the best of friends, but the little bird
followed the baby sheep wherever it went, calling out
with shrill, high-pitched quacks. It had adopted the lamb
as its mother, and the lamb responded by licking the
duckling and playfully nudging her with its nose."

I laugh, genuinely, at the memory of Quack being
knocked backwards by the lamb's overenthusiastic
olfactory apparatus, and of Moira's giggles. Perhaps, I'm
thinking, the best way to extinguish Moira forever is to
let her out into the open and giggle herself to death.

The children laugh too, but Rea only lies on the bed, her face dark with doubt.

"What is it?" I ask. "Didn't you like my story? It was true. That baby duck and lamb became the greatest of friends. Everyone in our Reservation loved to come and watch them play together. And Moira—" I stop. How insensitive of me! I'd not given a second thought to banging on about my friend from the past, as if Rea and I have no past to share. "I'm sorry, Rea. Just thought the children would like to hear—"

"We do, we do, don't we, Sara?" squealed Daniel. "Please tell us more stories or we'll have to bounce again!"

"Quiet, Daniel!" admonishes Sara. The older child's glance is enough to make me realise it's no easy ride for her to carry a brother like Daniel.

"The little girl in the story is no longer," I tell children—untruthfully, for I have no idea what happened to Moira. "And she's not important. Not like Rea. Do you know, Rea is the only woman I've—" On seeing a tear trail Rea's cheek, I stop again. All three of us stare at her, the children with puzzlement and me with guilt.

"It's not that," reassures Rea. At least, I try to feel reassured. "I've had no life. And there are nineteen others just like me who—and no, Peter, even you couldn't tell us apart. I was kidding myself when I told you we're all different. And we did know what each other was thinking. I had nothing to call my own before Texta—and you. No animals, no laughing, no bouncing. Nothing happened. Nothing to store in my head!"

I climb up onto the bed. Sara makes way for me then pulls at Daniel's arm. I hug Rea.

100

"Thank you," I say to the children. "Thanks for helping her. For bouncing! Come back any time. More stories later, ay?"

Sara gets down off the bed. She grabs Daniel and leaves the room with her brother who keeps looking over his shoulder at Rea. Perhaps he finds it hard to believe what his eyes are showing him: female perfection.

"What happened to the duckling?" asks Rea when I've wiped away her tears.

"A fox. Didn't last a week."

But I said nothing about the 'afterwards' when Moira and I searched the woods for days armed with home-made bows and arrows. Never before, nor since, until I planned my escape with Rea, have I felt such determination as during that period when I vowed to kill that accursed fox. But we never found it. Will this planned escape work out any better?

I get up, quietly close the door then return to the bed minus trousers. We make love, and as we do I enter not only Rea, but heaven. Finally, I can leave little Moira in the hell of my past.

Or can I?

***

"This is Texta," explained the Directress.

Moira looked but said nothing.

"You poor thing," said the woman called Texta. "You look done in. Did the wardens treat you well?"

The girl's back was feeling worse by the minute. She glanced from the woman in grey to the Directress, then nodded.

"Good! They're learning all the time. Like the rest of us, ay? So here you can learn, at long last. Your Chief said you're a fast learner. That's the main reason why you're here."

101

Moira had already learned to remain silent. She sought for human warmth in the woman's eyes but found nothing. The accompanying smile was empty of feeling.

"I'll take you to the dormitory. They'll all be back soon. It'll be your first test in your new life here at the school. See to it that you pass."

Texta left the room. For a few moments, Moira remained stationary, her thoughts melding with the pain across her back.

"Go on, then, girl! You heard what she said." The old woman in the red cloak scowled as Moira followed Texta out of the room and along the corridor.

A separate building housed the dormitories. It, too, was pink, almost cheerful, but the windows were small and, although colourful, there was something grim about the place. Maybe, as with the Directress and with Texta, this was because of the lack of any human warmth. Moira sat down on a low, firm bed, nursing her wounds, and she wondered how the arrival of other girls would constitute a test. If only someone could explain what on earth was going on...

Chapter 8

Rea cannot leave her past behind for she has none. No parents, no little friend like Moira—nothing. How can she leave behind nothing? I must try to understand. To keep memories of Moira at bay, I must know what it's like for Rea to emerge from the vacuum of a Parth Path childhood.

They told us that aphids reproduce by parthenogenesis but do it differently from the little South Vietnamese lizard with a weird name. When the First Controller, or, as she's known to Parth Path followers, the 'Great One', first came up with the idea, they told her it could never be done. Something to do with the role of special genes in the spermatozoa that serve as keys to open and close genetic doors. *'Nothing's impossible in science',* she told them. *'And what about Dolly the sheep? Anyway, there are sufficient numbers of men left to get hold of that genetic material and parcel it up in molecular wrappings that will confuse Nature till she gives up.'*

Whilst the Parth Path reveres the First Controller as the Saviour of Civilisation, I'm thinking about those men kept in cages in the laboratory. If civilisation is about life, can such existence also be called 'life'? Rea's 'past' is nothing, but their hideous 'present' must be something unimaginably worse than an empty past.

Nevertheless, she suffered. Perhaps suffering is a sort of 'something'. Food, clothes and water, she had in abundance. Materials to keep her alive. Nineteen lookalikes to play with, too, but—surprise, surprise—all wanted the same thing all the time. Plus, being in one of the later batches of cloned new-liners to emerge from the

103

Great One's laboratories, it seems that most of her waking life, as a child, was spent being examined with needles and scans and with prodding and poking from teams of white-coated women. Her changing lookalike image was stored a million times over in digital files peppered with meaningless figures and codes. Multiplied by twenty, she'd become a three-dimensional perfection of quantum bytes. The 'big event' for her and her fellow clonies was their final separation.

Alone, at last. A being with a purpose? Didn't happen like that. Solitude was accompanied by further scientific scrutiny, including interminable, and often painful, physical examinations. Rea became an existence in which she played only a minor role. At the age of eighteen she was transferred, via several other man camps, to Man Camp 7 where her existence seemed about to morph into hell because of an elephant of a red warden nicknamed 'Hellcat' until the moment I came up for seconds.

What drives those fiends to unleash feminine fury on girls like Rea? Probably the new-liners' genetic perfection. Bizarrely, this saves the girls from punishment beyond the limit, as I've seen happen regularly to new rattie boys and men reduced by whips to limp, lifeless forms suitable only for recycling. Whiplash marks striping the lovely legs and backs of new-liners? The Commandant would personally recycle any red warden guilty of such a defilement of perfection. So, they came up other ways of venting their scorn on girls like Rea. Depriving them of food, water and rest, if desired, were the least unpleasant. Having her stand tied to a post in the exercise yard in the blazing sun for red wardens to torment and tease was a favourite pastime of some. Worst was to become plaything of the night for one of these women. Even being consigned to the Commandant's bed chamber was preferable.

Or was it?

I wish I knew why I continually press Rea about the Commandant. I suppose I've always harboured an irrational fear that if there is something about the girl, past or present, of which I am unaware, then part of her remains lost to me. If part is lost, could this grow to take away the Rea whom I love? As happened with Moira.

No, nothing about the girl should be enshrouded in mystery. Not if we're to begin a real life together here on the Island.

When we have exhausted every precious ounce of passion in that bed, after we've become a single eight-limbed self-searching, writhing creature of silken skin (hers), lean muscle (mine) and moist kisses (both) too many times to count, we lie stretched out, legs overlapping, my fingers tracing those curves that give me so much pleasure.

"Is that all we have to do?" Rea asks.

I roll over, grinning, and drink in the love that flows from her eyes.

"To do what?" I ask.

"Make a baby?"

I laugh.

"How come you're asking this of a simple Single X-Why? Rea, I'm afraid we learned nothing about the truth during those Parth Path lessons. But Moi—" Damn it, I nearly let wee Moira's name escape again after our shared hour in heaven. "*Her* mother. Mother Agnes, she was called. She had us playing mothers and fathers. Babies come from mothers' tummies and—yes, I believe that's all there is to it. Loving each other. Nature's way."

"No needles? No tubes? No men in cages?"

I shake my head.

"No Parth Path. Not here. If we can believe Texta."

"Of course we can! You heard what her husband Tommy said. We're free. Please don't spoil it by being... being—I don't know—being stupid. About Texta." I stay quiet. I've just been to heaven and wish to go there again. Every day, if possible. So, I'll not talk about Moira, Texta, Tommy or Matt.

Rea, at eighteen, is still little more than a child because she had no true childhood to outgrow. One day, I'll allow my anger over Rea's lost past to surface, but not yet. Rea and I must first have a life together. She *will* have her baby—perhaps two, like Mother Mary—and then, piece by piece, I'll collect fragments of truth and fit these together. And perhaps Angela's children, Sara and Daniel, will find a way into my beloved's heart. But Angela and her shell-like state that gives out and takes in nothing? Is there a reason for this? Sara, I believe, knows a lot more than she's willing, at present, to divulge. When she's ready to tell me about her mother, perhaps I shall be a little wiser.

Meanwhile, the curvy bliss of Rea!

***

Why should I wish so much to know what happens to those men in cages? I believe there has to be a reason for the Controller to deploy young new-liners as 'cleaners' in the laboratories rather than use slaves for this purpose. Single X-Why slaves clean out the yards, the canteens and the dormitories, so why dirty the hands of those young jewels of biological perfection in the laboratories? My guess is that it's about forcing them to witness the ultimate in humiliation of a fellow living thing that no longer deserves a share in the wonder of life. An essential Parth Path experience for Rea and other new-liners, the

106

Controller might argue. One that should ensure these Double X creations will never choose to share their beauty with males. But with Rea, the reverse happened, helped by her revulsion at being 'pleasured' by the Commadant.

I tell myself it's because no part of Rea's straight-jacketed life to date must be hidden from me that I have to know these things, plus create an image in my mind of the woman who forcibly took my girl to her bed so many times. There has to be so much more to the Parth Path of which both Rea and Texta are unaware, involving, perhaps, all the commandants and the Controller. The ease with which we have escaped from Man Camp 7 cannot, I fear, be a simple matter of luck and determination. For now, I only wish to conceive of the past as something to be packaged in a sealed box and destroyed forever.

Would that the Moira in my mind could climb into that box and disappear.

But the future? Alone with Rea, at last? We fall asleep together, a twist of limbs, blended angles (me) and curves (her).

***

A strange sound awakens us. A sound that I've not before heard. I look up and see two familiar faces peering down. One belongs to Daniel who, laughing, explains:

"It's our cockerel! He's doing his job. Waking you two up!"

After disentangling our intertwined limbs from their dream-world confusion, Rea and I raise ourselves up onto elbows.

"What," I ask, "is your cockerel?" I'm thinking about the thing between my legs which was so busy with Rea before we fell asleep. In man camps, they call them 'cocks'.

"Husband of all the hens who lay the eggs. And Daddy to the little chicks. Only they haven't arrived yet. Still in their eggs."

Daniel looks at Rea, then giggles, whilst Sara, flushed, looks at me as if she wants to say something but doesn't know how to. With well-budded breasts, she must be at least as old as Moira when I last saw my childhood friend.

"Will you show us?" I ask.

"Of course!" agrees Daniel. "And everything else you need to know. That's why Mummy sent us to see you're awake."

"Mummy?" queries Rea. For her, a word without meaning.

"Mother," I explain.

"Is that what you were doing with him?" the boy asks her, pointing at me. "Starting to become a Mummy?"

"Shhh!" Sara admonishes.

I remember the term 'Mummy' from the Reservation. I nod to Daniel and he grins again, but Sara, clearly embarrassed, turns away. Neither Rea nor I have on any clothing and the bed cover barely covers anything.

"Come on, Daniel. They're awake now."

"But I want to show Albert to Rea."

"Leave them alone. You heard what Mummy said."

The children are gone. I playfully pull Rea from the bed.

"Get dressed. We have to meet Albert."

"No, we don't! Not yet," she protests, laughing. She wraps her arms around me. I need no persuasion to give in to her demands for more love-making whilst serenaded by Albert and his noisy harem of egg-laying females. And I wonder, as she climaxes in my arms, whether it's better or worse for Albert to have to fire more than one hundred and fifty females into orgasmic frenzy.

Later, when dressed, we meet Albert. Daniel chatters away about the cockerel's masculine habits whilst Sara with her keen, gentle eyes, listens. I sense she's a person who, unlike her mother, takes in everything and yet, like her, is still reluctant to give anything away. Not because she's selfish. It's enough to look at the child's eyes to know she isn't that. She's careful. And this seems to tell me something. Why, in this Island paradise, should caution be so important to her?

Rea and I exchange amused glances when Daniel talks about Albert climbing on top of a chosen hen and doing his alpha-male thing whilst flapping his wings. The boy wants to know why the hen just squats down and looks around without trying to escape. It seems to me that Daniel shares ignorance with the Man Camp 7 Commandant who encourages women to titillate rattie men for amusement. Does it not occur to her double X chromosome brain that females might sometimes not only appreciate, but actually enjoy male attention?

"Let's collect the eggs now!" Sara suggests.

Eggs sometimes appeared, scrambled, on the menu in the Man Camp 7 canteen, but Rea had no idea where that creamy-yellow mush comes from. I remember it all from the Reservation, of course, but she probably imagines we went around with a large spoon scooping scrambled egg from the guano-spattered ground of the poultry run.

Moira and I loved to collect eggs. There was one broody hen who barely left the nest and would merely

109

cluck contentedly as I lifted her up for my friend to retrieve whatever emerged from her oviducts. I always did the lifting, Moira the collecting. Because of beaks and claws. But this particularly gentle bird would never have used Mother Nature's weapons against my friend. Not even against the evil fox who gobbled up Quack. Nevertheless, I wanted no possible harm to come to little Moira and therefore insisted on sticking to the same routine we had for all the other hens.

How I failed that girl! I must never allow the same thing to happen to Rea.

Rea cannot stop laughing when she sees her first egg. Sara looks puzzled, so I have to explain to her how Rea has only ever lived in built-up places controlled by the Parth Path, where food is brought in by slaves, and the likes of Watchem. Humans, lizards and dogs are the only living things she'd encountered. She still looks puzzled, but I'm thinking, 'that girl thinks'. Meanwhile, Daniel babbles on about the different ways in which their mother uses eggs.

The children take us into their hut for the first time. It's as if we have finally been vetted and passed as fit to fraternise with Angela. There's a deliciously-fragrant smell in the hut, a smaller version of ours, and Angela hovers in the background, almost fearful of our intrusion. Sara takes over. Once again, I'm in the world of the Double X but a meaningful one. I notice how everything that Sara says and does serves a purpose whereas sentences seem to flow from her brother's lips merely because they need to escape.

Rea's eyes brighten as Sara shows her around the kitchen, explaining objects to do with food preparation that lie hidden behind doors and in drawers. I have the feeling that home life is going to appeal to my girl. I began to notice this about Moira, too. She always loved to take over from Mother Agnes in the kitchen.

"I do all the cooking," Sara explains. "Want me to teach you?" Grinning, Rea nods. "Plus, how to wash things. Come with me. I'll show you where I wash the clothes."

We follow the girl to a small room that surely budded from the kitchen by inanimate parthenogenesis. Buckets of water, neatly lined up against a wall, somehow remind me of slave culls at Man Camp 7. When food production is down in that place, or when there's a need for more man fuel, slave numbers are reduced by 'culling'. The slaves, waiting to be recycled, in tidy lines, are as passive as Sara's line of buckets of water.

Daniel sees his opportunity. I detect in him unease with this indoor world of women, despite his sister being the gentlest creature imaginable.

"Can I take Solem out to the fields?" he asks Sara, not his mother.

"Sure," she cheerfully replies.

I feel troubled. This isn't what I expected to greet us at the end of a perilous sea voyage. I still can't fathom the fear eating away at Angela's face, creating a mask of uncertainty. Who are these people and what might they do to, or with, Rea? It doesn't match up with my memories of the Reservation. I look to Angela for a chink of recognition, something with which I can connect to reassure myself that Rea will not be harmed in my absence. Sara notices.

"She'll be all right. I promise. Look..."

She beckons me over to a chest of drawers, looking up at me with eyes that are at the same time warm, wise and reassuring and way beyond those of a child of her age. I know now that Rea will be safe. Sara opens the drawer, standing in such a way that only she and I can see its contents:

A gun.

Protecting her mother and her brother? From what? From whom?

Sara snaps the drawer shut and continues to explain to Rea how she should wash the clothes with warm water heated on the brick oven in the kitchen, rinsing with cold water from the first of the row of buckets. I leave with Daniel, trusting Sara but not the Island. We run a gauntlet of stares from residents of other huts, but Daniel cheerily waves at them whilst talking to me about growing crops. We reach the fields, not unlike those beyond the Reservation of my childhood. Men and women, dressed not as slaves, in white, but in colourful clothes, are bent digging for potatoes in the first field. Children cheerfully run around their legs, picking up whatever their parents have missed, and tossing their gatherings into the wooden crates dotted about. On seeing Daniel and me, they come running towards us shrieking with delight. The workers look up. I recognise the dour face of Matt amongst them.

Soon, we're encircled by a group of chattering children.

"Can I touch him?" a boy of no more than six asks Daniel. "Can I see what the chosen one feels like?"

Daniel grins at me and I nod. A small hand touches my arm. Its owner giggles. Then another child reaches out and another and another until I'm being poked and prodded and rubbed and patted as if I were some sort of magical animal conferring untold fortune to those connecting with me.

"He's just like us, really," says Daniel. "*She's* the one that's special. You should see her! And they've started making babies, you know."

My face turns hot and red. Not through anger but because of something I haven't experienced since Moira once asked to see my dangly male thing on the beach.

I blushed then, too. I showed her so quickly she would have missed the vision if she'd blinked. All she said was "Oh!" No other comment was made and there was no further mention of the object in question, but I remained red-faced for the rest of the evening. I suppose she felt curious to see what it was that helped to make babies, but I remember fearing that, after seeing it, she might no longer wish to choose me when she'd 'started'. I remember wondering whether it might make a difference if I were to do something about it. By making it bigger, smaller or prettier? Moira often wore a pink ribbon in her blonde hair. Should I tie a pink ribbon around my dangly thing and show her again, I asked myself?

Matt comes over to join us.

"Potatoes," he says, as if the word explains every mystery of the universe. I'm thinking that young Daniel could well give this man lessons in communication.

"Potatoes grow easily if you look after them properly," explains Daniel. "It's like—well, they have to go in at the right depth after the soil's been dug over. Oh, and we use fertilizer. Do you know about fertilizer?"

Ground slaves' bones?

I nod whilst Matt stares at Daniel as though relieved to have discovered, in the boy, an external voice.

"The stuff stinks. We mix burnt animal bones into the compost and pee on it for weeks. Not Sara or the girls. Just me and my friends. Oh, and Albert's stuff too. And the hens'. Sara and I scoop all the shit off the ground

113

and mix that in too. Pfaw! You have to hold your nose. See that wheelbarrow?"

Daniel points to an idle barrow, tilted to one side. I nod. Matt turns to look at it too.

"We use it to carry the fertilizer in. When Sara tells us to. Jimmy fancies Sara, but I think he's too young for her because she's so clever, don't you?"

"Who's Jimmy?"

"Don't you know? Jimmy. The one they thought—" Matt grabs Daniel's arm and pulls him over. He stoops and whispers something into the boy's ear. Daniel looks back at me.

"What?" I ask.

"I've got to show you your growing land," the boy says, freeing himself from Matt. "Next to ours. I'll come back here later to bank up the rest of our late potatoes, but I'll show you where yours grow. And what to do. Follow me!"

I want to know what it is that Matt whispered about Jimmy whom I've never met. Again, I'm glad Rea's with Sara, but I'm more desperate than ever to find out what on earth is going on in this place.

We have a large patch of land, twice the size of Daniel's and Matt's. Beyond rows of sprouting potatoes are tall poles supporting twirled plants which I'm told are beans. I remember beans from the Reservation. Moira adored them. But this little bit of land? Why should it belong to us? Had someone as ruthless as the Commandant confiscated it from others and called it ours?

I asked Daniel, but he merely shrugged his shoulders.

"Everyone knows this is your land," he said. "We've been working it for you. And you're gonna have some of our hens too. Sara says. They're making a run for them now."

"Who?"

"Men."

Men?

I panic, turn and run back towards the huts. People digging up and harvesting potatoes stop to stare at me, much as cows used to back in the Reservation when Moira and I ran together across fields.

"Wait!" Daniel calls out. I don't, so he runs after me.

The boy's right. Three sturdy young men are working away at the back of our hut with posts, spades, hammers and wire. Wire like the stuff that kept us ratties inside the compound of Man Camp 7. I pull out my knife and enter the hut expecting the worst but, to my relief, Rea isn't there. I'd had this fleeting vision of her lying on our bed with another man on top of her. Instead, she's still in Angela's hut, seated at the table with Sara and her mother. All three are eating something pale and sloppy out of bowls. Rea looks up.

"This is delicious," she says, offering me a spoonful.

I take the spoon. Sara's wide eyes watch keenly as I taste the stuff.

Porridge!

I remember, and Mother Mary and Moira reappear in my brain as solid as the pine table on which Rea rests her arms. Every morning, in the Reservation, we ate porridge and already I had grown to prefer Moira's to my mother's. Daniel arrives at the open doorway, out of breath. He seems upset, so I reassure him that I suddenly had to check that Rea was all right. Sara looks offended.

"I'm sorry," I tell her, feeling stupid. "I should have trusted you."

115

"She's going to show me how to make this—um—" Rea looks to Sara, but I complete her sentence.

"Porridge," I say. "And the best I've tasted. Well done, Sara. You'll make a good teacher too, I'm sure of it."

The ice is broken, and Sara's porridge is better than both Mother's and Moira's. Daniel and I sit at the table to enjoy bowlfuls of the stuff. Rea looks happier than I've ever seen her and even Angela is grinning—until I ask her about the children's father.

It's as if a shutter comes down over her eyes, though whether to shut out the world from her sight, or hide her feelings from the gaze of others, I can't tell. She looks to Sara, but it's Daniel who answers:

"Which one?" he asks.

This is not what Rea wants to hear. I can tell this from the way her eyes seem to ask me to shut up, but I must know. Sara, it seems, is Tommy's daughter, and Tommy is Texta's husband. Does that make things any clearer for me? Not when I discover that Matt is Daniel's father yet, like Tommy, lives in another hut. Sara appears angry, whether with me for asking, or with Daniel for telling, I'm not sure, but I feel annoyed with myself for Sara is the last person on the Island I would wish to displease.

"Thanks for doing so much for Rea, Sara," I offer, a feeble attempt to pacify the girl. "Angela's taught you well. And I'm sure there's a lot more for you and Daniel to pass on to us. We must seem pretty stupid to you, but Rea and I have been like prisoners for so long—"

"Always!" insists Rea. "I was never free until you cut a hole in that wire. Thanks to Texta."

"Does she ever come here?" I ask Angela. "Texta, I mean."

No response from the mother, but Sara shakes her head.

"No. She can't. I only know this because—" Sara aborts her sentence and bites her lower lip as if she is suddenly reminded of something and her eyes plead for me to stay quiet. Angela gets up from the table, her face changed. She leaves the room, closing the door behind her. I hear sobs. Sobs like those of my own mother whenever Caitlin fell ill. My young sister always seemed to be suffering from something. Her short life was a story of head-to-toe illnesses and accidents.

"I'm sorry if I've caused offence," I apologise.

"It's not your fault," says Sara. "I'll see to her. Afterwards Rea and I can make things here whilst Daniel shows you how to bank potatoes. And he can tell you what to do with your hens when you get back."

Sara disappears into the back room, and I hear her comforting voice against her mother's crescendo then diminuendo of sobs. What a lucky young man Jimmy will be if the girl chooses him.

I soon discover how back-destroying work in the fields is, for after two hours of digging for potatoes I can barely stand up straight. The other figures in the field go fuzzy when I try, so I hang my head down again before coming up more slowly.

"What are you doing?" asks a small girl.

"Surviving," I reply, clasping both hands over the small of my back before easing myself into a vertical stance. "Surviving! Do you like potatoes?"

"What a funny question!" she said, giggling, before stooping down to help me.

And what funny people, I'm thinking. The scene so resembles the fields worked by slaves I used to peer at through the Man Camp 7 wire fence. Are these Islanders truly free?

Later, Daniel and I dig up turnips for Rea and Sara to cook. Back in our hut, we wash these, slice them and put them in a saucepan together with the early potatoes to await the attention of Rea and Sara. And that's when Rolem makes his first appearance since his whale-sized bulk disappeared through the doorway of his hut the previous day. Now it fills the doorway of our hut, cutting out the light.

"Rea?" he asks.

"With Sara."

"She'll be all right with that girl," he reassures. "It's you I'm going to have to watch."

"Because?"

Daniel's gone to request further orders from his sister, so I see an opportunity to press the gentle giant for more information.

"Mind if I sit down first?" he asks.

"If you can find a chair big enough."

He looks around and fixes on a large box of logs by the fireplace. He lifts this up as if weightless, places it beside me then lowers his broad backside onto it.

"There's only so much I know. Only so much any of us knows. Texta's behind all of this. But she's not who you think she is."

"Works in the canteen at Man Camp 7? The Commandant's bed maid?"

"She *is* the Commandant!"

***

She heard it before she saw it: a babbling river of voices that swelled to a torrent before bursting through the door. A flood of girls of all ages, dressed in blue. The voices dwindled as the flood filled the dormitory. A girl older than Moira stepped forwards.

"Are you the new girl?" she asked.

Moira had always hated stupid questions and stupid people.

"What do you think?"

"What's your name? They told us you were coming today but said nothing else about you."

"Tell me yours first."

Moira stood up and studied the red-haired girl who seemed as wide as Moira was tall. She decided she didn't like the other girl's self-satisfaction which had worked its way into a false smile. Their gazes locked swords. Moira would not give in.

The red-head turned to share her supercilious smile with the girls gathered behind her.

"The newcomer so obviously hasn't 'started' yet and she puts herself above me!" Moira immediately thumped a well-aimed blow causing the large girl to topple like a felled tree. The bang of the girl's head striking the floor triggered a gasp that rippled through her fellow students. Moira stood feet astride, peering down at her dazed rival.

"Are you all right, Thea?" questioned a small girl.

"It would have been easier if you, not she, had said who you are," Moira told the larger girl. "Now, will someone tell me what I need to know about this place or must I work it out for myself?"

The girl on the floor remained where she was whilst a sea of faces attempted to think collectively on its feet. Someone who dared knock Thea to the ground? Was this possible? All they had been told was that a new girl was arriving by boat and that she was 'special'. Thea's warning that pandering to this girl would be punishable

119

by 'exclusion' had, in an instant, become irrelevant. The red-haired girl stretched out on the ground, rubbing her head, was already excluded.

"That's your bed. The one at the top there."

The child who had informed Moira that the red-head was called Thea pointed to a solitary bed at the far end of the dormitory, placed at right angles to the rows lining the long walls.

"Thank you," said Moira. Mother Agnes had taught her to always be polite.

***

"What?"

I feel sick. The room seems to swim around me and Rolem's large face goes into a spin. I hold onto the side of the table for support, although I'm already seated. "What?" I repeat, as if Rolem didn't hear me the first time.

"Texta is the Commandant of Man Camp 7. But it's not enough for her."

"Wait a minute. D'you have any idea what Rea and I have been through? To get here? What Rea...?" I think of Rea's torment in the Commandant's bed and her telling me that Texta is like a mother to her. I think of the bother Texta took to arrange our escape. Escape from her? No way!

"I was a part of it. Remember?" Rolem emphasised. "That bastard Drackem? The scum on the boat who but for me would have—"

"But what about the Captain?" I interrupt. "Does he not work for Texta? Avoiding the Commandant's helicopter at the same time? Makes no sense. And Tommy? Texta's husband—plus Sara's father? And... no, I cannot believe this! I'm sorry!"

To think of poor Rea suffering, in bed, the Commandant's unwelcome advances on her beautiful body when it was Texta all along taking advantage of the dark! I want to rush next door and question my girl. Is she also playing games with me? Am I but a plaything in some strange circus of amusement to advance the Parth Path? Rather than enlightening me, Rolem has merely thrown confusion into a chaos of puzzles.

"Why?" I ask.

"Like I just said, Solem. There's only so much I know. And very few know more. The Captain knows even less, I reckon. Holed up in Man Camp 7 you must have thought of that place as your whole world."

"Wrong," I inform him. "I had a past. In the Reservation." I don't mention Moira.

"The past is dead. Like Drackem. You must accept that. Guess you once thought of Man Camp 7 as the ultimate that the Parth Path has to offer you. The only way forward before Rea appeared. Am I right?"

I nod.

"So, she was planted there, wasn't she?" I ask.

"Texta?"

"No, Rea. Texta had her transferred to Man Camp 7 not only for her own enjoyment, but to test me. I—I think I'm going to vomit."

Swamped by a wave of nausea, I turn to retch, then feel a ton-weight hand press down on my arm. Rolem pats my shoulder.

"Rea's special for many people. Not only Texta. And Texta's not the only one wielding power. Like the Captain always says, we should talk about the Parth *Paths*. Use the plural—not singular. Even the Controller—"

"Whom no one ever sees." I interrupt. I have a thought. One that I must share with Rea. It might at least put my mind at rest. "Wait here, Rolem. I'm just going next door."

I leave Rolem alone, wondering, whilst I run to Angela's hut. Rea and Sara have their sleeves rolled up and Rea is mixing something in a bowl.

"Look!" she says, proudly displaying an unappetizing buff-coloured mixture.

"Excuse us a minute," I say to Sara. Rea, frowning, hands the younger girl the bowl and follows me outside. I feel Sara's wide-eyed gaze follow us through the door. I take Rea to Albert's place, away from human eyes and ears.

"Have you ever seen the Commandant?" I ask.

"Of course not!" she answers as if this is the most ridiculous question anyone has ever asked of anyone else. Her eyes tell me she's truthful.

I hug and kiss her as tears threaten to tip from my eye-lids. I cannot describe my sense of relief. Rea touches my cheeks, adding tactile reassurance.

"What a crazy question. No one ever sees the Commandant. When in bed—" She looks distraught. This magnifies my relief. "...In bed with that cow, I have to wear a mask to cover my eyes. Even though it's pitch black. All the lights are out, and she has no windows in her bedroom. It stinks of her sweat. You can also smell this on Texta, poor woman. The Commandant never speaks. Just uses her hands. All over me! Why?"

Rea is crying.

"It's just that—" I falter. Maybe there are things Rea shouldn't yet know. I pretend to laugh. "Then I suppose I'll never know whether you find me better looking or not?"

"Peter—please stop worrying. You've just no idea how much I love you."

122

I kiss her again then watch as she disappears back inside Angela's hut. And I'm beginning to understand why Angela is as she appears to be, but Sara remains a mystery. Tommy's daughter? Is she Texta's daughter too? A young Commandant in training? Is Rea safe with her?

I must return to Rolem to press him further. I now wish to know more about the girl chosen for a boy called Jimmy (or is it vice versa?). But Rolem's gone.

***

I'm quickly learning that the Island in no way resembles the Reservation. This is no haven for natties. It's as much a part of the Parth Path as are Man Camp 7 and the laboratories. The roles that Rea, myself and Angela's children must play are at best unclear, at worst pre-determined by Texta-the-Commandant.

Jimmy is an idiot. The day after Rolem's revelation, I ask Daniel to take me to him, for I'm getting more and more curious about his sister's role in our unfolding story. Maybe Sara-the-Commandant would be no bad thing, for I see only kindness in the child, but Sara paired with an idiot? Why?

Jimmy is only slightly older than Tommy's daughter. Certainly younger than me. He's thick-set, like some of the male guards at Man Camp 7, and can hardly string together two words that make any sense. He can push a barrow in the fields, but that, it seems, is the sum total of his contribution to Island society. Daniel winks at me when he sees my jaw drop.

"She says she's gonna run away if they force her to lie with him. Don't tell anyone else I said that, or Sara would kill me."

"That's too cruel," I say on seeing that clown use his garden fork to play with clods of earth. "But why?"

123

"Some say—" Daniel turns to check that no one else is within earshot. "Some say my sister's the only girl kind enough to put up with Jimmy. But that's not true. Sara thinks it's Texta's fault."

"That woman again?"

Daniel comes up close and whispers. It's the first time I hear him speak without telling the whole world.

"I'll let you into another secret—if Sara's okay about it. Early tomorrow. Before Albert wakes up. I always get up before him anyway."

I'm not sure I want to know anything more concerning Jimmy and Sara, however secret. Shrugging my shoulders, I leave the field for I feel a sudden urge to make love to Rea.

***

It's Rea who awakens me.

"Peter—there's someone outside," she whispers.

A knock on the door. I forgot to tell her before we drifted off to sleep, wrapped together in each other's arms. I place a finger on her soft lips.

"Shhh! It's okay. It'll be Daniel."

"So early?"

"I'll tell him to come back later. You and I have important things to do."

Rea frowns. She still falls victim to my gentle teasing. I fondle her perfect new-liner breasts and the frown is replaced with a smile.

"Very important!" she whispers. "I agree!"

Another knock. Annoyed, I scramble out of bed, grab a towel to hide my firming erection and open the door to Sara, not Daniel. Taken aback, she turns her face away. I feel awful.

"I'm sorry, I... I thought—" I stutter.

124

"Daniel's going to keep a lookout here. Just follow me—when you've, um—when you're—" She looks down at my towel. Can she see?

Sara's not the sort of person to whom you might say, "wait a minute, just tell me what this is about first." I leave her standing at the door, and looking the other way, as I quickly slip into my clothes.

"What does that girl want?" asks Rea. She sounds cross.

"I don't know. Daniel was going to tell me something before Albert wakes up."

"Albert?"

"Rea too?" I ask Sara, ignoring Rea's query, but the younger girl shakes her head.

"Too dangerous," she says.

I kiss Rea and leave her nursing a frown. I follow Sara out of the village compound, round the lake and into the wood, away from the path that led us from the shore to the huts. Without a path, we brush aside bushes and branches as we push our way through the undergrowth in the dim light of dawn. Something bulges Sara's back pocket. The shape informs me it's her gun. This is more than "telling me a secret." As I watch the fabric outline of the gun move up and down on Sara's bottom, I begin to think what a fool I am. This isn't about Texta not being who she seems to be. It's about Sara. Sara, as Moira was when I last saw her being dragged away by those callous red wardens, a girl astride that bridge between childhood and womanhood. I find the changing shape of Sara's silhouette almost as pleasing as the contours of my beloved, and I feel shame. Then fear kicks this aside when I realise I'm alone in the forest with an armed girl whom I honestly do not know and who may even be the Commandant's daughter. And, from what I recently learned from her brother, *she* was supposed to be one of the chosen pair before Rea and I appeared on the scene. There is no other soul within at least a mile radius. Who would find my body in this dense scrub off the beaten path? There again, why kill me and not Rea who may already be with child?

I stop. So, does Sara when she realises I'm no longer behind her.

"It's not far," she calls out without turning.

"My execution spot? Thanks—but no thanks. Shoot me here if you must."

I see it now. Sara wishes to eliminate first me, then go back for Rea.

***

The boy with a grievance large enough to accommodate a boatload of girls like Moira could not stop smiling as he oversaw the completion of the Clearance. The Chief had lent him her whip and he used it with effect. 'Practice,' he called it as he playfully lashed the backs of those who, before the red wardens arrived, were very much his superiors. Practice needed no provocation when he flogged all those survivors who had failed to ensure Moira would become his. Now his dreams would no longer be trapped in fantasy. The Chief had all but promised him Moira's body, and the new Reservation under his leadership would be a very different place. It seemed unlikely that the Chief would interfere with his decisions.

When the large boat docked the following day, Luke was waiting on the shore, whip in hand. He'd disposed of his 'helpers'. He wanted no one from the old place around when he brought Moira back to the new Reservation—his Reservation; no one who might say unpleasant things about him; no one to remind him of Peter.

**

Leaving Thea lying face-up on the floor, the other girls crowded around Moira as she sat on her bed, testing it for comfort. She just wished they'd all go away and leave her alone with private thoughts of Peter. She had already tried to imagine what it would be like in bed with him after 'starting'. Mother Agnes had told her things that made little sense. All she really wanted was for the boy to hold her close and stroke her hair as he'd been so fond of doing of late.

"I'm hungry," Moira said to the girl who had so readily switched allegiance. This girl was the only one who had glasses on, and she wore the fixed expression of someone in a permanent state of fear.

"I'll get you some bread. That's all we're allowed before meal times."

"Just bread?"

"Texta's rules. But if you really are special you might be allowed more."

Ten minutes later, Moira was tucking in to a plate full of bread, cheese and fruit. Most of the girls had dispersed, leaving behind the timid girl with glasses and two dummies who never spoke a word. Thea had taken to her own bed and was looking up at the ceiling. Moira began to feel sorry for the older girl, though not in the least guilty.

"Thea!" she called out. "Have you ever played cricky?" Thea turned a blank face towards the newcomer. "Cricky! It's fun. Want me to teach you?"

Thea sat up, rubbed her head again then came across to Moira's bed. The other three stepped back, still mindful of her authority over them.

127

"Sit next to me," Moira said, patting the bed cover beside her. Not exactly a command, but the red-head seemed to take it that way. She obediently sat next to the new girl, looking at her all the time though green, cat-like eyes. Moira was far prettier, although Thea had never considered looks to be something that trumped size.

"What's cricky?" she asked.

"A game. We played it on my reservation. I always played with the boy I'm going to choose."

"Choose a boy?" Thea failed to conceal her disgust.

"Yes, a boy. My best friend. But I usually win."

"Of course," said Thea. "How could a boy possibly beat a girl?"

Thea had never seen a boy.

"Peter is very handsome. He's my protector too."

"A boy? Your protector?"

"You know nothing, I can see! And with a face like yours, never will. But when I've taught you cricky, we'll have teams and you can be in charge of one of them. All right?"

Moira had decided that the best way to keep on top of Thea was to allow her limited power. She got up and went to the window before the older girl had a chance to respond.

"Out there on that lawn. We can all play cricky," she announced as she peered at the world outside the school; a world into which she would one day escape and find Peter again.

"Aren't you forgetting something?" asked the girl with glasses. But her expression changed when Moira turned abruptly and froze her with contempt. "I mean— we do have classes. With Norma," she burbled.

128

Moira chose to ignore the remark. Instead she looked again out of the window and wondered where, in that world beyond the glass, they had taken Peter to; wondered whether she would ever see him again.

Chapter 9

"What are you talking about?" asks Sara.

Never, before, have I seen anyone look so upset. Seeing the hurt in those mellow eyes, no way could she be planning to kill me. How could I have misread her so badly?

"I'm sorry. Your gun," I explain, patting the back of my hip. Of course she would not have made it so obvious if she had planned to shoot me. For a few awful moments, Sara just looks at me, as if trying to comprehend the impossible—that I could believe her capable of such evil.

"I don't know how to use it," she says at last, "but I thought you might, being a chosen one."

I remember that woman threatening to shoot Moira if I didn't kill her first. I remember the fear.

"I think I know," I said. "Look, Sara, I'm so sorry. It's that man camp place. It makes a man wary."

"A man?"

"Your secret. It'll be as safe with me. Like your gun. Tell me. Now."

"It's a place. Like I said, not far."

Less than a stone's throw from where I stand is a nest of branches part-hidden behind a tangle of brambles. I help Sara pull these off a large circular wooden board from which protrudes a rusted handle.

"Matt says they made it during the Great Man War."

Together, we lift the board aside to reveal a ladder that disappears underground.

"Where does it lead to?" I ask.

"The hideout," she says. "I'll show you. Only me, Daniel and Matt know about it. We hope."

As I descend into the blackness, thoughts of death reappear. Not by Sara's hand but by that of Texta. If only I knew how I fitted into that woman's game.

"Does she know about this place?" I ask when I join the girl at the bottom of the ladder. "Texta, I mean." Sara's just close enough for me to see her shake her head. She strikes a match and lights a candle to reveal a space no larger than Rea's and my bedroom. There's a mattress, with a bedcover, on the floor, a small table, with two chairs, and a cabinet. Beside the wall are three buckets brimming with water. "Your secret hideout?" I ask.

Sara nods. I feel myself blush as I take in the mattress. In only a few years, she'll be as old as Rea and, much sooner than that, able to have babies.

"Why? Why are you showing me? If it's secret?"

"You and Rea are going to need it. I'm sure of it. Because of what you were doing together."

The flickering candlelight plays with Sara's features in a way that makes it hard for me to understand her expression, but I do detect a reddening of cheeks that matches mine.

"I don't follow you. Is this to do with Texta?"

"Everything's to do with Texta."

"She plans to kill me?"

"I—I don't think so. But Rea, yes. If it happens."

"What happens?"

Sara says nothing, but her eyes have me wondering. Ever since first seeing the girl, those eyes have confused me. Just as Texta is turning out to be someone so very different from the woman who planned and facilitated my escape from Man Camp 7, this child, with the mind of a woman, is changing my perception of not only the Island but everything that concerns me.

"How would I ever find this place again without you?" I ask.

"I'll show you. But first, a couple of things. Daniel and I re-fill the water buckets every week. To be prepared. And look inside that cabinet there."

She points to a lop-sided wooden cabinet, with feet missing on one side, that in any other circumstance might have appeared comical. I open it. Inside are many candles and bundles of salted meat and fish, wrapped in dried leaves, and some dried fruit.

"Matt says you don't need much food to survive on your own for long periods, but you have to have water. People die without water."

So, this place is about me—about us—and death. Or about not dying.

"Can I trust Matt?" I ask.

Sara nods.

"Doesn't talk much, does he?"

Sara smiles.

"There's a good reason for that. There are hidden ears all over the Island. Matt's no fool. Look, we'd better go back now. I'll show you how easy it is to find, but please don't tell anyone else. Not even Rea."

I prickle at the thought of keeping anything from Rea. Can I truly trust Sara? I say nothing as we emerge from the hideout before replacing the cover and pushing back the branches. By following black ribbons tied to trees, invisible until pointed out to me, we make our way to the lake and to our village of huts. Sara disappears into Angela's hut whilst I rejoin Rea in bed. She rolls over and kisses me.

Not even Rea?

"What was that about?" she asks.

132

"Nothing," I lie, then stroke and fondle her whilst attempting to drive out from my brain the fear stoked by Sara's words. Whoever Texta turns out to be, Rea is all that she seems. Beautiful, caring wonderful Rea. I will have a life with her. Nothing and no one will stop this.

Not even Sara.

***

Time plays tricks. It taints happiness with fear, need with futility, purpose with boredom, blending all into an existence that slips inexorably towards a quantum soup of fleeting thoughts and moments. Imperceptibly, things change because of time.

Not always for the worse! Rea's pregnant. Soon, the changing curve of her belly reveals this to the Island community. Even Angela appears pleased. Sara is over the moon about the impending arrival of new life whilst Daniel never stops chattering about how babies come into the world, about their needs and their nuisances. How can the child possibly know? Most of all, how can he, or anyone else, imagine the joy that Rea and I feel. I've all but forgotten about Sara's secret in the woods, for the branch-covered hideout seems of vanishing importance compared with the approach of a new life. To think I had even wondered whether a cloned girl could give birth to a child in the same way as a nattie woman! Now, I know that my Rea is not only 'normal' in every possible way, she's super-normal. The chosen one whose baby will be extra special for what I would like to call 'the free world': that world outside the Commandant's dominion in Man Camp 7 and out of reach of the Controller's ears. Whatever her supposed influence on the Island, there is no more than mention of her name, nor indeed that of Texta, the Commandant's alter ego.

Boy or girl? Double X or Single X-Why? For me it doesn't matter, but Rea seems so certain it's to be a girl that she's come up with a name from, for me, the old times. Like my mother, she's to be called 'Mary'.

Rea receives special treatment from all, particularly Sara. According to the Island girl, the daughter of the chosen ones, like her mother, must be protected from every possible danger. The girl is forever watching over our hut from her window and coming across with all manner of excuses to enquire about Rea's health so that she can fuss around doing things for us. She's even taken over most of our cooking and cleaning. Perhaps, I wonder, this helps her to avoid Jimmy.

Jimmy reminds me of Luke, for he's as obsessed with Sara as Luke was with Moira. I can tell from the girl's expressions and body language, in his proximity, that he's the very last person on the Island she would wish to bed. Despite this, the boy, who pretends to be friends with Daniel, jumps at every opportunity to hang around outside Angela's hut. Favoured by Tommy, he knows Sara will find it impossible to reject him when the time comes. I wish I could warn Tommy that Jimmy can only bring his daughter misery, but it seems that, as a 'chosen one', I have no influence on the affairs of the Island.

***

The chosen ones? Chosen for what?

My concern about Jimmy took a new turn when Daniel leaked something a friend once told him in confidence: that before our arrival by boat, Tommy had promised that not only were Jimmy and Sara to be the chosen ones, but that their girl baby would one day be used to create the 'Immortal Controller'. I intend to question Tommy about this when given the chance. Although babble and gossip pour from Daniel's mouth

134

like water from a tap with a faulty washer, he's not one to deliberately lie.

To tell the truth, I prefer that Rea and I live our lives apart from the daily affairs of the Island. Pampered by Sara and other children, we have time together; time to forget the horror of the Parth Path and, for me, time to forget little Moira.

***

Every morning, Rea and I oversleep. Not surprising considering the love-making that goes on in our bed each night: sessions of bliss that never succeed to quench my lust for Rea's body and her warmth of spirit. As always, I wake up late this particular morning. It's unusually quiet, for Albert and his harem are well past the noisy period of their daily routine. Then something happens. Something wonderful, but at the same time disturbing. Something that breaks the silence. Something unimaginably beautiful. It enters my ears and flows like silvered threads of curling sound that curve into my consciousness as if trying to seek out my soul; a voice-dance of dreams and desires. I hear Moira in those hanging notes, for she, too, used to sing. I thought my little friend sang well and I loved to hear her sing to the sea and to the trees, but the sublime beauty of the voice singing outside our hut is of a different order altogether. I hold my breath as if this might help me hold on to the sweet sound. It has to be Sara, but why have I never heard her sing before? Why should this extraordinary thing be happening now and outside our hut? I turn to see Rea's response. She's asleep. I reach out to touch her arm, then stop. Because of something that cools my cheek.

I barely cried as a child, and certainly not since the Reservation Clearance. What troubles me is that this single tear doesn't seem to relate to my love but to the owner of that voice outside. I don't want Rea to see me like this. I go to the door, hesitate, then open it. I open the door to get closer to that hauntingly-beautiful sound. Suddenly, it ceases.

Sara, also in tears, looks up at me. She's been taking clothes off the washing line outside Angela's hut and folding them neatly with the same care and precision with which every word of her song was delivered.

Curse the Controller, Sara stopped singing when our eyes met! I want to tell her to ignore me and carry on, but my mouth refuses to vocalise anything sensible. Hurriedly, the girl collects her pile of folded washing, turns and disappears into Angela's hut leaving me alone and feeling confused.

***

The Chief had a gun. Luke saw it beside her bed when he was allowed to hide inside her house during the Clearance. The woman was obviously afraid of reprisals. If the ratties had put up more of a fight, this might have been an issue, but it turned out to be the smoothest clearance she had ever witnessed. The boy knew that males could never be allowed to handle guns, but a repeating dream had him shooting Peter in the head every night. Plus, others who threatened to claim Moira.

"Where have they taken her?" he asked the Chief.

"Only one place she can go to."

"Which is?"

"School. To learn. The Controller has plans for her."

Not yet bold enough to ask whether such plans might include him, he could only hope that they would. Meanwhile he would have to make do by venting his frustration on the newcomers with his whip. He became an expert. Their screams extracted from him not sympathy but a hollow smile that would have chilled the most brutal adversary.

***

"Want me to teach you?" Moira asked. The girl with glasses and her two friends studied the larger girl for quality of response. A nod was all they saw. "So long as you do exactly as I say," added Moira.

The other girls said nothing.

"Like I said, I'll allow you to head one team if you get me all the things I need. And whenever I need them." How she hated these stupid girls they now forced her to be with, and how she longed to be with Peter again.

"We'll have to ask the teachers whether Texta would approve before we can do anything," blurted the girl with glasses.

"Things are going to have to change, then. Who is this Texta, anyway?"

The other girl shrugged her shoulders.

"Haven't you seen her?"

"Yes. Just another woman as far as I can tell. Why does she matter so much? It's not like she's the Controller!"

The ensuing silence was accompanied by open-mouthed stares.

It seemed there was no answer to her question, so Moira asked the four girls who were annoying her to leave, Thea included. They left. Moira returned to her bed, lay face down and wept. She wept for her parents, she wept for Peter and she wept for the loss of a happy life in the Reservation, the only life she had known until being rudely deposited in this vast, lifeless building called 'school'. It seemed to Moira that the tears would never cease.

*She spoke little during the rest of her first day at
school, exempted from classes. Dawn arrived the
following day after a fitful sleep for the new pupil. As
happened with the toy boats that she and Peter used to
float in rock pools on the Reservation beach, she seemed
to have lost direction. Float...? Moira had decided,
before finally floating into the oblivion of sleep, when it
had grown dark, that she would always float whatever
they might throw at her personal boat. She would never
go under. Her time at the school would ensure she
would forever remain on top. She no longer had Peter to
'allow' her to win, not that this had ever truly been
necessary. She, Moira, would see to it that she never
lost. Not even that woman called Texta would defeat
her. And so, the new Moira who attended her very first
lesson the next morning was even stronger than the
Moira who had humiliated Thea in front of her peers:*

*"And it came to pass that the Great Controller of the
Universe, from whose cosmic breasts flowed the milk
that spawned life in every one of her trillion galaxies,
decided to enter a chosen planet named Earth in the
flesh and blood of her likeness. The First Controller on
Earth worked tirelessly to undo the damage caused by
the dominant species that had abused the Great
Controller's beneficence. Not only had males,
contaminated by Y chromosomes, turned their violent
attentions against the pure sex, but they had engaged in
terrible wars that threatened the very survival of the
Great Controller's celestial jewel, Planet Earth."*

*Moira sat listening with pursed lips, not believing
one word read by the teacher, Norma.*

*Norma was a thickset woman who wore a red belt
into which was slotted a whip. Moira swore that if this*

138

were ever used across her back she would strangle the woman with it.

"And so, girls, never forget what the First Controller did to save our beloved planet. Nor why. Having been falsely named 'Homo' sapiens in place of the Great Controller's true name for us, 'Femina' sapiens, humankind faced untold miseries because of men. Which brings me round to the genetics of our near extinction and our ultimate salvation. Who can tell me why and how the Single X-Why came into being anyway?"

Thea's hand shot up. The older girl shot a triumphant sideways glance at Moira.

"To allow exchange of DNA during meiosis thus creating the opportunity for improvement in our species. Larger, fitter women. Leaders!" She stressed the word 'larger'. Moira bristled to think the stupid fat girl would dare to challenge her to do battle again.

"Diversification," Moira countered. She had no idea why she said this other than the need to trump the red-head. The woman called Norma smiled, and in that smile, Moira saw an opportunity for further conquest.

"Indeed, Moira. Diversification. Sometimes good. Sometimes bad."

Thea's next glance was uncertain. More of a scowl.

"Improvement is what the Great Controller expected, but instead of this, the introduction of the weaker Y chromosome had a devastating effect, culminating in her appearance in human form on Earth as the First Controller of our World. Hence 'Y' became 'Why'. A question with no sensible answer. Thereafter, it was decided that Femina sapiens should learn from her mistakes and, in the future, control the fabric of genetic change by using the wisdom handed down by the First

Controller. Girls, it's all about control. Control over what you do and say (Norma looked pointedly at Thea who seemed to shrink to a more acceptable size under her gaze) and control over the beauty of the planet that Our Lady personally chose from trillions of other habitable worlds."

Emboldened by Norma's comment, Moira went up to her after class.

"What have they done with Peter?" she asked. "And is this or is it not the Island?"

Chapter 10

A girl! An adorable, soft, warm, huggable infant girl, so helpless in my arms whilst Sara mops Rea's sweat-peppered brow. Every fibre of my soul yearns to protect both Rea and our daughter. Angela hands me a woollen shawl in which to wrap Mary. When Sara has done fussing over Rea, and when my beloved's frustration at not holding her baby becomes apparent, I return the precious bundle of delight to her mother. At this moment, I feel as if my happiness could reach the soft, white, sheep-wool clouds that drift slowly above the Island on this day of brightness and joy. Sara's warning in the woods is a fading memory, Texta's duplicity merely a troubled giant's fanciful delusion and Moira has gone forever. My consciousness is fully pre-occupied with our baby girl and her beautiful mother—the two true loves of my life.

Mary could not escape being beautiful. I did fear that my nattie genes might have damaged her looks, but whenever I stare at her little face, which, frankly, is something I do at every available opportunity, only perfection blinks back at me. And in the little wobbles of that small head and the purposeless movements of those tiny fingers, my thoughts become focused on the mystery of life in ways I never dreamt possible before I first held my daughter against my cheek. Those Parth Path teachings of genes and mutations seem totally irrelevant. Most of all, I derive intense pleasure on feeling my face up against Mary's inquisitive little features, feeling the soft silk of her breath, listening to nonsense baby noises which carry more meaning than all the adult ranting I've yet had the misfortune to hear to date. And I should never have worried that Rea's natural instincts might have been blunted by the Parth Path's interference with her chromosomes. Nor has the lack of having a mother distorted her maternal affection. Perfect baby, perfect mother.

Sara seems almost disappointed that it comes so easily to Rea. I believe she would have liked the young mother to struggle, if only momentarily, as an excuse for hands-on teaching of all baby-related matters about which her knowledge appears inexhaustible. This apart, the girl spends most of every waking hour of every day in our hut. I confess, her cooking skills are significantly superior to Rea's and her ideas of 'keeping a tidy house' for us almost scarily obsessive.

I suppose Mary has changed not only Rea and me, but also Sara. She seems older, her nubile breasts firmer and her shape fuller. I remember feeling embarrassed to have noticed, walking behind her that day in the wood, that her curves were already similar to those of Rea. About two weeks after Mary's birth, I casually asked the girl whether the attention she gives Rea is a preparation for her own motherhood. Daniel happens to be with us, as always babbling away about nothing in particular. I'm not prepared for his sister's response. At first, she stares at me with a look of horror as if I've just pronounced a death sentence.

"I love Rea," she begins, slowly, each word articulated with a gentle precision that I've grown to expect from the girl. "But I also—" She stops. Her eyes fill with tears. She looks straight into my eyes, briefly, but for long enough for something to pierce through to my soul. A sort of longing that neither of us understands. I feel my face get hotter by the second until Sara turns and runs from our hut.

"What was that about?" asks Rea, cradling Mary in her arms.

"Dunno," I lie. "I think I must've upset her."

"It'll be Jimmy," offers Daniel. "Always pestering me about Sara. 'Has she started yet?' he keeps asking. It's about all he can say these days. I think she has but won't let on. Mother must tell Tommy as soon as she finds out, see. Do you know, the other day Sara spent two hours washing her clothes—"

"That's enough, Daniel! Leave your sister alone. Growing up's hard for a nattie girl without having interference from little brothers."

One simple question seems to now turn my happiness on its head. The gun, the secret hideout and that talk of 'them' planning to kill Rea—these things take on a new meaning. Is 'them' Sara? I cannot believe this because of what I see in the younger girl's eyes, but I feel confused and, dare I say it, anxious.

This is heightened by an argument I overhear between Sara and Daniel a few days later. The girl seems to have put behind her that moment of embarrassment between us and is busy outside our front door washing Mary's endless supply of nappies. I overhear Daniel say something. Exactly what, I don't know, but from the tone of his voice something unpleasant. There's a pause, followed by Sara shouting, "How dare you!" Never once have I heard the girl raise her voice before now.

"You'll see, then. And don't say I didn't warn you," replies the brother.

I hear Sara sobbing. I want to go outside and comfort her—or at least find out what it's about—but after those unspoken words of a few days back, I feel discretion is called for. I listen. Silence from Daniel suggests to me that he's left. Maybe he'll return, and all will become clear. Could it be something to do with Jimmy?

Jimmy? Luke?

Luke and Moira reappear in my head. If my blonde-haired friend hadn't stopped me, I really would have killed the Reservation boy. Should I now kill Jimmy? I saw something flash in Sara's eyes in response to my prying question the other day. A curious mix of anger, fear and hopelessness.

Anger and fear about Jimmy or her father, Tommy? I do not want her to suffer. Of all people, apart from Rea, I really do not wish for that to happen. To be bedded by an idiot like Jimmy would be unbearable for a girl as bright as Sara. But is this about Jimmy? Might it be something far worse? Are things happening that I couldn't even guess at?

One thing about babies... they ensure little else occupies your mind, day or night. For the first six months, I forget all concerns about Jimmy and Sara. Daniel and his sister patch things up, though I never do discover what that verbal skirmish and those tears were about. We also see more of Angela who seems almost as taken with Mary as is Sara. Tommy has vanished for a while (to I know not and care not where) so I cannot question him about Jimmy. Jimmy is clearly missing out where Sara's concerned for Nature is screaming out for all to see: the girl is by now very much a young woman.

Shortly after sunrise one day, Daniel calls out and bangs on our door. Rea and I have barely slept since a six-months-old Mary caught something that turned her wee brow pink and as hot as fried pancakes. Grumbling, I roll out of bed and head for the door. More bangs. I curse like a slave, then hope this doesn't register with Rea who knows none of the bad language we men from

144

Man Camp 7 are so fond of using, even when under threat of a whipping... in fact, particularly when under threat.

I open the door to discover Daniel in a state of panic.

"They've taken Sara!" he says.

Am I dreaming or are my ears deceiving me?

"What?" I ask stupidly.

"The Commandant. She's here. With the wardens. And they've got Sara. Asking her questions."

"Where?" I ask.

"Gone to the woods. Jimmy told them about the hideout. I tried to warn her a while back. She didn't believe me, and we had a row. They must think Rea and Mary are there."

He looks beyond me at Rea who is now resting on one elbow and rubbing her eyes.

"What is it, Peter?" she asks.

I curse the Commandant, Texta, Man Camp 7 and the Controller. I curse Jimmy.

"I should've killed him!" I say, struggling into my trousers. "How did he find out?"

Daniel remains silent. I have an odd feeling he knows.

"Peter?" Rea enquires again.

For a few moments, I'm lost in a cloud of confusion before finding my voice:

"Quick—take Mary out of here!" I say. "I've got to save Sara."

"Take Mary out? Where?" she asks. I look at Daniel:

"Where can she—?" I begin.

"Albert's place," the boy interrupts, as if there is no other option.

Dressed in her nightie, flushed and clutching Mary to her bosom, Rea hurries out into the chicken yard. The

145

last I see of her is a rounded bottom squeezing through the small door beyond which Sara or Daniel would look for eggs every morning. I hear squawking and flapping. When this settles down, I follow Daniel into Angela's hut. I make straight for the drawer where Sara keeps the gun hidden. Angela watches, helpless, as tears trickle. All I do know about that woman is that she truly loves her daughter.

Praise the Great Controller, it's there. Sara, despite professing to know nothing about firearms, later gave me a detailed lesson on its use. She showed me how to kill. I follow Daniel to the edge of the village where we're met by Matt. I've long realised there's more to Matt than I first credited him with. He's canny. He knows silence is safer than a misplaced remark. He carries a knife and an axe. Little defence against Parth Path weaponry, but, curiously, this gives me confidence. At least I have one true ally. Then I spot Rolem and my confidence soars. I haven't seen him since Mary's birth. I was told he was away on a sea trip. If true, there'll be a boat in the harbour.

Boat? 'They've taken Sara.' Boat=Parth Path red wardens. Is Rolem with them after all?

Rolem raises a finger to his lips when I open my mouth to say something. He nods at Daniel. My confidence starts to slump as I follow the giant and the boy along the path. Daniel leaves the path and pushes through the undergrowth into the wood. Rolem follows him and Matt and I trail the big fellow.

I hear their voices before I catch sight of six red wardens with whips and guns and Sara with her hands bound behind her back. She's only wearing a short nightie, like Rea's, and I notice, with shame, how shapely her legs have become. Whether or not the girl told her

146

captors about the black ribbons, or whether Jimmy-the-Informer had done the dirty on us, is no longer of importance. When they discover the secret hideout with water and food but no Rea, one thing is certain: they'll execute the girl.

The giant uses sign language to tell Daniel, Matt and me to spread out. He wants us to attack from four fronts. How could I have doubted the man? He points to a tree then holds up both hands in front of his broad face. He's telling me to use a tree as cover.

I've already killed a man and a dog. Now I'm prepared to kill not one, but six women. Our speed and accuracy are all that can save Sara. I keep the execution party, heading for the hideout, in my line of vision. Cleverly, Rolem takes an arc (curves again!) to cut them off. Daniel, whom I'm about to discover is somewhat of an expert stone thrower, remains in the rear whilst Matt and I take up positions on either side of the wardens, me closer to Sara. Why they have no dogs puzzles me. Overconfidence?

Rolem descends on the wardens like an enraged bull. At the same time, Daniel fells a woman from the behind with a deadly rock missile. I waste no time. From behind a large tree, Sara's gun, my right hand and right eye work as a team. I down first one, then two wardens. Matt kills another with an axe. The two women guarding Sara turn, confused, in circles. In one bound, Rolem has their heads in his hands before cracking them together like hens' eggs. Without waiting to see whether any of Sara's captors are still alive, he picks up the surprised girl under one arm and runs with her to join me. Not one flicker of movement from any of the wardens' bodies. Moments later Daniel and Matt join us.

"The boat," Rolem whispers. "Tommy's on board. This is all his and Jimmy's doing. Do you have any bullets left?"

I look at Sara still dangling like a doll from the giant's tree-branch arm. She looks almost comical.

"Oh, Sara! Sorry!" apologises Rolem. He lowers her to the ground. Perhaps there is a little of the 'simple' in the giant. The girl appears too shocked to utter a word.

"How many more bullets in the gun?" I ask.

Sara holds up four fingers.

"How many others are there with Tommy?" I ask Rolem.

"Three," the giant replies.

"And the Captain? The crew?"

"You know them as well as I do. Like the boat, they go where the tide takes them."

I had thought, after our last encounter, that there was more to the Captain than driftwood flotsam, but maybe I was mistaken. Tommy seems to be the key; Tommy and his questionable link with Texta. Kill Tommy and we stand a chance. Plus, Sara will be free. No Jimmy for her to worry about. Somehow, her happiness means a lot to me.

But Rea and Mary are still cooped up with Albert and his harem back in the village. Hopefully, any noise emerging from the cockerel will be attributed to the time of day, but she cannot stay there. Neither can Sara return to the village. Solution: Rolem heads off with Sara, Matt and his axe to the harbour whilst Daniel and I, with Sara's gun, return for Rea and Mary.

**

Luke thrived on power and the pain of others. The Chief seemed only too happy to rule through her newly-appointed henchman. When he questioned her about

148

Moira, she always said: "In time, dear boy. Why must you always be in such a hurry?" "Because of her starting," he would reply. "And it has to be me! Not Peter!"

Gradually, he came to accept it wasn't going to happen straightaway, and no one could tell him where 'the school' was, so he gave up asking and concentrated on hurting others as he would have wished to hurt Peter. Every time he flailed his whip across bared flesh, he would imagine that flesh belonging to his rival in love, even if the recipient happened to be female. Quite soon, his methodical efficiency at maintaining order paid off. Discipline in the new reservation prevailed as never before. And none of the old inhabitants who remained dared complain about how much better things used to be. Everyone feared the boy with a grudge the size of a mountain. Months passed. They planted trees—Luke had a thing about trees—and these grew as months turned to years. Luke had a wife. Children, even. Like all the others, they too felt the sting of his whip for every conceivable reason. But never did he forget Moira.

Then the Chief died—unexpectedly—and in the wake of her death, Luke discovered his true purpose in the Reservation. He wasn't pleased.

Neither was the Controller when she learned what he did.

***

Moira was a model student. She listened, she questioned, appropriately, and she co-operated. On that first occasion when she met Texta, she was, though cared not to admit it, impressed. That the woman was to be appointed as Commandant at the nearby Man Camp 7, within easy walking distance, did not surprise

149

her. Texta was confident they had made the right decision choosing Moira and rewarded the girl with the status of 'Section Leader'. This meant that those like Thea, desperate to bully others, would always have to check with Moira before anything could get done. She was the 'controller' of the students' small world enclosed within the greater world of the school, itself a minute piece of the Parth Path universal jigsaw.

Moira knew that to survive she would have to thwart attempts by others to knock her off her pedestal as she had done with Thea. She had seen the effects of ruthlessness at the Reservation. Her beloved parents killed, Peter dragged away to she knew not where, a whole way of life erased in one sweep. Bitter? Yes, she was bitter, but the girl vowed to use bitterness to her advantage. She became feared for her temper, yet the driving force behind everything she did and achieved was a determination that one day she would be re-united with her one true friend, Peter. The silence she received after asking, following that first lesson, where they had taken Peter, told her one thing: that he was alive. And the lack of response to her question about the Island meant she was still on the mainland. But if she had known the truth—that he had been taken to a camp just a short walk away on the other side of a hill—she would have followed a different course. Nothing could have stopped her from absconding, then making her way to the man camp and demanding that they free her friend. As it was, ignorance was a blessing, for back in those early days even she would have been shot. Not, however, ten years later when, as Directress of the school, her power had spread way beyond monitoring the academic progress of her pupils. As a member of the Parth Path Council, she'd had the privilege of meeting the Controller herself. Deferential on the outside, internally Moira seethed and saw the wise old woman as yet another pedestal to be toppled, another Thea to be pushed aside.

Texta was a different matter. Moira found her hard to read. A total mystery, in fact. Whilst the Controller struggled to keep those following the Parth Path on course, Texta's goals seemed obscure and, at times, off kilter. The woman both fascinated and frightened the new Directress. And Moira began to suspect her senior also knew things about Peter. However, she did not yet feel she was in any position to test her hunch.

The Controller was delighted with Moira's alterations to the curriculum. For too long there had been too much focus on the Scriptures of the Great Controller. All that 'and it came to pass' nonsense left the new Directress cold. The truth, she felt sure, lay in the laboratories, the living science of the Parth Path. But not even she had knowledge of what really went on there.

In her early days at the school, Moira never truly believed that the First Controller was the Great One who came down to Earth in flesh and blood. Nor did she accept that 'Man' had been created from 'Woman' to diversify the human species. She knew, of course, of his innate inferiority from Peter's perpetual need to make her feel good and to win in the games they played, but all those years without setting eyes on a single Single X-Why convinced her that she also had a need. A need to be with Peter again, and for him to worship her, rather than for her to worship the 'Great One'. Behind the dazzle of her rise to power was the little Moira who yearned ever more strongly to be pampered again. By Peter. No other man would do.

The Controller agreed with Moira's decision to teach the girls more about the genetic realities of the Path. But parthenogenesis without the DNA exchange of meiosis would lead nowhere. Evolution, Moira reckoned, was a natural process, though to say so openly would have amounted to heresy. Nevertheless, what little she knew about the goings on in the Parth Path Laboratories made scientific sense. Selected Single X-Why 'donors' would be the source of exciting new DNA, allowing genetic manipulation on a grand scale. Parthenogenesis of the resulting super-women would enable the control of large numbers of XX individuals all serving different purposes: some, bed companions for the leaders; others female workers of sufficient strength to replace nattie men who had become such a nuisance that continued culling threatened to eradicate the male sex altogether. Then there were those women with super-big brains who could create a new world of near perfection such as had never before been seen in the Great Controller's Universe...

And so the 'Ultimate Plan' became the Path's new vision.

Few mentioned the 'Ultimate Plan' at Council Meetings, mostly because it was a divisive issue. Unlike the dreamt-up Immortal Controller, the present incumbent was mortal. What would happen after her death? Everyone knew that the man camp commandants had split into rival factions, secretly aligning in favour of just a few women whose names were never spoken. The present Controller had always feared a situation, mirroring the one that had triggered the Great Man War, might one day threaten her species again. This is why she had the insight to encourage Moira to teach the younger generation of girls that there can only be one Parth Path: a genetic one leading to the Perfect Woman who would one day take over and be cloned in perpetuity as the Immortal Controller. Only she could turn the 'Ultimate Plan' into reality. And the XX and Single X-Why chromosomes required would come from the 'Chosen Ones'.

Moira's interpretation of this was easy: one of the XX chromosomes would be from an ovum of hers. The other X, allowing genetic exchange, would derive from Peter's sperm. Their daughter would, one day, become the first Immortal Controller. From her, daughter after daughter after daughter would bud until Femina sapiens had extended her benign wisdom across the entire Universe.

But Peter had to be found. As far as Moira was concerned, Texta, not the ageing Controller, had to be the key.

Chapter 11

Even before we break cover, the noise coming from the village tells me something is seriously amiss. Shouts and screams flash me back to the Reservation Clearance. A small crowd of red wardens and islanders is gathered in a tight group on the grassy meadow that slopes down towards the lake. I hear the cry of a baby. *My* baby. Angrily pushing Daniel aside, I burst from the undergrowth with my gun raised. The shouting stops but the screaming continues.

Rea is kneeling on the ground, her hands bound behind her back, her beautiful face swollen and bloodied. She screams as though she cannot stop. The wardens, armed with guns, see me, move away from her then spread out in a line, their weapons pointing at me like accusatory fingers. Now the only audible sounds are coming from Rea and Mary and these are tearing me apart.

"Leave her alone!" I yell. "Don't you know that she's the Chosen One? What the devil are you playing at? Mary's special too."

The Devil? I once read about the Devil in that illegal book, 'The Holy Bible'. I read about God too, but only the Devil seemed real.

Those red-belted bullies say nothing. Preparing to shoot them one by one, I walk on. Rea, on hearing my voice, turns her face in my direction. Her eyes are lost behind a mess of broken flesh. I can't even be sure she's able to see me. My anger hits the gong. Using both hands, I raise my gun to eye level, finger on the trigger, until one of them grabs Rea's hair and jams the barrel of her weapon against the side of my beloved's head. I stop and lower my gun. I can only hope the warden will do the same with hers. She doesn't.

One of the intruders is holding Mary as if she's only a bag of rubbish. Mary responds by emptying her little lungs into the chill air. I look from mother to daughter, again and again, till I spot three figures striding towards us. They must have emerged from the huts. One is Angela, also with her wrists bound behind her back, one I recognise as Texta and the third is a younger woman with blonde hair. Tears distort my focus, but she seems to be one of those females who is neither attractive nor unattractive. They join Rea and her captors whilst my mind wonders who gave Rea away. There again, do I have to blame anyone? Mary's little cries could have alerted them. Or did they simply search every available hiding space?

The blonde looks at Rea as if she's a rabid dog then breaks away and approaches me. The realisation of who she is hits me like a brick to the head. My knees tremble, my already clouded vision blurs, I drop the gun. As I fight to remain standing, mouth agape, Moira bends down, picks up the gun and slots it into her belt. She, too, wears a red belt.

"Aren't you going to say 'hello', Peter?"

***

Luke's disappearance caused no detectable response in the higher Parth Path echelons. Indeed, no one even bothered to inform the Controller. He was to be eliminated anyway, having served his purpose: to provide living proof of Single X Why devilry. The Reservation was in revolt following their Chief's unexpected death; the nattie women were all convinced that allowing a man so much freedom and power had been a terrible mistake. The tenets of the Parth Path had

155

to be right. The social experiment had achieved its purpose and a new, totally female-led system prevailed for those privileged natties allowed to 'run' their own affairs.

Luke survived more through luck than cunning. Escaping across the moors, he hid in derelict farm buildings and outhouses, stumbling across the occasional lost soul whom he would rob, whip or both. He killed a sheep with a rock and pulled flesh from its bones. He drank from streams and puddles. Slowly, keeping within his sights the old road that led to the ghost city the Chief had told him about, and where he had convinced himself he would find the 'school', he travelled south. As with the sheep, he killed anything eatable and he rid himself of anyone who got in his way. If Moira had already chosen another man, which seemed likely, Luke promised himself he would conjure up an extra special way of dispatching the bastard. A blow to the head with a rock would be far too humane. It would have to involve the man's dangly thing if the foul object had invaded Moira. He hadn't yet decided how this would be achieved, but Moira could watch. She'd have to learn who she really was... his!

The road Luke followed did not, as he'd hoped, take him to the city but instead to a fenced-in collection of buildings and huts with trucks and a helicopter as well. There were watchtowers and, even from a distance, Luke could make out figures, with guns, manning them.

Manning? Pfff! Anyone who'd manned Moira was already dead meat.

He heard the barks of dogs and, in the fields around Man Camp 7, men worked in rows. Women with whips ensured these men stayed bent double and didn't look up and Luke envied them their job. Any one of those men

156

could have entered Moira, reason enough for him to criss-cross their backs with whip welts. But he had no intention of joining their number. Taking a higher route, he headed for some woods beyond which he picked up the road again.

Inside a ruined cottage, he found an old man dressed in rags and gnawing on a mould-covered crust. The man seemed to be alone and, rather than appearing alarmed at Luke's unannounced entry, seemed almost pleased to see someone other than his own reflection or shadow. He smiled and told Luke his name was Watchem. One thing was certain. He was far too old for his male member to pose any sort of threat where Moira was concerned. Luke sat down at the table and smiled back. He longed for water, he needed food but above all else he had to find Moira. It seemed likely that the old fellow knew things—things that might lead him to the girl-turned-woman.

***

Moira struck a deal with Texta.

Suppressing her initial shock on learning that Peter had been imprisoned close by, in Man Camp 7, for all those years, and that he had been chosen by the Controller for genetic experiments that had something to do with the Immortal Controller Project, she listened with ears as wide as satellite dishes. When she heard about Rea, she was unable to contain her disgust.

"You forced Peter to bed a clonie? One of twenty lookalikes? A budded bundle of engineered genes?"

"Didn't need much forcing."

"Poor boy! How could you?"

"No longer a boy. And he's no longer Peter. They call him Solem."

"Solem? What sort of name is that?"

157

"Look, I was only following instructions. But like you, I've had my doubts. About the wisdom of this. And about the Controller."

"Wisdom? The whole thing's crazy! Any child of his—and that creature called Rea—she'll be... well, even if Peter is the father, half of its genes will be corrupted. She'll be a freak! Immortal Controller indeed!"

The younger woman's anger flared like a flame doused with man-fuel. Texta, at first alarmed, allowed a grin to form as she stared at the Directress. Moira's looks and body were as nothing up against those of the canteen girl who had so often shared her bed, so Moira's infatuation with the Single X Why of her childhood was now of no consequence to anyone. One of Texta's greatest disappointments had been the day when the Controller visited Man Camp 7, incognito, and sat unnoticed in the canteen to observe for herself the genetic potential of those entering and leaving. Unfortunately, Rea was on serving duty. The Controller already knew about Solem. She had personally chosen the boy when, dressed as a red warden, she visited the Reservation and ordered him to club Moira to death. The respect he'd shown his Double X friend was obvious. The subsequent Island stories and lies, about Tommy's daughter being chosen, were calculated distractions. No one should know about Solem until the laboratory was ready to receive the fruit of his union with Rea. After engineering Solem's and Rea's 'escape' from Man Camp 7—all part of the genetic perfection programme—Texta had attempted to locate Rea's clone sisters but failed. That's when she decided to befriend the newly-appointed Directress of the nearby Parth Path School. Knowing about Moira's and Solem's friendship at the Reservation, she could perhaps use this to her *advantage. The fact that she and Tommy had been unable to bear children was now of little importance. She'd been perfectly happy to donate the man to Angela, for she'd always found sex with a Single X-Why boring and pointless. She had been less than happy with the special attention given to Tommy's daughter, but the genetic perfection programme had, at last, put a stop to that nonsense. Although she still yearned for the curves of a woman like Rea, her goal was to influence history of the future with her brain rather than her womb.*

"I know where they've gone," said Texta.

The other woman's response took her by surprise. Moira jumped up, grabbed a handful of Texta's greying hair, yanked her superior's head back and spat out her question inches from her face:

"You knew and said nothing?"

"Calm down!" ordered Texta. Moira relaxed her grip if not her anger.

"How long have you known?"

"Remember your position in the Path, Moira. The Controller may favour you now, but you are my junior. Considerably so. Of all the commandants, she chose me to oversee this top-secret project. And I was the one given the job of testing Solem."

"Peter!"

"Whatever—looking for leadership potential in his genes. Risk-taking."

"Putting him at risk, the poor boy."

"No longer a boy!"

Moira sat down with the eyes of her mind in the past. She saw Peter again, very much a boy.

"He is to me. He'll always be a boy. My boy. Do you know...?" she began, turning to face Texta who sat smoothing down her hair after Moira's unwelcome

159

attack on her head. "—That Peter's the only true friend I've ever had?"

"D'you think the Controller cares one chromosome about your past?"

"She might if—"

Moira's sudden smile puzzled Texta.

"If what?"

"Accidents happen."

"The baby?"

"Monster!"

"I'm not hearing this."

"You told me how you brought the clonie girl to your bed. Your choice or the Controller's?"

Texta's eyes hardened.

"I know exactly why the Controller made that decision in the canteen."

"This Peter—I mean Solem—and Rea business. For you. Bearable or unbearable?"

"Neither. Torture. The things I do for the Parth Path! For the Controller!"

"It's not her path. Remember that. She's only its guardian. Which means she's also our servant. Being Directress of the Parth Path School has taught me many things. Most of all—"

"What you're asking for is to join me when I go to collect the baby?"

Moira smiled and nodded.

"Waited a very long time. I've been patient. I'll forgive you for not saying about Peter only if you let me join you."

"And the baby?"

Moira's smile vanished. She looked away.

***

160

Sara stayed close behind Rolem whilst the giant crept, unseen, to the very edge of the wood, gauging his chance of success. He knew the boat, the Captain and the crew as well as anyone. The unknown quantity was Tommy. He felt Sara's hand grip his arm and understood why. Jimmy had appeared on deck with the man she called her father. Both knew why the boy was there. Jimmy's reward for spying on Sara and Daniel would be Sara. Instead of killing her straightaway, they'd planned to keep her prisoner in the hideout, for Jimmy to visit and do the necessary until the baby had been taken. Once Mary was on board the boat, Sara's inevitable fate would have been played out.

But no one in authority had considered Rolem.

Rolem loved Sara in a way no other man could do and for good reason. Tommy knew, of course, that he wasn't the girl's true father. After all, he had been unable to give Texta a child. The myth was a convenience to distract from his true purpose on the Island—to help his monster of a wife, after she had left to join the Parth Path, in return for 'concessions'. An island of his own to govern had been promised. Apart from Rolem, the only other person who knew the true identity of Sara's father was Angela. Sara remained unaware of the real reason behind the attention the big man always showed her.

Tommy and Jimmy disappeared as soon as the Captain appeared on deck—something that Rolem interpreted as evidence of friction on board. Doubtless, Tommy would be trying to throw his weight around, as always, though without impressing the Captain. Rolem emerged from cover, announcing his presence to those on board. A slight nod from the hardened sea-farer was enough to reassure the giant. He took his daughter by the hand and ran with her to the quayside. They stepped onto the plank, father following daughter, and were soon aboard. The Captain quickly took them below deck to his private cabin. The girl was now old enough to catch the attention of twenty female-deprived ruffians, but their respect for, and fear of Rolem ensured her safety. The giant whispered to the Captain that neither Jimmy nor Tommy should know she was on the boat.

The Captain went off, reappeared with food and drink then sat and listened whilst Rolem told the whole story to date.

"Six dead, you say?"

Rolem nodded. Deeply concerned for the welfare of little Mary, and her mother, Sara began to cry. The giant held her close.

"Tommy's gone back on land for you, Sara," the Captain informed them. "With Jimmy. When they return, he'll know you're here," he added, squinting at the girl almost hidden behind two huge arms.

"Not when, but if," Rolem announced, stroking Sara's hair. "Promise me you'll take good care of her whilst I go back on shore to finish what we started."

"No!" begged Sara, holding onto the big man. "I won't let you leave me alone on this boat. You've always been special for me, Rolem. What will I do if something happens to you?"

Rolem looked from his daughter to the Captain and back. He had an idea.

"You're right. We'll stick together. Solem and Rea haven't shown up yet—which is kind of worrying. We'll wait together in the wood. The only threat to me is from the wardens' guns. But they can't shoot through trees. And we'll have the element of surprise. Unless they've

162

forced Matt and the others to talk. Do you still have a gun?" he asked the Captain.

The other man shook his head. Rolem knew he was lying, but it was worth a try. All he really cared about was the Sara's safety plus that of the child of the true Chosen Ones. He had never believed all that nonsense about Sara being chosen, anyway. It was only put around by Tommy, and partly as protection for himself being Sara's surrogate dad. Uncertain, now, whether or not to trust the Captain (why won't he lend me his gun?), the giant took Sara off the boat, when the deck was clear, and hid her, not in the wood, as he'd said, but inside a quayside hut. He smashed open its door with a sledgehammer fist, and, with the door half-off, from inside he and Sara had a good visual of the stretch of concrete separating the sea from the trees, plus the rest of the coast-line. The path to the lake was a mere giant's step from the hut.

It wasn't a long wait. When the time came, Rolem was too much of a softie to kill the boy as well. Tommy's body was thrown aside as Jimmy, trembling, stepped back towards the boat, denying that he had any intention of taking Sara against her will. But he felt bold enough to tell Rolem one thing:

"It's over for you," he ventured. "They've given themselves up. So Sara will have to be mine anyway!"

Chapter 12

In that fleeting moment of recognition, all those years spent thinking about my past with Moira become lost in a blur of confusion. The friend of my childhood, who had never left my brain until Rea and I first made love behind that store shed in Man Camp 7, has now metamorphosed, like a butterfly in reverse, into something ugly. I try to avoid her eyes although only they can tell me the truth: that the woman with the gun isn't some creature manufactured in the Parth Path laboratories, pretending to be my one-time dearest friend. But the truth hurts.

Moira takes a step towards me. I fix my gaze on the butch brute still holding my bloodied Rea by the hair.

"Leave Rea alone," I say, struggling to blot out the face of Moira whose presence confuses me. "She's done nothing wrong. Shoot me instead. We only followed Texta's instructions."

"My instructions?" mocks Texta. "I've no idea what—"

"Shut up!" barks Moira, snapping at her superior like a dog turning on its mistress.

"Moira, what's got into you? I'll take the child, then you can do what you—"

Texta's last words. No one is prepared for what Moira does. Swivelling as if controlled by an unseen hand, she points her gun at Texta and pulls the trigger. The man camp Commandant is given no time to protest. The bang of the discharging gun transports me back to the Reservation Clearance, seeing my mother and sister transformed by identical bangs from living family to lifeless corpses. I never found out what happened to my father. I watch as Texta drops face down to the ground. I stare at the twitching of a dying woman's fingers, reduced to a silent dummy. A second bang hits my brain.

"No!" I yell.

I rush to Rea's body. I throw myself across her as if this might in some way save the girl. I push, pull and tug at her. I stroke her pain-distorted face, attempt to wipe away the blood, but the red ooze from the black hole in her right temple just won't stop. Her unseeing eyes glaze over.

"No, no, no!" I sob, hugging my love's limp body against mine. I hear Moira talk to the woman who has just shot her.

"Why did you do that?" she asks as if speaking to a naughty child.

"But Directress, you said—" begins the pig of a red warden.

Bang! No chance to finish her sentence. Her fat body slumps to the ground.

"Bukla, you went too far ten years ago as well. I never forget, see. Which is why I'm here, of course."

I look up. I'm still alive. Why? That last shot should have been for me. I look for Mary. Stupid, considering she's still bawling her little head off, but I can't seem to see her properly through the tears clouding my vision. Beside me lies the corpse of the woman who shot Rea, but I feel nothing for her death. With Rea gone, nothing else matters.

I stand up and, for the first time since we were parted ten years ago, I see into my old friend's eyes.

"Kill me," I say. "You seem pretty good at it now. Do your job!"

"Peter?"

"Bloody kill me!" I scream.

Disgust is a curious thing. Almost worse than blind hatred. I don't think I've ever truly experienced it before. Moira disgusts me. I could hate her no more than hate a spill of vomit or a squashed slug. Our past together suddenly seems like a deception. I feel I was cheated by letting that lively little blonde-haired girl befriend me and allowing the child to beat me in cricky when I would have easily won every time. Mary's gone quiet and I scan the circle of faces for reassurance that my baby—*our* baby, for she still belongs to my dead love—hasn't also been slaughtered because of this slug who calls me 'Peter'.

One of the red wardens is holding Mary. I see my child's tiny hands flail, her legs kick. I focus every sentient cell inside me on that little bundle of life, on Rea's joy. Without Rea, the little girl has only me. I approach the warden holding her.

"Peter, what do you think you're doing?" asks Moira.

I ignore her. I hit the warden when she tries to grab my arm to restrain me as, screaming abuse, I attempt to pull my baby daughter free. Moira shouts at me but I no longer hear words. Just a noise I wish to shut out, like everything else in this foul world apart from Mary.

Then... nothing!

***

"What do you plan to do?" Moira asked.

The sea was rough. Even before the boat began to pitch and roll like a drunken acrobat, she had emptied her stomach contents over the side several times. And the constant motion stirred her anger as well as her insides. For as long as she'd known Texta, she had regarded herself as the older woman's confidante. It was because of the Commandant that she had undergone a meteoric rise to power from top pupil to schoolteacher to Directress, plus gained a foot in the door with the Controller. And because of Texta, she was both respected and feared. So why the deceit about Peter? Texta had known all along, but, worse than that, Moira now knew it was she who was responsible for the Clearance that tore her away from her family, from her life in the Reservation and from her only true friend.

The younger woman was reminded of a game she and Peter used to play as children: turning over stones in the fields at the foot of the mountain. They would choose large stones, some of which required them to push and pull together until these were successfully upturned. 'Guess What's Underneath' they called the game. The winner was the child who had the most number of correct discoveries. Slugs, worms, spiders, snails, ants and centipedes were the most commonly suggested creatures. Any wrong offer meant a minus mark. This was one game in which the boy could not engineer a win for her. Oh, those winning games of 'cricky'! She knew he wanted her to win, of course, and loved him all the more for it. It felt like the boy was telling her he was already hers. But Texta? What evil lay hidden beneath that woman's exterior?

By separating Moira from Peter, Texta had destroyed what should have been hers. Worse still, knowing how she and Peter felt about each other, she then encouraged him to copulate with a genetic freak. Moira was now more aware of what went on in the laboratories, and it sickened her, like everything else concerning the Parth Path. She would use her power for a single purpose: to return to a future with Peter. She had repeatedly lied to Texta and to others in authority to get to where she was.

"Why should it affect me if I do see Peter again on the Island? I'm a different person. Besides, I no longer have any feelings for Single X-Whys. But out interest, what exactly do you plan to do with the father of the Special Child?"

The lies had become tinged with anger as Moira bobbed up and down and down and up in the stern of the boat, squatting beside Texta.

No feelings for Peter? He was all she thought about!

She recalled that time when she and Peter collapsed helpless with laughter on discovering a pair of woman's knickers when playing 'Guess What's Underneath'. The how and why of it was the cause of much speculation between them, associated with frequent bursts of giggles. But there was no laughter when she lifted her skirt and showed him hers.

Peter had already given her a glimpse of his dangly thing, a solemn occasion for both, so, after that find under a stone, Peter asked her to show him her knickers. It seemed a fair exchange of revelation, so she allowed him the briefest of viewing with a quick up and down of her skirt, but it was enough to tip the boy into a state of near ecstasy. This both puzzled and pleased the young Moira. It made no sense that his eyes nearly fell out or that he couldn't stop staring at her skirt where the transforming vision had appeared, but the shared experience somehow strengthened her hold over her friend. Afterwards, she didn't lose a single 'cricky' match.

"What do I plan to do?" echoed Texta as if the question were of no importance. "I don't plan to do anything. Just continue with my job. To ensure the success of the Parth Path. Moira, sometimes I just don't understand what you're—"

"Never mind," interrupted the younger woman. "Just put it down to this bloody boat." She stared at the back of the Captain until his see-saw motion made her heave again. She got up and went to lean over the side but this time nothing came up. She looked back at Texta.

"What'll happen to Peter?" she asked.

"He killed a dog," came the reply. "So, what, in your opinion, do you think should happen to him?"

"You told him to."

"I told him to escape if he could."

"Which he did."

"Proving we got it right about his risk-taking genes. The ones that also help to feed the brain with dopamine."

"So why kill him?"

"He killed a dog," repeated the older woman.

Fearful that Texta might see the exasperation in her expression, Moira looked at the horizon.

"How far now?" she asked.

"Not far. We've been on this boat for longer than it would normally take to go there and back. Listen, when we take the child just leave me to deal with Peter and his genetic doll. I'd like her back, you know. Those other girls are no substitute."

Moira smiled into the wind.

"Genetic doll? I like it. Must remember that." She smiled for Texta's benefit. "Yes, it's about time Peter stopped playing with dolls," she whispered for only the wind to hear. Tears dampened the corners of her eyes as she thought of the 'family game' they used to play together and the bizarre 'coming together' simulations between boy and girl. If it hadn't been for the Clearance, she'd have asked Peter to share her bed that very night. As it was she was still a virgin ten years later and had not the slightest sexual interest in anything with two legs and two X chromosomes.

Arrival at the Island abolished the nausea but intensified the anger. It was like stepping into a past that had been denied her for too long. Texta might not have had a definitive plan, but Moira most certainly did have. Those years of endurance and learning at the Parth Path school had not been wasted.

***

Whilst Luke waited, squashed inside in a large crate full of tools and other provisions for the Islanders, he began to doubt Watchem. How could he be sure the 'Directress' of whom the man spoke was the same Moira from the reservation? If the weather hadn't been so awful, he might have climbed out and done the old man in for deceiving him, but the tarpaulin cover was at least giving him protection against the elements.

Then he heard voices. Female voices. One, younger than the other, changed in pitch and tone, but still recognisable. As the two women waited with Watchem, beside the crate, talking—no, arguing—Luke smiled to himself. At long last Moira would be his. When his head banged against a jagged farm implement whilst the crate was swung on board the boat, his mind countered the pain by conjuring what he would do to Moira on the Island, working out how to make her yield herself to him plus suffer for rejecting his advances on the Reservation. Later, when the pitch and roll of the boat caused him to lose all sense of space and place, he controlled the nausea by reliving the past as it should have been: being chosen by Moira at her 'starting', entering both her hut and herself, having a home with the girl, a home in which he would be the indisputable master and his woman would have no chance to argue

170

with him or make him feel small. There would be children from whom one of the daughters would be selected as the special child destined to become the Immortal Controller, but always under his power. When the movement of the boat finally ceased, he heard her voice again, its owner so soon to be his...

***

I come to on my bed. *Our* bed. For a moment, I truly believe I've just awoken from the worst nightmare of my life until I roll over to see Moira's face, inches from mine and staring at me as if I'm the Great Controller herself. I spring upright and edge away from her. My head feels sore.

"I'm so sorry, Peter," Moira says. "I had to hit you to stop them from killing you. For the same reason, I had to shoot Texta."

I just scowl at the woman, wishing she would turn into Rea.

"What's wrong?" she asks. "I don't understand. Why are you behaving so strangely?"

My turn to stare at my friend from the past. Those eyes—yes, it's Moira. That frown I used to love so much hangs on her forehead. I remember once telling her I should try to blow it away. Back then, she laughed and said a kiss would be better.

Kiss?

How can I even speak with the creature who engineered the death of Rea, let alone kiss her? As in the past, she reads my thoughts. She, too, sits up, the frown still there.

"Peter, you must understand I played no part in the shooting. I only came to protect you and—"

"And not Rea!"

Moira goes quiet. She gets up from the bed and, with her back to me, looks out of the window.

"Your hens?" she asks.

I say nothing.

"This feels so like the Reservation." She turns to face me. "Do you remember Quack and the sheep?" she asks. I only remember telling the story to Rea, Daniel and Sara. "I'm not one of them. You must know this. They tried to turn me into a monster like Texta, but I used my brain to deceive them. Texta never told me you were in Man Camp 7 all those years... and so close to our school. She split us apart and wanted to keep it that way. That's why she arranged for you to bed a clonie—"

I jump up from the bed as though released by a spring. Moira gets up and backs away when she sees my clenched fists.

"Holy Controller, what on earth are you talking about, woman? You know nothing about me. I loved Rea. She was my life—my everything! We have a child. Mary. We're the Chosen Ones. Mary is... is... Pfff!"

The Special Child? Honestly, I have no idea what this means?

I swivel round and slam the top of the bedside cabinet with my fist. I want to break it. Instead, I hurt my wrist. Moira winces. I clutch my sore wrist with my other hand, rubbing as I face Moira. Her frown is gone and there's a look of genuine concern on her face. I wish so much to hate her, but can't, just as I could never erase her from my brain when I was with Rea."

"Mary's going to be all right. I promise. And you must believe me when I say I never intended any harm to come to Rea. I didn't know—"

"No, you bloody didn't!" I yell. Moira recoils. I feel bad. Why? "And where's Mary? What have you done with

172

her? And Rea. How do you know she's dead? Surely if you're so fucking clever you can do something for her!"

"May I sit down, please?" Moira timidly asks.

In the Reservation, whenever upset, Moira liked to sit down. I would always sit beside her and rest my arm across her, sometimes gently squeezing her soft shoulder. And I would kiss her.

Not now!

"Do what you bloody like! Like shooting the only person I've ever really loved. Apart from Mary."

Moira, now several shades paler than the face that was staring at me when I came to, sits on the bed again. She's trembling.

"The woman I killed was called Bukla. Bukla-the-Pig. She flogged me for trying to escape and get to you when they took me away. After they separated us. And because of my wrists being bound, I couldn't even rub the wounds—" A tear trickles down her cheek. I do not want to watch its journey towards the mouth delivering these words of self-pity, but I watch all the same.

"You haven't answered my question. When can I see Mary? And Rea?"

"They're digging a grave for all three—"

"Forget your bloody grave. Take me to see her!"

"I'm not as important as you think. Only a glorified teacher."

"Glorified, huh? Your own glory? Moira the Magnificent overcomes Texta the Terrible?"

Suddenly, Moira throws herself onto the bed face down and cries till I can bear it no longer. Something in me breaks. This is my friend from the past and the past can never change. Rea had nothing to do with that, which is why I could never forget Moira. Likewise, Moira had nothing to do with Rea. Why should I blame her for everything? Sara had warned me about Texta, and there on my bed—our bed—lies the woman who killed that monster. I sit beside Moira and gently run my hand down her back. Never, in Man Camp 7, could I have imagined myself trying to comfort a woman wearing that dreaded grey uniform and a red belt.

"Take me to her," I say. "Please."

Moira looks round at me. I see the same fear as when Luke appeared from behind a tree with the intention of ravishing her. Something in the woman's expression tells me that not only is she still a virgin, but, unlike Rea, is also untouched by female hands. She nods. I want to take hold of her hand, as I used to, but can't bring myself to do it. Instead, I follow her out of the bedroom and out of the hut, past Angela's place and towards the lake. I stop when I see three bodies on the ground. Moira walks on ahead and talks to a group of wardens digging a large grave beside the path.

The Parth Path? What the hell is this all about? I ask myself, looking at Rea's body, wishing she would spring back to life. The diggers back away and Moira gestures to me. Slowly, quietly, I approach Rea. I don't want to disturb her death-sleep. I kneel beside her. I can't stop crying. Once I would have done anything to prevent Moira from seeing me cry, but now the tears are as much for the friend of my past as for the loss of Rea. I feel sick and at first don't know why—until it's so painfully obvious. I look up at Moira who also weeps.

"Her eyes!" I say. "Couldn't you even do that for her? Didn't you monsters even think to close them before burying her?"

***

Luke, confined in the crate, rubbed the bruises caused by being swung over the side of the boat and

174

dropped from a height onto the concrete quayside. After waiting for what seemed an eternity, he was about to push open the lid, and make a run for it, when a commotion outside froze him: men shouting, a bang, then voices. A girl's voice too, but thankfully not Moira's, although ten years back it could have been mistaken for the voice of the one who should have bedded him. He remained still. The voices stopped. Discomfort from the bruises was slowly working its way up the pain scale until he could stand it no longer. Knife in hand, he burst free and emerged blinking...

***

After hearing a noise coming from inside the crate that had been dropped from the boat's crane onto the quayside, Rolem warned Sara to remain silent. They stood statue-still and watched as the crate lid, unsecured, was raised up a fraction, went still, then suddenly flipped over. Out sprang a bearded young man clutching a knife. He merely stared at them whilst they eyed him with horror. Tommy's body lay sprawled out beside the concrete hut whilst Jimmy had been safely delivered to the Captain on board.

"Who are you?" asked Rolem. He grinned when he realised the man was only armed with a knife. Luke's courage abandoned him as soon as he saw Rolem's size and Tommy's body. He focused on the girl. About the same age as Moira before they took her away, and quite pretty.

"I'm Luke. Come to claim what's rightfully mine," replied Luke.

For some reason, Rolem found this uproariously funny. Between uncontrollable guffaws, he kept pointing at Luke until Sara frowned her concern.

"Rolem, I don't think he has anything to do with Jimmy or Tommy," she said. "I've never seen him before."

"Oh dear, oh dear! I'm so sorry Sara. I must try to control myself. If only Solem were here—"

"Peter!" corrected Sara. "Remember his proper name!"

"Peter?" questioned Luke. His courage found new strength. He approached the girl and pointed his knife at her. "Peter?" he asked again. The anger in his face caused Sara to grab her father's arm. "There's only one Peter I know of. Is he here? With her?"

Rolem chuckled again.

"Oh, I get it," he said. "You're after Rea, right? No man can take his eyes off her, she's that perfect. Well, forget it. She and Peter are the Chosen Ones and their daughter Mary is the Special Child we've all been waiting for. So, climb back into your crate and he can decide what to do with you before the boat leaves. You could join Jimmy in the hold, maybe?"

"I know no one called Rea. Texta's woman never—"

"So, you are with Texta, then?" Rolem gently removed Sara's hand from his arm and sidled up to Luke, looming above the man. He squeezed his hands together as if deciding on the strength needed to break Luke's neck. "I'd better finish you off now if you've anything to do with that woman."

"Me and Texta? You must be joking."

"I may laugh a lot but I never joke."

Luke turned and bolted for the wood but got no further than the first tree from behind which Matt appeared and aimed a punch at his jaw, jerking his head back. The knife fell. Matt stooped to pick this up

176

whilst Luke, on his back staring at the sky, rubbed his jaw before easing himself onto his elbows.

"I'm telling you, I know nothing about anyone called Rea," he protested. "Only Moira. She was going to choose me all those years ago, before ..." He glanced at his knife now held firm by Matt's slender fingers. Matt proudly cleaned the blade of his new acquisition by wiping it on the other man's sleeve. "Moira!" implored Luke, turning to face Rolem and Sara. "Her name's Moira. I've no idea who this Rea is you talk off. Must be another Peter."

"A name like that? Unlikely," responded Rolem. "So, what about you and Texta?"

"Evil! She's the one who tore me and Moira apart. It's all her fault." He looked again at Matt and at the knife in his skeleton hand. "I'd kill her given half a chance."

Rolem nodded.

"Yes, you would. I can see that. Give him back his knife, Matt. He might be useful to us whoever he is. But Peter and someone called Moira?" He looked at Sara. "You know him better than me. Has he mentioned a Moira?"

Sara blushed. Her expression revealed a reluctance to talk about Peter.

"Well?" persisted Rolem. "You can at least tell your father." Sara shook her head. Peter in bed with Rea was bad enough for her, but Peter with some strange woman called Moira somehow seemed ten times worse.

"Come here," Rolem said to Luke, now back on his feet and reunited with his knife. Matt retrieved his axe from behind the tree whilst Luke went as close to Rolem as he dared. "We're waiting for Peter to arrive with Rea and the child but they're taking an awful long time. I'm

beginning to worry that Texta and her red-belted bullies have caught them. Peter's no fighter."

"Can't be the same Peter then," suggested Luke. He remembered how, but for his beloved Moira's intervention, the bastard would have smashed his skull with a broken-off branch.

"We'll have to go to the village. Cut through the woods," continued Rolem.

"This Peter you go on about... is he—I mean, was he a Wrathie Rattie?"

Rolem looked at Sara. The girl nodded, unaware that this simple gesture would influence destinies in such a profound way. They were about to head off into the wood in the direction of the lake when a shrill voice called from the undergrowth:

"Sara! Rolem!" Daniel emerged from the line of trees, panting like a dog. He stooped down to regain his breath.

"Daniel?" queried Sara. She knew her brother well enough to realise that something was seriously wrong. The boy straightened up.

"They've killed Rea!"

Sara clapped her hand to her mouth.

"Peter?" she whispered into her palm.

"They shot her when Peter found the red wardens with Mary. Rea's face was covered in blood," announced Daniel. "Bet Jimmy's behind this. Jimmy and Tommy."

Tears spilled from the girl's eyes.

"Is the baby all right?"

Daniel shrugged his shoulders.

"Didn't wait to find out. But I heard two more gun shots."

"Two more? Oh no... Peter! Please no!"

Rolem, fearing the girl might pass out, held onto her.

"I'm not sure we can trust the Captain any longer either," continued Daniel. "I think—"

"Stop babbling!" interrupted Matt. "Did they see you?" Daniel shrugged his shoulders. "They'll have followed you, Daniel. You, Sara and Rolem in the hut over there. This Luke person and I can hide in the crate till the red wardens arrive."

"No," insisted Rolem. "We stay together. Safety in numbers." He glanced at the line of trees. "One tree each, right? They'll be coming by the path. You and Luke on one side, me and Matt on the other. Sara, my dearest—just stay back. If anything happens to me, hide wherever you can. And try to make contact with Peter. We don't know for sure he's been shot. Or Mary. Whatever happens, look after Mary. She's more precious than anything you can imagine."

Chapter 13

I hug Rea for the last time before gently closing her unseeing brown eyes forever. Once, when there was life there, these were surely the two most beautiful objects in the universe. Now they're empty of all meaning. I wait until the grave has been fully dug, then carefully lift my love's stiffened body and place it to rest in the freshly-dug ground. I look up at the grave-diggers leaning impatiently on their shovels. I know that each of them is only waiting for word from Moira to swipe at my bruised head with her shovel before heaping the dark earth onto both of us, but Moira shows no sign of betraying me. Perhaps I've misread her. One of the red-belted wardens walks towards Texta's corpse.

"No!" I yell. "Not in the same grave as Rea."

To know that Texta defiled my beloved's precious body with her groping hands is bad enough, but to have her lying for eternity beside Rea is unbearable. Moira acknowledges my request by ordering her minions to dig a separate grave. When they begin to strike the sod with their spades, I shout again at them:

"Further away! The other side of hell if possible!" My eyes search for a spot for Rea's tormentor. "Beyond those bushes there. Where Rea won't have to smell that animal. She hated her smell!" I point to a cluster of evergreen bushes further down the slope, some way off the path. "Or you could use her stinking body as fuel to power a helicopter with. Whatever, just get the fucking Commandant away from here. Her fat pig, too!"

The wardens, unable to take any sort of order from a Single X-Why, look to Moira. The subservience in their eyes tells a different story from the one given to me by my one-time friend.

"Do as he says," she commands. Grudgingly, two red-belted women set off, trailing their spades, whilst four others follow, between them dragging two foul corpses, and leaving their shovels on the ground. I pick up one of these and start to refill Rea's grave from the surrounding hillock of earth.

"For Controller's sake, help me!" I say to Moira. "Show me you're still human."

I said this without expecting any response. It was a stab at what she'd become, but to my surprise, and, dare I say, annoyance, she picks up one of the other spades and dutifully sets to work beside me. Together we gradually cover Rea's body with fresh soil.

I stop and lean on my spade, watching as Moira continues to layer the love of my life with earth.

"They used to call it penance," I tell her. "Got that from one of those illegal books. Expect you've read them all, being a teacher."

She looks up.

"What books?"

"What books?" I mimic in a thin feminine voice. "You bloody know what books!"

"Peter... I, too, am a victim of the Parth Path. Becoming Directress and getting one step closer to the Controller was my only way to—" She pauses, lost for words.

"Become her?" I suggest.

"No, Peter. I'm still me. Moira. Your friend. Did it mean nothing to you, all those years we spent together playing on the—?"

"Where's Mary? She's all that matters to me."

"Somewhere safe. She'll be on the boat by now. I told them to take her to my school where I have friends who'll—"

I drop my spade, grab a fistful of her dress just below those same breasts that filled me with so much fascination when they started to sprout in the Reservation, and I raise her up till her feet leave the ground."

"You what?" I snarl. Her fear pleases me, though I can't understand why.

"Peter—put me down. Just listen!"

I lower her but maintain my hold on her grey uniform dress.

"You sent my baby away without even consulting me!" I cry.

"She's just not safe here now that Texta's dead."

"What are you talking about? Hardly safe when the bitch was alive, ay?"

"She really believed that Mary was born to be special. To start a clone of future controllers with her genetic design. After a few changes in the laboratory. Tommy, her old husband, is the dangerous one. He wouldn't have dared do anything when she was alive, but now... who knows?"

"So—wait a minute, you're saying that Rea and I were just part of some sort of weird experiment."

"Not so weird. Not if you've had your head filled with Parth Path doctrine like I got for the past ten years. I could only bear it by day-dreaming about the times we used to have on the Reservation. See, inside my head you protected me from the Parth Path. You were still my saviour."

"Bollocks!" I say, relaxing my grip. "Cut the self-pity, Moira. So, what'll happen to Mary at that school?"

182

"There they'll still think she's the future seed of all Controllers. The first Immortal Controller. She'll be more than safe. She'll be worshipped."

"Yeah. I read a book called 'The Holy Bible' at Man Camp 7. All about worshipping. But Mary's just a baby, for Controller's sake! And milk on the journey? In the boat? Who's gonna give her milk? Only mothers can do that."

"What about cows? Cow's milk's what they use in the cloning laboratories all over Parthpathia. Only us natties are brought up on human milk."

"Why didn't you kill Texta before if you're not one of them? If you believe the Parth Path is a load of shit."

"Precisely because I'm *not* one of them. But—" She looks at the wardens in the distance standing over the bodies of Texta and Bukla. "—I had a score to settle with Texta as well as with Bukla. For separating us. And threatening to kill you after taking Mary. She wanted Rea for herself, you know. Neither of us intended for Bukla to shoot Rea. And I don't kill babies, Peter. Besides, she's yours. I could never—"

"Shut up!" I snap. "I've heard enough."

I return to my duty of burying Rea and, reluctantly or not I cannot tell, Moira continues to assist me. As I dig I think of only one thing: being reunited with little Mary, feeling her warm cheek up against mine and drinking in the sweet innocence of the little sounds emerging from her small lips.

***

Behind large trees bordering the path to the lake and village, Rolem and Sara stood, barely daring to breathe. Across the path were hidden Matt, Luke and Daniel.

183

Daniel had amassed a pile of stones chosen for shape and size. Having perfected the art of stone throwing, he was very particular about such things. Too large and the trajectory would never reach its target; too small and the target might survive. Irregularly-shaped stones had a habit of going off course. So, only smooth, rounded stones of a certain size ended up snug in the cup of his hand. He barely had enough time to collect half a dozen before the sound of red wardens' voices filtered through the forest vegetation. With stones bulging his pockets, he selected a tree trunk broad enough to conceal him.

There were only three red wardens. One carried baby Mary and two younger gun-bearing women walked on either side of her. They laughed when the older woman made funny faces at the infant. Mary was silent, either through fear or curiosity. Obviously, the wardens' leaders were confident that all rebels had been obliterated or there would have been a greater force accompanying the Special Child of the Chosen Ones on her journey to safety. The deaths of Texta and Bukla seemed of no concern to them, perhaps because neither woman had been popular with Parth Path minions. Moira was their true leader. After all, Moira also knew the Controller.

On the quayside, one of the women, with her gun raised, kicked open the flimsy hut door just in case a rebel had escaped unharmed from the battle in the woods. She opened the lid of the crate on seeing that this was unsecured. She gave her colleagues the thumbs up, but immediately staggered to one side, clutching her head. Her gun dropped to the ground and she fell to her knees.

Daniel cursed aloud when the stone failed to kill the woman. If he'd kept his mouth shut, things might have turned out differently, but Daniel being Daniel, an expletive just popped out. The other armed warden swivelled, aimed and shot the thin boy as he stood on the path about to throw another stone.

"No!" screamed Sara when her brother dropped face forward without any further sound. The stunned warden retrieved her gun whilst her companion fired two shots at the tree behind which Sara trembled with grief and terror. Slowly, this red warden, built like a bullock, approached the tree that had cried out, panning the barrel of her gun in wide curves from left to right and right to left, all the time covering any potential living target within firing range. What had seemed like over-confidence by dispatching only three wardens for the task of delivering the baby to the boat was balanced by the fact that these armed women were expert shots. Because of this, a small army had been deemed unnecessary by Moira.

"Show yourself, whoever you are," called the warden as she approached the tree. If Rolem had not stepped on a dried twig that cracked when it snapped, he might have survived. The woman swivelled and shot as Matt's axe swung down into her skull with a force that almost split her head in two. Rolem-the-giant and the large warden fell in balletic unison.

Sara emerged and dropped beside her dead father, weeping and cradling his huge head on her lap whilst Matt and Luke ran after the third warden, a slightly-built woman who fled towards the boat with Mary held firm against her flattened breasts. She was fast, though slow compared with Matt who grabbed her from behind and yanked her off the gangplank. Although skinny, the *man was strong. His axe still lay embedded in the larger woman's skull, but he easily pulled the child free. The unarmed warden punched and slapped at him until Luke arrived. The Captain, leaning on the side of the boat, alerted by the gun-shots, watched as the woman grunted and clutched at her belly after Luke's knife had been thrust into it. She stumbled back, Luke stabbed her again in the chest, slashed the knife across her face then kicked her corpse off the quay into the water. By then, other bearded faces had joined the Captain's at the side of the boat.*

"What now, Matt?" called the Captain. "Plan B or Plan C?"

Matt, afraid to even look at the squirming baby in his arms, felt lost without Rolem.

"Sara!" he shouted. Sara looked up. Luke briefly turned to her, then faced Matt again.

"Give the baby to me," he said. "I know all about them. Had two of my own, once. At the Reservation."

True, but he'd never held either of them. They'd only come into his world because he had practised on his 'wife' what he planned to do with Moira. For days after being 'entered', the poor woman would sit nursing her bruises. Matt-the-silent-one, who had spent a good deal of his life studying and trying to understand others, could read Luke like an open book. Luke raised his knife and stepped towards Matt, gesturing with his free hand for the other man to yield up the little kicking bundle.

"Give her to me! Come on! Or I'll take the girl!" He glanced at Sara.

Luke saw the baby as a bargaining tool with Moira. Sara, likewise, with Matt. But Matt merely shook his head and backed away, clutching Mary to his chest. Sara, unnoticed by Luke, pulled the axe free from the

186

slain woman's head. Matt, not taking his eyes off Luke, saw the girl, out of the corner of his eye, advance slowly, holding the axe with two hands above her head. The axe shook. Matt knew that he was only safe from the other man whilst he held Mary.

"No," he said. "Tell me first why I should trust you." Not used to using speech, speaking now was the one thing that might give Sara time to reach them unnoticed.

"You've got it all wrong, man," Luke told him.

"Why the knife?" asked Matt. Sara now stood directly behind Luke, the axe raised high. She hesitated. Matt realised that the girl could not kill. In her hands, the axe was no more lethal than a twig. "Shoot him," he called out to the Captain.

But the Captain only laughed.

"And spoil the fun?" he said. "You there! The one who thought I didn't know he was hiding in the crate. Let the girl bring the child to me."

Luke briefly looked over his shoulder at Sara, but before he could take advantage of the girl's terror, and her reluctance to inflict harm on any living creature, Matt brought his leg up smartly between Luke's legs, catching the other man's balls with his foot. Luke cried out, dropped the knife and scissored his legs against the excruciating pain. The Captain and his crew guffawed like a line of screeching monkeys.

"Quick!" Matt exclaimed, handing the girl the baby in exchange for the axe. "Take Mary. On board. Take her to the Controller. And never leave her side until you're sure you can trust the woman. I hate the Parth Path more than anything, but I do believe in the Special One. And that has to be Mary."

Sara skirted around a hopping, cursing Luke, swopped the axe for Mary, then ran towards the gangplank. Matt picked up the knife and slotted it into his belt. Angered by the deaths of both Rolem and his son, especially his son, the gentle, thin man was transformed into a one-man army that would take on anyone and anything. Sara stopped and looked back at him.

"Aren't you coming with me?" she asked.

"I've a score to settle with the woman who did this." Matt indicated with his axe the bodies strewn across the quayside.

"Please don't," begged Sara. "You'll be outnumbered. They all have guns."

Matt taps his head.

"And I have this. It's called a brain."

"What about him?"

Sara glanced at Luke who was still clutching his crotch and taking in deep breaths to override the pain.

"He might just prove useful. If he can forgive me," he added.

"There's something else I haven't told you."

"I know," said Matt.

Sara frowned.

"You can't. How can you know?"

"Peter? You?" replied Matt. "I've known all along."

"Please don't tell him. I've started, but with Jimmy—or any other man—I just couldn't!"

"You have his baby. Just treasure her like your own."

"They'll kill him, won't they?"

"With Peter, nothing is certain. It's why the Controller chose him. Hurry now before they realise that something's happened to their trained killers." Matt

188

stepped forward and kissed the girl on the forehead. "I think he knows. Deep down. And knows you're a good girl, too."

Hugging Mary against her young bosom, Sara, in tears, climbed on board, helped by the Captain.

"Take her straight to the Controller!" Matt called out. "And Sara, always think of Peter to remind you why your father died!" Sara just looked at him. "Rolem was your true father. Not Tommy!"

"I've always known!" the girl said quietly to little Mary.

But this knowledge gave the girl strength. She ran with the baby up the gangplank to be confronted by a line of female-starved sailors who stood gaping at the pretty Island girl. A shout from the Captain dispersed them.

"They'll not harm you or the child, I promise," he said to Sara. "But never leave my cabin without an escort. And it's a long journey all the way to the Old City. The one they used to call Edinburgh. That's where she lives. In a building known as The Castle."

When Sara turned to call out to Matt about something that she'd not dared to mention before, something she wanted Daniel's father to pass on to Peter, something she wished the man she loved to know if she were to die, but both he and Luke were gone.

***

I'm sitting at the table where Rea and I shared every meal together, apart from those served by Sara at Angela's. Already, I miss Sara. To think I'll never again hear that beautiful voice compounds the agony of losing Rea. Moira is talking outside to her red-belted wardens. She talks quietly, thinking I can't hear, but she seems to have forgotten how acute my hearing is.

189

I recall little Moira from my other, earlier, life also talking quietly, even whispering, outside the window by my bed inside Mother Mary's hut in the Reservation.

"Are you there, Peter?" she would ask through the thin wooden wall of our hut. Once I jokingly whispered back, "No." And I giggled, but this only confused her.

"Why did you say, 'No'?" she asked moments later when we were happily reunited outside as dawn began to break in a pink spill over the mountains beyond the fields.

"Because whatever I say, the true answer can only be 'yes!'"

She still didn't get it, so I kissed her, and we ran off down to the beach to watch the rising sun make dappled patterns on the sea.

This time, I not only hear every word, but try to understand what's happened to my one-time friend. She sounds angry.

"What do you mean, they've taken the child?"

"The boat's away. The two gun wardens are dead on the quayside. The skinny one's floating in the water. And there are two rebels shot through the head. One a giant of a man, the other a boy. But there were others. Must have escaped."

Rolem dead? And a boy? Daniel? Did he open his mouth one time too many? Have Sara and Matt escaped with Mary on the boat? Can the Captain really be trusted? And what about Sara? Have they already changed her as they've changed Moira? As for Mary...

"Are there no other boats on this blessed island?" asks Moira.

I hear no reply.

"A helicopter?"

Silence.

"Someone's going to have to pay for this! And did you pay the Captain fully in advance with proper provisions this time?"

No response.

"Well, did you? Provisions is all he thinks about."

In my head, I can picture Moira grabbing the owner of the other voice by the front of her dress and giving her a shake. "Then, we'll just have to hope for a storm, won't we? Those clouds look promising. And find me someone amongst the villagers here who can cook."

A storm? She wants Mary dead? I will kill the cow!

"There's a woman on her own next door."

Angela? Yes, bring Angela here. Who knows, maybe she can sing as well as her daughter? We could all sit around just listening to her. What else is there to do in this fucking nightmare?

Moira re-enters our hut and smiles. How I used to love those smiles. They truly brightened up many a long day in the Reservation. Same face, albeit older, same lips that I kissed so many times after her breasts had sprouted. She sits at the table beside me and gently places an arm across my shoulders.

"I'm so sorry about Rea, Peter. I honestly had no idea you loved her. I suppose—" She stops as if to gaze into her past. Our past.

"Suppose what?" I ask bluntly.

"I suppose I believed so much in what we had together on the Reservation that nothing else seemed real."

"Well you supposed wrong. So... why did you wish for a storm? To destroy Mary without getting your own hands dirty?"

"You were listening?"

"I do have flipping ears, woman!"

191

"Why do you get it so wrong all the time? About me! The Captain will have to take shelter on the mainland if there's a storm. And Mary will be safe there once they get her to the school. Otherwise the Captain might prefer to stay adrift and use her as a bargaining tool. Please don't think badly of me whatever I say!"

"I'm not staying, you know."

"No one can leave the Island till the boat returns. Unless the Controller decides to send out a helicopter."

"No, I mean this hut. Memories."

"Of course!" She smiles again, and I feel my anger slowly begin to melt.

"I can stay with Angela."

A flash of jealousy straightens her smile. Already, I miss that smile.

"Who's Angela?" she asks.

"The woman next door." I turn and squint into her eyes. "Excellent cook, too. Like her daughter."

"Daughter? They said she lives alone."

I shake my head. Moira remains silent. I play with cutlery on the table. Should I stab the fork into her neck? Never again enjoy that sweet smile?

"She does, now. I expect," I say. "Live alone, that is. Your lot killed her son and maybe the girl too."

Horror, not jealousy, now plays tricks with Moira's features. Horror caused by a sudden awareness that the girl might have taken the baby onto the boat? That voice outside had made no mention of a girl being amongst the dead.

"*My* lot do not kill for no reason," she said after a long pause. "They control situations that threaten us all, Peter. I just want the baby taken to a place of safety. My school. Can this daughter you speak of be trusted?"

I say no more. Moira could never understand the love inside Sara. There again, do I *really* know the girl with the beautiful voice? But discussion with Moira seems pointless. Plus, I'm tired and hungry.

"I'll ask this Angela person to come round. Cook something for both of us," Moira says.

"Order her to come, you mean!"

"That's not fair, Peter. You speak as if I'm a monster. All I've ever wanted is to be with you again. Now I can't seem to do anything right."

"You said it!" I agree.

Moira starts to cry. What a bugger! A woman's greatest weapon! My guard drops.

"Look, I'm sorry," I blurt. "I, too, had you in my head all those years in Man Camp 7. Even when with Rea, I had trouble getting rid of you."

True. Moira's face brightens.

"You really thought about me?"

I nod.

"Like every day?"

I nod again, and when she puts her arms around me, and kisses my lips, I feel the same hardening of my dangly thing that so excited me when we last kissed ten years ago. She leads me into the bedroom and starts to remove my shirt. Something snaps, my dangly thing goes limp and dangly again.

"Not now," I say. "Not so soon after what's happened." I still find it impossible to believe that I'll never again hold Rea in my arms.

"You're still the Chosen One for me," she says. "There's been no one else."

Perhaps a part of me wishes I could say the same to her, for in truth I was even happier with Moira on the

Reservation without sex than when I was trying to make sense of the Island with Rea, plus sex.

***

"Move!" snapped Matt, prodding the larger man in the back. Luke, groaning, was in no fit state to refuse Matt's demands as he staggered along the path towards the lake. Halfway there, Matt told Luke to stop. He pulled at some broken-off tree branches until he found what he was looking for. A black ribbon. He then pushed his 'prisoner' into the undergrowth along a zig-zag course, periodically stopping to look for more ribbons. Eventually they reached the clearing around Sara's and Daniel's secret hideout. From one of his pockets hung the ribbons he'd removed from the branches. He cleared the dead foliage obscuring the brick opening and slid back the cover.

"Down the ladder," he ordered.

"I am not—"

"Down the bloody ladder, I said. You want this Moira person for yourself, correct?"

"She's mine by rights. If they hadn't taken her and that bastard away, we'd have been together long ago. I ran the new reservation for the Chief, you know."

"I've no interest in your past. I only know that Moira, who- or whatever she may be, is a danger to Mary. And to Sara. You see, you should never have threatened my little boy's sister."

"The dead boy was her brother? They don't look at all alike."

"Didn't!" corrected Matt. "Different fathers."

"So, you were you his—?"

"Never you mind! Stay with me and do as I say, and I'll do my best to get Moira to you. Only because I hate her more than I hate you."

194

Luke peered into the darkness below.

"What's down there?" he asked.

"Lamps, food, water. And a couple of mattresses."

"Now you're talking. But I'll only need one mattress with her. Any rope?"

"To hang yourself with?"

"Secure her. In case she struggles."

Matt's first assessment of the other man seemed confirmed whenever Luke opened his mouth. He was evil personified, but might yet serve a purpose.

"Go on down. I'll show you everything. Of course, you're free to leave any time you want but I guarantee they'll kill you. Do what you will with that creature called Moira, and it won't be me killing you."

In the hideout, Matt showed Luke everything he needed to know. To the larger man's delight, there were even a couple of knives in a drawer. Matt left Luke lying on a mattress, nursing his wounded manhood. When Matt was gone, and the lid closed, this turned into masturbation fuelled by thoughts of what he would do to Moira. He had no reason to doubt the skinny man whose only agenda seemed to be one of separating Peter from Moira. That far, their paths ran parallel. Afterwards, when Moira was well and truly his, Peter would suffer in ways the bastard could never dream of, not even in his worst nightmares.

Luke climaxed alone and in the dark, with images of Moira and Peter, as they were ten years back, dancing like ghosts in the hell of his mind.

***

Heavy with fatigue, my head is still sore after being walloped after Rea was killed, and Mary had been snatched away. I lie curled up on our bed—Rea's and mine. It seems that my life-lights have been turned off, as happened with the electricity in Man Camp 7 every evening whilst the Commandant pleasured herself on top of a clonie before flopping into sexual exhaustion. Something touches my back. I cannot believe I'm feeling Rea's warm hands stroking me. No, I'm not dreaming, but for a few moments I try to convince myself that the earlier events of the day—Moira appearing as if out nowhere and Rea and Texta being shot—were simply a nightmare. The hands travel round to my front, one finding its way to my firming erection. Rea never does that. She's totally passive, at the same time passionately responsive. Something to do with being a clonie, brought up in a laboratory, I used to tell myself. This feminine assertion can mean only one thing. I turn over. That smile from my past again, now only inches away. My anger gone, my erection feels all-encompassing. I cannot stop myself from kissing those lips again, so soft and loving, so eager, and only when I collapse, spent, on top of Moira's yielding body, can I safely remember Rea. As Moira tries to hold onto me to prolong her orgasm, I feel overcome by shame. I know that Moira can never replace Rea, yet no longer can I hate the only friend from my childhood.

Chapter 14

Stretched out on the bunk in the Captain's cabin, Sara fed Mary from a bottle of cow's milk for babies. She'd been shown how to make it up with powder from a carton using water boiled on the Captain's gas ring, and leaving it to cool till the temperature equalled that of the back of her hand. Mary burped when raised to the Island girl's shoulder, then giggled in response to playful tickles. Sara, too, laughed. Now that she had 'started', it seemed so natural not only to be holding the infant but to be her sole carer and protector. She was impossibly happy but for one thing. On that matter, hope would have to be her only companion.

"You'll need help when we reach the mainland," the Captain said. "I'll fetch him when we touch shore."

"Him?" Sara's eyes lit up. Hope pushed aside her fears and seemed to fill the small cabin.

"Watchem. He and I go back a long way. You can trust him."

The girl's eyes dimmed. Having hoped for something else, she cuddled Mary against her face... Mary, possibly the only part of Peter she would ever get to know.

"He helped Peter and he'll help you. The Controller respects him. He's told her a lot about Texta and the others."

"Others?"

"It's about time you learnt a few things, my dear," replied the Captain. He came across and sat beside Sara. "Things about this place they used to call Scotland which has now become the world. The human world, at least. Because of what happened in the Great Man War.

197

Parthpathia now, but perhaps not forever. Once. a very long time ago, it was called Caledonia."

***

Moira falls asleep in my arms. I kiss her forehead, climb out of bed, turn and look down at her. Up until a year ago, making love to my childhood sweetheart was a paradise forever beyond my reach. And I could tell it was her first time, so she had not deceived me as I had her, with Rea.

Who really was that genetic perfection called Rea? Something inside me should hold up a board for my inner eye to read and written across it in large bold letters would be the words *'Rea not real!'* And yet I loved the mother of my baby more than I could ever love my friend from the Reservation. And now she's dead.

Once, I jokingly promised Rea that I would seek out one of her nineteen sibling clonies should anything ever happen to her. This upset her, and I virtually kicked myself for saying it, for I knew humour was not her thing, but then I truly did believe life with a second-best Rea-lookalike would be better than lifelong masturbation inspired by memories of both Rea and Moira. Although Rea was in my head during our foreplay, Moira took centre-stage there as we climaxed together on Rea's bed. It was Moira who fired that burst of primordial energy we call 'orgasm'.

I leave Moira asleep and seek out Angela. Angela will restore normality for me. Perhaps Angela can also bring back the old Moira. Instruct her in the ways of a nattie woman even if she's not much of a cook herself. But what, Controller forbid, has happened to Sara? Will she come back to the Island? Will I never again hear the liquid music of that heavenly voice?

198

My head spins as I leave the hut. Matt is the last person I expect to be standing there, holding an axe. I quickly scan the street for lurking wardens and half-concealed eyes.

"Come inside," I say to him, opening the door. "But stay quiet. Moira's asleep!"

***

"Know this first, Sara. Inside every man lurks a demon. It leaks out, like an oil slick, from his Y chromosome to smother his single X, sometimes whispering, sometimes shouting, often silent, but it's always there, waiting for the chance to do harm. And to others of his own sex as well as to women."

Sara shook her head though said nothing. There were many men she knew for whom this was not true. One in particular.

"Across the world, scientists, mostly females, warned that those in control, men of course (apart from here in Scotland which was already run by women), of the dangers of damaging the climate, the sea—indeed life in all its forms—beyond a point of no return, but the greed seeping out from four billion Y chromosomes across the planet prevented them from listening. Or if they did, they took no action."

Sara, who had no interest in chromosomes, rocked baby Mary in her arms and watched as tiny eyelids shut out the cruelty of a world of which the Captain spoke.

"It began with what the First Controller called 'Accelerated Tribalism'. Throughout the history of womankind, humans formed tribes that competed for land and resources. Result: wars. But it got more complicated. Tribes within tribes, tribes spanning other tribes, and when food, water and resources began to run out, because of disregard for nature, the wars

escalated. Two tribes in particular vied for global power, each claiming a divine right to destroy the other at whatever cost, and both driven by Y chromosomes."

Sara stifled a yawn. She couldn't see where this leading.

"Weapons of mass destruction. Nobody believed they would ever be used, but in the Great Man War that followed there were so few survivors that, but for the First Controller, humanity would have perished altogether. Perhaps one day we'll discover what remains of the old civilisation south of the two big cities, and in those lands across the sea, but for the present we have to rely on the Parth Path to give babies like Mary a future. And Mary, of course, is a part of the path."

"Do you believe she really is the Special One?" asked Sara. "Because of Rea and—?" The girl could no longer say his name. Not without weeping.

"The first Immortal Controller? Who knows? If she isn't, does that make her any less precious?"

Sara smiled at the sleeping baby.

"No," she replied.

"Look, get some sleep now. I'll make sure you're both safe."

Sara and Mary slept together on the cabin bunk and the Captain never left them. He peed into a jar and emptied this out through a porthole. His new pilot was a reliable man, but not even he could be trusted to guard Sara and the child of the Chosen Ones alone. He did, however, bring food and drink to the cabin, and, thankfully, the sea was calm, so they made good speed across the grey water. The girl and the baby slept for most of the time.

Sara was grateful to have learned so much about babies from Rea. The genetically-perfect woman turned out to be a perfect mother, and Sara, teacher of housekeeping and culinary skills, became, for a change, her eager student. All the more so to impress the baby's father.

The boat had stopped moving when the Captain tapped her arm to awaken her, and she felt frightened. Sara had only ever known the Island. She expected the mainland to be different. Huge and strange. Yet once out on deck, it seemed she'd returned to the Island with the quayside, trees and hills just re-arranged into an unfamiliar pattern. Hope that Peter was about re-enter her life abandoned her when she saw an old, white-haired man dressed in tattered rags standing beside his horse and cart on a path at the top of a steep bank. She watched him clamber down the slope, surprisingly nimble for a man of his age.

"Watchem," the Captain said to Sara. Watchem gave the girl a short bow as she stood with Mary on the quayside. The old man looked baffled.

"So, you're the replacement chosen female? So young! But where's—?"

The Captain, holding a bag full of baby milk powder, took hold of Watchem's arm, led him aside and whispered into his ear. Watchem repeatedly glanced at the girl and nodded. Taking the bag from the Captain, he led Sara up the bank to his cart, helping her onto the seat beside his. Behind this was a blanket-lined wicker basket already prepared for the child of the Chosen Ones, but Sara held onto Mary.

The girl turned to wave at the Captain, now just a face in a row of faces all bearded save one: Jimmy. On leaving the boat holding Mary, she had felt more convinced than ever that everyone was wrong about the Y chromosome. Her true protectors had all been *furnished with Y chromosomes and one of these she could hardly bear never to see again. On seeing Jimmy amongst the sailors, she wondered.*

***

"Rolem and Daniel are dead," whispers Matt.

The words hit like bullets. Perhaps making love to Moira softened my anger over Rea, but now I'm more confused than ever. I feel light-headed and have to sit down. Matt sits beside me to unravel the full horror of what happened on the quayside. I don't know whether I'm more concerned for Sara's safety or that of my daughter.

"So... she's on the boat? With Jimmy on board? Couldn't you have killed the boy too? You know how she hates him."

"Couldn't do it. He's little more than a child."

"I'm going with them. To protect Sara and Mary."

"Too late. The boat's gone. The Captain didn't want to take the risk. They'll be taken to the City of the Castle. To the Controller."

"And you think *she's* responsible?" I glance at the closed bedroom door.

"The one they call Moira? She's with you?"

I don't want to believe any of this. After entering Moira, I could almost imagine myself back on the Reservation. She, too, had been harmed. Even whipped. Together, we might be able to re-live our past here on the Island.

"She had reason to kill Texta. Plus the fat one. But Daniel and Rolem? No way! She says those at the school are to be trusted. And that she's not like the others. Moira promised me that Sara will be safe with the Captain."

"Safe from Jimmy?"

202

"It's not Sara you should worry about now. Look to yourself, Matt."

"They killed Rea, Rolem and Daniel and now they're going to kill you. Or *she* will!"

Having enjoyed the virgin delights of Moira's body, I cannot believe this. And I swear she must have kissed every square inch of mine in our foreplay.

"You're wrong. I'll ask her. We used to share everything, you know."

"She's a monster. She's using you. Playing a game you cannot win."

Game? Cricky? Did I truly control those winning games on the Reservation? She was a virgin before we made love. Of this, I have no doubt. But a virgin out of choice or circumstance? No opportunities with another Single-X Why at the school, I imagine.

"Guess you played together as children never knowing she'd turn into a monster, huh?"

"A tune," I said, remembering the whistled tune we shared when calling on one another to come out and play. "A very special tune back then. Like one bird calling another with a very special song."

Matt nods his head thoughtfully. I wish I could make him out. He's only ever been a puzzle to me.

"There's a place the other side of the Island where you can hide," he says. "Not even Sara knows about it. I'll fetch you when the boat returns. You do want to see Mary again, don't you? It'll be a few days, but there's water and food there. Salted chicken meat as well."

Chicken? I think of Rea being dragged, struggling, out of Albert's harem. What part did Moira really play in her capture and death? Was Texta just a convenient excuse? Being dead, the older woman could no longer expose Moira's complicity. How convenient for my old

203

friend! And me? Does the young woman who has just responded to my caresses, like a fresh flower opening out in the first light of dawn, truly wish to kill me as well? Maybe one fuck was enough to give her what she *really* wanted: a child of her own, child to call 'special', and destroy Mary?

"Go!" says Matt. "Whatever *she* says, they'll kill you when they learn the truth about Sara's escape. I can hide you. When the boat comes back, the Captain will get you to the mainland. Then they can take you to Mary."

Take me to Mary? If only!

His words are enough. Moira's still asleep. Believing I'll return, one day, to her embrace, if she's true, or kill her if she's not, I follow Matt round the back of the hut, past Albert's place, across the potato fields over the hills to an unfamiliar coastline of jutting rocks and wave-hollowed coves. One of these, deeper than the others, will, I learn, serve as my hideout. There's a ledge furnished with blankets and a box containing food and bottles of water. The highwater mark tells me that the cove, which fades into darkness, is cut off, for periods, by the tide. Part of me wishes to disappear into that darkness in the hope of finding Rea there; part of me wishes Moira had shot me instead of Texta.

***

The old man called Watchem said nothing more. Sara was thankful, for she felt sure she would have screamed in response to any further mention of chromosomes, X or Y. Her brother and true father had been killed, and here she was in a cart with a total stranger on her way to meet the Controller. Until then, the woman who controlled what remained of humanity was, for the Island girl, no more than a word revered by all. And now Sara was carrying the baby who would one day become the first Immortal Controller.

Mary was awake. She smiled when the Island girl stroked her cheeks. If only for the father's sake, Sara swore she would look after the child with every sentient fibre of her being. Perhaps, if he still lived, he would thank her when she returned Mary to him. Just to be thanked would be enough, for nothing more could be hoped for.

"Did you know him well?" Watchem asked, as if reading her mind.

'Did' not 'do'? Tears appeared as Sara hesitated before nodding. Of course, she knew him well! Perhaps better than anyone alive. But what more could she have done to save Rea whom he so adored? It was the guilt of this failure that caused the tears to flow. Failing Peter.

"The Chosen One? Aye!" Sara nodded again. Watchem reached sideways and hugged the girl close. "The Controller will be proud of you."

Sara looked up at him. He seemed impossibly old and wise. Was he alive during the Great Man War of which the Captain spoke, the girl wondered? Did he really know the Controller? Was the woman only flesh and blood after all? And might she, Sara from the Island, also get killed, like her father and brother.

"Get some sleep," suggested Watchem. "It's a long ride to the City of the Castle."

***

As soon as Matt has gone, I see that the water level is already rising. Doubts enter my brain. Why should I trust Matt-the-Silent-One? He knows nothing about Moira, about the beauty of our past friendship nor indeed what she went through during the ten years after we became separated by the Parth Path. Has he gone back to kill

205

her? How could I be so gullible? If the water level hadn't already blocked off my only escape route, I would flee from the cove and run back to Moira. But I'm stuck here with only anger and confusion to comfort me. I help myself to salted chicken and fruit as I wait for the tide to turn.

***

"He's waiting for you," announced Matt.

"Who?" questioned Moira. "What are you talking about? And who are you, anyway?"

"Solem. Peter. Whatever you like to call him. There's a secret place. He's afraid you'll not be safe here. Not now, with that woman being dead. They'll know, by now, that you killed her. And he didn't want them to find you two together. That's why he fetched me."

Moira rubbed her eyes as she stared at the gaunt figure standing in the doorway. The woman called Angela from the hut next door stood looking on as if curious to see what might happen next.

"Explain!" Moira demanded. She wasn't used to being told what to do, least of all by a Single X-Why. Matt glanced over his shoulder at Angela, his wink unseen by Moira. Angela left.

"May I come in to explain?" asked the thin man.

Moira stepped back, her hand resting on the gun slotted into her red belt.

"Where is he? Where's Peter?" she asked.

"He told me to take you to him."

"You're lying. He'd have said something."

"You saw Angela staring like that. She hates Peter for what happened to her son. Plus Peter and Rea becoming the Chosen Ones instead of her daughter Sara and that boy Jimmy. She'll betray both of you."

Moira raised her gun, flicked the safety catch then pointed it at Matt. The man, now even more convinced that the blonde had ordered those wardens to shoot his son, did some quick thinking.

"Shoot me if you like, but you'll never find him on your own. Not before they do."

Moira's experience of Single X-Whys was restricted to a blissful childhood with Peter, plus memories of the men on the Reservation including Luke. Parth Path teaching had warned her of their treachery that culminated in the Great Man War. There again, were they any different from the likes of Texta and Bukla? And what if men could become friends? She had certainly known boys play together, on the Reservation, as she had played with Peter.

"I can wait till I find out the truth," replied Moira. "I'll follow you. Don't try anything. This gun has already killed two women."

"Stay quiet," warned Matt.

Angela had disappeared into her hut. Moira followed Matt through the village. Pairs of curious eyes watched from windows as they headed off in the direction of the lake, and, from there, on into the wood.

Moira longed for Peter to take her again. She recalled seeing his dangly thing twice when they were children. She had asked him to show her again after she'd obliged him with a quick glimpse of her knickers. Neither had said anything on either occasion, but she knew then it would one day bring her joy as it finally did only hours earlier. His hands and his lips as well. For ten years, she had thought about a bliss that should have happened on the Reservation. But for Texta, they could have been the Chosen Ones and the Special Child would have been theirs instead of the screaming baby *that emerged from that clonie. By now, ten years later, they would have had a daughter together. As Moira followed the skinny figure through the undergrowth, she re-enacted in, her mind, that explosion of ecstasy when she and Peter climaxed together. The first thing she would do, once she had dispensed with the thin man, would be to make love to Peter again... and again and again.*

Chapter 15

Watchem knew the road well. He had a gun in his hand. A gun without bullets, but those human animals, shacked up together in what he called the 'Badlands', would be none the wiser. They feared him. Maybe a collective consciousness had branded their DNA with a warning about guns. Standing in groups, they would only stare at the old man who drove the horse-drawn cart, unaware of the fresh young girl and the baby hidden beneath the stinking tarpaulin. The girl, they would have group-ravaged as eagerly as they would have demolished a hunk of stale bread, but the old man was to be respected. Because of his gun.

Once beyond the clusters of broken buildings, villages of the past, and out of earshot of their miserable inhabitants, Watchem stopped the horse and helped Sara and Mary down from the cart. The Island girl, carrying Mary, sat beside him in front, and he urged the horse on with his whip.

"The Skeleton Wall," he said as if that explained everything. When Sara looked at him, puzzled, through keen bright eyes, he chuckled. "Yes, the Skeleton Wall," he repeated. "That's what the Parth Path calls it. A human wall. A wall of death."

Sara gently covered Mary's ears to protect them from yet another cruel truth from the past.

"A human wall?" she queried.

"Aye! Pretty much most of the population of this place they once called Scotland. Dead and piled high. See, the First Controller had already been quietly working away in her laboratories and was close to finding a solution to the problem of re-creating human

life without the involvement of Single X-Whys when the war broke out. Scotland wasn't a part of the fighting, but she saw it coming and worked feverishly hard both in the laboratories and in the streets of the cities to promote the Parth Path. It was she who suggested a wall. To keep them out."

"Them?"

"The millions down south. Once, a great leader called Hadrian built a wall of mud. wood and stone to keep the people of Scotland out of his territories to the south."

"When?"

"Of that, I have no idea, my dear child. But it was the First Controller's inspiration for a wall of people. Men, women and children. Half a mile deep, spanning their country from coast to coast, armed with whatever they could hold that was sharp enough to cut through human flesh. And when the hordes came, from the south, it was in waves. Cars, trucks. Mostly men or women dressed as men. They called them soldiers."

"Double Xs dressed as Single X-Whys?"

"In trousers. Women just like men. They say that's when women lost the power to stop it. Effectively turned into men."

"In trousers? How strange!"

"And they, too, were armed with guns. Whether they planned to bring the Great Man War to this country called Scotland, or wished to escape the terrors down south, we'll never know. No living person has been beyond the Skeleton Wall."

"Why a Skeleton Wall?"

"Bones left behind. Everywhere. Finally, they stopped coming. Probably because there were none left to come with their guns and their rockets. The bodies of

people from both sides were piled as high as houses and when they rotted, the stinking flesh fell from them. It's said that the stench of those decomposing corpses even reached the City of the Castle over seventy miles away. The bodies became alive again with maggots, flies and worms until only bones were left."

Sara had to take in deep breaths to stop her throwing up.

"Now, all these years later, they say it's just a wall of skeletons and brambles."

"Have you been there?" asked Sara.

"No, but do you know what they say happens once a year on the anniversary of that battle?"

Sara shook her head.

"Apparently, the skeletons stand up tall and proud again. Then they dance on delicate white feet to tunes played by the wind whistling through the flutes of their dead comrades' hollowed bones."

"Do they sing?" asked Sara, wondering what dead people might have left to sing about. Watchem laughed.

"Sing? Now why would they want to sing about getting slaughtered?"

Sara said nothing. For her, anything was worth singing about, happy or sad. Mostly sad. And when Watchem fell silent, and when the only sounds were those of the horse's hooves and the heavy roll of the cartwheels, she began to sing. She sang for Mary and for the baby's father and became so lost in the flow of the song that she failed to see the tears streaming down Watchem's wrinkled old face.

***

Moira stood back, her gun raised, as the thin man pulled the branches away from the rectangular brick wall to reveal a large metal lid which he slid to one side.

211

"You still here, Peter?" he said quietly. Silence. "He's afraid to call back in case there are red wardens hiding in the wood."

"It's a trap," challenged Moira. How could she have been so stupid? Of course, Peter would never have gone off without saying anything, and certainly would not have entrusted the secret of a trysting place to a man with the face of a skull.

"Peter, whistle your special tune for her," Matt whispered into the hideout. He beckoned to Moira who edged towards the open hole. "Peter told me. A special tune. One known only to you two. Tell him you're here and he'll whistle your tune. He said you both used to whistle it outside each other's huts in the mornings. Said how you loved to play games together. Go on. See if he remembers."

Still warm between her legs from Peter's lovemaking, Moira allowed her instincts to give way to temptation. She wanted Peter again so badly. Right now! If there was any possibility of truth in what the man told her, she would grasp it. Besides, she had a gun which gave her more power than all the men of the Island lumped together.

"Peter—whistle our tune," she spoke to the hole.

Luke remembered the tune well from his childhood stalking of Moira. He often hummed it to himself as he pictured what he would do with the girl who should have been his. Pitch perfect, he whistled the phrase. Moira up above smiled. The Moira in Luke's mind didn't. She shouldn't. Not after what she and Peter did. Matt peered from the top of the ladder into the hideout. Down below, in the darkness, Luke watched Moira's legs appear feet first. Legs that rightfully belonged to *him, followed by a body far shapelier than that of the child-turning-woman of his past.*

Moira, once down, could barely make out anything in the dim light.

"The woman who killed my son is all yours. Like I promised. Have fun!" called the thin man before closing the lid above her.

Total blackness!

"Peter?" the woman whispered.

A hand shot out of the shadows, knocking the gun from her hand. Before she could respond, her head was forced back, in the crux of an elbow, lifting her feet off the ground. Moira screamed. He, the owner of the arm, laughed. She struggled to breathe, let alone speak, as the arm tightened around her throat. She kicked out and attempted to dig her assailant with her elbow whilst squirming and twisting to free herself, but he was too strong.

The laugh wasn't Peter's, and when a voice said, "You should've chosen me back then, Moira—it would've made it easier for you now!" everything came back to her in a rush: a tree, a knife and a boy called Luke.

***

Miserable and shivering from cold, I lie on the stone ledge, hugging myself and wishing that my body was Moira's. It's getting dark, yet still Matt hasn't returned. Inside my head, something dawns: knowledge that I know nothing about the man of few words. Why, if he truly was Daniel's father, does he not live with and care for Angela. Was that Sara's doing? Did she know something about her step-father no one wished to tell me? As I lie here, waiting for the tide to go out, my brain picks over memories of Moira and our blissful friendship, of Daniel and Sara and Rolem and of ten years of hell in Man Camp 7 until Rea arrived.

Why can't I feel more anger over Rea's death? Perhaps it's as it was when Mother Mary and my sister Caitlin were killed. Something beyond anger takes control and turns me into a puppet; a walking, talking puppet that climaxed with Moira and now wishes only to do that again, over and over. The one person who made Rea real, little Mary, has been taken from me. Moira said she must be taken to the school, her domain, safe from the Controller. Matt tells me she's been taken to the only safe place, the City of the Castle from where the Controller rules what remains of human civilisation. Whom should I believe? If only I had learned more from Sara about the people on the Island. I was so caught up with being a loving husband and a caring father, it had never entered my mind to press the girl for further information. She served us, the Chosen Ones, like a dutiful servant—but we were chosen for what and by whom? And what purpose does Sara serve for the Parth Path?

***

"Where are we?" asked Sara.

The cart had stopped with jolt and awoken her. In the darkness, she could just make out a high wire fence and a dimly-lit tower. She sat up. Mary still slept but wriggled and jerked about in her slumber. Sara stroked the baby's short, silky, black hair.

"Under the tarpaulin again, my girl. This is the man camp where Peter spent ten years."

"Peter?" Mention of the man's name fanned her hope.

"A terrible place, but it's a part of the Parth Path. One of many man camps. You do not want to know what goes on there."

If Peter had been in that man camp, she did want to know, but for the safety of Peter's baby she crawled under the tarpaulin with Mary, thankful the child still slept. The cart moved forwards then stopped again. She heard voices. Watchem's and a woman's voice as harsh as the icy wind that blew off the Island hills in the winter. The tarpaulin was lifted and Watchem's hands pulled out a couple of crates. The cart jolted forwards again. Mary began to stir and make noises, but Sara felt safe with Watchem and with the memory of Peter. When she was sure that they had left the man camp, she raised the edge of the tarpaulin and peered out. Dark forest trees seemed to be on the move, not the other way around, until she sat up. Exhausted, Watchem sat slouched forwards over the reins.

"Can't we stop somewhere?" Sara asked. "You must be tired. And I need to change Mary's nappy."

Watchem reined the horse to a halt and turned to face the girl.

"For the second reason, yes. The other, no."

He alighted, took the baby, then helped Sara down. Whilst the girl set about cleaning Mary's bottom, wrapping a fresh nappy around those little kicking legs and feeding her from a bottle, Watchem shared, with the girl, his fears about what they had told him at the man camp.

"The one they call Hellcat already knew about Texta," he said. "She's taken over. Texta was bad, but Hellcat—" He shook his head. "It's only a matter of time before the inevitable happens. Then it'll be too late. We have to get to the Controller as quickly as possible."

215

"You mean she might harm little Mary?" questioned the girl.

"Worse. But she'll not deploy the helicopter at night. I've got to warn the Controller."

"But your poor horse—"

"Florrie? Oh, she'll be as desperate as me to stop Hellcat from doing her thing?"

"Doing her thing?"

"If Peter were here, he'd explain."

If only Peter was with her. Rea too. She had never felt jealousy of the woman who shared Peter's bed. If Peter had loved her, so did Sara. As they rode on into the night, and before she and Mary slipped once more into slumber, Sara dwelt on how she would look after Mary's father when they were re-united. Surrogate mother to his child, servant, house-keeper, cook—all these things—and if she could achieve perfection, just maybe something else might happen. After all, she had already started. She was, as they would say on the Island, 'past her time'.

What she saw when her eyes opened again took Sara's breath away. Dawn had broken and, silhouetted against the pink sky, was a miniature mountain bearing a grey building quite unlike anything on the Island. The path had become a wide street dotted with stationary red-belted wardens. The surface of the street was hard and without holes, so the cart no longer bumped and bounced.

Sara, who had been asleep resting on Watchem's shoulder, sat forwards and looked up at the high buildings and down at groups of women who stood and watched as the cart trundled to the end of the street before turning a corner and climbing a hill leading up to the Castle. The cobblestones caused the cart to judder

216

till they came to a halt in front of an iron gate flanked by two sentry boxes. In each of these stood a warden with a gun and a whip. Both recognised Watchem. One went to open the gate with a large key that dangled from her belt whilst the other stared at Sara, a hard, cold stare that bore right through the girl. Sara snuggled against Watchem, holding Mary, as Florrie pulled the cart past the sentries and on into the Castle precinct.

"No helicopter?" observed Watchem, looking at the wardens. One stepped forward.

"Watchem, what are you doing here? And who is this girl with a baby? Is it yours? At your age?"

Incensed at the thought of being mother to Watchem's child, Sara was about to blurt out, 'Mary's the Special One, you fool,' when Watchem gripped her arm. A warning for the girl to keep her mouth shut.

"I have to see the Controller at once," he said. "Moira the Directress has killed Texta."

***

Determined to ignore Matt's warning and return to Moira, I fall asleep. That we *will* resurrect the Reservation, and play forever a *real* game of 'family', unburdened by the pretence of childhood, are the thoughts that fill my mind as I drift off. When I wake up the tide is out, leaving in its wake a path of wet pebbles that curves around a protruding rock half-blocking the entrance to the cove. I drink what's left of the water, stuff my pockets to near bursting with dried fruits and biscuits and leave the beach, heading over the hills, across empty potato fields... then stop. Half a dozen red wardens lie stretched out in twisted contortions of death. I breathe a sigh of relief that none are blonde and run to my hut: mine and Rea's or mine and Moira's?

"Moira!" I shriek. The door is wide open and the hut is empty apart from, in the bedroom, her grey dress and red belt. They lie on the floor as if hurriedly discarded, and the dress is torn.

Matt? Curse that crazy fool! And curse myself for trusting him!

One of Rea's three dresses is missing.

Several times, I check each room, every cupboard, underneath the bed, and outside, including Albert's hut, but Moira is nowhere to be seen. I find my gun and slot it into my belt. In escalating panic, I run across to Angela's hut and bang on the door. Nothing. I knock again then push it open.

"Angela! Moira! Sara!" I call out. I say Sara's name for the hut always seems to me more Sara's than Angela's, but the hut is deserted. All the other huts are empty too, but a further six red-belted wardens' bodies litter the paths and the hen yards but, thank the Controller, not one of them is Moira's.

Could something worse than a bullet through the brain have happened to my childhood friend? Has Matt flipped, because of Daniel's death, as I have witnessed happen so often to men in Man Camp 7 when pushed beyond the limit? The thought that he might be torturing her somewhere out of my reach drives me to distraction. The only place I can think of is Sara's hideout in the wood. Two more dead wardens float face down in the lake, tingeing the still water around their bodies red. Sara's black ribbons are gone, so I must rely on memory to guide me through the tangle of bushes and branches. When I reach the hideout, it's no longer hidden by foliage. A large stone rests on top of the metal lid. Before I can summon courage to remove it and call down into the hideout, I stop to think.

It was as ugly as yielding to Peter's embraces had been beautiful. Moira spat in Luke's face. He slapped her twice, hard, each blow forcing her head round. Proud of his 'conquest', as he saw it, Luke stepped back and pulled up his trousers. Moira, sobbing, kicked at him but so feebly that he laughed.

"Like I said, it would've been easier for you if you had chosen me back then. Anyway, we got here at last and don't pretend you didn't enjoy it, slut!"

She could think only of killing him, the one sure way of stopping it from ever happening again.

"Now all I have to do is to kill that creature called Peter as you have already done for his girl. He never really liked you, anyway. Only pretended to so he could get at me."

Luke was lying, but as long as he kept talking and she could hear him, it meant she was alive, and if she was alive she would be able to kill him. That's all she had space for in her brain, apart from memories of Peter. But it would have to happen soon, and before Luke found her childhood friend.

***

Watchem drove the cart on into the castle precinct, halting outside a large wooden door. He repeated what he told the others about Moira killing Texta and the need to speak with the Controller. After helping Sara and Mary down from the cart, he led the way into the castle.

Sara's eyes circled walls hung with weapons from the past, with large portraits of people probably long dead, and with furnishings which, even in a dream, would have seemed strange. But this was no dream. She was in the Castle of the Controller holding the Special

219

Child destined to become the Immortal Controller. Clones of Mary would, like the baby she held, have the genetic perfection required to steer the surviving rump of humanity away from total extinction.

Each room was guarded by a red-belted warden in grey; each warden was given the same tale and the same excuse by Watchem, and as they passed from room to room, Sara began to wonder whether they would ever get to see the Controller, until...

A room without a warden, smaller than the others and with a bed, a desk and piles of books and papers. A white-haired lady wearing a red robe looked up at them. Her spine curved into a 'C' for 'Controller', she stood, took hold of a walking stick resting against her desk, flicked her hand at Watchem, grinned then shuffled towards them.

"At long last," she said. "Did you have a really hard time getting here?"

Before Watchem could reply, she turned to face Sara.

"So, this is the girl they speak of? Sara?"

Behind the warts, lines and wrinkles decorating the old woman's face was a warmth that sparkled in her grey-green eyes. Something there caused Sara to want to hug the Controller, but holding Mary made this impossible.

"Yes," replied the girl. "And this is Mary."

She held Mary aloft like a holy offering for the old woman—a gift. Mary flailed her arms and made gurgling noises, unaware that she was in the presence of the most important person in the living universe.

"Of course," acknowledged the Controller. "So, you're going to tell me that Texta is dead, Watchem?"

"Worse," said Watchem. "That monster Hellcat has taken over in Man Camp 7. The cities are running out of supplies. I've no idea what's happened to Peter—"

"Solem, please. No more of that Reservation nonsense."

"Texta's warden killed Rea which is why—"

"Which, I'm afraid to say, had to happen. She would never have agreed to what is needed for little Mary."

"So—Peter too?" queried Watchem. He glanced at Sara for reaction.

"No!" gasped the girl.

The Controller looked again at Sara, her smile gone.

"Have you—with Solem—?" she began.

"No, no, no!" the girl emphasised. "But they mustn't kill him. They can't."

"If Moira has any say, they won't, unfortunately. They go back a long way, Solem and Moira. But first let me show you to your room, child. Next to mine. They'll have to destroy me before they can harm you and, as you'll soon discover, I'm almost indestructible, except..." When she looked at young Sara again, those warm eyes had turned hard.

"Except for what?" asked Sara.

"Time," replied the Controller.

"May I leave now?" asked Watchem. "Florrie needs feeding and—well, I've been all night without sleep. Not much use to anyone at present."

"You were so good to me," insisted Sara. She reached up and kissed his cheek whilst still holding Mary. "When can I see you again?"

"Ask her, not me."

"What would the Parth Path do without you, Watchem? You're my ears on the outside world. A bat

221

screeches on an island in the far north, and because of you I know about it."

Humble as ever, Watchem merely smiled and left to tend to Florrie.

"Where's he going to sleep?" Sara asked.

"In his cart. As he's done ever since I've been Controller. Even when he was my eyes over the sea in that tower, he slept with Florrie."

"He could have my bed for a few hours."

"He could not! Remember this, child. He, Solem and that giant called Rolem are mere Single X-Whys. They should feel privileged to be allowed to live. If—"

"My father's dead. My real father, that is. Rolem. The red wardens shot him. My brother too."

"My dear, I'm so sorry. But you now know why Mary is so precious."

"I don't understand. This Castle is full of wardens like the one who killed my father. What am I doing here? What is the Parth Path?"

"Put Mary on my bed, sit down and we'll have a talk. Then you'll know everything."

***

With Luke gone and the lid pulled back across the opening, shutting out the darkness above from the darkness below ground, Moira rolled over onto her front and struggled to her knees. Often, in the Reservation, particularly during the winter months, there was no light and she used to rely on the feel of things with her hands. When finding her way to the outside toilet at night, looking for the jug of water or, with her pubertal growth spurt, food, it was her hands that would guide her. Now, in this underground hole, damaged and in pain from Luke's violent intrusion on her body, she crawled forwards till her hand touched a wall. Then, by travelling along the wall, her fingers came into contact with what seemed to be a cupboard. They journeyed up and down all over the front of this and finally touched a curved metal handle. She pulled at it. A drawer opened. Her searching hand extracted a box containing biscuits. She opened another drawer. More food. In the bottom drawer, her fingers discovered something from her past. Several of them. Candles plus a box of matches. She lit one and a tiny point of light illuminated her only hope of escape. The thought of killing Luke magnified the light and she saw the ladder. A broken-off branch lay at the foot of the ladder. Perhaps it got caught and was snapped off by the heavy metal lid when Luke closed the hole. She removed its twigs and side branches to fashion what would become her most treasured possession: a club with which to kill the man who had raped her. If only she had allowed Peter to complete the task ten years back this would never have happened.

With candle and club clasped in one hand, Moira mounted the ladder, but the metal lid wouldn't budge. The brute must have weighed it down with a heavy stone, trapping her till he could return. She pushed against it with her shoulders to no avail. She was about to give up, and rely on surprising Luke on his return, when she remembered Peter once demonstrating to her how force transmitted via a stick could be greater than with hands alone. It was during a 'guess the creatures hidden under rocks' game. At first, the boy could not lift a particularly large rock, but by stabbing into the ground, driving the stick into the yielding earth, her friend managed to dislodge the rock. She won the game plus learnt a lesson in science.

Moira stabbed at the lid with the end of her club. Something bounced and rattled. Repeatedly, she thrust her weapon against the metal. Gradually the stone above shifted until, with one final blow, it fell, and the lid sprang open. Moira climbed out. The candle dropped into the hideout, but she held on to the club. There was enough light from a quarter moon to see by as she replaced the lid and the stone before choosing a tree with the broadest trunk behind which she stood and waited, holding the club with both hands.

She didn't have to wait long. Like an animal returning to its excreta, he was back, removing the stone, shifting the lid, and grinning like a naughty child.

"Peter's dead, my little beauty. So, you can forget all about him!" Luke called down into the space below, unaware of the silent figure standing right behind him. "We'll go back to the Reservation, just you and me. "Start a—"

In one forceful sweep, the club cracked the man's skull apart like a spoon opening a boiled egg.

"Never!" screamed Moira. Again and again, the club cracked into that skull till nothing of its owner above the shoulders was recognisable. His soft brain dripped into the hole below. "Never, never, never! You always were a bad liar!" she screamed at the sticky, pink substance before pushing what remained of Luke into the hideout and closing the lid, shutting out the horror of what happened to her in that hole.

***

I don't think I can handle finding Moira dead. With Rea killed and Mary taken away from me, my future's gone. All I have left is Moira. Maybe no longer 'wee Moira' from my past, but she could still become my new future. With Moira gone, I have nothing. I must know.

I see congealed blood. I lift the stone off the lid, toying with the fantasy of breaking Matt's skull with it. I push aside the lid with my eyes tightly closed. When I open them, and peer into the space below, I laugh. Never believed in nervous laughter until now.

As I'd feared, there is a body down there. Its arms are splayed out as if hugging the earth, and the broken head is twisted to one side, the neck snapped. But, joy of joys, it's a Single X-Why. And bearded. My mind trawls a longlist of bearded men on the Island, but the bloodied figure below is too broken to recognise.

"Moira?" I call down in case she's down there cowering in a corner. No reply. The figure remains still.

I return to the village and to Rea's and my hut. I feel hungry and help myself to food before lying back on the bed on which I have made love to the two women of my life, thinking what I should do next. How can Moira simply disappear? And where are Matt and the other villagers?

Chapter 16

Over the following few days, I spend every waking moment, when not eating or urinating, combing the Island for Moira. It's not a large island, but large enough to occupy me in daily searches from dawn till dusk. I believe I now know every tree, every gully and more hidden coves than I can count on my fingers and toes, but apart from a discarded grey dress and that red belt of authority, I can find no trace of my friend. I did discover what happened to Matt and the Islanders, however. From Angela...

All shot! Beyond the wood, not far from the quay.

Trapped in that cove, by the tide, on the other side of the Island, I would not have heard the screams and the commotion. In the courtyard of an old, long-neglected farmhouse, I discover the bodies of familiar faces scattered like discarded puppets, some cruelly connected in death by embraces: a white-bearded old man's head with half a skull missing rests peacefully on the leg of a girl younger than Sara; Seb-the-joker, a simpleton with an impish sense of humour, is stretched in a bow-like curve over the body of Fat Janice, a jovial woman who was one of the few people who could extract more than a sentence of speech from Angela. Then I see a face framed in an open window, gone in a flash so still alive. I run to the building where I find Matt's body, a gun still gripped in his rigid hand. And I see Angela.

Terrified beyond words, she squats in a corner of the roofless building, shaking. I approach her, sink to a floor sprouting with weeds, and place an arm around her.

"How?" I ask.

After a long pause, she tries to explain:

"He just—just... I don't really know. Brought us all here. To start over again, he said. He'd shot a few red wardens. Got their guns and handed these to the others. Single X-Whys. He was laughing when they shot the last of the wardens. Never stopped laughing. When we got here he collected all the guns. 'New life,' he said. Told me to stay inside. Out of trouble. Then—" She pointed to the window. "From there. Shot them all one by one. And when—"

Angela starts to shake again. I hold her close.

"When the noise stopped, he came in here, looked at me then pointed the gun at his own head. There was a bang and—"

Finally, the woman finds the courage to cry. She weeps as if all the pain of the Island is being poured into those tears. I fear she'll never stop.

"Sara?" she asks. "Where's Sara? He wouldn't say. Only promised me she'd be safe."

"The boat," I reply. "That much I do know. But Moira—?"

"The Directress? Who stole Rea's bed?"

"No, Angela. She didn't. She was my greatest friend once, before Rea, I loved her very much."

"'Because of the Directress! What she did to Daniel. That's why,' he said before killing everyone."

"Moira did not kill Daniel. You've got to believe me. Matt flipped. He went crazy."

"Said he'd given her to him. To the man from the boat. As a present, he said. To do what he liked with."

That body?

I grip a handful of Angela's dress, but let go when I see the fear in her eyes.

"Him? From the boat? Who?"

"Him. That's all he said. Before it happened."

227

"The boat at the quayside. The only escape from the Island. Maybe it's back already. We'll go there. You're coming with me."

Assuming 'he' was the bludgeoned, bearded man in the hideout, I can only presume that Moira, forever feisty, got the better of him, whoever he was, and persuaded the Captain to take her away. I have to find her. Watchem will know where the school is. Where else would she go?

First, Angela must face the horror of seeing Daniel's body. It seems that she has no more grief left inside her as, kneeling beside her dead son, she strokes his blood-smeared face.

"So bright for a boy," she says without tears. "Could almost have been a girl, he was that clever. Do you think they shot him because he opened his mouth too much? Never could stay silent for long, you know."

I shrug my shoulders. Recalling what Moira and I did with Rea, I tell her we should at least bury him. Rolem's body is too large for us to move. Tommy's doesn't even deserve a mention. Only a brief glance. I go back to the village and return with a spade. It takes me half a day to dig a grave for Daniel, but Angela seems happier when he's finally laid to rest. She even smiles.

Then we wait. Periodically, I disappear, hoping to find Moira, and return with food and water. We wait for three days, and during that time I listen and learn as the woman who was always a stranger to me opens up about her past, about Tommy (whom she always hated) and Rolem and Matt. But there's one person she avoids telling me about. One person whose story I yearn to know more of. Sara.

"Tell me about Sara, please. What was she like as a child? She seems so grown up already I just can't imagine her ever doing childish things."

At first it seems that Angela wishes to avoid the subject of her daughter.

"You say Daniel was clever, but Sara is—she seems so—" I pause, before offering a word that might come close to describing the girl: "Special?" Yes, the word that applies to Mary is surely also meant for Sara.

"You know she started a while back?"

Who wouldn't have guessed? For size and shape, she closely matched Rea.

"I understand she liked Jimmy no more than you did Tommy," I say. "Why did Tommy insist she should choose the boy?"

"She knew she wasn't the Chosen One. Not even with a lovely man like Rolem for a father. Only the other day, before they arrived, she told me all that she now wanted was to be with—" Angela stopped as if unsure whether to tell me what her daughter had confided to her. "You'll not be seeing her again, so there's no need to say more."

"If she's with the Controller, and me being a Single X-Why, no, I shan't be seeing her again. Mary, neither." It seems both fate and the Parth Path are determined to remove all traces of Rea from my life, including our shared happiness, little Mary. "Unlikely, at least. But you, perhaps?"

"She'd never forgive me if I were to tell you what else she said."

"Wants to be special?" I suggest. Angela looks at me in a funny way.

"Actually, she always wanted to become Controller herself. You see, Rolem once told her she's the only one who could make the Parth Path work. She'd be far better

229

than the present one. Better than anyone else. Then you showed up." For the first time, I see anger in Angela's eyes. "You!" she repeats, accusingly. "She *wanted* you. In bed. After seeing you and Rea together. Couldn't you even guess how she felt? Spending almost every minute of daylight working away for you two. Yes, she loved Rea, but only because that brought her closer to you. See what you've done! Torn us all apart ever since you arrived. And Mary—why *is* she so special? No one explained it to us. All they said was 'genes', as if that's enough to explain everything."

I feel too confused to respond. All I wish for is to see Sara—to tell her how strongly I feel for her, and about her, but not in *that* way. She's only a child, for Great Controller's sake! As I'm painfully discovering, Rea could never have replaced Moira and no way could someone as young as Sara replace either of them. Perhaps I should go to the City of the Castle to seek out Sara, tell her not to be so stupid, and maybe, just maybe, I'll be allowed to see little Mary.

"Please allow me to make amends," I say to Angela. "I'll take you to Sara. For your sake, not mine." I suggest. "Then I'll find Moira, even if it means spending the rest of my life searching every damned hole and building on the mainland."

I don't mention Sara or Moira again, although it's several more days before the boat returns. When it does, I first ask the Captain why Jimmy was in the line of faces peering at us from the deck when Angela and I mounted the gangplank.

"Good worker," he says. "Never gives me any trouble."

"Did he get anywhere near Sara and Mary?"

"No chance! Look, I thought you were dead."

"Is that what Jimmy told you?"

"No. Sara. Didn't exactly say you'd been killed. But she—"

"What, then?"

"Just how she was with the baby. As if protecting the only surviving bit of you. Were you and Sara—?" No way can I allow such a ridiculous question to be asked:

"Shut up! She's only a child! Just tell me how she'll get to the City!"

"Watchem."

"Ah—Watchem! The old man. Still going strong, then."

"Even stronger since his old lady passed away."

***

In the dark, Moira found her way back through the wood by tracing broken branches and disturbed undergrowth. Something Peter taught her to do as a child. 'Tracking', the boy had called it. She returned to Peter's hut hoping to find him. Although common sense told her that the man who raped her had killed him as he'd said, memories of Peter would not allow her to believe this.

She stopped at the lake and stepped into the black water. Her uniform dress, torn and defiled by that man, disgusted her so much that she took it off. Her underwear too. She squatted down and splashed water over the foul stickiness left by that creature. If only she could have washed away all recall of what happened in the hideout.

Naked, she walked through the corpse-strewn village. She was still holding her discarded clothes when she reached Peter's empty hut. There, she found a yellow and blue dress that once belonged to Rea. It was pretty, and doubtless had come from the nearest dead city on

231

the mainland. More importantly, she hoped it might please Peter. Of course, he loved her. He told her this, in between kisses that helped her to hold onto that delicious orgasm, her first ever. Holding the dress up in front of her spoiled body, she thought how well those women of the past must have looked as she stroked the silky-smooth material with the palm of her hand, the same hand that had brought the club down onto Luke's skull. She thought how awful it must have been for women of the past, living in a world dominated by men like Luke. If most Single X-Whys had been more like Peter, perhaps the Great Man War would never have happened.

Ignoring common sense, Moira swore to Rea, via her dress, that she would find their shared lover, Peter, and hold on to him forever. But now she also knew how necessary the Parth Path was. All other paths would be destroyed by Y chromosomes.

She found a bag, and filled this with dried fruit, a screw-capped bottle, which she filled with fresh water from the well, then set off in the blue and yellow dress for the strip of coast beyond the quay. She discovered a shallow inlet from which the seaward approach to, but not the quay itself, was visible. She would be able to see the boat and be seen by those on board.

Shattered and damaged, Moira sat back against a steep bank beside a shallow cove, invisible in the darkness. She fell asleep until awoken by high-pitched whistle. She crawled into the cove. A lone figure in a small boat bobbing on the dawn pink-flecked swell had already spotted her and he waved.

The boat was similar to craft she remembered seeing in the Reservation harbour. To run away would have been senseless. Besides, this wasn't Luke. Luke was dead. She beckoned to the man who pointed to the quay. She scrambled over the rocks and waited for the boat to dock, standing as far as possible from the bodies of a giant, another man, a boy and two dead wardens. As the boat edged towards the quay, close to the bloated floating body of a third warden, the man picked up a rope and flung it ashore. He told Moira to tie up the boat, which she did.

"Who are you?" she asked.

"Does it matter?" he replied.

"A lot," she said. "Who—?"

"You're in trouble, right? Things have gone wrong here. I can tell." His grey-blue eyes took in the bodies decorating the quayside. "So, you were waiting for the Captain's boat, correct?"

"No," she lied.

"To get you off this godforsaken Island?"

"No. I'm waiting for—"

"They've left already. I passed the big boat. The Captain called out to me. Tell him to get off the Island, he shouted. It's cursed."

"Peter?"

"You mean the one called Solem?"

"Peter," Moira repeated.

"The Chosen One? Father of the Special Child?"

Could she believe him? Or was this man in with the murderers who'd killed her wardens?

Moira was about to say something, to beg the man to help her find Peter, for her brain still refused to accept Luke's claim, when the unmistakable sound of gun-fire and screams in the distance broke the silence. It had to be Matt, the fiend who had deceived her.

"Quick, onto the boat," the boatman urged. "I'll come back for Solem. Or Peter. From what I hear, he can take care of himself, but against guns—who knows?"

"So can I," insisted Moira raising the club. "He taught me to take care of myself. And I can't leave him behind."

"The child's safe. Look, between us, the Captain and I will look for Peter. If he's still alive. Right now, you're coming with me—or you'll end up shot. Can't do much dead, can you?"

Moira hesitated until shrieks of children silenced by gunfire knocked sense into her brain. Engulfed by despair, all she wanted was to lie in Peter's arms again. Only Peter could remove from her the shame of what happened in the hideout.

The man helped her into the boat and, sitting in the stern, she started to plan inside her head:

Still Directress of the school, Moira was a woman of importance. She had no need to reason with the Controller. Shooting Texta had been a justified execution and Bukla was evil personified. If Peter wasn't found soon, she would persuade the Controller to organise a search. They could disperse the helicopters across the country, all five of them, whilst she would return to the Island with as many red wardens as could be squeezed into a fleet of Parth Path boats. Once the perpetrators of the massacre had been dealt with, she would order every square metre of the Island to be searched. They would look behind every tree, bush, building and boulder, and once reunited with Peter, she would bring back the good she'd known in the Reservation and destroy the bad. She and Peter were essential to the Parth Path.

"Hungry?" the man asked, when the horizon had swallowed the Island and there was only a sea of sun-flecked white waves between the boat and the horror of what happened in that hideout.

Moira nodded.

*****

Sara held Mary up against her chest in an embrace that she hoped might shut out what she'd just heard.

"You've still so much to learn," the Controller added.

"But I don't understand," the girl said. "He's good. You told me yourself. Not like the other Single X-Whys. Like my true father. He'd have saved anyone loyal to the Parth Path, boy or girl. And Mary's his child."

The Controller sighed. She reached across and patted Mary's head.

"He's given her to us. The first Immortal Controller. Of what further use can he possibly be? Anyway, his name will become immortal."

"I don't know anything about mortal or immortal. Just people. Tommy was bad. So is Jimmy. Peter's good."

"Oh dear. I do believe—look, if it makes it any easier for you, they'll make it quick. A single bullet. And here, in the Castle, we'll build a shrine to the Chosen Ones."

"What's that?"

"Do you remember his face?"

Sara narrowed her eyes at the Controller.

"If I didn't, I wouldn't be here with Mary. Saving her from what's going on."

"Saving her?" The Controller chuckled. "Look, I'd like you to draw a picture of Peter. They say you can sing. Sing whilst you draw. Let your voice flow into the lines of his face. Our stone worker can then re-create

235

Peter in stone from your drawing. A Peter that'll live on forever in the home of his eternal daughters."

Sara, whose mind flipped back to that moment when Peter opened the door whilst she was outside his hut, merging her soul with his through her voice, winced at the words 'eternal daughters'. Mary, although genetically part of Peter, was herself. What was this woman planning to do to the baby, in her laboratory, that would ensure she'd never die? And how could a clone of the child also be Mary— clone after clone after clone?

"The Great Controller wouldn't like it. It would be like making a mockery of Her," Sara objected.

"Wise girl, but don't let yourself get too wise. It's because Peter is good and liked by all that who knew him—"

"Not all!"

"Most, then. It's precisely because of this that he must be moved on, as I prefer to put it. Did you not see the evil things Single X-Whys were doing on the Island?"

"Your wardens killed my father and brother."

"Good people, I grant you. But if I allowed enough good Single X-Whys to live and group together, who knows what might happen? Soon they'd re-establish themselves as leaders. Make armies and weapons—"

"Like the guns your wardens use?"

"Child, you know nothing of the weapons the Single X-Whys used in the Great Man War. Weapons that in a few seconds could wipe out whole countries, destroying both the land and the people. Listen, you'll stay here with the child till she comes of age."

"Her starting?"

236

"No. Long before. When our scientists can be sure we have the right genetic mix. And stability. Important genes may be affected by environment and switch off. Usually through something called methylation. Can't have that happen with the Immortal Controller."

Sara's opinion of the Controller was slipping into reverse. When she first heard her speak about the terrible times women had before the Great Man War, about the genius of the First Controller who saved a rump of Double X humanity in a land shielded from the horrors that had scarred the rest of the planet, she felt proud to be a girl and proud to have the privilege of the old woman's confidence. Now it seemed to her that all humanity was bad, the Controller included. Why should they kill Peter if he was a good man?

"How old are you, child?" asked the Controller.

Sara couldn't see what this had to do with anything.

"Fifteen," she lied.

"Hmm!" The Controller's eyes seemed to bore through to the truth. The girl was fourteen. "Multiply that by five and you have us as we were five years ago."

"Us?" queried Sara.

"Us! Two dead, three left. Show her!" she called out.

"I don't under—" began Sara, but her mouth remained open before she could finish the word when two identical old ladies in red cloaks appeared in the doorway to the next room.

"Numbers two and five," explained the Controller. "I'm number One. Three and Four are gone, and our days are also numbered. No way can our genes continue for the benefit of future generations. Not one of us was fertile like Rea. But we were the start of the Immortal Controller Programme. A clone of five."

237

"Can... can they—?" Sara stared at the silent figures in the doorway. "Can they talk?"

"Yes, but they won't. Not till I'm dead. But they know everything I say and do, and if I die tomorrow, Number Two will become me. After her, Number Five. You'd not be able to tell any of us apart. And I know exactly what you're thinking." Sara turned away and looked down at Mary. "If you kill all of us, Peter will still die."

***

Jimmy worked hard on the boat. Unlike most of the other men, he always did as he was told, but he wasn't sure how to handle it when he saw Peter and Angela board. He knew how Sara felt about Peter and how Angela felt about him. Thankfully, Peter had no interest in Sara. Besides he was too old for a girl who hadn't yet started. Perhaps a man with Peter's experience might help him. Instruct him on ways of gaining the affection of a Double X.

***

"Tell me about the girl's mother," the man asks.

The Captain and I stand side by side as he steers the boat through the drizzle towards the cloud-covered mountains of the mainland. He speaks without looking at me, which underlines what I suspected when we first boarded. That he's taken a liking to the woman.

Angela has her own cabin. When Jimmy was assigned to guard her, I told the Captain that this was not a good idea, so Jimmy was sent down to the engine room instead. A large loner, who reminds me of Rolem, and whom the Captain trusts, guards her instead.

"Sad," I reply, watching the mainland tip this way and that, like the see-saw on the Reservation that used to so delight little Moira and me.

238

"She has reason to be. I never had children, so it's difficult for me to understand, but one dead and the other taken to the City of the Castle. Too much for any woman to have to bear."

"Even before this, she was sad. Rarely spoke. Sara did everything for her on the Island."

"That doesn't mean she's not strong. So, Tommy was the girl's—?" *Father? I can't let the man say it:*

"No! She hated him. Rolem was the true father of Sara and Matt the father of Daniel."

"Yes, Rolem. What will we do without him? The Controller made a big mistake there. He was the best. But Matt? He must have changed. Very quiet, but I only ever knew him as a good man."

"I don't think they—you, know. That is, not apart from having Daniel together. He no longer shared Angela's bed is what I mean to say. But Daniel getting shot must have really screwed him up."

"Lonely," the Captain announced after a pause.

"Matt?"

"No, Angela. There's a need in Double Xs that the Parth Path does not recognise. I see it in Angela."

Not only Double Xs! I bloody see it in myself.

My anger over Rea's brutal killing blinded me to my need to love Moira. My friend from the past was right. Rea had never been truly 'real'. A clone too perfect for a simple human like myself. As friends in the Reservation, Moira and I often argued. True friends do that. Rea could never understand the hurt of conflict or the joy of patching up rifts between those close to each other. Her genes were too polished, their edges too soft. Perhaps, by adoring her to the point of idolisation, I was merely acknowledging the molecular perfection of her love for me. I feel I could tease, cajole and shout at Moira without

239

ceasing to love her; so very different from when I was with Rea. Before they shot her. Moira, not Rea, had always been my true soulmate.

Curse Matt for deceiving me and tearing me away from her. A self-aimed bullet through the brain was insufficient punishment!

"So, what did happen to Matt?" asks the Captain as if reading my mind. "Love for his son?"

I shrug my shoulders and focus on the quay, now just discernible on the moving horizon. I can make out a horse and cart, grey on grey. Watchem, no doubt.

"Daniel's death pushed him too far. Preferred to go mad rather than talk about it. Never was a talker."

A madness that kills? And whose body was that with its brains spilt out in the hideout? Perhaps Moira knows.

"Do you know anything about the school?" I ask.

"Me, a mere boatman? Ask Watchem!"

I say nothing more. From the upper deck, as we slow down, coming into shore, I watch the seaweed and the jellyfish drift lazily past. When the boat has docked, Watchem approaches and I can tell from his expression he has something to tell. I fear for Sara and Mary. The journey to the City of the Castle would be perilous.

"Tell me the worst," I ask as he ties up the boat. The Captain is talking to Angela. I can only guess at the curved course of their conversation, for Angela also wanted to know more about the Captain. A man of the sea was all I could tell her.

"Sara," says Watchem. "She—"

"She's all right, yes? And Mary?"

"Don't worry about the girl. Or the child. Safely delivered to the Controller. It's you Sara's worried about."

Serious little Sara, forever a worrier. I imagine neatly-parcelled packages of worry hidden away inside that young head, one for every conceivable eventuality. Poor girl! Life on the Island was enough to contend with, but with a near catatonic mother, and a brother who always spoke before he thought, hope must have always seemed pointless.

"Me?" I question.

"The Controller wants you dead. Like Rea. No further use for you."

"Shit! What about Moira? The school?"

"How do you know you can trust your old friend?"

I look back at the boat. The Captain is holding both Angela's hands in his as he talks, and neither appears to be in any hurry for her to disembark. I can only guess what he's saying, but I see trust there and it seems to me that both already know far more about each other than I do. Finally, he lets go, leaving her hands to hover like bees reluctant to abandon a flower before they drop to her sides and before she steps down the gangplank and onto the mainland for the first time. She turns and looks up at the Captain.

"I trust Moira," I reply, turning to look at Watchem. "She may be the Directress, but she has good reason to hate the Parth Path. They destroyed everything we had on the Reservation.

"All the more dangerous for both of you. To stay here, I mean."

"We can't go back to the Island."

"Never said you should. So, you think she's returned to the school?"

"Is the school like Man Camp 7? Wardens with whips and guns, dogs and men in cages?"

241

"Not as far as I know. Just silly little girls, their crushes and jealousies, a handful of teachers and the Directress. So, what do you propose to do with Moira? She can't protect you. As soon as they know you're still alive, they'll hunt you down and eliminate you. Her, too, from what you say. There's only one solution. For both of you."

"The City of the Castle? To join Sara?"

"Are you mad?"

***

"Just get on with your drawing of him and feel proud, in the future, to have known both Chosen Ones. Make it a worthy tribute."

"I have to thank Watchem first," insisted Sara. "It's my duty."

"Duty? Your only duty, child, is to the Parth Path. But, yes. See him before you get stuck into that picture. Vekia will take you to him."

"Vekia?"

The Controller nodded at an old lady in a black cloak sitting with her back to them in the far corner of the room. Hidden by the high back of the chair, she'd been hitherto invisible to the girl. Vekia stood up slowly, as if struggling against gravity, and came over to Sara.

"You wish me to take you to Watchem?" she asked.

Even her voice sounded impossibly old, like a voice scratched out by bones on age-parched skin. For a few moments, Sara simply stared at the bent old lady. Tommy, whose hair had only recently turned white, was the oldest person, apart from Watchem and the Controller, she had yet seen.

"Please," the girl replied. "But what about—?" she began, looking down at Mary asleep on her lap.

"I think Mary and I need to get to know each other," interrupted the Controller.

"But I promised Peter I'd not let her out of my sight." That is, the Peter inside her head whom she'd been asked to draw.

"Sara, just remember one thing: there can be no Parth Path with a Single X-Why like Peter up front, here in the Castle. Thank Watchem, a harmless man if ever there was one, then come back and do what you must do for Peter's memory. Do you hear me? I don't want to have to call in the warden with a whip standing outside that door. Don't push me any further. Two and Five would have had you flogged already for impudence."

Sara, always reluctantly submissive, handed Mary to the Controller without further questioning and left the room with Vekia. She did not wish to look at the whip-wielding red warden. Once outside the Castle, and out of earshot of all wardens, Vekia spoke in her thin, flaky voice:

"Always stay close to me, child. I, too, was once an Island nattie and know things from long ago that not even the Controller knows."

Her eyes flickered like ancient jewels. Jewels of truth. Sara loved those eyes.

"What things?" the girl asked as the old woman, ignored by the wardens, led her to the Castle gates beyond which Sara prayed they would find Watchem still there.

"When the time's right, I'll show you, my child. And as I said, stay close to me. Not even the Controller would dare to harm you when you're with me."

There were wardens outside the gates as well, so Sara had to speak softly into Watchem's ear whilst the old lady distracted the nearest warden by conversing with her.

"It's Peter," Sara whispered. "They're going to kill him. Please, please warn him. I couldn't bear it if—" Vekia tapped her shoulder. She turned.

"Thank Watchem from the Controller, too," the old woman said loudly, winking again at Sara. Right behind her stood a red warden. Sara could not be sure her whispers hadn't reached the wrong ears.

"Thank you from all of us," Sara repeated loudly. "The Controller too." Watchem also winked and Sara felt reassured. The red warden wandered off, Sara reached out, took the old man's hand and gave it a squeeze.

"Please find him!" she begged.

She turned, not wishing for her tears to be seen, and returned with Vekia to the Castle. As she drew that picture of Peter, she struggled to keep the tears away. She sang to stem their flow. The same song that she sang for Peter outside his and Rea's hut. It merged with a drawing more beautiful than her memories of the man. The picture was free from the worries that forever bore into her brain; worries that turned bright into dark, light into heavy and joy into sadness.

But the picture had no genes and therefore no life.

***

"Will you take us to Sara now?" Angela timidly asks Watchem.

Watchem looks from Angela to me and back several times, his eyes like butterflies uncertain where they should land. He shakes his head.

"They'll kill you both," he replies. "You've given them Mary, so they have no further use for you. Angela, being

244

Sara's mother, would be an annoyance. As for Sara...
they'll let her live until Mary comes of age."

"I have to see my daughter! She's all I have."

Watchem looks up at the Captain on board, waiting
patiently for him to untie the boat.

"Just a moment," he says to Angela. He walks to the
quayside and speaks to the Captain. From the other
man's face, I can guess what he asks. Even promise of a
barrel of whisky from the City would not have
transformed it in quite the same way. Watchem turns
and calls out to Angela.

"Back on the boat," he says.

Angela looks at me. I agree. It's the only solution. I've
seen enough death. Angela is a gentle soul, though
simple. Her gentle genes were passed on to her daughter,
but not the simple ones. The Captain will look after her
on his boat until Moira and I can come up with a
solution.

"I'll find Moira," I tell her. "Then we can see what's to
be done about Sara and Mary. No one's safe from the
Parth Path, but for the time being they'll not harm Sara."

I don't truly believe what I'm saying, but Watchem is
right. Angela should stay with the Captain. If he can
control the scum working the boat, she'll be safe. There is
one person I'm uneasy about as Angela steps back on
board, but fate, it seems has other plans for him. "Wait!"
shouts a young man. He says something to the Captain
who, concerned only for Angela's safety, shrugs his
shoulders. Jimmy climbs over the side of the boat and
leaps to the quay.

My heart sinks!

"Curses, not him!" I mutter as Jimmy approaches.

"I'm Sara's," he says boldly to Watchem.

"Sara's what?" I ask.

"You know. For when she starts. Tommy promised me."

"Get back on that boat," I hiss between teeth that would happily bite into the boy's neck. I don't know why I feel so negative about this simpleton, but I do have a curiously overwhelming wish to protect Angela's daughter from the pain of being saddled with such an idiot.

"I can help you," the boy insists. "Take me with you. I'll be your servant. I'm pretty agile. You saw me jump from the boat, didn't you?"

Perhaps my experiences with Luke have caused me to misread Jimmy. Luke was evil. Jimmy is just stupid. Stupid could, as the boy suggested, prove useful. After all, I have no idea what I'll be facing in my attempt to meet up with Moira again.

"Can you kill?" I ask him.

"Anyone who stops me and Sara coming together is dead."

"So, all the armed Parth Path red wardens are already dead ducks, ay?" I tease.

"Wherever she is, she'll need a man."

"You're not a man."

Jimmy looks around forlornly for something that might prove to the world he's more than a dim seventeen-year-old.

"Ask the Captain," he says. He turns and shouts out to the Captain who stands comforting Angela on deck. "Tell him. Tell Peter how good I am."

"It's true," affirms the Captain. "My best deck hand. He might yet surprise you."

Reluctantly, I agree to let Jimmy join me on Watchem's cart as we begin the bumpy ride away from the shore towards Man Camp 7 and the school where, for

246

all those years, Moira was held captive whilst I whiled away my time as a privileged Single X-Why in the nearby man camp. Had I known this back then, Rea, and therefore Mary, might never have happened.

Chapter 17

Moira shook her head. Already, she felt sick, and the mention of food made her lean over the side of the small boat and retch. With her eyes streaming, she sat back again and stared at the boatman in the stern.

"Who are you, really?" she asked.

"Think of me as the Captain's spare hand," he replied.

Moira's muddled mind flashed back to Luke's animal hands tearing at her clothes in the dark, invading those parts of her only she and Peter had touched. Her own hands had frantically grabbed at his when he fumbled with her breasts, as her legs tried to close against the advance of his erect manhood and she recalled how she'd tried to turn her face away from his foul stench. If only the water of the lake could have washed away the smell of these memories, leaving just those of Peter's tender love-making.

"I killed a man," she said.

The boatman chuckled.

"Is that all? Look, I know how important you are."

"You know nothing about me."

"The Directress, right? And you're on the Parth Path Council?"

"Who told you?"

"Like I said, I'm the Captain's other hand and the Captain knows everything. I'll not harm you."

"All of you lot out here, you're—you're so ignorant. Stupid!" Although the boatman was clearly no threat, Moira felt vulnerable wearing Rea's dress without the usual extras—belt, whip and gun. "Take me to the

mainland and stop talking. Your voice makes me feel sick."

She closed her eyes to shut out the man and the sea as the boat bobbed and bounced over the grey water towards a strip of mainland mountains balanced on the horizon. But excluding the man and the sea created a blank mental sheet that filled with images of Luke; Luke, the boy who emerged from behind a tree, holding a knife to her throat; Luke, the man who raped her in the dark.

Although dead, could he still destroy her? It all depended on Peter. Would Peter help to remove Luke from her mind for good, or would he reject her? This happened once when he replaced her with a clonie called Rea. Would he now seek out a young Rea lookalike, one of nineteen dispersed across the land north of the Wall?

The boat danced on the swell. Moira watched the foam in her wake form a broad white strip that faded into a haze that blotted out the Island. If only the mist could hide what happened there. She flipped between despair that urged her to end her life with a bullet through the head, and a determination to hold onto Peter wherever he was and whatever he said or did. Only one thing was certain: Peter was not dead. On the Reservation, it always seemed as if each child could somehow sense where the other was and how they felt. This had been stronger for her than for her bosom friend. Although she had no idea where he might be, that he was no longer alive was not even a possibility, despite what Luke had said.

The man in the stern remained true to his word. Silent for the remainder of the crossing, he gave Moira no cause to fear him. She closed her eyes again, repeatedly half-opening one eye to make sure he wasn't edging towards her, but he stayed stuck in the stern steering the small craft with a gritty resolve that reminded her of Peter.

When close to the shore, she made out a line of red wardens and two trucks. Her escort back to the school or to a cruel execution? Texta had many allies on the Parth Path Council. Word of the Commandant's shooting would have already reached the Controller's omnipresent ears.

The man in the boat—Moira never did discover his name—graciously helped her to disembark. For a few fearful moments, she stood alone in that yellow and blue dress which set her apart from the line of uniformed wardens. One of these stepped forward, her gun still lodged in its holster. Because of this, Moira knew she was safe for the time being.

"Welcome back," the young woman said. "The Controller sends her congratulations."

"Oh?"

"The child is safe within the Castle. And the initial laboratory tests are looking good, so well done! Plus, the deceased Chosen Ones, Solem and Rea, will soon be immortalised in stone. By a newly-appointed Parth Path artist."

"But—why isn't the child at the school? Why the Castle?" Moira looked from the woman to the other wardens. "Didn't they tell you about—?" she began, but the woman's eyes were warning her not to speak of the death of her superior.

"All part of the plan. Texta's support dropped to zero when it all leaked out. About her underhand scheme. Seems someone in the canteen let the devil out of the bag. A new-liner girl that Texta was bedding after losing Rea."

"A clone of the chosen Double X who got shot?" asked Moira, fearing another Rea.

The warden shook her head.

"You must be tired," she said. "You can sleep in the truck on the way back to the school. That dress your wearing—"

Something was wrong. For a start, she wasn't being addressed as 'Directress'.

"What about the dress?" queried Moira, knowing only too well that in anyone of lesser status such attire would have earned them a flogging.

"It suits you. We've all felt for some time that a Directress deserves something that sets her apart. Yellow and blue. A step towards the red cloak of the Controller, maybe? Until the scientists have done their job and the child comes of age. So perhaps you should give it to her, though I doubt it would fit."

"Her?" queried Moira. She felt herself struggling to reclaim authority. The other red wardens remained silent. Their cold stares unnerved her. "I'm tired. Tell the driver to take it easy. The potholes get worse every year."

In the truck her eyes remained shut but her mind was razor-sharp alert. The reference to her dress confused her. After all, was she not still Directress? Would she be able to gather enough support to search for Peter? But why did that woman say he was dead? She knew he was alive. And did Luke have anything to do with the Parth Path? After all, he'd been hand-in-glove with the Reservation chief.

Sleep was out of the question whilst her mind tussled with the impossible and the unthinkable. Sleep,

sleep, sleep… damn it! Why, oh why, had she allowed sleep to overcome her after her first true taste of heaven with Peter?

***

"South of the Skeleton Wall," says Watchem. There's a finality in his words that sends shivers down my spine bones.

"Certain death?" I suggest. Am I, or is Watchem, the crazy one?

"Perhaps, but worse would happen to you should you get caught. You saw what went on in Man Camp 7. The Controller isn't yet convinced that you're already dead, although Sara whispered to me that she's been told to draw your likeness for immortalisation as a statue. Rea's too. It's what they do for executed favourites."

"Sara? She's one of them, now? Great Controller, nothing makes sense anymore!"

"I don't know what you mean. Sara's a sweet child. But why should anything make sense? Look, they have Mary and as far as the Controller's concerned that's what matters. You, the girl's father, are too much of a threat."

Sara too? Wishing me dead? I say nothing. Not with Jimmy beside me. But why would the girl want to warn Watchem and me if she's with them and is part of the Parth Path plan? Can I even trust Watchem? I study the man for a few moments.

"Well, I'm not going anywhere without Moira," I inform him.

Watchem's face goes blank. I've seen that happen before. It means he's churning things around in that old brain of his.

"Is it far to the City of the Castle?" asks Jimmy.

"Shut up!" I grip Jimmy's arm. I may be skinny, but I'm strong. Jimmy winces. He must know that he should

252

only speak if I tell him to. "Just cut your prattle! We're not going there. Are you bloody deaf?"

"Potatoes!" Watchem suddenly exclaims. Jimmy and I stare at him. "Outside Man Camp 7. You'll have seen them, no doubt. Through the wire fence. In all weathers. You and Jimmy. Potatoes."

I get his drift. He wants me and Jimmy to join the team of slaves who dig the potatoes. Pretend to the wardens that Moira sent us there for punishment. Then he'll drive on to the school to find her. Seems risky, and if Moira isn't at the school, my days as a man camp slave will be numbered. Slaves do not last long. Jimmy, of course, has no idea what he's let himself in for.

"Potatoes?" he queries.

"What makes you so sure Moira will be at the school?" I ask, ignoring Jimmy.

The last time I'd seen her, only the top half of her face was visible above our bedcover on the Island, blissfully asleep after our gentle love-making. It had been so different from the sexual frenzy of entering Rea-the-Perfect. More like a natural extension of our friendship that had evolved into love way back when we were children untroubled by the Parth Path.

"The Captain's other hand has seen to it."

"Never knew he had three hands!"

Watchem chuckled.

"More than three. You're looking at a fourth. So, how d'you fancy life as a slave for a day or two?"

Seems I have no other option. And if there's no Moira, there'll be no curve to lead me away from slavery. Only a straight line to death at the hands of Hellcat. I can almost see the bitch's slit-eyes twinkle as she tweaks the handle of her whip and slow-steps towards me. But I'm beyond caring. Without Moira, it's turning into a direct route to hell anyway. No avoidance path. Only Hellcat then death.

I recognise the road I took when carrying Rea towards our new life together, and for a few brief moments I fantasise about finding one of her clonie sisters, if Moira doesn't appear, and starting over again. Then there's the wood where we hid from the helicopter, and the slope down which we scrambled away from the terrors of Man Camp 7, helped, we thought, by a woman who turned out to be our greatest enemy.

"Wait here," says Watchem, climbing down from the cart. He approaches the whip-wielding warden.

He talks to her, and curiously I no longer care what he's saying. Something like this, I expect:

'This is the man the Controller wants dead. His friend too. Make it slow and painful. She wants him to suffer for raping the Directress.'

Raping? Hardly. Moira was so loving when she yielded up her divine body to my caresses it almost blew my mind away.

Watchem looks back at us. I jump down, a directionless automaton.

"What's happening?" asks Jimmy.

"Shut up. Just follow me. Do as they say. Dig potatoes."

Jimmy and I halt when the slave-minder approaches, a woman whose face and size resemble those of Florrie the horse. She stops, glances, nods and beckons to me. On Watchem's instructions, I've left my gun behind in the cart. I say nothing as the Double X mountain of fat and muscle comes up and squeezes my arms and legs then does the same to Jimmy. The boy looks to be on the verge of tears. I feel sorry for him. I now understand why he fell for Sara. For someone so simple, she must have

254

seemed like one of those goddesses of the past that I'd read about in illegal books.

Those books! Never, in Man Camp 7, could I have imagined myself journeying with the man who had brought the hidden books to us. A man called Watchem.

"The young one's not up to much," the mountain remarks. "Still—might get a couple of days' work out of him. The other looks tough enough, though. They need food and water, you say?" Watchem only grunted. "Take 'em to the man camp, then. Tell the wardens to feed 'em in the canteen. Slave food only. Tell the warden at the gate to put 'em in whites then bring 'em back out when they've been fed."

Watchem says nothing more as he escorts us to the man camp gate. The camp seems larger than I remember. Has it grown, like a beast that feeds upon the misery of the weaker sex before plumping out into something ever more grotesque? I look up at the watchtower where I killed a man and a dog in my bid to escape with Rea. What a cruel irony it is to return, not as a free man to liberate those imprisoned behind the high wire fence, as had once been my delusional dream, but as a slave.

Why did I trust you, Watchem?

***

She tore it up. If Peter was dead, so was she. Life no longer had meaning. The Controller said nothing at first, when she found the paper in pieces beside the bed on the floor of the Island girl's room. She stooped, stiffly, to pick them up. "Solem, not Peter!" she muttered before going off with the torn scraps and leaving Sara alone with Mary. "Stubborn child!"

Peter... Solem? Did it matter anymore?

255

The baby was all Sara had to link her with Peter. Mary was unbelievably beautiful, like Rea, plus spirited in her own little way, like Peter. The Island girl took the bubbly bundle of life from the cot beside her bed, sat and cradled her in her arms. She so wished that she could be together with Peter and the wee child, just the three of them, for only a minute; a minute to know the comfort and protection of another. She had never properly experienced this on the Island. She had always been the protector, protecting her own poor mother who at times barely had the will to stand unsupported let alone guide and care for her children. She, Sara, had effectively been 'mother' to little Daniel, now dead. Her true father, Rolem, she had loved more than anyone before Peter arrived, but he was rarely around for reasons she could never comprehend. Matt had been a mystery whilst Tommy she had always hated. Just a minute in Peter's arms would have given her the strength she needed to carry on. Now all she could do was to play mother all over again to little Mary, but she did not resent this. The baby girl was precious to her, but not because she was the 'Special One'. She loved his child as she loved him.

They pieced together Sara's torn drawing and the Castle artist set to work creating a lasting likeness of 'Solem' as the Controller insisted he should remembered. One that would stand proud forever in the Great Hall where the Controller met with her council. All three of her.

***

A sudden jolt, when the careless driver braked too hard, awoke Moira. She cursed herself for falling asleep, but thankfully everything in the back of the truck seemed unchanged. The youngest red warden smiled.

256

"It's good you've had a sleep," she said. "You'll need your wits about you for the de-briefing."

"De-briefing?" Moira looked at the other three wardens. They said nothing. None smiled.

As she climbed out of the truck, she was reminded of the day of the Clearance when she arrived at the school after being flogged by Bukla. She truly enjoyed putting a bullet into that woman's head. But something felt wrong. Being taken into the building, with wardens on either side of her, felt as if she were a prisoner being led to a place of execution rather than the Directress with a place on the Parth Path Council returning to regain control of her school.

"Where are we going?" she asked as they escorted her, not to her office, but to the gymnasium where future red wardens were trained in the art of inflicting pain.

"She said to bring you here," said the youngest warden.

"She?"

The door was opened. The gymnasium, a place she'd not been to since graduating five years back, seemed huge. She'd never had any interest in the team games that went on in there and she'd played no part in red warden training. The games that she and Peter had enjoyed remained safely inside her head whilst her smart brain ensured a dazzling rise in power. Before she left for the Island with Texta, no one would have dared to question her about anything, yet now she was to be 'de-briefed'. Interrogated is what the woman really meant. But by whom?

'Can it be?' wondered Moira. A squarely-built, red-haired woman stood alone at the far end of the gymnasium beside a solitary chair. She held a whip. As they approached her, a memory flapped into Moira's brain like the trapped crow that had frightened her and Peter in an old shed in the Reservation. The shed was used to store grain and hay, and on rainy days, in the last year of their childhood life together, she and Peter would sometimes go there to do what they mostly did on the beach: cuddle and kiss. That is, before a large black crow flew at them, shrieking like a creature from hell, the moment they opened the rickety door. Moira had to cover her face against its beak and claws and the beat of its wings. It was gone in seconds, but the terror of the bird remained stuck in her mind and thereafter she refused to return to the shed.

"We'll just have to get wet when it's raining and we need to kiss," she remembered telling Peter. "I'm never going back into that beastly shed!"

The shock of seeing the fat girl Thea, whom she had so easily displaced after her arrival at the school, reminded her of that crow. The memory of that ugly face beat at her mind as that big black bird had attacked her face, but, unlike the crow, did not fly away. She stood vulnerable, wearing Rea's thin dress and unarmed, as Thea approached with her whip. Moira's rival from the past did not smile. She stopped right in front of her, slotted her whip into her belt, folded her arms and stared at Moira through cold blue eyes.

"Sit down," said the youngest of the other wardens. "We know you're tired. But the Directress must have the truth. About you and Solem."

***

I have to trust Watchem!

At the gate, I turn to watch the old man return to his horse and cart. It's like watching hope being swept away by the tide of time. Moira and I once sat on the beach together watching the tide go out, and we giggled whilst the drift wood we threw into the sea bobbed about close to the shore. We giggled because I said the way the wood wobbled on the water reminded me of her swelling breasts. I'd seen these for the first time in the shed where father kept his tools, and had told her I loved the way they wobbled when she allowed me to touch them before hiding them away again.

"You'll be able to share them with me very soon," she'd promised. "And whenever you want after that... until we have our first baby. Then they'll be needed to give her milk."

'*Very soon*' took ten years to happen because five days later the red wardens arrived for the cruel Clearance that destroyed everything we'd known. And now, will it be another ten years before I see them again?

"So, you've returned to us, Solem. As a slave, I hear. And who's your little companion?"

I throw Jimmy a sideways glance. I recognise that look in his eyes from my years in the man camp. Blind, bloody fear!

"A friend," I reply.

"Hmm! Not much man-fuel there. I'm supposed to get you two fed. Have a little surprise waiting for you in the canteen. Follow me."

Hellcat, no doubt. With Texta the Commandant dead, the fat terror of Man Camp 7 would have free rein to flog anything that moves for one reason only: self-gratification. Poor Jimmy. I bet he'll soon wish he had never known Sara and was still safely on board the Captain's boat.

We pass the hut behind which Rea and I first made love and where I discovered what the thing that dangled from between my legs was truly about. But it's Moira, not

Rea, in my head when I look at it. Then, along a familiar path and into the main building to the canteen. The door opens and my heart stops. I hold onto Jimmy for support when what I'm trying not to focus on fades, blurs then becomes horribly clear.

***

Vekia understood all about babies. She'd had two, she told Sara, although what had become of them she had no idea. She didn't even know whether they were still alive, yet once she loved them more than anything in the world. The pain, she told Sara, was unbearable when they were taken from her in the confusion five years after the Great Man War. She was twenty-three at the time, and only survived because of her dead father's connection with the First Controller. A computer scientist, he had helped the woman fix her digital problems during a long period of intensive research leading up to the war. When Vekia (her name back then was also 'Mary') appeared, dishevelled and desperate for help, in the laboratory where the brilliant scientist was finalising what would form the basis of the Parth Path, the First Controller took pity on the daughter of her computer fix-it man. What her father taught her about computers helped her, after his death, to sort out the digital gremlins that kept bugging the scientist's work. In those early days, before the First Controller became virtually deified, Vekia, her sister and the genetics scientist became friends, but the woman's authority perished with the First Controller's death. The sisters became little more than maids to subsequent controllers, and the present surviving clone of women ignored Vekia's presence in the Castle as 'they', all three of the present Controller, got on with implementing the path set out by the First Controller. At eighty-five, Vekia knew that her life, too, would soon come to an end, but the young girl from the Island, who had brought the 'Special One', was like the last breath of air from an almost-forgotten past. She vowed that before they died, she and her sister would pass on to the child everything of importance they had ever learnt during their long lives, starting with where it all began: computers.

The old woman in the black cloak was wise enough to recognise a brilliant brain, and this is what impressed her about Sara. The girl was stunningly clever, an attribute that the present Parth Path leaders, unlike the First Controller, would fail to recognise. But the girl was more than just a brain. She had a curious sensitivity about her that, if detected, could become her undoing with the present Controller. Vekia had no doubt that the Controller would, given the chance, follow the Parth Path to infinity without questioning a single step along the way. The Island girl would, Vekia feared, question every step. There was no time to lose. Lessons would have to start immediately, before her own death could put an end to them.

Sara looked up, with the baby asleep and snug in her arms, when Vekia entered. Tears streamed down the girl's cheeks. The old woman sat beside her, placing a comforting arm across her shoulders.

"I know why you're crying," she whispered. "You cared about him, didn't you?" Sara nodded. "A lot?" Sara nodded again. "Do you think he's still alive?" Vekia asked.

"Sure of it! Can feel him. Ever since—" She looked up at Vekia. "Ever since he came to the Island I've been able to sort of feel him. I can't explain it. He's alive but in terrible trouble."

261

"From the shape of you, I can tell you've started. Were you and this man Peter ever—you know—ever in bed together?" Thinking of Rea and Peter, Sara shook her head. How she wished that she could have been Rea in that bed and, like the clonie, now be dead. At least she would have shared something with Peter. "But you're not like them, are you?"

"Who?"

"You know who! All of them from the Controller down to the bedroom maids. Double X fanatics."

"You're a maid, aren't you?" observed Sara.

"So I am," agreed the old woman as she dabbed with her sleeve at a tear on its journey down the girl's cheek. "At least they think I am. You know, one thing I learnt first-hand from the First Controller is that nothing is exactly as it seems."

The girl's eyes sparkled.

"You really knew her?"

"We were the greatest of friends. Because my father helped her with those experiments before the Great Man War. Look, Mary's fast asleep. She'll be safe in her cot. The Controller's in her room. Not to be disturbed for at least an hour. I've something to show you."

"Now?"

"Now has many more possibilities than 'then'! Yes, now!"

"There's one thing that terrifies me."

Vekia stroked the girl's cheek then patted it gently.

"Tell me."

"You asked if I'd shared a bed with Peter. And I said 'no' which is the truth, but I've never stopped thinking about exactly that."

"And it terrifies you?"

262

"No. I spoke with Rea a lot, you see. She used to talk about what happened to her in the laboratories and when she worked at the man camp. And about—" The girl stopped and looked down at her hands as they played with the hem of her skirt. "She had to do awful things. With the Commandant. And sometimes with the red wardens. I swore I'd kill myself if I ever had to do that sort of thing. With a Double X, that is."

"But not with Peter, right?"

"That would be so different. Anyway, it can never be."

"Look, don't worry. I've put it about that you wet your bed."

"You what? How could you!"

"To protect you from all of that, you silly girl. There aren't many younger maids in the Castle to service the three Controller clonies. And none as pretty as you." The woman chuckled. "Thankfully, my sister and I are too old for them, so we're both perfectly safe."

"Sister?"

"You'll meet her very soon. Now, I'm going to show you something that might just change everything."

Vekia stood and offered Sara a wrinkled hand. The girl took it and held it to her bosom. For the first time since leaving the Island, she felt in command of herself. She grinned at the old maid.

"I think I might even enjoy wetting my bed knowing that it'll save me from her. Or them! Thank you!"

***

"Wait!" exclaimed Thea as Moira approached the chair. "That obscene dress you're wearing. Did Peter give it to you?"

Moira wished he had. She shook her head.

"Remove it!"

263

Slowly, Moira slipped off the dress and placed it on the chair, then stood uneasily in her underwear trying to hide her bulging breasts with both hands.

"Those too! The ridiculous little garments you're flaunting. As if any of us here would be interested! Take them off too. Then sit down."

Moments later, the woman who thought she was still rightfully Directress sat naked on top of her dress, her legs crossed, her hands failing to conceal her breasts.

"Have you or have you not given this body I see to that man?"

Moira said nothing. She sat as stiff as a statue, fighting back the tears. Thea placed a chubby hand on her whip handle. Moira's mind clung to the memory of the man to whom she'd already given the body of which her old rival spoke. 'A winner', he had always called her and would make sure she won at anything they played together. She had only become Directress through winning. She would not allow tears to appear. The only tears she would ever shed would be for the man she loved now with both soul and body.

"Yes, I have," Moira replied looking up at the bully who'd displaced her in her absence. She stood up, unashamed of her body or her 'crime'. "I shared it with him because I love him." Moira heeded the surprise of the other four women. They reminded her of the anxious chickens that she and Peter, as small children, used to playfully chase in the Reservation. "I gave my body to that man because I'm a woman. A true woman. But you lot—you've become like them. Like the Single X-Whys of the Great Man War and Texta and her bullies. That's why I had to kill those two women. The Parth Path—"

Moira's sharp eyes fixed on the smallest of the women,

her ex-pupil. "The true Parth Path can never succeed if you become like them."

Thea flicked her whip free from her belt. It dangled to the ground like a dead snake. The large woman pointed to the chair and addressed the youngest warden.

"You know why the chair's here. Do what you must. Let's get this over with before I send you to the local man camp as damaged trash for the new Commandant to play with. Oh, you didn't think this out very well, did you, Moira? Texta was your only ally and you went and shot her."

None of the six women standing in the gymnasium had a gun. Thea, as before, was proving to be overconfident. It was now down to numbers. Moira saw uncertainty in the eyes of her ex-pupil and in those of two of the other wardens. The youngest woman still stood beside Thea. Moira knew what Thea expected this novice to do: drape the body enjoyed by Peter over the back of that chair face down for a flogging that would scar her for life, physically and mentally. Instead, Moira picked up the chair. It felt heavy, but she felt curiously strong. Damaged by Luke, but still strong, she raised it high and, imagining Luke to be at the receiving end, smashed it down so hard on the floorboards that two of the legs snapped off. She picked one up and kicked the other towards her ex-pupil.

She was right. Thea and her young protégée now stood together whilst Moira, proud to be naked, and the others, one now armed, half-encircled the Directress in a curve of defiance. Thea's whip remained limp and useless. The protégée looked terrified.

265

"Oh, I get it," taunted Moira. "You've already bedded the poor young thing. Used her body. Given her favours in exchange for favours, right?"

Thea said nothing. Moira was beginning to enjoy the encounter.

"Just like Single X-Whys used to do before the Great Man War. Tell me, you little whore, have you actually read the First Controller's Parth Path scriptures?" Moira saw mounting discomfort in the eyes of the young trainee warden standing beside the red-haired whale. She stared into those eyes and slowly nodded.

"I see it all, now. Power. Like the power of the men who tried to destroy our world. No, I'm proud of my woman's body. It gives me power over Single X-Whys and keeps us safe. Whips only make them angry."

Luke re-appeared in her mind. The man who had defiled that same body now mocked her. She felt her grip on the wooden chair leg weaken. Balance of power or numbers? She looked into the distance, fearful that those who had sided with her would also see in her the shame of being damaged by Luke. What happened next wasn't what either she or Thea expected. The younger warden joined the arc formed by her colleagues, thus completing a circle around Thea. The new Directress returned her whip to her red belt.

"Take her away! Send her to the man camp. Let the new Commandant there flog her. I'm too tired to do the job properly, anyway," she said, then left.

Moira's ex-pupil picked up the dress and undergarments off the floor and handed these to her old boss. Moira hurriedly dressed before being escorted out of the gymnasium. They took her to the dormitory building. She felt confused. Had she won a victory or had defeat merely been delayed. As she passed present *pupils they stopped to stare like curious cattle. Seeing their old Directress being led away puzzled them. She remembered feeding the cows with Peter in the Reservation. She recalled laughing when he told her that people who stared at them like cows, as some of the other Reservation children used to, should be fed with grass like cows.*

They found a room for Moira. The door was locked behind her. She was left alone. Was she being protected from Thea or was she still the fat bitch's prisoner?

***

"Rea?"

The girl serving food at the bar looks up. She frowns as Rea used to. It *has* to be my love brought back to life… but it cannot be!

"Is it really her?" asks Jimmy. "The chosen one?" I stare at the girl for a few moments, drinking in her beauty, then shake my head.

"No," I say. "Just a poor copy."

We're taken to a table, given bowls and sent to fill these with mash and brown stuff like on the day I first met Rea. I find myself marvelling at the delicate hands of Rea's clone sister and fantasise about enjoying her delicious body behind the shed in the evening, but common sense tells me that can never happen again. Rea's gone and must remain in my past. Moira, my past when I lay with Rea, is now my future. I deliberately avoid looking at the girl as Jimmy and I prolong our meal for as long as possible before being taken out to the potato fields.

The Mountain turns out to be not as bad as she looks. Jimmy works well, and both of us are used to potato digging, head down, back high. I amuse myself by wondering about the lives of our fellow diggers, the slaves. Have any of them killed, as I have, slept, like me, with a woman... or loved two? I consider myself fortunate. If they shoot me now, I'll have blissful memories to take with me to that place of spent slaves beyond the grave.

The Parth Path never mentions what happens after death. Unlike that illegal book, The Holy Bible, which I read from cover to cover, and which touches on heaven and hell, what happens after death seems irrelevant to its leaders. But if they do shoot me, they'll also preserve, forever, wee Moira of the Reservation, a perfection called Rea, and my re-discovered friend from the past when we got to know each other again during that brief but heavenly reunion on the Island. My brain will die with these fluid images fixed firmly in a place somewhere outside time and space; a place where no red warden nor Commandant will be able to them take away from me.

The Mountain clearly has no intention of either shooting or flogging me. When she sees the abundance of potatoes that Jimmy and I, experts, manage to free from the dry earth she smiles and praises us.

"Good workers, I see. Can always trust Watchem to give me what I need. Workers that'll earn me privileges."

"An honour," I say, smiling. I think this monster of a woman rather likes me. Nevertheless, I must avoid being cocky, for I also have to look after Jimmy. I've grown rather fond of the stupid boy.

Compared with the Island girl, Rea wasn't particularly clever, but this didn't matter to me. For Sara, though, I can understand how awful it would be for a brilliant girl like that to be forced to bed a blockhead like Jimmy. I reckon that it all boils down to Double X and Single X-Why balance. Men are inferior. Must be bad enough for a Parth Path Double X to have to mate with a

Single X anyway, but if that Single X is tediously dull, this would magnify a girl's misery. Poor Jimmy. Sara can never be his.

But Sara working with, and for the Parth Path? How could she?

We labour for several hours. Frankly, I enjoy it. There's something uniquely satisfying about working on the land, feeling the earth slip through your fingers, discovering life in that earth, for potatoes are alive. I read that once. A book on biology that appeared one day in the man camp dormitory hut. I tried to relate what I read to what was spilled out for our edification during Parth Path lessons. Things to do with genes, mutations and DNA. Thirsty for knowledge, I lapped it all up but only believed what I chose to believe. And I tried to merge some of these beliefs with that book I kept coming back to: The Holy Bible. It seemed to me that they were merely trying to recreate Jesus in female form but failed because none of it was real. Only the First Controller was, and the more I learned about her, the more human she became, and therefore to be pitied, not revered.

After the day's work, we return to the canteen. I'm thankful that Rea's lookalike clonie is no longer there, for digging potatoes has made me randy and I might have had trouble keeping both eyes and hands off the girl. Jimmy, thankfully, looks fine. We eat with the slaves, so I'm spared the humiliation of jeers from my previous inmate friends, if I can call them that, on seeing me dressed in white. The Mountain joins us. I've already learned how slave wardens regard their slaves as personal property, working and eating with them. Will she sleep in the same slave hut as us? Hopefully not. She'll snore like a bloody belching volcano, that's for sure.

She comes across to our table clutching a tray-sized plate of food.

"Watchem," she says, then walks over to sit at a table by herself. Just 'Watchem'. I would hug her if my arms could encircle her massive girth.

How stupid I've been. Of course! Watchem! Out of all the slave teams in the fields, he took us to one overseen by the Mountain not because he thought she might kill me but because she'll protect us. That is, until he finds Moira. This massive woman is with him. Maybe he slips her sacks full of food on the sly to keep her happy, but, for whatever reason, I feel safe and know I can trust the woman. And Watchem. He *will* find Moira.

Bless the Great Controller, the Mountain does not bed down with her team. I sleep deeply my first night back at the man camp, and dream not of Rea, nor of Moira the child, but of Moira the woman. But it's a disturbing dream and I wake up in the middle of the night. I see Jimmy lying awake on the hard mattress beside mine. He's crying, and I suddenly realise that he's little more than a child lost in a cold, unfriendly world.

"I promise you everything will be all right," I whisper. "You've no idea what goes on in this place and I pray to the First Controller you never come face-to-face with Hellcat, but if Watchem does his job we'll soon be out of here."

Then it dawns on me: south of the Wall? Will Watchem take us there? Might the unknown be a better option for Jimmy than remaining here to be kissed by Hellcat's whip? But will Moira truly risk everything by coming with us? Knowing my old friend, she's sure to find a way out of the embarrassment of having slept with me on just one glorious occasion should she decide to stay behind. Moira the winner! She has to be.

"Get some sleep now!" I say to Jimmy. "I can't do with dragging a moping zombie over the Wall." I give the boy a gentle punch on the arm, roll over and drift off once more. Moira again, but dead. Dead in my arms, shot in the head like Rea. This time it's Jimmy who does the talking when I wake up.

"You cried out," he says. "In your sleep. 'Moira, Moira, oh Moira!' Over and over. What went on in your dream? I know there must be things I'll never find out without Sara."

I remember little of my dream apart from the bang of the gun and the blood and Moira's empty eyes. But I also remember making love to her again before she got shot. I ease myself up and see a curve of faces peering down at me.

"Best thing ever," I say to the lot of them. "Make love to a woman once and you've lived!"

One of the men smiles.

"I had a woman once," he says. "Till the red wardens came and took her away. And brought me here. The thought of her keeps me alive."

"On a reservation?" I ask.

He nods.

Why he should come straight to the potato fields whilst I spent ten years as the unwitting 'Chosen One' is a mystery. Like everything to do with the Parth Path. Whether or not Moira believes in it, I never had enough time to find out. At first, on linking the woman with Rea's death, I truly hated her. Conversation was impossible. Then we had sex, the healer of all hatred, and spoke little both during and after intercourse. Words so easily confound and confuse.

"Well, I don't know about you lot, but I'm looking forward to a day out there digging potatoes." I

271

announced, springing upright. "How about a contest? Jimmy and me against the lot of you? For numbers of potatoes?"

I grin at Jimmy. He gapes at me as if I've gone mad. Then I see a problem. The Mountain might protect the pair of us but perhaps not the others. No mortal could survive a Mountain whipping.

"Maybe not," I say, "but I'll tell you one thing that I learnt before in this bloody place. No sense of humour and you're done for!"

I slip into my whites, then Jimmy and I leave for breakfast before digging again out there in the fields. Each day, over the next several days, is the same, but my humour wanes. *No Watchem, no Moira!* But on the seventh day...

My heart leaps when I see Watchem's cart in the distance. I remain stooped over my row of withered potato plants. If the Mountain turns nasty, I'll never make the Wall. I hear the cart stop but don't dare to look up for fear my friend won't be with the old man. Jimmy looks instead. I watch his feet disappear as he walks carelessly off towards the cart. I hear a woman's voice. Then another. I tilt my head a little to take in the picture...

Watchem, you're a wonderful old man!

Moira and another, younger, woman stand beside Watchem and Jimmy. The Mountain waves at the them. I throw down my fork and run. Several slaves cheer. I run to Moira. Fast. *Really* fast. Run into her open arms and fall into those eyes from my childhood.

And I weep like baby.

Chapter 18

Sara followed Vekia out of the Castle to the esplanade. When the red warden at the castle gate asked where they were going, Vekia replied, "the Shrine".

Beyond the esplanade, packed with trucks, tents and boxes of provisions, was a cobblestoned road leading downhill from the Castle and flanked by tall, dark grey stone houses. Men, women and children dressed in filthy, tattered clothes, stopped and gazed at the old woman and the young girl as they emerged from the other side of the open gates. Their eyes seemed to tease out Sara's fear.

"Is the Shrine far?" she asked.

Her companion chuckled.

"Far? Why, these old bones can barely get me outside the Castle. It's just there!" she answered pointing to a building on the corner. "And don't believe what it says. 'Whisky'! That's from before the Great Man War. A drink containing a poison that drove men mad and destroyed their insides. Women got poisoned by it too. Some say that without that poison coursing through their veins, there might never have been a war. I don't believe that. Anyway, the First Controller used this building for her work. Close to the Castle, see. Only certain people know what's really inside. And that list of two is about to include you."

"Why? Why should you show me these things? I'm only here to look after little Mary."

"Oh, you're more than a baby minder. Much more. And your life is about to change, big time."

Vekia took Sara by the hand and banged on the door. Whilst they waited, Sara turned and looked up at the tall building on the other side of the street. It resembled a watchtower.

"Yes, they watch over the city from up there," observed the old lady on seeing the child staring up at the high building. "It's got a huge mirror at the top that looks down on the street. They're supposed to check on anyone who enters or leaves the Castle. They know me of course, and by now they'll know you too. You'll be written down in their ledger book already. Can you guess what you're known as?" Sara shook her head. "Island Sara. Sounds romantic, don't you think?" Sara thought it sounded silly but said nothing. "And me— well, they can never remember my name, so I'm just 'the Woman in Black'. I come here all the time, so I expect they've given up recording my visits."

"So why do you come here? What's so special about the place?"

"The Shrine. That's all. Listen! She's here already."

There was a rattling on the other side of the door. It creaked open. In front of Sara stood a white-haired woman even more bent than Vekia. She had a single eye paired with an empty eye socket. Sara should have found her scary, but that single eye shone with such warmth and wisdom that the girl could not stop herself from smiling at its owner.

"She's awful young, Vekky, but I can see what you mean. Also, why you say she should have been the Chosen One all along."

"No longer important. The child in the Castle isn't the one who really matters now, anyhow."

Sara's smile vanished. She had no idea what the two old women were talking about other than the fact that Tommy had always tried to convince everyone on the Island that she and Jimmy were the Chosen Ones. She was so relieved when all of this changed following the arrival of Peter and Rea. Chosen for what, she used to wonder? She had never relished the title.

"You haven't introduced me, Vekky. I should rap your old knuckles for such an oversight."

"Sister dear, I confess I forgot. I assumed everyone in the world knows Omnia, the all-knowing one."

"Your sister?" questioned Sara. Out of respect, she held out her hand to the one-eyed old lady. Omnia took this and gently squeezed it.

"We should keep quiet about that chosen business, Vekky. Do remember, you're only a maid."

"A maid made by the Great Man War, ay? You should take over from here. With the explaining, I mean. And Sara, listen to every word my dear sister has to say. You and this place hold the key to the future of our world. You, plus whoever the father of the true Special Child turns out to be." She glanced over her shoulder to make sure there were no listening ears nearby. "And I think we know who that is, Sara, don't we?"

Sara blushed the colour of the wardens' belts. She'd already drawn his likeness for a memorial monument and torn it up in a burst of frustration because it was so lifeless. A lifeless Peter was worse than no Peter. The Controller had only scolded her before retrieving the fragments.

"This way, my child," beckoned Omnia, stepping back for Sara and Vekia to enter.

They descended a short flight of steps. Omnia flicked a switch. In an instant, a dazzling display of lights illuminated a large room with long, high benches and rows of shiny, blank rectangular screens. A complex system of wires connected these to metal boxes underneath the benches.

"Show her the books, sis," urged Vekia. "She has to read these before she gets stuck in. I can take some away hidden under my cloak. No one will know."

"Not even the Controller has the faintest idea what these are about," said Omnia. "Which is why this place has become a shrine. The Shrine! Now, see that candle over there?" Omnia's single bright eye twinkled with the flame's reflection as she indicated a tall lit candle in front of the largest screen. "They all think this has something to do with the Great Universal Controller somewhere up there in the sky. And that we have to keep the candle lit to remind Her that we're still here. All of this is supposed to somehow connect us with Her. What utter nonsense, ay sis?"

"But the books aren't nonsense, Omny."

"Books?" questioned Sara.

"Come. I'll show you. Remember me telling you about our dear father and how he worked for the First Controller?" Sara nodded, fascinated by everything she saw as they passed by the screens and the wires and boxes under the benches. "Well, only we, and now you, know what I told you earlier. About Father fixing her computer problems. Because he was a Single X-Why, the First Controller had to pretend our father was a slave playing with electrical toys for her amusement. When she died, with her work unfinished, they took him away."

"Never saw Dad again," said Omnia.

"But he taught us a lot about these computers. And he always wrote everything down. 'Backup', he called it. Gave all the books to Omnia, being the elder daughter, the day the First Controller died. Of a heart attack, the Castle doctor said. But we think she was poisoned."

Sara stopped in front of the large screen which mirrored the flickering candle.

"What a waste of good candles," observed Omnia. "Do you know what those numbskulls in the Castle call me, Sara?"

"Not Omnia, then?" queried Sara.

"The Priestess of the Shrine. Whenever one of the Parth Path Council comes to pay her respects to the Great Universal Controller, I bow in front of this computer and mumble rubbish. They call it praying."

"Rubbish?"

Omnia put her hands together, bowed her head then chanted in a loud monotone:

"Ram, cram, megapixel, megabyte... hard drive, soft drive, internet, outernet... upload, download, phishing... Amen."

"What's it mean?"

"Nothing at all, but it keeps them happy. Plus, I'm able to guard Father's books and—" Omnia indicated the row of screens with a sweep of a hand. "And all these."

"The books, Omnia. Show her the books. This is all so exciting. I can almost hear Father's voice again whenever I hear the word 'books'."

Omnia, bent, as was her sister, like a human question mark, shuffled towards a heavy wooden chest at the far end of the long room. She opened a small pouch attached to her belt, removed a key and slotted this into a keyhole in the lid of the chest.

"Help me lift this, child. My hands are barely as strong as a kitten's paws these days."

Sara helped the old lady ease open the lid. A strange smell rose up from the open chest. It engulfed Sara in a past that seemed both sad and inviting. The smell made *the girl wonder how many hands from years long gone had touched those books so neatly stacked inside the chest. How many pairs of eyes had read the wisdom contained between those stiff covers peppered with neat little rounded woodworm holes?*

The girl took out the top book and read the cover: 'Computer Programming and Cybergenetics.'

She opened it and started to read the first page. Although she understood little of what was written, the words had a strange hold over her. She picked up the next book: 'A-Z of Computer Science.' It seemed to call out to the girl, like a map that might lead her into the mystery of those screens and boxes. Gradually, under the gentle gaze of the two old ladies, the girl extracted a mounting pile of old books from the chest. Books covering not only every aspect of computing and of genetics, but many that reached out to other corners of the scientific universe: human evolution, animal behaviour, physics and astronomy. There was a heavy tome on advanced mathematics that intrigued Sara with its scrambles of figures and exacting diagrams.

"Of course, these represent only a fraction of our father's knowledge," Omnia informed the girl. Sara looked up at her from a spread of algebraic signs and symbols. Omnia grinned when she saw the astonishment written across the girl's face.

"Oh, you were so very right about this child, Vekia. Always a better judge of character than I was."

"That's because you've been forever stuck in these books of Father's."

"Still am. But at last I can let go now."

"Will you teach me?" asked Sara. "About everything in these books?"

"Child, to have a purpose in life for the first time in ninety years will be my one pleasure before I die."

"Don't you dare die, sis! Not yet. Not before you've taught her everything you know."

"But the books are nothing."

A shadow of disappointment clouded the girl's young features.

"What do you mean? I've never before seen anything so wonderful as these books."

"Don't get me wrong, child. They are wonderful. It's why Father kept them. But the greatest wonder is what he stored behind all those screens. Inside the computers. The books are merely a door to a world of knowledge you couldn't possibly imagine. Pictures—moving, talking pictures—plus everything the First Controller did. All here, Sara. For you."

When tears welled in Sara's eyes, Vekia placed her arm across the girl's shoulders and hugged her.

"I think she's a little overwhelmed, Omny. We should go back now. Must be Mary's feeding time, anyway. I'll take a couple of Father's books with me under my cloak. You can choose which ones, Sara."

"Can you turn one of the computers on, please?" the girl asked.

Vekia glanced at her sister who shook her head.

"Not yet, dear. Read some books first, then we'll introduce you to the computers. And when you're ready, you, not me, will turn her on."

"Her?"

"What the First Controller called 'the Mistress'. The big one. No one's turned her on since she died. And you, not me, will do that. Not for the Great Universal Controller, if she exists, but for the future. Your future and that of your baby."

Sara turned and hid her face on Vekia's shoulder. She began to cry.

"There, there, my child! It's all been too much to take in, I know. Just think of this place as the start of a journey. Your child's journey."

"I don't have a baby of my own."

"You will do. You must, one day. His child."

***

"Enough of that!" says Watchem after Moira and I find each other's lips in a kiss that I wish would never end. "Do you want those poor bastards to get flogged for playing with themselves."

I see what he means. The diggers have stopped digging. They stand resting forwards on mud-encrusted digging forks. A row of sex-starved eyes fix on a man—me—and a woman—my childhood friend—embracing as if we are alone together in another world. I hold Moira at arm's length whilst our eyes continue the kiss.

"Rea's dress?" I query. "Yes. It suits you."

Moira says nothing. I wipe away her tears with the tips of my fingers, then laugh. I've made an earth-stained smear on her cheek.

"Into the cart with you two lovebirds," shouts Watchem. "Before that goon in the watchtower realises something's going on."

I take hold of Moira's hand before we run to the cart, followed by Jimmy. I help my childhood friend up, Jimmy too, before squeezing in between them. I can't bear the thought of even a young boy touching Moira, for she looks impossibly beautiful in that dress. More so than a thousand Reas put together.

Watchem climbs up, cracks his whip and we're off.

"This is Jimmy," I say. "From the Island."

"Hello Jimmy!"

I don't want to share Moira's name with the boy. Everything about Moira must stay mine. Even the dress that had been chosen by me for Rea; one in a batch of clothes brought to the Island from the mainland by the Captain. "Clothes," he told me, "worn by women of the past before they invented that awful grey uniform."

"Where are we going?" asks Moira.

"Yes, where *are* we going?" I echo, looking at Watchem for a reply.

"To the Wall."

Moira appears shocked but says nothing. I take hold of her hand again. The same hand I held a thousand times on the Reservation, and little has changed between us since then.

"I'm so very sorry," I say. She's shaking. I fear her tears will never stop. "For what happened on the Island, I mean. That bastard Matt. I never imagined he'd trick me. How—?"

Moira silences me with two fingers on my lips. I know not to ask, but the pain in her eyes is enough to turn everything red for me. I'm angry with myself beyond words for leaving her alone in our hut. Being upset over Rea's death was no excuse.

"What's beyond the Wall?" asks Jimmy.

"Maybe it's better you don't know," I suggest.

"I'll tell you," says Watchem. "A place where little boys like you can live free. No slaves. No man camps."

"Imagine that, Jimmy, ay?"

"But I want Sara! She's *all* I want," he protests.

I laugh.

"The little boy wants his little girl. How about that, Moira? Just like we used to be. Another reservation? Without the threat of a clearance?"

281

But Moira looks away. She still doesn't smile. Something has changed her. It's as if she's staring at something I'm blind to.

"So, what happened to the Moira the Directress?" I ask, stroking Moira's hand. "At the school?"

"A new Directress. Her! And because of you, she was going to flog me."

The red turns deep crimson. I fear my face might burst and splash the whole world with red.

"Surely my Moira got the better of her?"

"A big fat girl called Thea. Had me stripped naked—"

"Turn around, Watchem. I'll bloody kill that woman!"

"No, Peter, you won't," insists Moira. "There's been enough killing. I have friends in the school, see."

Friends? Confused by the red rage, my jealousy hits a gong. My mind regurgitates Rea being bedded by Texta, the dead Commandant's hands crawling like venomous spiders over that heavenly body.

"What sort of friends?" The suspicion distorting my face frightens Moira.

"Peter, I enjoyed teaching. I was good. The girls listened to me. I only wish, now, I hadn't loaded their brains with all that Parth Path nonsense, but they respected me. One of the wardens there had been my pupil. It was a question of numbers. Ended up five against one. None of us had a gun, see."

"Guns, guns, guns! And we've only got one."

"That's where you're wrong," interrupts Watchem. "You've got three. Two more in the back. And enough bullets to kill a thousand Theas. But you'll need every one of these where you're going."

"Can't you just take me to the Castle," asks Jimmy. "That's where they took Sara, isn't it?"

"Like Moira said, my boy, we've all seen enough killing."

Moira rests her head on my shoulder. A sign that she's done with talking. She often did that back on the Reservation when she wanted me to stay silent. 'Savouring the moment', she used to say. Red turns to pink merging gradually with the soft blue of the sun-soaked sky above as I savour the warmth of our reunion, bumping along a road towards an unknown future—unknown except for one thing: that it'll be different from anything we could possibly imagine even in the maddest of dreams.

**

Sara hid Omnia's books underneath her bed. Being both maid to the Controller and surrogate mother to Mary, there was no risk of anyone else, apart from Vekia, knowing. As soon as Mary had been fed and changed, she sat by the window with the baby asleep on her lap and an open book on the basics of computing leaned up against the little bundle. She read for hours till the next feed, then again till the one after that. Vekia was the only other person she saw in her room. The Controller made it perfectly clear she didn't like babies. At least, not those in which a Single X-Why had played a part. Mary, she said, was a Parth Path necessity, but one day, after she (all three of her) had gone, things would change. Her scientists would see to that. Like Peter, all Single X-Whys would be virtually exterminated.

"He isn't dead," the girl whispered to Mary when alone again. "Your father's still alive. I know it."

She read on. And later, when Mary was settled for her long sleep of the day, Sara and Vekia returned with those books to the Shrine. The girl had her first lesson, during which her eager brain absorbed everything the wise old woman said about mathematics. Numbers and their relationship to the things around her had always fascinated Sara, even as a child. She was way better than any of the other children on the Island when they got taught by Matt. The man called her his 'little star', which angered Daniel, but after lessons, she would go over everything again with her half-brother. Teaching him helped her to learn, so back in the Castle, Sara would tell baby Mary all about numbers of importance and those equations that explained why the Universe held together. She talked about electrons, fundamental particles and the Theory of Relativity. The String Theory was unravelled in simple words for the infant, the mysteries of Nature explained at length. The baby girl grinned on learning about chromosomes, DNA and mitochondria. Then Sara would read on from more books, and more and more. Days, weeks and months passed. Little Mary learned not only about meiosis and the epigenome, she learned to walk and talk. Still Sara had not switched on the Mistress in the Shrine, but she had every confidence in the two old sisters when they told her this could only happen when she was ready.

No one seemed bothered when little Mary started to go with Sara and Vekia to the Shrine every day.

"The Immortal Controller of the future must connect with the Great Universal Controller," was Vekia's official excuse. "She must worship every day."

The Controller was glad to have the Castle free of the child for long periods. The constant childish chatter, the screams, the crying annoyed all three of her to the point that she was tempted to relocate Sara and Mary to a tiny room at the far end of the Castle.

"Too cold, Controller," said Vekia. "The Special Child would die."

On matters of health and dying, everyone paid heed to Vekia. Her knowledge of these things was all that separated the sick from the mortuary, a short cart ride down the hill from the Castle. Unbeknown to the authorities, one of the books Vekia suggested to Sara that she should read was about 'Medicine'.

Mary was a three-year-old toddler when Sara, now a young woman, turned on the Mistress. She knew what to do from what Omnia had taught her and from the old woman's books. When the large touch screen lit up, and words and icons appeared, Sara's fingers gently opened the digital door of a past that Omnia promised would take her to the world of the future.

"The Parth Path is doomed," the girl's teacher repeatedly told her, "but you, my dear, and Mary are not."

Sara, however, found little comfort in these words.

The chest now remained closed, for all the books within it had been read. Instead, Sara and Mary, who in time was allowed to play games (educational, Omnia emphasised) on a smaller computer, spent most of every day in the Shrine, returning to the Castle only for meals, toiletry and sleep. They rarely saw the Controller, and when they did she never spoke. What went on during increasingly rowdy Parth Path Council meetings in the Great Hall was neither of concern nor interest to Island Sara.

What really troubled the girl was a growing shortage of supplies and, as became apparent on the short walk from the Castle gate to the Shrine, a gradual descent into chaos. Vekia, more bent and frail, now demanded that two armed red wardens should accompany them for the daily journey. All day, these would stand on guard at the top of the steps whilst Mary made patterns and pictures on her screen and Sara struggled, on hers, with ways to save the world. One thing she was thankful to Omnia's father for was the 'autofix' button. Whenever things went wrong, and that happened frequently, a single touch on this rendered the screen blue, then white, after which the system would re-boot and normality return.

After three years, Sara had all but forgotten the Island, though not Peter, when Vekia, with three more years of wrinkles puckering her face, came to take her and Mary to the Shrine one morning. There should have been a Council meeting that day, but Controller Number 1 was ill, and Sara hadn't seen the other two for weeks.

"Someone to see you," the old woman said. Sara, now almost eighteen, looked up from brushing Mary's long hair. For a brief, blissful moment, the young woman thought it would be the child's father, for Vekia's eyes informed her that this 'someone' was very special. She'd not given up hope of seeing Peter again, although every time she passed by the sculpture of the Chosen Ones her brain would try to persuade her heart that this had to be all that remained of him. She was totally unprepared to meet, again, the person who walked nervously into her small room, looking from side to side as if expecting the walls to close in and squash her out of existence.

***

Rounding a corner, several hours' ride from Man Camp 7, Watchem reins Florrie to a halt. Moira clutches my arm for good reason. A Parth Path truck is parked on the side of the road. Watchem climbs down. Convinced of his betrayal, I pull out my knife, ready to slit the man's throat as I'd once done to the guard in Man Camp 7. The killing gets easier each time.

"This is where I must leave you. Unless you want to be tracked down by one of the helicopters."

"But that truck? What's going on?" I ask.

"This is only the beginning, Peter. From here to beyond the City of the Castle you must travel by truck. My dear old Florrie would die on us if I tried to force her to complete the rest of the journey. Besides, we'd take too long. Your enemies at the school, Moira. They have contacts. Connections with those who know the Parth Path must destroy you and us if it's to remain under their control."

"How can we escape from them?" asks Moira. I detect despair in the tone of my friend's voice.

"In a different future. Not mine, but yours," says Watchem. He transfers his gaze to me. "Please trust me, Peter. Would I have risked everything just to deceive you?" Those old grey eyes fix me with the warmth of his wisdom. I reckon he knows me better than I know myself. I shake my head then help Moira down. Jimmy is as excited as a puppy.

"Wow! I get to travel in a truck? Sara's gonna *have* to choose me now!"

I can tell Watchem wants no prolonged farewells, no ceremony, no fuss. He hands me a bag. I look inside. Another gun and handfuls of bullets. He's held on to the third weapon for obvious reasons.

"Run to the truck. Now! Stay under cover in the back. And listen to your ex-pupil, Moira."

Ex-pupil?

Sure enough, Moira discovers the driver is the young warden who stood up for her against Thea and saved her from being flogged naked.

287

"Hanna? What are you doing?" she asks.

"Anything to stop our new Directress from gaining power on the Council. When she learns you've not been flogged by that brutish Commandant at Man Camp 7, as I promised you would be, she'll go berserk. But they'll soon replace her. It's all falling apart, Moira. Get into the back with your Single X-Whys. And no one except me speaks if we're stopped. Right?"

Jimmy is less excited when he sees the cramped space, behind crates of provisions, into which we're forced to squeeze to remain concealed. The journey is uncomfortable, and for most of it I keep one arm firmly around Moira, holding her body up against mine. Hanna drives as if her life depends on reaching our destination within the shortest possible time. Perhaps it does. After all, apart from crossing the dreaded Wall, I have no idea where we're heading.

When we reach a bridge over a wide river, Hanna stops the truck. We all need a pee. The women squat behind some bushes whilst Jimmy and I spray the roadside with urine.

"Do we pass by the City?" the boy asks as he douses a dandelion. "Perhaps I could hide in one of the crates. I keep telling you, I'm only here because of Sara."

"Jimmy, she's already started. A while back. And she did not choose you. Get that into your thick skull. You can help me and Moira or you can get yourself killed in the City."

He shrugs his shoulders and returns to the truck.

"It's over there somewhere, isn't it? On the other side of the river. The City of the Castle where you used to come for those Parth Path Council meetings?" I ask Moira.

"Came by truck once a month. Not so much meetings but contests. Because of what you taught me in the Reservation, I made sure I never lost."

"What's she like? The Controller?"

"Not stupid. A clonie, you know."

"Could've guessed. Will they really clone Mary? I did love Rea, you know. But something felt wrong with her being—well, a clonie. She knew this, too, I think."

"The younger ones are dying off. The Controller was different. Nearly all the others have a problem with a particular gene. Caused by the cloning process. Gets switched off. And this leads to cancer. Rea would have died within a few years anyway. A very painful death. Texta knew this. She, too, loved Rea."

For me, these words are like a punch in the brain. That question reappears. How real *was* Rea? A Parth Path pleasure puss whose fate, and body, had been in the hands of one of its leaders? Or a willing partner along the Path, the 'only path'?

"They'll want to test Mary for this epigenetic potential. Maybe they've already done that. If she has it, she'll be of no use to them. They'll kill her."

Sara took Mary to the City knowing all this?

I feel sickened. Either way, it seems my precious wee child is doomed. Like Jimmy, I'm tempted to steal myself into the City to rescue her, even if it means killing Mary's 'protectress', Sara. Or perhaps we should give the Island girl to Jimmy. Her punishment for being a part of this charade could be a life-come-living-death with that numbskull.

We return to the truck and continue our journey. I see the City in the distance through a gap in the truck's tarpaulin cover. It has two small mountains projecting like unequal ancient twin breasts bursting above its careless sprawl. The larger one stands proudly bare, whilst the smaller bears, like a rugged nipple, the battlements of the Controller's Castle. To think that Mary has been taken there by that girl Sara angers me. In my mind, Sara's face turns red. Both Rea and I had always trusted her. That she's deceived us makes me feel isolated. With Watchem gone, and Mary lost to me, Moira's all I have now. Jimmy's too stupid to count and Hanna remains an unknown quantity.

Beyond the City, the truck trundles over a series of gentler hills, past small communities of nattie folk with hatred in their eyes—hatred for what they perceive as a threat to what they've built up from nothing.

As we approach the Wall (Hanna said "not far now"), I conjure images of heaped-up human remains, bones whitened by the wind, clothing torn by the talons of the great birds of prey that dominate the mainland. I see the opaque eyes of death staring at oblivion from worm-riddled, dried-mud eye sockets and, in my mind, I smell the heavy stench of a war that, but for the First Controller, would have destroyed all humankind. I wonder what on earth I'm doing by leading Moira away from a life that should have catapulted her into the Castle as the next Controller. Moira-the-Winner would have put a stop to the horrific practices of the Parth Path. Moira would have recreated the bliss of the Reservation throughout the land. But I look sideways at the woman I've always loved, see her tears and realise I'm doing the right thing by taking her away from all of this to face the terror of the Wall and the uncertainty that lies beyond.

Chapter 19

Hanna stops the truck. Surely this can't be the Wall? I breathe in, deeply, expecting to smell the long-dead corpses of those hordes that tried to escape from the horror of the south, inhale the stench rising from the mile-deep bone-wall of men, women and children from the both sides who fought for survival.

The air is clean and fresh.

"I'm staying inside," says Moira.

"The bodies!" exclaims Jimmy, a teenager eager for gore. "I must see them. Will they be covered with barnacles like those bits of wood on the beach back home?"

"Barnacles, Jimmy? I don't think so. No sea." I climb down from the back of the truck and walk over to Hanna who stands staring out across the rugged, open landscape. Jimmy joins us.

"Where are the bones?" he asks.

"No bones, Jimmy. Just lies. There. See for yourself. Or rather, don't see."

Curling over the hills like a man camp slave's whiplash welt is a grey braid of earth and stone, visible only in parts. No death or decay. Quite the opposite. Nature has brought life to these bare-flesh hills, spreading her green gown over every ridge, bump and gully. And there's a beauty in the silence of the place. Somehow, I expected to hear echoes of the shrieks and screams of those who had died in that final battle, worse than anything that might emerge from a flogged slave. Hearing nothing is serenely beautiful.

"There never was a battle for survival," says Hanna. "Moira taught me, and others who listened to her, one thing: to seek out the truth. All those lies were to frighten us. Stop us from finding out. No dried-out bodies. No bones. Nothing. Just a wall built two thousand years ago. By men from the South. From across the sea."

"The sea? So there would have been barnacles if there were bodies," chirps Jimmy.

"Shut up!"

Jimmy, as always, annoys me but Hanna puts a comforting arm around him, claiming his stupidity for herself.

"We'll find you some barnacles. At the Castle by the Sea." Hanna turns to face me.

"Another castle?" I ask. I'd assumed there was no sensible human life south of the Wall.

"Moira should have been Controller, you know. She's the only one who really cared about us at the school. For the others, it was—well, all about power."

"And this Castle by the Sea?"

"Don't tell Moira. About the other castle, that is. Not yet". Her eyes fix meaningfully on me. "We kept quiet about it. Look, when she went to fetch the Special Child from the Island, some of us knew there was another reason for her. You. Plus, an opportunity to get rid of that woman."

"Texta?"

"Uh-huh. But Thea took over—"

"The one who threatened to flog her?"

"Never was much risk of that. Even before Moira returned, we were divided. Most of us hated Thea. Then we heard about the new Commandant."

"Hellcat?" I offer.

Hanna chuckled.

"Calling her that is too kind. But she was the downside to getting rid of Texta. Man Camp 7 is the only one of any importance now. Because of what goes on there."

"Rea told me. Lizards and men in cages and things."

"See, we all knew that those rumours about the Skeleton Wall were lies. As is almost everything else to do with the Parth Path. I and two others came down here. In the truck. We told Thea we were going to get support for her. She sees herself ousting Hellcat. We discovered there *are* people south of the border. Not many, but some. Normal people. All natties, of course. They know nothing about cloning. They were horrified when we told them. When we got back, I overheard Thea tell her girls how she planned to break Moira on her return. And this was before she knew about Texta. Or Peter. This other castle might well change everything for Moira."

"I don't see a connection. Moira has no interest in castles. She just wants a life."

"Something no one will have if the woman you call Hellcat ever becomes Controller."

"Aren't there several Controllers? All clonies? Oh, to think that Sara could let them mess around like that with my baby!"

"That girl from the Island? But she *is* them. Has been all along. In on the deception. Oh, you ratties are so easy to deceive."

So, as I suspected, Sara has deceived me all along! Was that beautiful voice outside our hut but music of the devil? The hills turn red. Particularly the whiplash ridge of that old wall. I'm tempted to tell Hanna to turn the truck around, drive me to the City, hand me her whip and use it across that little bitch's back. Then strangle her with it. There again, can I trust Hanna whom I barely know?

293

"You're saying you want to set Moira up as Controller in this other Castle? The one by the sea with barnacles on it? Then challenge the Parth Path Council?"

"Not a council any more. And without Moira, there's no one there with any common sense."

I suggest the inevitable:

"War?"

"We hope not. Whatever the Parth Path does or doesn't stand for, war must never again be an option."

Nevertheless, if Moira and a troupe of breakaways were to take on the Parth Path fighters, she would win. I personally taught her never to lose. But is fighting what she now wants?

"I'm tired. It's getting dark. We need to find somewhere to sleep for the night. Maybe Moira will feel up to giving you an answer tomorrow."

We return to the truck. Hanna starts the engine and we follow a curling road which finally gives up its curves and straightens out. She pulls into the courtyard of a farm no different to the ones I saw north of the Wall. A young woman, surrounded by three children, appears in the doorway. They look impossibly thin and I see hunger eating into their eyes. Hanna tells us to get out, then picks up a small box of food, of which there are several in the truck.

"Take these, Eileen," she says to the woman. "And please put us up for the night."

"Where are we?" asks Moira.

"South of a wall which doesn't exist."

"You haven't answered my question."

"On the way to the Castle by the Sea. With barnacles on it." The words popped out of Jimmy like shit from the backside of a pig. "And Moira's gonna be the new Controller," he adds. How foolish of me to have left

Hanna in charge of Jimmy's stupidity. Hanna turns to Moira like a naughty schoolgirl about to face the wrath of her ex-teacher.

"No more castles. No new Controller," my friend from the past says quietly.

"But Moira, it has to be! What else can we do?"

"Go to Hell! Because that's what everything's become. Everything except for Peter. No, we're staying here. Eileen, do you have room for two nattie slaves on your farm?"

Before Eileen can answer, Moira disappears into the small house. I follow. There seems to be no man about, a relief for me as I cannot help but match up the shape of Moira's figure in Rea's flimsy dress with the Moira I rediscovered in bed on the Island. Eileen follows us inside. We're looking at an untidy, cluttered room with empty plates on the table, all that remains of the family's last meal whatever and whenever that was.

"I'll ask Frank. When he's back from digging potatoes," Eileen says.

"Digging potatoes? A job for Jimmy, then," I grin.

I go to the front door. Jimmy, the truck and Hanna are gone. With our other gun and most our ammo. It dawns on me that Hanna perhaps had no intention of setting Moira up as the rival Controller in that Castle by the Sea. Deception, deception, deception! Whatever her plan, I reckon she wants to steal glory for herself. Poor stupid Jimmy. Surely she can't be hankering after his dumb genes?

Moira shrugs her shoulders when I tell her. She seems too upset about something to even speak; something that she's been holding back from me. Perhaps, after a sleep, she'll awaken refreshed enough to begin a new life. Then she can discard all her fears like an opening flower shedding its sepals. My new Moira! No Parth Path, no red wardens, no Chosen Ones, no Controllers, no Special—

Mary, oh dear little Mary, what are they doing to you? Is it true what Hanna says about Sara? Did Sara betray my darling Rea as well as me? Was that fiasco over the hideout in the wood all fake? To draw me out? In trusting that girl, have I consigned my baby to unimaginable torments in the Parth Path laboratories?

I'm haunted by visions of Double X devils in white coats. I still have my gun with a single bullet in my pocket. Should I ever meet the girl from the Island again, it'll not be a red warden's whip but a bullet to the head for her. And I pray that this might happen before my baby daughter is turned into a genetic monster. I shall use the same clinically-efficient method with which Bukla dispatched Rea.

But would this be sufficient? Unlike Sara, my gentle Rea was no pain-deserving monster...

I'll never find out what happened to Rea's original genetic phenotype—the young woman from whom she and her nineteen sisters were cloned. And no one can tell me whether Mary-the-Immortal-Controller will still be Mary or become like that other canteen girl who both was and wasn't Rea. A beautiful, lookalike face that was more fantasy than reality, teasing me because the loving face of Rea had been taken away.

***

"*Mother Angela?*"

"*Shhh!*" *warned Vekia.* "*Don't let them hear you call her that. The good lady seeks employment, don't you my dear?*" *Vekia looked pointedly at Sara's mother, but there was no response.* "*Well, let me close the door against the ears of the Castle before you two talk.*"

The old woman left Angela and Sara staring in disbelief at one another before the girl ran into Angela's open arms. The mother slid her fingers through her daughter's red hair.

"It's so much longer," she said. She held Sara, weeping, at arm's length. "And don't you dare cut it!"

Sara sensed a new confidence in her mother. This wasn't the timid woman who scarcely had the courage to breathe, and whom she'd left behind on the Island when she fled with Mary.

"Sit down. Tell me everything," her mother demanded. "How you're coping, what Mary's up to and as much about the Controller as you can." She winked. Before, if Sara had been lucky, the woman might have vocalised a sentence of no more than half a dozen words. Now it was like the verbal release of a dammed river. And after Sara had said as much as she safely could, the girl heard about the terror of Matt going mad and shooting everyone on the Island, apart from her mother. When Angela began to talk about Peter and Jimmy, the girl looked the other way.

"Did Watchem warn him?" she asked.

"Warn Jimmy?"

"No, Peter. About what they planned to do to him?" Angela's eyebrows rose up. She had no answer.

"Jimmy wanted to come here. To see you—" she said.

"Pfff! The stupid pig!" Sara looked away with disgust as if said pig were in the room with them.

"He's changed, Sara. We all have."

"What about Peter. Where is he? Is he still alive?" She turned to look straight into her mother's eyes. She had to know the truth, and she'd learned as a child how only eyes can reveal the truth.

297

"Went to the school. For Moira. Years ago. That's the last I heard. They vanished together after that."

Sara winced as if she'd been stung.

"Moira the Directress? The fiend who had Rea shot? Maybe... maybe he risked his life to get revenge on that woman."

"It's not like that, Sara. They're friends. Always have been. Grew up together on a reservation on the mainland. Seems it was rather like the Island. Until the Parth Path ordered a clearance. But Peter was always the Chosen One—"

"I know that!" interrupted Sara. "I just want to know—" Her eyes left Angela to hide her tears.

"Oh dear! It happened, then? You and Peter together?"

"No, mother! Stop it. None of that. Nothing happened between us. Yes, I'd started as you know, but no, I hadn't chosen. Still haven't! Just kept quiet back then because of Jimmy. And Tommy. Anyway, I knew how much Peter loved Rea."

"You know that Tommy was Jimmy's father?"

"Yes, that figures! The piglet son of a pig."

"Sara, I too fear for Peter. Even though it wasn't Moira who shot Rea, how can we trust her? She was the Directress of the school, after all. The place where they teach all this Parth Path stuff."

"But you say she came from a reservation? Makes no sense. Oh Mother, just tell me more about yourself! How did you get here?"

"A long story. The Captain took us on board. Peter and me. Don't think there was anyone else left alive on the Island. Jimmy was already on the boat."

"I know. I saw him myself."

"Once on the mainland, I wanted to come straight here. To see you. But they warned me not to. Besides, the Captain was especially kind to me."

"Especially kind?" Sara grinned at her mother. "What do you mean?"

"Took a liking to me."

"Like my father Rolem did?"

Angela nodded shyly, then laughed.

"Sara, being with the Captain has been a dream. You've no idea how wonderful he is."

But Sara could only think about Peter. What had they done to him? Why should he and Moira have vanished?

"How could you let them take him to the school?"

"The Captain?"

"No! Peter. And that woman—"

"My child, we neither of us know anything about 'that woman'. Nor about Peter, for that matter. Like I said, people change. Jimmy was a good worker, the Captain says."

"Mother, no! Look, I know you've come here for a reason. Not just to tell me how wonderful your captain is."

"My captain? (Angela chuckles.) Oh Sara! What's happening out there doesn't bear thinking about."

"Well, don't think about it, then! Float away with the Captain in that boat of his. Float off to paradise!"

Sara couldn't understand why she was taking her anger out on her mother other than it had to do with Peter. Everything that mattered had to do with Peter.

"I want you to come away with us. The Captain says it's for the best. Because of what's happening. Watchem too. He's waiting outside."

Sara went silent. She felt pulled in opposite directions by two equal forces: one trying to make her relive a past paradise somewhere across the sea, the other urging her to remain for an uncertain future protecting the child of the man she loved.

"Mary..." she began. "The baby. I'm all she's got. And you can't even tell me whether he's still alive."

"She's theirs now," insisted Angela. "She's the Special One. You've no part to play in what happens to her once they get going with her genes in that laboratory."

"What laboratory? Like you said, it's all falling apart. But I've also seen things, Mother. At the Shrine."

"Shrine?"

The girl bit her lower lip and looked down at her feet. Had she said too much to her mother already?

"That old lady who showed you in. She and her sister know so much. Omnia is teaching me everything she knows. Including what the First Controller really said."

"Hmm! Seems they've taken over your brain, child."

"I'm no longer a child! And no one's taken over anything of mine. Mother, it wasn't supposed to be like this. They killed her. Back then."

"Who?"

"Who do you think?"

"The First Controller? The all-powerful, brilliant saviour of Femina sapiens? If the old ladies told you that, either they're soft in the head or they're telling lies."

"I've seen her. On the computer screen. Moving, speaking. (Angela looks puzzled.) She was such an amazing woman, Mother. Had so much love in her! And

300

this is where it has to happen! Not out there on the sea somewhere, but here in the Castle."

"So, you won't come with me?"

"I have to stay with Mary. I promised Peter."

"Ah—so this is still about Peter, then." Angela stroked Sara's hand as it lay motionless on her lap. *If only Peter could stroke me like that,* the girl thought. *"Peter the Chosen One, ay?"*

"You saw the statue of him, I expect. In the grand hall."

"Couldn't miss it. Incredible likeness."

"I did it. The drawing at least. Forced to by the Controller. I tore it up, but she put the pieces together and got their artist to make the statue. I remember thinking, 'if I tear it up perhaps they can't kill him.'"

"Well that's all you'll ever see of him from now on, my dear girl. The Captain says he's not been heard of for years. Not since he vanished. Probably got taken as a slave. You'll know how long slaves last, being one of 'them' now!"

"A slave?" A tear dropped onto one of Sara's slippers. She wiped it away with her other foot.

"Bring the child."

"I can't. Besides, there are other things keeping me here. Things to do with what the First Controller said."

Not even Omnia knew about the file inside the Mistress that Sara had discovered. She'd opened it out of curiosity. Possibly the great woman's last spoken words: that the Chosen Ones would be just that: chosen by each other since this was the only way forwards. Natural selection, she called it. Anything else was no better than the Great Man War. Humanity destroying itself through greed and lust for unbridled power. There was something about the way in which the woman

301

delivered her speech, perhaps only minutes before her death, for she ended by saying, 'They're at the door'. But there was something she said that made Sara listen to her words over and over: 'A man from a reservation and a woman from the Island.' Just that. Nevertheless, Mary was the true reason for staying at the Castle. Mary was the girl's only link with Peter.

Angela stayed for a couple of hours, during which time mother and daughter reminisced about happier times on the Island, about Rolem who, as Angela tearfully put it, also had Sara's determination.

"Oh, I'd say living on a boat with all those Single X-Whys needs some determination, Mother," teased Sara. Angela looked offended.

"It's not like that. Just me and the Captain. His name's Mallem, but no one calls him that."

"I'm sorry, Mother. I'm really happy for you. But me on a boat? With all those sailors? Men like Jimmy? I couldn't."

"Well, I must go," announced Angela, standing up.

"Mother, you can do one thing for me. Like you said, things are changing. Can you be my eyes and ears out there. Come here whenever you can. You're so quiet, you could pass by those wardens like a shadow. It's just that the Controller's getting so old."

"That woman in black?"

Sara laughed.

"Vekia the Controller? No way! She's a maid. The sister of Omnia I spoke about. Look, when the Controller's gone, all three of her, I really don't know what's going to happen. You should hear them shouting out there at the Council meetings. Such a horrible noise!"

"That's what I was trying to tell you, Sara. It's not safe here any longer."

"Which is why Mary needs me."

Angela left, but she did return, at times, as promised, full to the brim with knowledge about new reservations, other cities, man camps plus, most importantly, what was going on in Man Camp 7 and at the school.

***

We sleep apart.

Frank, a dour man of monosyllabic speech, who says more with his eyes, refuses to leave us alone. Slit-like eyes convey messages of warning. He's seen my gun. I assume he doesn't have one, but I know he has a knife. Several. On a rack by the door. Eileen, friendly before he arrives back home with a basket of potatoes and green leaves, morphs, afterwards, into a ghost. It's growing dark outside, so too late for Moira and me to seek refuge elsewhere. After we share one potato and a lettuce leaf, the family retreat into another room. There are two beds there. One for Eileen and Frank and the other for the three children aged, at a guess, between two and six. Like Frank, they stared at us all the time but said nothing. I tried to find out more about life here, south of the Wall, but only discovered a wall of silence. Moira sleeps under the table, myself on the floor by the door. Near the knives.

The following morning, Frank has already left when I awaken. He must have climbed over my body, but I secretly thank him for not plunging a knife into it. The children are eating at the table with Moira still underneath, asleep. It's their chatter that must have whisked me out of a dream; a dream of being back in the Reservation with Moira, Mother Mary and little Caitlin.

How like Eileen's children my poor ailing sister was: skinny and timid with eyes that reflected only fear from the world around her. I pretend to remain asleep until they've finished their breakfast of porridge and are gone to help their father.

"You can get up now," Eileen says cheerfully. "You must be hungry."

I struggle to my feet as Moira crawls out from under the table. I know from her expression that whatever it was that troubled her the previous evening is still on her mind. She says little, but Eileen, now warm and friendly, talks at length.

The nearest habitation is a day's walk away. They just about manage to keep themselves alive, but Eileen fears for her children. There used to be neighbours in another farmhouse only two hours walk away along the road, and life was easier then. This was before the youngest child, Jonathan, was born. The families helped and supported each other. The neighbours' teenage children loved to play with Eileen's little girls and promised to teach them to read and write, for neither Eileen nor Frank are literate. This idyllic life ended when raiders, as Eileen calls them, killed the father, raped the mother (Moira winces and looks away) and took the children. The mother stayed with Frank and Eileen until she was found, one morning, hanging from the branch of a tree.

"There was a gang of them," Eileen says. "All men. Surely it has to be better north of the Wall. Where only women rule."

She grins at Moira. Wee Moira from my past would have talked non-stop about the Parth Path, the Reservation, the Controller and her Council, but this Moira merely shrugs her shoulders. Eileen then tells us how things have changed since the first truckload of red wardens passed through on their way south. Sometimes they bring things from north of Wall. Food and clothes for the children.

"Living up there must be heaven. So why are you here?" she asks.

My eyes seek a response from Moira. She merely shrugs her shoulders again.

"Look," I say, "we can't stay. But that farmhouse you mentioned... is anyone there now?"

"Not that I know of."

"Two hours walk away?"

"With the children, yes. You'll make it in an hour."

I glance at Moira. She nods and shortly afterwards we leave. Eileen gives us a bag containing a few provisions, including potatoes and one of the knives.

"Don't tell my husband," she pleads. "And you'll find potatoes there too. In the field behind the farmhouse. Growing wild. They used to have chickens and cows. In the woods. Some may have survived. She said the raiders weren't interested in the animals. Animals themselves, I guess."

We wave at Frank and the children in a field, but they ignore us. It's as if we'd never entered their lives, and soon Eileen, Frank and that little farmhouse are no more than a memory as we walk on, hoping that Eileen wasn't leading us on. Beyond every curve in the twisting road, I expect to discover death, dormant yet waiting for us. Our only true friend, perhaps?

The farmhouse, marked by a rotten wooden gate, is set back, off the road. The gate will have to go, I tell Moira.

"It must be how those bastards who raped that poor woman knew that there were people here."

Moira freezes. Her expression, previously blank, changes. She starts to shake.

"Moira?"

She drops to her knees and screams. Her hands clutch at dead leaves and hit the ground, over and over she beats the earth beside the road. Not like the little Moira of my earliest memories, who would just go quiet if she didn't get her own way. I would sometimes try, unsuccessfully, to copy her, thinking that her way was sure to be the better than my red rages. No, this is a different Moira. One I have never known before, and I cannot understand what's happening to her. I kneel beside her and place an arm across her shoulders. She turns and presses her face up against my chest. I feel her nose and her chin there. I feel the quivering of her lips as she sobs and I know they're telling me, without words, that something awful happened to her.

At the school? That bitch Thea?

"Look, you don't have to tell me out here on the road," I say. "Let's get to the farmhouse. All right?"

I help Moira up as everything around me starts to turn red. How is it that Double Xs can be so cruel to their own kind? I swear to kill Thea in the worst possible way. No—I'll take on the whole bloody Parth Path instead. No whip-wielding red warden will be safe from me! Even that conniving little bitch, Hanna, who brought us here, will have to watch out. Then I'll track down Sara with my gun and my only bullet before Moira and I can get on with the life we began together in the Reservation all those years ago.

Moira holds onto me as we push through the undergrowth, that has taken over the path, to the farm buildings. The farm is large. Far larger than Eileen's and Frank's place. Larger than anything we saw in the

Reservation. It has windows, too, although this unnerves me. Eyes, hidden by the undergrowth, could peer at us... at Moira in her pretty blue and yellow dress. Worse still, out of that dress. We'll have to block out the outside world with curtains like those that Mother Agnes made for others on the Reservation. I've never known anyone so gifted at creating beautiful patterns with cloth as Moira's mother. Surely the gene responsible for this lies embedded somewhere in her daughter.

Inside the main farm building, horror of what happened to that family unfolds after I leave Moira sitting alone in the spacious kitchen. A doll, lying on her side at the foot of the stairs, stares at a black splash daubing the wall and trailing in lazy dribbles to a flat cake of black-brown blood spread out on the floor. Doubtless where the father of the doll's owner met his death. But that's not the worst of it. In thick, rough strokes of dried blood are printed above the stairs:

FUCK THEIR WOMEN

I try to imagine what those women went through upstairs whilst the man of the house lay butchered on the floor. I find four rooms, each furnished with a bed, one with blood-stained linen pulled back, connected to the floor with a dried blood waterfall.

Please, not the daughter's blood, I whisper inside my head.

I spend what seems forever cleaning off the blood. There's water from a pump outside, buckets and plenty of other utensils, cloths and kitchen implements like those we used on the Island and in the Reservation. It's a home defiled but crying out for resurrection. Our home. Exhausted, I join Moira in the kitchen.

"What were you doing?" she asks.

"Getting rid of the past. Preparing for our future."

307

If only I could get rid of whatever horror lies concealed inside Moira. Perhaps one day she will tell me what really happened when she returned to the school. And the reason for Hanna's pretence about Moira becoming a rival Controller in the Castle by the Sea. Meanwhile, in our new home, I've already seen enough of what the past has done.

"A bed upstairs?" she asks.

"Beds!" I reply. "Four of them. We've a choice. But I'll understand if you wish to be alone." Moira shakes her head.

"Can we go upstairs now? Please?"

Maybe she'll tell me in bed. I follow her as I used to in the Reservation whenever she said she had a secret to show me. Once the secret was a cuckoo's song. It was morning, and she led me to a glen that cut a gash into the mountains beyond the fields. The call of the cuckoo was both magical and terrifying. I couldn't understand why it made me think of death, though not with sadness but happiness. Like a release. Now I fear death more than anything. Fear how it'll separate Moira and me again, and this time forever. Moira looks in all the rooms and, to my relief, chooses the one with a double bed similar to what we shared on the Island, and on which we made love for the first and, so far, only time.

"Do you still want me?" she asks, looking at the bed.

I've had enough. I hug her, gently, from behind, then run my hands over her shoulders, her breasts, tummy and buttocks, turn her around and ask her, again, to tell me what happened. She's crying.

"I can't," she says, "but please be gentle with me. In bed. Like before. On the Island."

"You really won't tell me? No need to feel ashamed. I promise one day I'll get my own back on Thea and her bullies."

"It's not that. Not her. But I can't say."

I slip off her dress and her underclothes, then lift her up in my arms and tenderly lie her down on the top of the bed, as if she might fall apart with anything more than the softest of handling. She feels cold. The bed linen is outside, in a tub of water in the yard, having the smells of the dead farmer and his family and the curse of their fate leached out of it. I lie beside Moira to provide warmth, if not comfort.

"Do you really want me?" she asks again. "I can never be like that perfect clonie."

"I want nothing else," I reassure her, stroking her hair. "And remember, it's only you who has always been perfect for me."

I first took to stroking Moira's hair after that episode in the woods when I almost killed young Luke. One of the things that made her seem so vulnerable, as she struggled against his arm-hold, was her dishevelled, curly, blonde hair after she twisted and fought to be free. Afterwards, it felt as if I were protecting her again whenever I stroked her hair. I remember praying to an invisible force, that I've always believed in, that she would soon 'start' and that I would be the boy of her choice. Never did I imagine then that this choosing would take ten years.

Now, she makes it clear I am indeed her choice, but why should she believe I might refuse her? I do not have to compare her with Rea. I have loved both women.

We come together, but although she responds sweetly to my caresses, I feel something has been left behind. Has an experience in the school soured her desire for a Single X-Why? Has the Parth Path forced her to want sex with Double Xs? When I flop over onto my back, with one arm still around Moira, I stare at the low ceiling and wonder: *how can we ever return to the past that we knew before the Clearance without understanding the present?*

Give her time, encourages a voice from within me. *We've both been through so much since then.*

Again, I stroke her blonde curls, vowing that I'll protect my love from the pain of all that has happened to her since the Clearance.

***

Those in charge were so wrapped up with spite and venom that they seemed to forget all about Sara and Mary. The child grew out of nappies and ate the same food as her young protectress and the servants. She toddled, crawled, toddled, walked then ran. She learned to talk early, much earlier than children on the Island, but that came as no surprise to Sara. His child would. And as the child grew strong, so did Sara's knowledge and wisdom from Omnia, and from the Mistress.

The Council meetings stopped. They had become so violent that Sara was amazed no one had been shot. During the last one, the woman from the school and the woman from Man Camp 7, the one built like a truck, walked out after an explosion of shouting and table thumping.

What happened next took the girl by surprise. It was all there, hidden away inside the Mistress, of course, but she had not yet discovered the folder about health, illnesses and treatments. So far, this had been left to Vekia.

Omnia fell ill with high fever and rash and within five days was dead. Soon afterwards, Vekia informed the Island girl, now eighteen, that the Controller was gravely ill and covered with red spots. All three of her. Vekia knew what it was. Together they went to the Shrine, for which Vekia was now keeper in the place of Omnia, and Sara learned all there was to be known about the β-haemolytic Streptococcus, a tiny round creature called a bacterium which could turn itself into a deadly string of beads. These strings would invade humans and produce all manner of problems including the 'scarlet fever', often fatal. Before the Great Man War, doctors could treat this with medicines known as antibiotics, but now, without these, it spread through communities like wildfire. The elderly and very young were particularly at risk, so Sara was told to remain in the Shrine after it had been 'disinfected', and she and Mary ate and slept there alone. Vekia, who said she must be immune, acted as go-between. Even the crowds in the street outside vanished, replaced by an occasional sick passer-by as the little beaded beasts swept through the City leaving rash-covered corpses in their wake.

One morning, Vekia brought with her not only food and drink for Sara and Mary, but a last message from the dying Controller; the only survivor of the three aged clonies. She, Sara, had been named as the new Controller till Mary came of age. Simply that.

After a few weeks, the new Controller emerged from the Castle when Vekia considered it safe for her to do so, and, together with the young child, entered a changed world. An even more dangerous world. She held a meeting of a few senior survivors of the ravages of scarlet fever, together with Vekia, and they hung on her every word as she spelled out what she had learned from the First Controller.

The uniform would no longer be grey, but white. Red wardens were to be abolished, belts were to be white. Whips were banned.

"But Controller, what about the Parth Path?" one woman queried.

"No Parth Path. Just humanity. What's left of it."

"They'll never accept this. They'll come down from the north and take the City. Kill you and all of us here."

Sara had never, until then, realised how much respect, even love, these other women held for her. Perhaps it was because she was guardian to Mary, their continuing link with the sacrosanct Parth Path.

"Then you'll have to see to it that they don't," Sara replied. "You have guns, trucks and helicopters enough. Fuel too, I imagine." She looked pointedly at the warden whose duty was 'fuel'. The woman flushed then nodded. "And we have friends. Contacts. My own mother for one. Don't worry. The Mistress in the Shrine will help us."

True. Battle strategy was one of the first things she had researched in the Mistress after becoming Controller. Plus, she remembered Peter once saying how important curves are. They had helped Rea and him to escape from that man camp, albeit into a trap set by Texta. Nevertheless, she had thought about curves ever since. Including her own. Every day she'd look at them in the mirror, hoping that if he ever did return he would find them pleasing.

***

Somehow, we survive.

We find a few animals. One cow and a clutch of hens, wild in the forest but easy to lure, with food, back to our farm. Moira laughs at the panicky hens; laughs properly for the first time since we met up again outside Man

Camp 7. How I love it when she laughs. I build a little enclosure for the hens and there's already a barn for the cow. We visit Eileen, when Frank's not around, and she gives us grain and seeds to plant, plus flour for bread. I'm pleased to see Moira, having grown thin, start to reform those curves that so excited me on the reservation years ago.

One curve forms more than the others. When I tell her that perhaps she now needs to cut down a little on the food, she bursts into tears.

We're sitting in the kitchen. The conversation starts because I suggest that perhaps she doesn't need yet another slice of my freshly-made bread. We have a large oven in the kitchen. Moira seems to have retained all the cooking skills handed down by Mother Agnes, but I make the bread. I tell her you need a Y chromosome to make bread.

"Baby," she whispers through the tears.

"What? Having a baby? That's so wonderful. Have as much bread as you want!"

But she can't stop crying. Not until it comes out; the reason for her tears, her behaviour and the loss of the Moira I once knew. I feel so foolish for not having helped her to tell me before. She fears the baby may not be mine.

"Of course it is!" I insist. "They didn't mess with you in those Parth Path laboratories, did they?" I imagine Thea and others poking her with needles, discharging into her the semen of science from syringes. She shakes her head.

"Luke," she replies looking at the window as if he were out there, peering in and enjoying her misery.

Luke? How on earth can she even mention his name?

313

Then the truth flicks out and stabs at every cell in my body. The hideout! How did I not see it?

"He—he came back. The Island. When you went off—" I can feel the pain in her words. I know what's coming and I don't want to hear any more... yet I must.

"Because of that mad bastard Matt?" I ask. "Great Controller, why did I listen to a madman?"

"You'd disappeared when I woke up. That man told me you were in hiding. Waiting for me. I'd killed Texta, see, and—"

"And he said they'd be after you? And that we mustn't be seen together, right?"

"It reminded me of our games back on the Reservation. You and I. Remember?"

"Hide and seek?" I'm now stroking her hair to control my anger as Luke's gloating face looms up in my head.

"Matt took me to a place in the woods."

"Covered with a heavy metal lid?"

"I went down the ladder, so excited after the time we'd had together in bed... and after I heard our special tune being whistled."

"Fuck the Controller... is this true? Luke was down there? And he—he—"

Suddenly, I feel guilty for peering down at that battered body and feeling so happy that it wasn't Moira's.

"I'm so sorry," Moira sobbed. She keeps repeating the word 'sorry', but I know what she means.

"He raped you?"

The word stings but I have to say it. It's almost a relief when Moira nods, for at least I know she wasn't a willing victim, but it hurts all the same. My childhood friend raped? No longer is that single bullet intended for

314

Sara. I'll return to the Island and slam it into Luke's corpse.

"I killed him. Later. After I escaped and hid behind a tree."

"A tree?"

My mind returns to another time when Luke might have raped her as a child had it not been for the broken off branch of a tree. It seems Moira, too, remembers, for she tells me how she clubbed him to death when he came back for her, and wanted to continue hitting him forever. She had hoped that would kill the memory of him, but he's never left her in peace since. It seems that now, in death, he's come to own my friend.

"Only once?" I ask, but I feel bad for it seems I'm belittling the worst moment in Moira's life. "I mean, is that enough for the child to be his? You and I have made love so many times since crossing the Wall. Once before and a thousand times since. Surely—?" I can't seem to stop talking. Perhaps it's the only way to prevent a red rage in me from exploding into something that'll destroy us both. "Surely the baby's mine. It has to be."

But Moira can't stop crying, and I see how I'm hurting her with my words. To be uncertain about the father of her child in such circumstances must be a weight almost impossible to bear, and yet poor Moira has had to carry this burden alone until now. I must forget my anger and my own uncertainty. I must help her as we always helped each other in childhood.

"Moira, it's mine. You killed him. He can't hurt you again. Forget him. Please."

She holds on to me, trembling, before asking me to make love to her again. I agree, but to my disgust I find myself imagining I'm Luke penetrating her in that cold dark hole on the Island.

From that day on we become closer. We have to cope. As the curve of Moira's belly swells, I fight off my insecurity by being more loving, more considerate and by watching her all the time.

One morning, Moira tells me she knows something is wrong. She no longer feels the baby kicking. And it's too early in the pregnancy. After all, I am already a father. I know seven months is wrong.

It comes almost as a relief when the baby enters our world stillborn. We'll never know whether it was mine or Luke's, but the Luke possibility helps us come to terms with the sadness of seeing the pathetic creature as we stare at its little body in the bedroom. Just a dead thing. Never will we have to worry about bringing up a child that might have carried Luke's genes.

But Moira sinks into depression that I struggle to understand. I promise her that she can have more babies. I try to reassure her that they'll know their true father and giver of half their genes. It makes no difference. Only a lengthy time with Eileen, when I'm out of the room, changes her. I daren't ask what they discussed, if indeed they even spoke, but gradually she recovers and life on our little farm resumes.

Moira never does become pregnant again. It doesn't matter to me, for I already have a daughter and I'm now making plans to recover the child for Moira to look after, but being childless clearly upsets her, so I avoid talking of this until I've finalised the details of my plan: to return north of the Wall, kill Sara with my last bullet and steal my own daughter for Moira. But Moira and I are so very happy together the plan is always shelved till 'tomorrow'. And tomorrow and tomorrow.

It happens almost three years later, but not as I had planned. A strange illness inflicts Eileen's children. They

316

turn bright red, shiver and take to bed. Eileen, convinced it was brought south of the Wall by the red wardens on their way to the Castle by the Sea where Hanna, as I guessed she might, has set herself up as rival Controller. Feeling unwell, Eileen begs Moira to help her. When she, too, develops the same rash, I try to dissuade my love, but she overrules me.

"They're desperate, Peter. Frank is hopeless, as you might expect of a Single X-Why. I must help her. Who else do they have?"

They die within days. Eileen too. Only Frank survives. A broken man, he struggles on, but the next time I visit, the house is deserted. All that remains of the family are mounds of earth in the potato field. I return with a bagful of potatoes to find Moira tired and fretful. I feel her forehead. It's hot. When the rash appears later in the day, I know already that it's over for us. I hold Moira up against me all night, praying that I, too, will become ill and die for I cannot face more of this life without my little friend.

She dies two days later. Her last words are:

"Thank you, Peter."

Yes, I want to die, but first I have a job to do. A journey to make. A shot to fire.

Chapter 20

I stagger on in a curve. A curve conceived by sheer animal instinct to avoid certain death at the hands of those who seek to destroy me only because forces beyond human control configured my paired twenty-third chromosomes with an X and a Y. Now that Moira, the other half of my personal life pair, has gone, why should it matter whether I live or die? Perhaps it's the mode of death promised by the Parth Path that encourages me to avoid confrontation with wardens in a man camp at the foot of the hill, blocking my route to the City beyond. Even from this distance I can see their dresses are white, not grey. How odd! Plus, they have no red belts. I still have my gun, but with only one bullet which is destined for the one who tricked me.

I'm too hungry to dwell on the irony of offering myself up to the leader of those who would see me killed. I know I'm not thinking straight, but I hope to discover a brain in the Controller. Something that's missing inside the heads of brutes like Hellcat. Something that might agree to me killing Sara for what she did before I too get shot. But one thing puzzles me, and I must ask the girl before discharging the bullet dormant for too long in the barrel of my gun. Why did she tell Watchem to warn me? The only answer I can come up with is that she knew I wanted to kill her and that no one in their right mind would expect me to survive south of the Wall, the only safe haven for me back then. Well, I did survive, and if she, too, is alive, she must face me and my bullet.

I scour an abandoned farmhouse for food. A stale, green-mould-covered chunk of bread sends me into raptures as I dig my teeth into its crusty hardness, washing it down with handfuls of water scooped from a puddle outside.

I've always loved the rain. I remember how Moira and I once sheltered under a spreading oak tree outside the Reservation village. Our game of cricky had to be abandoned when clouds appeared from nowhere, opened and emptied themselves. We ran, soaked and giggling to the huge tree under which we shivered and laughed, huddled together. Then we kissed with that innocence of blossoming adolescence. And I remember Moira saying how comforting the sound of the rain bouncing off the leaves was because it meant that no one would come and interrupt us. And when the storm was over, we ran hand-in-hand across the meadow to the huts. Moira suddenly stopped and sank to her knees. For an awful moment, I feared she had just died because Mother Mary was forever warning me about "catching my death" when playing in the rain. But Moira, bursting with life, rolled onto her back then spread her arms out, moving them up and down to create angel wing curves in the wet grass. I've read about angels in The Holy Bible. Moira will always be my angel.

"The smell of the grass when it's just rained, Peter! Don't you just love it?" she cried out.

No. I loved Moira and still do even though she's dead. What possible purpose can I now serve by pleading with the Controller. Pleading for what? Sara's death?

Yes, Sara's death.

The curve of my journey continues over the flat land beyond the hills, then on towards the City's unequal twin breasts. I detour through back gardens of houses, abandoned like that farm house. Here and there, I find bits of food and plenty of water. It's obvious to me that the illness that killed Moira, and many others in the

Castle by the Sea, I was told, also swept through the land north of the Wall. The bodies I come across, some decomposing, are cruelly decorated with that now familiar rash. For all I know, the Controller may also be dead.

The scraps of food filling my belly give me sufficient strength to power my legs up the hill to the Castle. The road, it seems, is called 'The Royal Mile' and is so full of angry people shouting and shoving each other around that there's little risk of me being spotted and recognised. Besides, after more than three years, who would remember the nattie who escaped execution on the Island by sleeping with the Directress who should have become Controller? No regrets! For three years, Moira and I had a life together and it was beautiful.

I worm my way through the crowd to the top of the hill. Three armed wardens, also in white dresses with white belts, stand guard at the castle gates. No red belts and no whips. I approach one. The smallest. Why this should make a difference if she's carrying a gun, I have no idea, but I choose her because of size.

"I'm here to see the Controller," I say.

She looks up at me, she looks at the other two wardens, looks over my shoulder at the unruly mob in the street, then back at me.

"It's him," she calls out.

So much for failing memories after three years. The others approach, looking me up and down. They say nothing. Nor do they shoot me.

"I said I've come to see the Controller. I'm giving myself up."

"So, it's true then," the smallest warden says. She reaches up and touches my beard. "Just like the statue. The Chosen One. Have you come to save us all?"

What an odd question!

"The Castle, please. Let me in."

"You'll not find her in there. Not at this time of day." She nods in the direction of a building on a corner opposite a taller one with a tower. "That's where she hides herself."

She takes me across to the building, also guarded by three white wardens. Again, I'm the object of incredulous stares before one of these women opens the door with a key. I'm taken down the steps then left in a long, dim room full of bright screens and wires. I'm not alone. Lit by a single, large screen is a young woman in a red robe. Her red hair, which used to be shoulder length, has grown longer. The last time I saw her, over three years ago now, she stood balanced between childhood and womanhood, like one of the red rose buds outside Angela's hut just before opening out. Now her flower is fully formed. How can I shoot a flower in full bloom?

"Sara?"

She turns and stares. My hand travels to the gun and I free it from my belt. I point the thing at Sara and walk slowly towards her. I see her happiness change to uncertainty then to fear. My hand is shaking.

Do it before you're deceived by that beautiful hair.

But those lips are trembling. And they, too, are beautiful.

Do it! Do it now! Like Texta, she deceived and used you!

But she's too young. And see that hair? See how the light from that bright screen picks out each wondrous filament? They're like threads of Life itself. And she's crying.

Oh, she's only crying because she knows she's going to die.

No, her eyes are saying something different. She's happy—

"Where is the Controller?" I ask. I want to hear her voice before I kill her. To make sure, for voices are as recognisable as faces.

"I *am* the Controller," she says.

Her voice, Sara's voice, is now as beautiful as her face. I recall those moments of bliss listening to that same voice singing outside our hut on the Island. Then I remember a spider in Mother Agnes's hut. It ran out from underneath the kitchen cupboard whilst Moira and I were playing a game with shells. Fearing spiders, I slapped my hand hard on the floor as it zig-zagged in a frantic effort to escape. I missed.

"Don't kill it!" my little friend cried out. "It's beautiful. You mustn't kill beautiful things."

Why did Sara have to become so beautiful? Every day for three years, her face grew uglier inside my head. Surely this can't be the same Sara—and she most definitely *cannot* be the Controller. The Controller has to be a nasty old woman.

"Stop playing games. You're no longer a child. I need to see the Controller. Explain to her why I have to—"

Kill you?

I can no more say the words than do it.

"Mary!" Sara calls out.

A small child comes running from an adjacent room. I drop to my knees and open my arms wide, but the child stops, her wide brown eyes looking at me. They show the same fear that I see in Sara's eyes.

"Who's this, Mummy?" she asks.

"Drop the gun, Peter. You're scaring your little daughter."

The thud of the gun dropping to the floor makes the child flinch. Even when she blinks, her eyes remain fixed on mine. The baby I so lovingly cradled in my arms is terrified of me. I lower my arms. There's so much of Rea in that pretty face that I'm almost as afraid of this little ghost from the past as she is of me.

"Mary, sing for your father. That song I taught you."

My mind travels back to that morning when Rea lay asleep and I stood in paradise, spellbound by Sara's sweet voice. Perhaps I already knew back then, in a strange sort of way. Knew that the 'Special Child' had to be ours... a child born of Sara and me, not Rea's little girl.

"I thought—they said—" I began, stumbling over confused thoughts. "Mary. The laboratories. Getting cloned. Destroyed. And you were in on it. Destroying my little girl."

Sara comes over to me. No, in her robe she doesn't just 'come', she glides. And the closeness of her smell excites me in the same curious way that her song outside our hut did. She kneels beside me.

"Come to Mummy," she says to Mary. *Mummy?* I recall Rea using the word whilst cuddling baby Mary.

The child—my child—runs to the young woman beside me.

"Peter, you need to see something. On the Mistress. The First Controller's key to the future."

"Mistress?"

"Over there. The computer with the big screen."

Sara stands and holds out her hand for me. Small, like Rea's, but firm and strong. Not tentative, as Rea's would have been. And as she leads both little Mary and the girl's father, me, to the Mistress, I now know why the girl I'd set out to kill has become the Controller. She has everything: the beauty of Rea, the humanity of Moira and the wisdom handed down by the First Controller.

"She's very like Rea," I say of my own daughter.

"Of course," answers Sara. "But there'll only ever be one of her. See here. The last words of the First Controller before they killed her."

I stand behind Sara as she sits and flicks her hands over the screen with the same grace as her silken voice when it entered our hut on the Island that morning.

"There," she says. "I knew the Parth Path had it wrong. All this time she's been misunderstood."

I watch the woman on the screen, so very human, brought back to life on the command of Sara's hand. She talks to us:

"These are the final words of Marion McGrath, First Controller of a country, once called Scotland, that appears to have become the last surviving remnant of human civilisation on Planet Earth. I was a scientist, never a politician, but a scientist who cared. They called me a lesbian because I loved another woman, and yes, I did hate men and what they were doing to the world, but, both morally and scientifically, trying to create a world of women free from men through parthenogenesis is wrong. My best friend, now, is a man. They call him a slave, but I see him as my saviour. I love both his beautiful young daughters, but I won't let that get in the way of what is right. It has to be by choice. Their choice. The choices of all of us left behind. This is how God—"

"God?" I question. A flick of the red-haired girl's hand freezes the First Controller. "Like in that book that got handed around the man camp when Hellcat wasn't looking? The Holy Bible?"

"That's on here too. Together with a million other books. But see, Peter. See how little Mary listens to her every word?"

True, Mary's eyes seem to drink in everything the woman on the screen says. I long to hear her little voice, too, but for the time being it's all about what I see in her eyes. Sara makes the First Controller speak again:

"—*Has always worked. Natural selection, the early scientists called it. There's nothing wrong with the Y chromosome. My anger that drove me to start along the Parth Path was no better than the anger that has wiped out ninety-nine-point-nine-nine percent of humanity. But I still believe there must, one day, be a Special Child. One with the genetic perfection to lead our species back from the brink. Whether the child's twenty-third pair of chromosomes are the same, XX, or different, XY, is of no importance. The child must be born out of the choice of one for another. The Holy Bible—*"

Sara freezes the screen again. I look at her.

"I must tell you something," she says, smiling for the first time since I dropped the gun. I recall how the quiet child, Sara, rarely smiled on the Island, unlike her brother who never stopped smiling, laughing and talking, often at the same time, but when Sara did smile it was like a visitation from heaven. "She speaks of a 'second coming', like a clone, but I believe the Special Child will be a first coming. No links with the past."

Still smiling, Sara switches the Mistress back on...

"*The Holy Bible talks of a second coming to save the world. I pray those two girls I love in secret will be able to protect the Mistress and all the wisdom she holds for this child.*"

The screen goes blank, Sara turns her face to me and her tears tell me she knew these girls.

"One died from the fever. Like the Controllers. All three of them. The other girl the Mistress talks about, her sister, an old lady called Vekia, died from her loss. I'm sure of it."

"Three Controllers?"

"Three. One of the very first batches of cloned women. By some genetic fluke, they survived to old age, but others, like Rea, have all died young. Around the age of thirty, they suffer what the First Controller calls 'genetic collapse'. Genes protecting against cancer and serious infections get turned off. Epigenetics. She was working on this before she got wind of the rebellion."

"Rebellion?"

"They never called it that. Only the First Controller did. I think they feared her wisdom. In the end, she knew there was no way she could escape from here. But by calling this place a shrine to the Great Universal Controller, she hoped her legacy might continue."

"Legacy?"

"What she stood for. Saving humanity. Now, with that little bug having killed so many people—"

"Little bug? Moira... she, too, died. And I blamed you lot. For sending whatever it was south of the Wall."

"Beta haemolytic streptococcus is its proper name. Centuries ago, before they invented antibiotics that fought against those bugs inside peoples' bodies, it killed folk in droves."

"And women invented these anti... whatevers?"

"A man. From our country. Scotland, as it was called back then."

"You were saying..."

"Just that by wiping out so many people, including the Controller and most of the Parth Path Council, it leaves us with an empty screen to start over again."

"Not entirely empty," I say, thinking of those final words of the First Controller. A Special Child? But not, I'm thinking, Mary. I sense Sara's thoughts merge with mine, but neither of us says anything. This must wait until we're alone.

"Can I show Daddy my pictures?" asks Mary. Her first words in my presence, since her gurgles and googles as a baby over three years back, moisten my eyes.

"In a moment, sweetie. I have to tell him about the war first."

"Oh, I know all about the Great Man War from my man camp days," I inform my daughter. "Pretty much had it forced down my throat—via my ears. You know, Hellcat—"

"Body like a truck? Easy with her whip?" suggested Sara. "Became Commandant at Man Camp 7 after Moira shot Texta?"

"Yeah, that figures!"

"It was *her* doing. Objected to those old ladies appointing me as Controller. 'Too young,' she said. The Parth Path Council split in two. Rumour has it that she promised to return to the City, not as the new Controller's Man Camp 7 Commandant, but as the 'Invincible Controller'. With an army."

"An army?"

"Just like the men would've done before the Great Man War. And as the First Controller foresaw in her writings."

A thought occurs to me.

"You're not—you know, like the First Controller, are you?"

"No way as wise or clever. Why?"

"I didn't mean that. I mean the way she—you know, how she says, on the Mistress, that she loves the daughters of that man?"

Sara first smiles, then laughs.

"I loved Vekia and Omnia, as they were called, like my own mother. Or mothers! But the person I can only ever love in that way is standing right beside me."

My tears mingle with her laughter, telling me only one thing: that I too have always loved the girl from the Island. Sara stands up and wipes my tears with the long sleeve of her robe of office.

"And I remembered you once saying how important curves are. You told me this when I was cooking in your kitchen. You said I was developing the curves of a woman. I felt sad. I thought I already was a woman. For you, I mean. The things that went on in my mind told me I was."

"You were. It's why I said that. I'd noticed you looking more and more like Rea every day."

"Well—you also said how you and Rea escaped from the man camp by running over the hills in a curve. To confuse the red wardens and the dogs."

"Why are all the wardens here dressed in white?"

"I'm coming to that. Angela—"

"Your mother?"

Sara nods.

"She'd been with the Captain all that time. She was the only survivor on the Island after Matt went berserk..."

"Because of Daniel. He really loved that boy."

"I wasn't there, so I don't know exactly what happened. Only Angela says it's a miracle she survived. Anyway, my silent mother has ears like sponges. She absorbed information from all possible sources between here and Man Camp 7. We knew what route the Commandant would take and—"

"And curved around her? Split into two groups? One in front of and one behind her army."

"I couldn't go myself. You know I can't kill."

I think of Moira, the spider and Texta. She 'couldn't kill' either, though did when she had too. But perhaps Sara is even stronger than the friend from my childhood.

"They said that once the woman you call Hellcat was shot dead, that was the end of it. The others put down their weapons. What remained of her supporters fled south of the Wall. To the Castle by the Sea."

"Which explains a lot. To think I almost believed them!"

"Let me show you something."

Whilst Mary searches for her pictures on her own computer, Sara sits in front of the Mistress again and flicks her hand across the screen. This becomes a map that shows a world from south of the Wall to the Islands in the northwest. By spreading her fingers over the screen, the image enlarges. She brings Man Camp 7 and the school into focus. These are now combined as 'Reservation 7'.

"So, no more cannibalism? No more fat man's blubber to fuel helicopters?"

Sara frowns.

"Never happened. No way can you make helicopter or truck fuel from human fat. They get oil out of the sea. And men were needlessly killed, yes, but not eaten. Rumours, Peter. Sad men's rumours."

"But man camps are truly gone?"

"Yes. And when the Special Child arrives, there must be no surviving traces of the Parth Path. See there. 'Caledonia' instead of Parthpathia."

329

I see the word written across the top of the page.

"It's what they used to call the land both north and south of the Wall many years ago. It's started, Peter. As the First Controller predicted, nothing that happened before you came back is now important. Not after we've—" Sara blushes. I know what she means so she doesn't have to spell it out. I place two fingers over her lips as Moira used to do so often. "It won't hurt too much, will it?"

I remember Rea asking me the same question. I shake my head, praying that it won't, and turn to Mary who stands waiting patiently beside me.

"Please show me your pictures now," I ask.

"Can I, Mummy?" she checks with Sara. Sara nods.

My daughter takes hold of my hand. For the first time since Moira's cruel death because of that little round bug with a ridiculous name, I feel joy. Joy of human company, joy of being loved and of being alive. Mary leads me to a computer at the far end of the room. It's decorated with small flowers plus other bits of nature collected from around the Castle. Her little hands, as graceful as the new Controller's, change the screen until a picture comes up: *her* picture, drawn, she tells me, with brushes hidden inside the machine.

Two curves come together. That's her body, the child says. The legs and arms are straight lines, like sticks, the eyes are dots, but the mouth is a curve that turns up at both ends.

"Mummy told me to do this for you, Daddy. For when you came back. You have come back, haven't you? For always?"

I look away. I don't want my child to see the shame of wet cheeks.

"Yes," I say to the empty space in front of my face. "Yes, I'm back."

"Good! You see, that's the baby you and Mummy are going to make. The Special Child. The First Controller said so. Everything the First Controller said comes true. But I don't know yet if it's going to be a boy or a girl. Do you know, Daddy?"

I turn to look at Sara. Our eyes meet. In an exchange of looks, they tell each other that what my daughter says must come true.

"Not yet, Mary," I answer. "But it really doesn't matter as long as it's born out of Love. Tell me, my child. What do *you* know about curves?"

Mary looks to her surrogate mother for an answer. I've always known that Sara understands curves. Sara smiles at me. Little Mary laughs, too young to understand the meaning in that smile. Sara, who played mother to her mother and brother, and who is my daughter's perfect mother, knows that the curve in tail of the 'y' is important to Humanity and therefore to all Life on Earth.

Instead of answering with words, Mary brings up an image on the screen. An image that is made up entirely of curves. She turns to look at me, to read my reaction

"It's thousands of years old," Sara explains. "From a country called China. I learned about it from the Mistress, and Mary loves it."

"It's called 'yin yang' and is very special," enthuses Mary. "Like my daddy and my mummy are special too. And they're going to make the Special Child together. Will that be soon?"

My eyes haven't left Sara's. They glance briefly at the black and white circles, curves and blobs on the screen then return to Sara as if, in her, they have finally found their true home.

"Yes," I say. "Soon. Would you like to have a little brother or a little sister?"

"Can it be tomorrow?"

Together, Sara and I laugh. But behind my laughter is a certain knowledge that I've finally completed my personal curve. I've come full circle to find, in Sara, the mother whom I never truly mourned because she was never truly killed. Mother Mary's spirit exists wherever there's life. The Parth Path failed because it refused to recognise that spirit. It craved that same dominion over others that culminated in the Great Man War. If humankind is to survive, it must listen to the girl from the Island who has already proved herself to be not a mere 'Controller', but Universal Mother.

The Author

After Oliver, a doctor, woke up one night with a ghost story in his head, he took to writing short stories, several winning prizes. During a visit to his Chinese wife's mother country in 2006, he became interested in Chinese mythology, thus inspiring his first middle grade readers' novel, *Moon Rabbit*. A winner of the Writers' and Artists' 2007 New Novel Competition, and long-listed for the Waterstone's Children's Book Prize, 2008, this was followed by its sequel, *Monkey King's Revenge*, a People's Book Prize finalist, plus two other children's novels. His writing for young adults includes a trilogy set in North America, *Beast to God*, a time travel post-apocalyptic novel, *The Terminus*, set in the London Underground, and *The Kelpie's Eyes*, a story of sisterly love and rivalry incorporating Scottish mythology. Of his two published adult novels, *A Single Petal*, set in ancient China, won the 2012 Local Legend Spiritual Writing Competition; the other, *Voices*, is a tale of family love spanning three generations against a background of murder and child abuse. A collection of adult short stories, *Lost Whispers and Other Stories*, was published in 2012.

Although not constrained by any particular genre or style, Oliver feels most comfortable in that magical space between reality and fantasy; the space into and out of which children slip so easily in their play; the place of dreams, myths and legends and deeply ingrained in diverse cultures across the globe; the magical realism of Latin American writers like Gabriel García Márquez and Isabel Allende in her young adult novels.

Oliver lived and worked as a doctor in England, America and finally Scotland where he and his wife now live. His daughter and youngest half-Spanish granddaughters live in Switzerland whilst his son and eldest granddaughters, also half-Spanish live in Texas.

Website: *www.olivereade.co.uk*

Blogs:
http://olivereade.blogspot.co.uk
http://runawaywheeliebin.blogspot.co.uk
http://childrenaswriters.blogspot.co.uk

Books by Oliver Eade, most also available as e-books:

For middle grade readers:
   Moon Rabbit: Stevie Scott from Peebles, Scotland befriends Maisie Wu, a new classmate from China, when she when she gets teased for being different. Early one morning, he takes her to the river to see some ducklings, she falls into the water, can't swim and he dives in to rescue her. They emerge in mythological China and must undertake a perilous mission before they can get back Peebles. A fun introduction to mythical Chinese beasts and legends.
   Monkey King's Revenge: Sequel to *Moon Rabbit* (available as print book only). Stevie and friends from Peebles High School have to get back to mythological China to rescue Maisie from the Monkey King after he kidnaps her out of revenge.
   Northwards: a brave young girl from Texas is called by Earth Mother to the High Arctic to save the world from a terrible evil.
   The Rainbow Animal: Rachel takes her pet hamster for a birthday ride on a strange-looking animal at a local mall carousel only to end up embroiled in a paint war between the funny little Colorwallies and Dullabillies.

For young adults:
   The Terminus: Oliver's debut young adult novel in which he returns to the city where he was brought up, a city now changed beyond recognition from the drab post-World War II era of his childhood and which, in a post-apocalyptic world, gives Mankind a second chance: London.

The Kelpie's Eyes: Scottish Borders sisters, Caitlin and Rhona, are transported, through a famous waterfall taken over by a kelpie, The Grey Mare's Tail, to a fairy-tale land consumed by evil, and to the backstreets of Victorian Glasgow, in a tale of sisterly love and rivalry. Won first prize in 2018 Words for the Wounded Young Adult Novel Competition.

For adults:
A Single Petal: A widowed village teacher in Tang Dynasty China links the death of his merchant friend with the disappearances of local Miao girls, endangering himself and his daughter as he digs more deeply into the mystery. Winner of Local Legend 2012 Spiritual Writing Competition.

Voices: A story of murder, family love and turmoil set in London.

Lost Whispers: A collection of short stories inspired by travels across the globe.

Plays:
The Gap: Staged in Scotland 2012, a one act surreal comedy about a dysfunctional Peacehaven family split apart when the earth divides into two along the Greenwich Meridian. Short-listed for the Rowan Tree One Act Play competition, 2009.

Pool Britannia: Full-length farce about British ex-pats sharing a condominium pool with locals in Turkey. Short-listed for the Sussex Playwrights' 80th Anniversary Competition, 2014.

Give the Dog a Bone & ***The Other Nathan***: One act black comedies, both long-listed for the British Theatre Challenge, 2015.

Schrödinger's Cat: Surreal black comedy take on the physics of quantum realities: was she or was she not killed? Runner-up winner in international competition for one act plays, 2017.

For other Silver Quill Publishing books for young adults, adults and young readers, visit:
www.silverquillpublishing.com

For young readers:
Shadows from the Past series by Wendy Leighton-Porter. '...Wendy has written a fantastic series of books (Shadows from the Past) filled with mystery, suspense, and adventure.'

Firestorm Rising & Demons of the Dark by John Clewarth '...Children learn that there are far more terrifying things in the universe than they ever learned at school, as a terrifying monster is awakened from a long, hot sleep.'

For adults:
Crying Through the Wind by Iona Carroll. '...Sensitively written novel of love, intrigue and hidden family secrets set in post-war Ireland... one of those books you can't put down from the very first paragraph...'

Familiar Yet Far by Iona Carroll. Second novel in **The Story of Oisin Kelly** series follows the young Irishman in *Crying Through the Wind* from Ireland and Edinburgh to Australia.... 'The author has a genius, bringing you into whichever country she is writing about. You can smell the rain in Ireland and the dust in the Outback...'

The Manhattan Deception, The Minerva System, Seven Stars and **Bomber Boys** by Simon Leighton-Porter. '...Fast paced thriller with a plot which twists and turns.' 'I loved it...' 'As soon as I picked this book up I knew I wouldn't be able to put it down...'

The Devil's Stain by Pamela Gordon-Hoad '...Gripping debut novel... tense fifteenth century English murder mystery... compelling story-line and believable characters...'

The Angel's Wing by Pamela Gordon-Hoad. Second novel in the ***Trials of Harry Somers*** series. '...A great plot with totally believable characters, and I look forward to the next book!'